NOTORIOUS DECEPTION

"Let us begin with the truth, shall we? To start with, I know you were never married to my cousin or anyone else for that matter," Derek stated.

"What?"

"You were a virgin, Diana," he said evenly. "Married women are not virgins."

Diana's mind raced. How could she possibly explain her relationship with her husband? "Giles never wanted me," she said finally. "On our wedding night he became quite drunk and took great delight in telling me he had married me only for my fortune and had no intention of being intimate with me. I slept alone that night."

"That was only one night. You claim to have been married for four years. There were other opportunities."

Diana's voice trembled. "Giles was most adamant in his rejection of me. During those few years that never changed."

"Tell me the truth, Diana," Derek beseeched softly. "Who put you up to this ridiculous charade?"

"No one," she whispered brokenly. She studied his grim face. "You don't believe me. I have told you the truth, yet you refuse to believe me."

Derek walked away from the bed, then opened the door, slamming it hard behind him.

Notorious Deception

ADRIENNE BASSO

LEISURE BOOKS   NEW YORK CITY

For Rudy, who encouraged, supported, and always believed. My endless love and thanks.

A LEISURE BOOK®

November 1994

Published by

Dorchester Publishing Co., Inc.
276 Fifth Avenue
New York, NY 10001

Notorious Deception

Chapter One

London, England—1818

The steady, rhythmic pounding of the rain atop the roof of the hired cab lulled its occupant into a false sense of security. Diana felt her eyes closing, her lids heavy, as the exhaustion she had been fighting for days finally threatened to overtake her. Her entire body was weary and sore from lack of sleep and the endless jostling of the poorly sprung vehicles she had ridden in for the past two weeks.

Diana drifted sleepily on a cloud of exhaustion until the abrupt stopping of the carriage woke her. Instinctively she thrust her arms out to keep from falling onto the floor of the hackney carriage as she was propelled forward.

"We're here, missy," the driver called down to her. He had to shout to be heard above the downpour.

Diana, now fully awake, scrambled upright and

squinted out of the grimy window in an effort to gain a better view of her destination. It was impossible to see very much of the building through the rain and the dirt on the glass. Sighing wearily, Diana gathered up her battered satchel and, clutching her black reticule in her hand, descended from the cab unassisted.

The driver sat hunched over on the top of the carriage, water pouring off his wide-brimmed hat. He announced the fare, which Diana, though she had no experience of city ways, knew was exorbitant. But she did not bother to quibble with the driver. She was only relieved she had enough coin in her purse to pay the man, and once she did, he disappeared quickly down the soggy street.

For a moment, Diana stood in the rain craning her neck skyward, taking in every detail of the impressive town house—from the carved stone front to the elegantly curved bay windows, balconies, and trellis work. Diana felt a moment of panic, wondering if she indeed was at the correct address, but she pushed that disturbing thought quickly toward the back of her mind. She had journeyed for too long and from too great a distance to be deterred any longer.

Squaring her shoulders, she marched up the wide stone steps and stood before the arched front doors. As she reached up to grab the large, shiny knocker, she saw a coat of arms discretely etched in the brass work. Her spirits soared as she recognized the family crest of the Earl of Harrowby.

"I've done it," she muttered under her breath in relief. "I've actually done it."

With renewed confidence, she lifted the heavy brass door fixture and banged loudly. Her knock was answered quickly by a footman, elegantly garbed in silver-and-blue livery. A sudden gust of wind drowned out Diana's voice as she spoke to the servant. Feeling utterly ridiculous standing outside in the pouring rain while shouting at the man, Diana entered the house uninvited.

The young footman gaped at her in astonishment and called for someone named Dobbs, who appeared instantly. Diana assumed that Dobbs was the butler.

"The servant's entrance is in the rear, miss," the man named Dobbs announced with a sniff, his long, pointed nose perched stiffly aloft. "Kindly remove yourself at once."

Diana swallowed back the scathing retort that sprang to her lips and deliberately dropped her soggy, rumpled satchel on the floor. Drawing her wet, travel-stained cloak regally around herself, she met the butler's eyes squarely. In her opinion, the only people more snobbish than the English aristocracy were their servants, and she refused to let the butler's superior manner intimidate her. She knew that she looked a sight, but it was hardly her fault she was wet and dripping water all over the finely polished marble floor. After all, it was raining heavily outside.

She raised her chin haughtily and spoke firmly. "I am the Dowager Countess of Harrowby. Please inform the present earl that I wish to speak to him at once."

Her announcement was met with a stunned silence. The butler opened his mouth several times, but seemed suddenly incapable of speech. The footman stared at Diana as if she had lost her wits. Diana was beginning to grow uncomfortable under their astonished scrutiny, when the butler finally regained his voice.

"One moment, milady," he sneered, and with an expression that could only be classified as malicious, the butler left the hallway.

The footman assisted Diana out of her cloak routinely, his astonished expression remaining as she tentatively smoothed out the wrinkles from her black crepe mourning gown. Diana willed herself to ignore the servant's rude stare when he picked up her satchel and placed it in the corner of the entrance hall, hidden from view. Nervously licking her lips, Diana waited for the disapproving butler to return.

"A toast to your health, milord," Lord Tristan Ashton called out jokingly as he raised his glass of French brandy high above his head.

"Stop it, Tristan," his companion admonished. "I swear, if I have to put up with any additional ribbing about this bloody title, I shall renounce it."

Tristan laughed at his friend's discomfort. "The boys still giving you a hard time, Derek?"

Derek merely snorted his response and picked up the half-empty brandy decanter. He refilled both his glass and Tristan's before answering.

"I'm surprised you haven't already heard. Pierrepoint, Coventry and Grantham fell all over each other at White's last evening, bowing and scraping. They put on quite a show."

Tristan smiled, despite his attempt not to. "They were only jesting Derek. They're probably a bit jealous. It will be a long time before Grantham comes into his title. After all, it isn't every day that a scoundrel such as you is raised to the rank of earl."

"It is still hard for me to believe I have been an earl for three months, Tris," Derek said. "While it is scarcely a secret I was not fond of my cousin, I never seriously contemplated inheriting his title.

And as unscrupulous as Giles was, I never thought he would come to his end in such a brutal manner. Being left to die in a London alley with his throat slit is hardly a fitting end to anyone's life."

"Just be glad you managed to keep all the sordid details out of the newspapers." Tristan grimaced. He had also held a low opinion of the former earl, but he had been suitably shocked at Giles's sudden and bloody demise. "It has been several months since the body was discovered. Is there any further information about Giles's death?"

"Not from the authorities," Derek replied. "Although I can hardly be surprised. They are an incompetent lot at best. I have hired a Bow Street runner to conduct an investigation."

Tristan nodded his head in approval. "He should have much better luck."

A thoughtful silence fell over the room as each man sat lost in his own thoughts. A sharp knock at the drawing room doors broke the companionable silence.

"Come," Derek barked loudly.

The butler, Dobbs, entered the room. "You have a visitor, your lordship," he said, wilting slightly under Derek's cold, hard stare. "May I show the lady in?"

"Lady?" Derek asked. "I was not expecting any visitors this afternoon."

"If you wish me to send her away, I shall," the butler replied smoothly, his eyes darting swiftly about the room. "I am sure the dowager countess can visit with you at a more convenient time."

At the butler's comment, Derek's expression changed to one of exasperation. "Henriette," he groaned. "She is not due to arrive until later this evening. Show her in at once Dobbs." With a casual

Adrienne Basso

wave of his hand, Derek dismissed the servant.

"Henriette is here?" Tristan inquired, rising to his feet. "Perhaps it is best if I take my leave."

"Don't even think about it Tristan," Derek warned, turning toward him. "'Tis punishment enough that I will have Henriette in residence here for several days. I have no intention of facing the grieving widow without reinforcements by my side."

"You're damned lucky I'm such a good friend," Tristan grumbled as he resumed his seat. "There aren't many who would stand by you at a time like this."

Tristan's quip helped to ease the tension in the room. Though meant as a joke, his comment was not far off the mark. Both men had little tolerance for Giles's widow, the overbearing and dramatic Henriette.

Dobbs opened the door without knocking, announcing with a sneer, "The Dowager Countess of Harrowby."

Diana heard a gasp of astonishment as she entered the room and hesitated near the doorway, her eyes moving nervously from one man to the other. She had expected the earl to be alone and was caught off guard by the appearance of a second person. She felt extremely self-conscious as the men continued to stare rather rudely at her. She was also at a decided disadvantage since she did not know which one of the gentleman was the earl. Her hands clutched the sides of her black gown and she unconsciously balled the material up in her fists, crushing it. Finally, one of the men spoke to her.

"I am sorry, but I did not catch your name," he said in a smooth voice.

"Diana, sir. I am Diana Rutledge, Dowager Countess of Harrowby," she stated in a clear voice, pleased that it sounded steady to her own ears. She expectantly held out her hand to the gentlemen who had addressed her.

He moved forward quickly and clasped it in greeting. "Charmed to make your acquaintance, madam," he said. "I am Tristan Ashton. And this is Derek Rutledge, current Earl of Harrowby. But of course, you must already know that."

"Well, actually, no, I didn't know that. I am not acquainted with the current earl." Diana looked in confusion at Tristan and then at the earl. Tristan was smiling pleasantly at her; the earl was glowering. "I am pleased to finally make your acquaintance, my lord." Diana dipped a small, graceful curtsy toward the silent man.

The earl regarded her with a cool glance, his handsome sculptured features set in a firm line. Then he faced the other man, his lips curling up in the mere hint of a smile.

"Is this some sort of game, Tris?" he inquired dryly.

"If it is, I can assure you it is not my doing, Derek," Tristan insisted.

The earl advanced and Diana stood utterly still, holding her body rigid. He circled her slowly, assessing every nuance of her soggy, travel-stained appearance. By sheer strength of will Diana subdued the tremor of panic invading her body as she met the predatory speculation in the earl's intense blue eyes.

"Will you kindly explain, madam," he finally said, unable to keep his fury from his voice, "exactly how you happen to have acquired the title Dowager Countess of Harrowby?"

Diana wrinkled her brow in confusion. She had thought very little about the kind of reception she would receive when she first encountered the new earl. She had been too busy concentrating all her efforts upon reaching London safely. His open display of hostility toward her was both unwarranted and unwelcome.

"I was married to the former earl," she said, in response to his question. "Giles Rutledge."

Her announcement brought a darker scowl from the earl and a hoot of laughter from Tristan. The earl turned away from Diana and walked toward the fire. Despite Diana's puzzlement at his rude and hostile behavior, she could not help but admire his ruggedly handsome features and his lean frame, which was displayed by his perfectly tailored clothes.

"Pierrepoint," Tristan announced with authority in his voice. "Or perhaps Coventry. But I would put my money on Pierrepoint."

"Another prank?" Derek inquired, his tone conveying his annoyance as he picked up his brandy glass and took a long swallow.

"What else," the other man replied, shrugging his shoulders. "I suppose we might as well see it through. Come over by the fire and sit down, madam. You must be chilled to the bone. And please do tell us your tale."

"For heaven's sake, Tris," Derek said, "don't encourage her."

Ignoring Derek, Tristan escorted Diana to a chair near the fire. He strode over to the sideboard and poured her a glass of sherry. Returning to her side, he handed her the glass and waited while she took a tentative sip.

Lifting her eyes, Diana studied the two exceedingly handsome men staring down at her while she slowly sipped the wine. Both men were tall and well proportioned, with fit athletic builds. Tristan was slightly taller than Derek, but Derek was broader of shoulder.

Their coloring was similar, but Tristan's hair was a darker shade of brown and his eyes a deep, warm sapphire blue. The earl had blond strands in his close-cropped hair, which was in disarray because of its natural curl, and his eyes were icy blue. Even though it was early April, both men sported golden tans, attesting to their preference for the outdoors.

Tristan had a boyish smile and an easy charm. Diana could not be certain about the earl's smile. He had not ceased scowling since she entered the room. As Diana continued her covert study of the two men, they, in turn, took in every aspect of her appearance, from her moist walking boots to her hair, which was simply braided down her back and fastened with a black velvet ribbon.

"You were going to tell us about yourself," Tristan said after he had given Diana sufficient time to compose herself.

"I am not sure exactly what you want to know," Diana replied hesitantly. She twirled the sherry glass nervously in her hands, absently noting that Tristan wore a wedding band. A quick glance at the earl's strong hands verified he did not.

"Surely you have more to say than that," Derek said flatly, looking pointedly down his nose at her with very cold, arresting eyes. "Were you not sufficiently coached?"

Diana blinked at his obscure remark. She could feel his animosity. Yet his arrogant stare gave her just the courage she needed and she indignantly straightened her back. Diana did not have a clue as to why they were treating her in such a strange manner, but she decided it was time to assert herself.

"I have come a great distance, sir, in order to settle the affairs of my late husband," she said in a strong voice. Diana faltered a bit as the men exchanged glances. Tristan's face was alight with amusement; the earl glowered with annoyance.

"He has been dead for over three months," Derek stated flatly. "What has taken you so long?"

Diana looked up unflinchingly into the man's cold blue eyes before she said, "News of Giles's death has only recently reached me. I have been traveling for nearly two weeks now."

"Exactly where have you come from, madam?" Derek asked mockingly.

"Cornwall," Diana responded calmly, determined not to lose her temper no matter how cruelly provoked.

"Cornwall? Near Truro?" Tristan asked.

"No," Diana answered, turning her attention to him. "Farther down the coast from Truro, nearer to St. Ives. The closest village to my home is called Zennor."

"This is really too much, Tristan," the earl interrupted with annoyance. "I am not about to sit through a long discourse on the geography of Cornwall." He shifted restlessly from foot to foot. "I do believe that I have had quite enough. I think it is time to summon Dobbs and have her *ladyship* escorted out of here at once."

Diana felt her anger ignite at both the earl's words and his sarcasm. She had been wrong to go there. She should have known better. It was only fitting that Giles's relations would treat her in such a disgraceful manner. Diana turned sharply to the earl and, with as much dignity as she could muster, rose to her feet.

"It will not be necessary for you to call your servant, my lord," she stated. "I will take my leave of my own accord. And gladly. I can assure you, I have had quite enough of your rude and ill-bred behavior." Diana fumbled momentarily in her black reticule before pulling forth several crumpled sheets of paper. "Here is a list of the properties Giles managed while we were wed. I still own them, as the marriage contract clearly states. I am requesting your solicitor forward the deeds of ownership to my residence at once. The address is listed on the copy of the marriage contract."

Derek reluctantly took the papers she offered him, his eyes gleaming brightly with speculation. "Bravo, madam," he sneered. "You seem to have found both your spirit and your imagination." He turned to Tristan and remarked further, "She appears to be warming to the part, don't you think?"

But Tristan was no longer smiling. "Perhaps we have been a bit hasty, Derek. I think we should listen to what she has to say."

The earl lifted an eyebrow. "Not you too, Tristan?" he responded suspiciously. "Don't tell me that you are somehow tangled up in this ridiculous farce?"

While the two men argued the point, Diana decided to make her escape. She sped swiftly past them, determined to leave the room as quickly as possible. Now that she realized her mistake in coming, she wanted nothing more than to leave and forget the entire incident. She would not subject herself to any more rude and hostile behavior. Diana did not know precisely where she would go once she left, since she did not know a soul in London, but it didn't matter. Uppermost in her mind was the need to be free of the Earls of Harrowby, both former and present.

Diana had almost reached the drawing room doors when Tristan called to her to stop. The strength of command in his voice caused her to

17

react automatically and she obeyed him.

It was a good thing too that she did, for a split second later the doors swung open, barely missing slamming into her head. A short, slender figure, clad entirely from head to toe in black, swept regally into the room.

"Derek," the woman called out in a throaty voice. "I have only just arrived, but I insisted to Dobbs that I see you immediately. The trip from Darford was positively draining, yet I felt I should greet you before I went to my rooms. Dobbs actually tried to dissuade me, and then he insisted on announcing me. Can you imagine—announcing me in my own home? The very idea. I told him I would not stand for it, of course."

While the woman paused a brief moment to catch her breath, the earl said, "Henriette—" but was cut off as she began speaking again.

"Tristan," she exclaimed, seeming to recover instantly from her exhaustion as she spotted the other man. "How very lovely to see you." She held out her hand dramatically for him to kiss and Tristan reluctantly complied. "And who is your friend?" Henriette inclined her head toward Diana.

Tristan didn't answer the woman, and she waited only a mere heartbeat before walking up to Diana and introducing herself. "I am Henriette Rutledge," she announced. "Countess of Harrowby."

For a brief moment Diana felt a flicker of sympathy for the earl. She couldn't imagine how he survived being married to such an overbearing woman. No wonder he scowled all the time. Diana turned her attention back to Henriette, who was talking about her difficult journey into town. She was pretty, Diana conceded, with her brilliant green eyes and dark hair, and probably near to Diana's age of twenty-two. And yet, Diana thought, Henriette resembled a black magpie, chattering away, her slim figure encased in a long pelisse of black silk with puffed sleeves and a half-dress cap of silk with its small black feather perched on top of her head.

Finally, Henriette ceased her tirade and looked expectantly at Diana. Since Diana did not have the faintest idea what had been said, she merely smiled. When Diana saw that Henriette had regained her breath and was about to begin another soliloquy, she spoke quickly.

"I was just explaining to your husband," Diana said. but Henriette immediately interjected.

"My husband," Henriette shrieked. "You cannot possibly mean Derek?"

"You did introduce yourself as the Countess of Harrowby, Henriette," Tristan said.

Henriette shot Tristan a positively chilling look and said, "'Tis a reasonable mistake. After all it has only been a few short months since my dearest Giles was so cruelly taken from me."

"Your dearest Giles?" Diana said. She made a low, choked sound as she stared at Henriette.

"Yes," Henriette responded, enjoying the intense attention everyone was now affording her. "Tristan was right however. I did make a mistake. Although I am far too young for the title, I am actually the *Dowager* Countess of Harrowby. Giles's widow."

Chapter Two

For a brief moment Diana thought she would faint. The room swam dizzily before her eyes, and she felt as if all the blood had just drained from her head. Suddenly, she felt Tristan's strong grip on her arm.

"Steady, my dear," he whispered in her ear as he encircled her waist and directed her toward the settee on the far side of the room.

Diana was instantly comforted by his gentle concern and strong presence, and she leaned heavily against him for support. When they reached the settee, she sank down gratefully on the lush velvet upholstery, her eyes staring straight ahead, unseeing. Her mind was completely blank, and she sat rigidly, as if in a trance. Henriette's voice droned on in the distance, a faint buzzing in Diana's ears.

The loud bang of the door awoke Diana from her trance, and quickly looking around the room, she saw that the other woman was gone. She then looked at the earl.

"I can assure you, my lord," Diana whispered, her voice vibrating with emotion, "I do not find your little jest in any way amusing."

"Nor do I find your jest amusing, madam," the earl countered calmly.

"Who was that woman?" Diana asked, pointing at the door, still not believing what she had heard.

"Precisely who she said," Derek answered. "Giles's widow, the Dowager Countess of Harrowby."

"But that is not possible!" Diana exclaimed, her voice rising with alarm. "I am Giles's widow."

"Indeed?" The earl's mouth twisted into a mocking sneer. "And may I ask precisely how long you were married to my cousin?"

"Over three years."

"Oh, damn." That expletive came from Tristan, who then moved back across the room to retrieve the brandy decanter and refill his glass.

Derek rubbed his hands across his chin in frustration. "I must tell you, madam, I am becoming increasingly annoyed with this whole charade. I demand you come clean of this entire matter and tell us who sent you here to play this ridiculous practical joke."

"No one has sent me here!" Diana screeched in reply. She bit her lip firmly to keep from saying anything else until she regained her temper. Finally, Diana said in a chilling tone, "My father always warned me the gentry were a queer lot. If this is not a childish prank, then I can only assume it is some sort of elaborate plot to cheat me out of my property. I can assure you, sir, it shall not succeed."

The bravado of Diana's statement did not lessen the fact that she was badly shaken by the entire incident, but she vowed she would die before allowing the earl to witness any of her distress. He had been cold, arrogant, and insulting from the moment she'd arrived, and she refused to be intimidated any further.

"I am afraid, Diana, it is neither a prank nor an attempt to cheat you," Tristan said softly. "I think we need to hear your entire story, from the beginning please, before we can make any sense of this."

Diana glanced uncertainly at the two men, who were regarding her even more intently than when she had first arrived. She was not entirely convinced of their sincerity, especially the earl's, but she reasoned that the only way to get to the truth would be to explain her situation.

"I grew up in various parts of England," Diana began in a soft, clear voice. "My mother died when I was six and my father was always pursuing some business venture, and he did not wish to be tied down to any particular location. Therefore, we were constantly moving. I had various nurses and several governesses during my childhood who saw to my care and upbringing. When I reached the age of fifteen my father sent me to Mrs. Elliston's Academy for Young Ladies in Sussex to complete my education. I graduated from the academy soon after my eighteenth birthday, and I took up residence in the new house my father had built outside of Bath.

"I was introduced to the earl by my father the summer I returned from school. Apparently Giles and my father were involved in several business ventures together. I was never able to clearly ascertain the nature of their business dealings. The earl came to our home for dinner on occasion, and since I acted as hostess for my father, I spent several evenings with him.

"At the time, Giles had recently come into his title, and my father was rather impressed to have a peer of the realm as a business partner. I suppose it is the curse of the merchant classes to be in awe of the nobility. No matter how successful he became, my father always worried he still carried the smell of the shop about him. Anyway, my father was extremely successful in his business dealings and was considered a man of very affluent means. Much to his dismay, however, he was not included in the upper echelons of society owing to his lack of appropriate connections. I believe that served to heighten his interest in Giles.

"Later that summer, my father informed me he had approached Giles with the idea of entering into a marriage with me. Having previously led a somewhat sheltered and secluded life, I found the notion appealing. Giles was charming, clever, and witty during the brief time I had spent in his company, and I must confess I was captivated by him. When I pressed my father for details about the possibility of a marriage with the earl, he admitted Giles was a bit reluctant to agree because of my lack of social stature. But father felt confident he would bring Giles up to scratch. My father was an extremely forceful man. He was fond of success and not easily deterred. Giles presented a challenge to him. It wasn't until much later that I realized my father had a substantial monetary hold on the earl, and that was how he was finally able to force the match. It was a fact Giles took great delight in pointing out to me during our marriage."

Diana paused for a moment, lost in her memories. After a brief hesitation, she said, "Eventually, my father's will prevailed, and before the summer ended, Giles proposed. Naturally, I accepted. My father had worked so hard to bring him around, and I was naive and impressionable enough to be taken in by Giles's winning ways. We were married in September of that year."

"When and where?" Derek asked, eyeing Diana irritably.

"The year was 1814. The wedding took place on September third in Chippenham, a small hamlet north of Bath. Only my father and my old nurse, Agnes, were in attendance. We stayed overnight in the village and the next morning Giles and I set out for Cornwall."

"Impossible," Derek said while pacing the room in agitation. "I was back in England during that time and I took up residence in London. I distinctly remember seeing Giles several times during the month of October. He never once said anything, nor in any way acted as though he were married. If memory serves me correctly, he began courting Henriette that season."

Diana swallowed hard at that statement and fell silent. She glanced out the long French window and dully watched the pelting raindrops slither down the glass. She felt strangely numb and lethargic.

"Calm down, Derek, and allow her to finish," Tristan advised. "Please continue."

A bit less sure of herself, Diana began speaking again. "There really is very little left to say. The journey to Cornwall took nearly a week. Giles became increasingly annoyed with the endless traveling and took to projecting his anger at me. He became strange and unaccountably hostile at times, gloomy on other occasions. I was seriously beginning to doubt the wisdom of our marriage when we arrived in Cornwall. We immediately moved into Snowshill Manor, a lovely restored Elizabethan estate my father had purchased as a wedding gift for us, and Giles proclaimed an interest in acquiring a tin or copper mine."

"This cannot possibly be accurate," Derek said, interrupting again. "How could Giles have been in Cornwall playing the devoted husband and here in London at the same time?"

Diana's face flushed with heat and she looked down at her hands. "I did not say, my lord, that Giles was playing the devoted husband. He left me in Cornwall only two days after we arrived. It was many months before I saw him again."

"Come now, madam," he said, disbelief etched in his voice. "You expect us to believe Giles deserted his new bride in the wilds of Cornwall and did not return for several months? Did you not question your husband's absence?"

Diana squirmed uncomfortably on the settee, the earl's statement bringing all the endless days and nights of uncertainty back into her heart. "Of course I questioned my husband's absence," she snapped. "He told me he was going to London to settle some business affairs and would return to Cornwall to take me back to the city with him before Christmas. But Giles did not return for over six months. By that time, my father had suddenly taken ill with fever and died, and I was quite distressed. Giles insisted I observe at least a year of mourning before I considered accompanying him to London. Naturally, I agreed. And then Giles left again."

"When did you next see him," Tristan inquired gently.

"Not until September of that year," Diana said, feeling the telltale warmth of humiliation rising again. "He brought several papers pertaining to my father's estate he wanted me to sign. It was at that time I learned my father had made a separate provision for me in his will, allocating the bulk of his wealth to me and not my husband. He also had certain properties held in trust for me that Giles was allowed to manage, but not sell without my permission."

"I don't imagine Giles was pleased to learn of that," the earl stated knowledgeably.

"No, he was not," Diana said, almost whispering as she recalled her late husband's angry reaction. "Giles was furious when he discovered I controlled the purse strings. He shouted names at me and accused me of all sorts of horrible things. He claimed I was in league with my father to cheat him out of his rightful due. Truth be told, I was glad when he left. Giles returned to Cornwall only three times during the following two years. On each occasion he brought a large folder of documents for me to sign. He said the papers allowed him the use of certain funds."

"And you signed them?" Derek asked, a trace of sympathy creeping into his voice.

"Yes," Diana whispered, hanging her head. "I quickly learned how ruthless Giles could be when denied what he desired." She shuddered when she saw the two men exchange concerned glances.

"How did you learn of Giles's death?"

"I read of his death in the *Times*. Cornwall is a bit remote, but we are not totally cut off from the rest of the country. The newspaper was several weeks old and the obituary notice rather brief. I noticed the announcement was placed a month after the date of his death. Was Giles ill for a long period of time?"

The earl's blue eyes did not waver. "No. My cousin died suddenly."

"Oh." A fleeting sense of guilt invaded Diana as she struggled and then failed to evoke a feeling of sympathy within her heart over her husband's death. "After reading the notice in the paper, I reasoned Giles's relatives had probably tried to locate me, but were unable to, so I decided it would be best if I came to London on my own. The obituary mentioned the earl's widow. I assumed they were referring to me." Diana's voice trailed off in a mixture of exhaustion and disbelief.

The room fell silent. Tristan rose from his leather wing-back chair and nearly dragged Derek out of his seat and across the room.

"I've always held the opinion that your cousin was a bastard, but even this seems too low for Giles. A bigamist for heaven's sake!" Tristan hissed, keeping his voice low so Diana would not overhear the conversation.

"This is extreme, even for Giles," Derek admitted. "Do you believe her story, Tris?"

Tristan shot Derek an incredible look. "I know you are not a man easily given to trust, Derek, but even you cannot doubt her sincerity. Good Lord, man, who in creation would make up such a bizarre tale? And for what possible gain?"

Derek looked past Tristan to the settee, where the young woman sat. She looked forlorn and helpless, but even her distress could not diminish the glow of her golden hair, the pink coloring of her high cheekbones, the charm of her full, lush mouth and finely chiseled nose. Her eyes were an elegant and expressive brown with long, thick golden lashes. Her features proclaimed her a pretty woman, but the creamy alabaster sparkle of her complexion declared her a rare beauty.

She was fashionable and expensively dressed and had the unmistakable look of quality. Her distress was obvious; her agitation seemed genuine, her manner genteel. She was not, by any means, a common woman. Yet Derek was still not entirely convinced. There was one other remote explanation. He crossed the room toward her.

Diana felt rather than heard his approach. She raised her eyes slowly, taking in every measure of his attire from his gleaming black Hessian boots and tight-fitting, buff-colored leather breeches to his ivory shirt, white cravat, and double-breasted green coat with its shiny brass buttons. Her eyes widened in surprise when they reached his handsome face. For the first time since she had entered the room, the earl was not scowling at her. He looked, she thought incredibly, almost kind.

"Is it possible, madam, that the husband of which you speak is not, in fact, my late cousin, Giles Rutledge?" he asked in a quiet voice.

Diana drew her brows together for a moment and pondered his question. "It is, I suppose, a possibility, my lord," she answered slowly.

Relaxing slightly at this last hope, Diana sank back against the comfortable sofa. She took a deep breath and absently looked around the drawing room, taking note of her surroundings for the first time. Green watered silk covered the walls and elegant swags of the same fabric draped the tall, narrow windows. The center carpet was white with an intricate design in shades of green, gold, and brown. The furnishings were very English in style. A Sheraton satinwood cabinet with painted oval panels instantly caught her attention. The overall effect was warm and inviting.

Diana's gaze shifted to the massive hearth, where the large fire blazed. Then her eyes drifted over the fireplace to the place where a huge painting depicting a hunting scene was hung. Something about the artwork seemed oddly familiar, and almost unwillingly Diana rose to her feet and strolled across the room, her eyes never leaving the painting.

"Giles," she said calmly, pointing at a mounted rider in the foreground. He sat regally upon his black stallion, one arm raised in triumph as he held a limp fox aloft. His eyes seem to be bearing down arrogantly at her, as if mocking her.

"I beg your pardon?" Derek asked.

"Giles," she repeated simply, her finger reaching up to trace the likeness. "This is a picture of my late husband."

Derek moved closer to gain a better view of the painting. "Yes, that is him," he confirmed with a sigh. Turning toward the south wall to another painting he added, "I believe Giles commissioned this work after Thomas Lawrence completed that portrait of Henriette and Rosalind."

Diana also turned so she could view the second painting in question. Her eyes beheld a strangely quiet Henriette in a stiff, formal pose. Diana gasped loudly as she noticed Henriette held a young girl in her arms.

"A child," she said in a strangled voice. "They had a child?"

A look of alarm crossed the earl's face. "I presume you do not have any children, madam, since you have not previously mentioned any?"

"No, no children. Whenever I broached the subject of children, Giles became exceedingly cross." Diana continued to stare at the portrait, unable to lift her gaze from the sweet-faced baby. "She is very pretty. Did you say her name is Rosalind? How old is she?"

"Rosalind just celebrated her second birthday this past February," the earl replied.

Adrienne Basso

"I see," Diana said in a flat tone. "When did Giles marry Henriette?"

"Early summer, 1815," Tristan said. "In June. Theirs was the last large society wedding before the Battle of Waterloo. Derek and I used to jest there was a connection between the wedding and the battle."

Diana let out a deep sigh and brought her hand up to rub her temples. It was all too difficult to comprehend. Her head pounded with tension and confusion. "Can you please explain to me what my position is? I married Giles first, but produced no issue. Am I his legal wife?"

"I have no idea," the earl answered honestly.

"Nor do I," Tristan said. "I suppose the best thing to do is to make some very discrete legal inquires."

"Do you have your marriage lines with you?" Derek asked.

"Of course not," Diana said. "They are not among the usual items I carry on my person. And I was certainly not aware it would be necessary for me to prove my identity."

"There is no need to worry about that now," Tristan interjected. "There will be plenty of time to sort all of this out later."

Diana shook her head in dismay and moved closer to the picture of Henriette and baby Rosalind.

Derek pulled Tristan off to the side and asked, "What are we going to do with her?"

"I'll take her," Tristan said.

"What!" Derek exclaimed. "What in the bloody hell do you mean by that?"

Tristan cocked an eyebrow at Derek's indignant expression and broke into a smile. "Don't look so worried, Derek," Tristan teased. "I'll take her back to my house. Caroline is in town with me; she will be glad of the company. Unless you prefer that Diana stay here with you and Henriette."

"Good Lord, no," Derek quickly countered. "It would be a great help if you could keep an eye on her while I have this outlandish story of hers checked out. This could still turn out to be an elaborate hoax, Tris."

"It could," Tristan reluctantly agreed. "But I strongly doubt it, my friend."

Diana finally turned her eyes away from the portrait and glanced over at the earl and Tristan where they were quietly speaking together on the far side of the room. She was too emotionally spent to get annoyed at their rude behavior. What could it matter now? The past four years of her life had been a lie. Giles had tricked her father. And used her. And most likely would have continued to do so if he had not died so suddenly. Diana felt sick to her stomach.

It was true that her marriage had been a far cry from a happy one, but being the Countess of Harrowby was an intricate part of her identity. It was decidedly unsettling to learn she had been living a lie these past years.

Diana's mind whirled. Much of Giles's strange behavior and unusual attitudes toward her finally seemed to have a reasonable explanation. He had been leading a double life. Though Giles had never gone so far as to profess love for Diana, she had believed that he at one time had held her in regard and respect. She realized that belief must have been a lie too. She had merely been a means to an end.

Diana had always known that Giles had married her for her fortune; he had never hidden that fact from her. But she wondered if she had even been legally married at all.

She bit her lip tightly, feeling the tears prick her eyes. It would certainly not help matters any if she broke down into sobs. Above all else, she must contain her emotions and keep a clear head. With a deep sense of foreboding, Diana felt the nightmare she found herself embroiled in had merely begun.

Chapter Three

When Diana saw Tristan and the earl approaching her out of the corner of her eye, she squared her shoulders. It had been difficult enough discovering Giles's betrayal, but her humiliation was intensified having these two men witness her disgrace. She drew together the last shreds of her pride and faced them.

"We thought under the circumstances, madam," the earl began, "you would be more comfortable staying at Tristan's home, which is only a few blocks from here. Unless you have made other arrangements?"

"I have made no other arrangements," Diana responded quietly. "But I cannot possibly impose on you, sir. If you would be so kind as to recommend a respectable establishment, I will be on my way." The last thing Diana wanted at this point was charity, although she was not certain she had enough coin in her purse to pay for decent lodgings.

"Nonsense," Tristan insisted. "I wouldn't hear of it. My wife, Caroline, will be delighted to have company."

"It would be best," the earl quickly agreed. "I shall tell Dobbs to have your carriage brought around."

The eager note in the earl's voice piqued Diana. He was very anxious to be rid of her. She thrust her chin up and stared hard into his blue eyes. "I do not have a carriage, my lord."

"Don't have a carriage?" Derek repeated. "How the devil did you get here?"

"In a hired vehicle," Diana said, bristling. "I set out in my own coach from Cornwall, but I am afraid the vehicle was not up to the long, arduous ride. We broke an axle on the fourth day out and my coachman, Richards, was injured. I left him, along with my traveling trunk and my maid, Amy, who is his wife, at a posting inn in Salisbury, and I continued the journey on my own. Upon my arrival in town I was left at the yard of the Bull and Mouth in Piccadilly, where I engaged the services of a cab."

"You traveled from Salisbury to London on a mail coach, without the benefit of a maid or a traveling companion?" the earl inquired in disbelief.

Diana shrugged her shoulders, refusing to be intimidated by the incredulous looks she was receiving from both the earl and Tristan. "I had no other choice. I could hardly abandon Richards with his broken leg. His need of Amy's services was simply greater than my own."

"Oh," Derek muttered uncertainly.

"We have no need of a carriage on any account," Tristan said. "The rain has finally let up, and if we leave right now, we should arrive at my house before it begins to shower again."

The matter decided, Derek rang for Dobbs. The butler appeared soon thereafter, his eyes deliberately avoiding Derek, who knew he would have to discipline the butler at the first opportunity. It was obvious from Dobb's overall demeanor that he was aware that he had acted with great impropriety concerning Diana. Derek sighed heavily. He sensed the household servants were wary of him, and many felt he did not deserve the title he had recently acquired. Though Giles had hardly been a kind employer, the staff was still loyal to him and, to some extent, Henriette. Derek knew that the staff still regarded him as an interloper.

Derek bid his farewells to Tristan and Diana in the privacy of the drawing room, deciding to spare them all a public good-bye in front of the curious servants. He could only imagine what tales were circulating through the servants' hall at that very moment. Damn nuisance.

Once alone, Derek stared moodily at the hunting picture of Giles, his dislike for his cousin intensifying. Even as boys they had not been on friendly terms. Their fathers, who were brothers, were not in any way close, and Giles always enjoyed taunting the younger Derek about his lack of title and wealth. As he grew to manhood, Giles had become even more of a bully, but Derek was not intimidated by his older cousin. Derek's father purchased a commission in the army for his only child, and Derek spent several years on the Peninsula fighting the French. After Derek had faced the horrors of war, he found that Giles's petty barbs were indeed inconsequential.

Derek's thoughts then focused on Diana Rutledge. He was still not entirely convinced of the truth of her tale. It was not his nature to easily trust, especially where women were concerned. Yet he had to admit, Tristan had made a valid point. Who could possibly make up such a bizarre story—and for what possible gain? It seemed unthinkable that such a lovely woman had been treated so shabbily by a member of his family. But as Derek once again looked at Giles's likeness, his anger intensified.

Derek finished his brandy with a flourish and left the room in search of Dobbs. He intended to give the servant a severe dressing down for his disgraceful behavior concerning Diana. It was a task he decided he would enjoy since, of all the servants in the house, Dobbs, in a sneaky and underhanded way, displayed the most disdain for the new earl. Derek, in turn, distrusted the butler immensely. As soon as he could produce a replacement, Dobbs would get sacked, Derek decided, walking toward the servants' quarters. He would not tolerate such insubordination under his own roof.

Diana enjoyed the feel of the cool air on her face as she walked down the street with Tristan at her side, his firm grip on her elbow guiding her along. The crisp air was refreshing and somehow cleansing to her spirit. She had only a vague recollection of bidding the earl a rather hasty good-bye, watching Tristan take her satchel from the curious footman, and leaving the house. With each step she took away from the house, she felt her confidence renewing itself, as her memories gradually faded into the background. Slowly, her mind began functioning again, and she started plotting her next course.

"Here we are," Tristan announced as they stopped before the large stone steps of his elegantly appointed house. He looked down at Diana expectantly.

"I do thank you, sir, for all of your kindness today," Diana said clearly. "But I cannot impose on your good nature any longer. If you would kindly hail a conveyance for me, I shall be on my way."

"Where will you go?" Tristan asked softly.

"I'm not precisely sure, sir," Diana admitted honestly. "But I am confident I shall find respectable lodgings before nightfall."

"Nonsense, and please call me Tristan. If you will allow me, I shall call you Diana." He once again firmly grasped her elbow and propelled her up the stone steps. "Now, Diana, I could not, in good conscience, abandon you. For one thing, it is beginning to rain again. And for another, Derek would skin me alive if I lost track of you."

At the mention of the earl, Diana's calmness erupted into anger. "It is hardly any concern of the earl's where I choose to spend the night. He has made it abundantly clear he does not believe my story. I feel certain he has no interest in what happens to me. In fact, I got the distinct impression that the earl would vastly prefer I disappeared from the face of the earth and was never heard from again."

Tristan flashed Diana a brilliant smile, but did not comment.

"And I also find it difficult to believe, Tristan," Diana said, her voice growing stronger with each word, "that you are in any way afraid of the earl."

"Oh, but in that instance you are wrong," he said quickly, as a young footman opened the door and Tristan led her into the house. "I have known Derek for more years than I care to recall. We fought side by side against the French, and I have witnessed firsthand his skill with both saber and pistol. He is not a man easily dismissed or deterred."

"The earl would never come to blows with a friend over an inconsequential woman," Diana responded.

Tristan turned to her in surprise at her correct assumption. She had a keen mind and she was astutely observant, he thought. How then had Giles managed so easily to dupe her? Tristan was prevented from further considering the matter by the sudden appearance of his wife, Caroline, on the staircase.

Caroline paused a moment on the staircase, her hand tightly clutching the oak banister, her lovely face unreadable as she called out her greeting.

"Good afternoon, Tristan," Caroline said in a level voice. "Back so soon. And how is Derek faring today?"

"He sends his regards, Caroline," Tristan responded evenly, feeling a sudden unpleasant tension grip his chest as he watched his wife descend the staircase. "I've brought a houseguest, Caroline."

"How nice," Caroline said calmly, her eyes narrowing suspiciously as she stood before Diana and her husband. "Are you a friend of Derek's?"

Diana turned questioning eyes to Tristan, clearly seeking guidance.

"A relative," Tristan stated firmly. "This is Diana Rutledge. Diana, my wife Caroline."

Caroline favored Diana with a slight, cool smile, but quickly turned her attention back to her husband. "Was there no room for Miss Rutledge at the earl's residence?"

Tristan cast his wife a chilling stare, surprised at her rudeness and irritated by her unfounded jealousy. Caroline's moods had become so unpredictable lately that he was unsure how best to handle her. He had every intention of explaining the entire situation to Caroline, but he refused to do so in front of a collection of curious servants. Annoyed at her churlish behavior, Tristan turned away from his wife, refusing to answer her question.

"Diana will be staying with us while she is in town," Tristan declared in a firm voice.

"'Tis a bit late, but if you wish, I shall instruct the servants to bring tea for you and your guest, Tristan," Caroline said briskly.

"I do not care for anything, thank you," Diana said, speaking for the first time.

Tristan nodded in understanding. "You must be exhausted, Diana. Mrs. Roget, our housekeeper, will show you to your room."

He signaled to the short, plump woman who hovered at the end of the vast entrance hall. She quickly came forward and bobbed a small curtsy.

Diana thanked him again, noting with alarm the increased tension between husband and wife. She felt a momentary pause of regret, knowing she was the catalyst for it, but she felt too emotionally drained to try to rectify the problem. If Tristan did not thoroughly explain her bizarre situation to his wife this evening, Diana decided she would do so herself in the morning before she left. Satisfying her conscience with that notion, Diana wearily followed the housekeeper up the long staircase.

Silently, the housekeeper led her down the short hallway and opened the door to a corner bedchamber. Two maids were busy placing fresh linens on the large four-poster bed in the center of the room, and a young footman was dragging a copper bathtub before the blazing fire. Diana noted her satchel had been placed conveniently near the bed by another footman.

"Shall I have a tray sent up while you wait for your

bath to be ready, madam?" Mrs. Roget asked.

"That would be wonderful," Diana responded, thinking she would enjoy a cup of hot tea in privacy. She crossed the room and sat in a comfortable overstuffed chair near the window, gazing down at the garden below as the servants bustled about the room. A pretty young maid placed a large tea tray on the table in front of her. Diana wanly smiled her thanks.

Within minutes the maids left, and Diana sipped her tea while absently staring at the stark trees, their buds just hinting at the splendor the warmer weather would produce.

"May I assist you with your bath, madam?" Mrs. Roget asked after the footman poured the last of the steaming water into the tub.

"That will not be necessary, Mrs. Roget," Diana responded, rising to her feet.

"Don't hesitate to ring if you need any further assistance, madam," Mrs. Roget said before she left the room.

Diana moved slowly about the chamber, her hands automatically undoing the long line of buttons down the front of her gown. She dipped her hand into the bathwater, testing the temperature, and she admired the luxurious size of the bathtub. The slight dampness of her dress and hair permeated her flesh, making Diana suddenly realize how cold she felt. Intent upon soaking herself in the warm comfort of the tub, Diana moved her fingers faster, releasing the fastenings of her undergarments and hastily pushing them off.

Once naked, she slipped languidly into the hot water, shivering slightly until her body accepted the heat and finally relaxed. She stretched her legs out,

letting her aching muscles float on the water's surface. Heaving a tremendous sigh, Diana looked into
the crackling flames of the nearby fire and felt the
first tears begin to trickle down her face. Then suddenly, the floodgates broke, and she gripped the
sides of the tub tightly with her hands as the hard,
bitter tears fell.

Tears of regret, tears of anger, tears of betrayal—
all the pain and anguish came rushing forth, the
wrenching sobs shaking her body, and the salty
tears cleansing her deep, raw wounds.

When Diana was finally able to regain control
of her emotions, she realized how cold the
bathwater had become. She plunged her face
into the cooling water and picked up the small
bar of lavender-scented soap. Quickly she washed
and then dunked her long tresses into the water.
She scrubbed her scalp hard and reached over to a
nearby bucket, which held clean water to rinse her
hair. That too had turned cold, but Diana welcomed
its reviving chill.

Once out of the tub, she quickly dried herself and
donned her long-sleeved, high-necked flannel nightgown. Its familiar warmth was comforting and she
wrapped her arms around herself. She sat before
the fire in the brocade striped rosewood chair, alternating between brushing her hair and eating the
assortment of sandwiches and pastries Mrs. Roget
had thoughtfully included on her tea tray.

When her long hair was finally dry, Diana tied
it back with a small yellow ribbon she pulled from
her satchel and then climbed onto the bed. She sat
down wearily on the soft feather mattress, pulling
the deep blue satin comforter up over her legs.
Twisting around, Diana piled two of the pillows
on top of each other and lazily stretched out on her

back, her tired eyes coming to rest on the ornate silk bed trimmings on the canopy above her.

Diana was prepared to spend the remainder of the afternoon tossing and turning about, but she had underestimated her exhaustion, both physical and emotional. She would just rest for a few minutes before supper, she decided. No sooner had she closed her eyes than she was fast asleep.

Diana came awake slowly, the brilliant sunlight streaming through the open draped windows warming her with its intensity. Gradually she opened her eyes, allowing them to adjust to the brightness of the sun. Strange, she wondered sleepily, the window curtains almost looked blue instead of white in the sunshine today. She blinked several times before realizing the window dressings were indeed a soft shade of blue. She sat up quickly, her mind momentarily disoriented as she surveyed her surroundings.

The events of the previous day came rushing into her mind with startling clarity, and it took her a few moments to regain her composure. She rose from the bed and walked barefoot across the deep, lush carpet to close the draperies and shut out the sunlight. The room immediately became dim and dreary without the golden warmth of the sun.

Diana heaved a deep sigh, turned back to the window, and reopened the drapes. She was having enough trouble keeping her mood steady without creating an atmosphere of depression, she decided. She rang for a servant to bring fresh water and assist her with her toilet. A young maid, who introduced herself as Gwen, first brought the requested water, then produced a tray with hot chocolate and freshly baked rolls.

"Mrs. Roget thought you might be hungry since

you missed supper last evening," Gwen said, placing the heavy tray on a small table near the window. The maid left to retrieve Diana's clothing, which had been cleaned and pressed the previous evening.

Diana ate her breakfast thoughtfully while she waited for the maid to return with her things. After she dressed, Diana sat patiently, watching the young maid skillfully brush out her long hair and, upon Diana's instructions, secure it in a tight coil at the base of her neck.

"You have the most beautiful hair I've ever seen," Gwen said sincerely, winding the soft, silky tresses. "Even Lady Caroline's hair isn't this light in color, nor as soft."

At the mention of Tristan's wife, Diana felt a sharp pang of guilt, remembering how distressed Caroline had been at her arrival yesterday. Her first order of business that day had to be a discussion with Caroline, Diana decided. No matter how awkward the situation, Diana would not allow two innocent people to suffer a misunderstanding on her account—especially after Tristan had been so kind to her the day before.

"Has the family breakfasted yet, Gwen?" Diana inquired.

"Just Lord Tristan, madam," Gwen replied. "Lady Caroline is not feeling well today. She is still abed."

"I see," Diana said, hoping that she was not in part responsible for Caroline's confinement to her bed. "Please convey a message to Lord Tristan that I would like to have a word with him at his earliest convenience."

"Yes, madam. But his lordship has left for his club, and he is not expected back until late this afternoon. Shall I give the message to Higgins, his valet?"

"Umm, no, I don't think that will be necessary," Diana replied, unsure as to her course of action. She was hoping to leave before luncheon, but that would not be possible until she had an opportunity to say her thanks and farewells to her hosts.

"Mrs. Roget told me to escort you to the morning room, so you can have a proper breakfast," Gwen said when Diana grew silent. Diana nodded her head in agreement and followed the maid out the door and through the house.

In the brilliant morning sunlight, Diana was afforded a splendid view of the interior of the house, and she was impressed with what she saw. The furnishings were tastefully understated and elegant, from the highly polished marble floors to the thick, lush, pristine wool carpets, gilt chairs, satinwood tables, and large, ornate vases filled with artfully arranged, freshly cut flowers.

The morning room was a cheerful place decorated in shades of white and peach. As the footman held out the chair for Diana to be seated at the small table, she realized she was indeed hungry. She ate in peaceful silence, doing justice to the sumptuous meal of eggs, thin slices of ham, delicately fried potatoes, crisp toast, and fresh fruit.

After conveying her compliments and thanks to the cook, Diana wandered among the rooms until she discovered the library. She took a deep breath as she entered the room, enjoying the smell of beeswax and lemon oil, and looked with genuine pleasure at the beautiful tooled-leather volumes lining the walls. She ran her hands lovingly over the obviously much read volumes, searching for an appropriate title to spend the afternoon reading.

Diana paused briefly among the works of Shakespeare, but decided against *Romeo and Juliet*,

Othello, or *Hamlet*. She had no desire to read about tragic love or scheming families, Diana determined, hoping that somewhere among the classics she would stumble upon a few volumes of popular fiction. Reading a Penny Novelette by Mrs. Radcliffe was just the thing she needed to escape from her own difficulties for a few hours. She wanted to immerse herself in a story set in a fantastic Italian castle with vaults and dungeons and secret passages, screams and the clanking of chains coming from dim corridors, haunted chambers, ghosts, doomed noble families and long-lost heirs.

Unfortunately Diana was not able to locate any novels of that genre and settled instead on a heavy volume of medieval history, another interest of hers. Comfortably nestled in a leather wing-back chair near a sunny window, she read her book, losing herself in the descriptive passages of the age of knights and chivalry. Her quiet solitude was suddenly interrupted by a female voice that was low, forceful and full of venom. Diana looked up in surprise and saw Caroline standing in the doorway.

"So, I see you are still here, *madam*," Caroline spat out, her voice slightly slurred. The spite in Caroline's voice was lethal and in direct contrast to the pretty blonde loveliness of her appearance. "Derek came by last night to see you, but Tristan did not think you should be disturbed. Then they both proceeded to tell me a totally deranged tale about you and Giles Rutledge. Naturally, I did not believe a word of it."

Caroline took only one unsteady step into the library before stopping. Then she leaned back heavily against the doorjamb for support. "Tristan was most protective of you. I didn't like it. Not one bit." She took a deep breath, focusing her eyes intently on Diana's startled face. "I do not have the foggiest idea who you really are, madam, but I warn you, if you have any designs on my husband, you had best abandon them. Immediately. I have no intention of letting some distressed female capture Tristan's attention. Despite our current state of marital discord, I love my husband. And I keep what is mine."

With that said, Caroline took another tentative step into the room and, without warning, collapsed into a heap on the rug.

Chapter Four

Diana jumped up from her chair and raced across the room.

"Caroline!" she exclaimed breathlessly, kneeling down next to the fallen woman. Gently Diana turned her onto her back, trying to determine if she had been injured by her fall. "Caroline, can you hear me?"

When she received no response, Diana rose quickly and ran into the hall, calling for help. Immediately a footman appeared, followed by a maid.

"Summon Mrs. Roget at once," Diana instructed the footman. "And bring me some fresh, cold water," she said to the maid. The servants quickly scurried off to do her bidding.

After what seemed like an eternity, Mrs. Roget arrived, followed by the butler, Sutton.

"I am not quite sure what happened," Diana said

to the worried servants. "One moment she was speaking to me and the next she fell to the floor."

"Shall I have Lord Tristan summoned?" Sutton asked.

Mrs. Roget leaned closely over Caroline's prostrate form, examining her mistress. "I don't believe that will be necessary, Mr. Sutton," the housekeeper concluded. She looked over at the young footman speculatively.

"Do you think you can carry madam up to her bedchamber?" Mrs. Roget asked the footman, who nodded.

Following the housekeeper's instructions, the footman carefully lifted Caroline into his arms and carried her up the long, winding staircase. Diana automatically fell in step with Mrs. Roget and they kept pace directly behind the servant. In the entrance foyer, they met the maid, who was coming from the back of house, lugging a pitcher of water. Mrs. Roget instructed the maid to take the water upstairs.

After Caroline had been placed on her bed, the housekeeper dismissed the footman and maid and poured out a fresh glass of water.

"Is she all right?" Diana asked, her eyes never leaving Caroline's pale features.

"She will be fine," Mrs. Roget insisted.

The housekeeper propped Caroline up in a reclining position and brought the glass of water to her lips, but was unable to get her to drink. Mrs. Roget put the glass down and walked over to Caroline's dressing table, searching among the bottles of makeup and scent.

"Here it is," the housekeeper declared in relief, holding up a small, half-empty brown bottle. "I know that when the mistress is very uncomfortable, she occasionally needs to take this medicine. She must have taken a bit too much today."

When she is uncomfortable? Diana thought with distress. "Do you think I might be the cause of this discomfort, Mrs. Roget?" Diana asked candidly.

"Good heavens, no," Mrs. Roget replied with astonishment. "The medicine is for the cramps she gets with her monthly courses."

"Oh," Diana said, flushing at discussing such an intimate matter, even with another woman. "Are you sure she will be all right? She is very pale."

Diana and the housekeeper turned to stare at Caroline, and the housekeeper said, "Well, perhaps it would be best if someone stays with her. I'd summon her maid, but today is Lucy's afternoon off and she has gone walking in the park with her young man. Would you mind sitting with her?"

"Of course not," Diana answered, hoping Caroline would not awaken and be too distraught at seeing Diana in her bedchamber. Diana doubted that Caroline, drugged or not, would want to be reminded of Diana's presence in the house.

"Very good," the housekeeper replied, obviously relieved. "I'll make sure his lordship is informed of madam's condition the moment he arrives home."

After the housekeeper left, Diana took up a position in the far corner of the bedchamber. It afforded her an unobstructed view of Caroline, but was not so close so that the first thing Caroline would see upon awakening was Diana's curious face.

Just a few minutes passed before Caroline began moaning. Concerned, Diana moved closer to the bed, trying to decipher what the other woman was saying. She placed a firm hand on Caroline's brow to determine if there was any sign of fever. At Diana's touch, Caroline immediately fell silent, and then she called out clearly, "Alyssa, is that you?"

49

Caroline did not open her eyes when she spoke, and Diana assumed she was still under the influence of the medication. When Caroline continued to call for Alyssa, Diana decided it would be best to placate her rather than allowing her to be further agitated.

"I am here, Caroline," Diana responded in a very low voice.

Caroline instantly relaxed. "Read to me," she pleaded. "Read to me from Byron's book."

Diana's eye speculatively swept about the room, coming to rest on the mahogany night table near the bed, where a slim book lay. She picked up the well-worn volume and read the title on the spine: *Childe Harold's Pilgrimage*. Diana opened the book and was impressed to read the personalized inscription and signature of the author, Lord Byron. Hoping to calm Caroline enough so she could sleep, Diana pulled her chair closer to the bed and spent the remainder of the afternoon reading to and watching over Caroline.

Derek arrived at his club on St. James Street at four o'clock, two hours later than he had told Tristan to meet him. He strolled purposefully through the rooms searching for his friend, giving only the briefest nod of acknowledgment to those acquaintances he passed on his way. He finally located Tristan comfortably settled in a quiet corner, hidden behind a copy of *The Examiner*.

"Becoming a reformist, Tris?" Derek remarked, reading the headline of the weekly paper.

A few seconds elapsed before Tristan lowered his paper. "Well, Derek," Tristan said in a dry voice, "I've been waiting for you for so long it was either read what the Hunt brothers have to say or join the young dandies lounging in the bow window up front. They are busy eyeing the women as they walk by and passing rude remarks about the men. You should be glad I chose the paper."

Derek smiled down at his friend before sitting in the chair next to him. "No, you should be glad you chose the paper. Liberals they may be, but the Hunts make a damn sight more sense than the fools sitting up at the windows."

"Perhaps," Tristan said with a grin, demonstrating that he was not really angry. "I was beginning to wonder about you, Derek. It isn't like you to be so late."

"Sorry," Derek said and signaled for a waiter to bring refreshments. "I've spent the most frustrating day. I swear I've been all over London this afternoon on the most complex document trail you can imagine."

"I wish I had been with you," Tristan remarked, tossing his newspaper aside. "Were you able to learn anything to substantiate the lovely Diana's most unusual story?"

"Not precisely. I have, however, made a rather bizarre connection between my cousin and the lady," Derek admitted. "I spent the better part of last night and this morning searching through every scrap of paper in the house, hoping Giles left some clues behind."

"And," Tristan said, "what have you discovered?"

"Not very much, I'm afraid. I found a letter dated September of last year from a solicitor who requested a meeting in his office with Giles. The solicitor's name was not familiar to me; he was not the same man who handled Giles's estate. I decided to pay this man, one Mr. Jonathan Marlow, a visit, but when I arrived at the address I was told he no longer kept an office at that location."

"Has he moved somewhere else?"

"If he did, it was very sudden. There were still a few files left and the odd bit of furniture, but the landlord said Mr. Marlow hadn't been in for over a week. And he did not have the slightest notion where Mr. Marlow might be located."

"That is odd," Tristan said, rubbing his brow thoughtfully. "What did you do next?"

"Since the solicitor was a blind alley I decided to investigate the properties Diana demanded the deeds for yesterday. She claimed Giles managed these properties, but they were in fact owned by her. As I read through the papers she had given me, I discovered one of the properties in question was, of all things, a tavern located on the outskirts of London. So I took a ride out there to have a chat with the proprietor."

Derek fell silent for a few minutes as the waiter placed a heavy silver tray containing a bottle of wine and two glasses on the mahogany table at the earl's side. Derek waited until the man poured out the drinks and left before he continued.

"Luck was finally on my side and I was able to speak with the owner. In fact, I not only saw the current deed of ownership, but I persuaded the proprietor to let me borrow the deed for a day or two."

"How on earth did you manage that?" Tristan asked.

"It wasn't easy," Derek answered with a slight laugh. "I first had to consume several tankards of the inn's very watered-down ale, and when all else failed, I left my new phaeton as collateral."

"This deed must be very important for you to part with your new carriage, even if only for a short time," Tristan said and leaned forward eagerly in his chair. "Well, don't keep me in suspense any longer,

Derek. Let me see the damn thing."

Silently, Derek handed the document into Tristan's outstretched hand, and then he sat back in his chair. His keen eyes never left his friend's face because he wanted to witness Tristan's initial reaction, hoping it would be as astonished as his own had been.

Tristan let out a long, low whistle as he scanned the page and read the signature of the seller, clearly written at the bottom of the document. There was no mention of either the Earl of Harrowby or Giles Rutledge, but the signature of the previous owner was distinctly written in a firm, bold hand: Diana Maria Crawford Rutledge.

"At least we know she was telling us the truth," Tristan said.

Derek merely grunted and shot Tristan a quelling look. "We know nothing of the kind, Tris," he insisted. "All this proves is that Diana owned this inn at one time and has since sold it. The name Rutledge is not an uncommon one. It in no way indicates that she was ever married to my cousin."

"What about the tavern keeper? Could he tell you anything about Diana?"

Derek squirmed uncomfortably in his seat for a moment. "Actually, that is where the rub is. It seems the innkeeper never met the previous owner. His only contact was with the owner's solicitor."

Tristan gave Derek a boyish grin. "And would, by any chance, this solicitor be Mr. Jonathan Marlow?"

"The very same," Derek reluctantly admitted as he absently fingered his wine goblet. "But you needn't look so smug, Tris. It still proves nothing."

"I disagree, Derek. 'Tis obvious the solicitor is the connection. Too bad Mr. Marlow is not available to answer our questions."

"That does seem to be rather convenient, doesn't it?" Derek said with a wry smile. "It puts me of the opinion that Diana and Mr. Marlow are somehow working together in this matter."

"For what possible purpose, Derek?"

The earl raised an eyebrow in surprise, displaying his amazement at his friend's naivete. "For the purpose of extorting money, Tristan. What else?"

Tristan frowned and shook his head. "I find it extremely difficult to believe Diana is an adventuress. She just does not fit the part."

"Why not?" he shot back. "Just because she is beautiful does not mean she is also honorable. Your head has always been too easily turned by a pretty face, Tris. I know only too well how a lovely exterior can conceal a faithless heart."

Tristan grimaced. "Can you not finally put Charity to rest, Derek? It has been almost two years," he said, his voice low and sympathetic.

"I was under the impression I had done just that," Derek murmured and curled his lips cynically. "Charity would probably find it vastly entertaining to know how her memory occasionally haunts me."

"Charity is a fool, Derek," Tristan stated vehemently. "She should have never chosen Winchester over you."

"She might finally be having second thoughts about it, Tris. After all, I am now an earl, and Winchester is merely a baron," he responded mockingly.

"You are well rid of her," Tristan insisted as he had countless other times.

This was not the first occasion he and Tristan had discussed Miss Charity Worthington, and even after two years, the memories still wounded Derek. He had yet to understand how he, a normally sensible

54

and levelheaded man, had become totally besotted with Charity, seemingly overnight. Hapless fool that he was, he had allowed his happiness to overflow when the lady had claimed to return his affection with equal ardor, and with pride and confidence, he had pressed his suit to Charity's father. Baron Worthington, a fair and unpretentious man, had looked with favor upon Derek's offer of marriage. Although untitled, Derek had a long and noble lineage; moreover, although he was a man of modest means, he possessed ambition. He had a proven head for business and a strong, determined character. Derek knew that he was exactly the sort of man that the baron sought for his youngest daughter.

Charity, it appeared, had had other ideas. When Derek had informed her of their impending marriage, she was clearly horrified. She had no intention of throwing herself away on an untitled man, no matter how well turned out. She demanded, in a voice full of spite and venom, that he immediately withdraw his suit so she would be free to peruse other offers of marriage.

Stunned, Derek had complied, still reeling from the shock. How could he have so grievously misjudged the angelic beauty? But Charity's scheming knew no bounds. After Derek reluctantly broke the agreement he had made with her father, Charity immediately circulated the rumor that Derek had jilted her, rallying the sympathies of the *ton* around her and turning respectable society against Derek. Charity had assumed an air of wounded fragility and shy innocence that successfully awakened the chivalrous instincts of Lord Winchester. They were married a month after Charity had refused Derek, amid all the pomp and circumstance Derek had come to despise.

Though his love for Charity had been of a short duration, it had had a profound and lasting effect on Derek's attitude toward women. He vowed that he would never again allow himself to be so easily taken in by a pretty face. He now avoided any entanglements with unmarried women of society and instead confined his relationships with women who were willing to engage in brief sexual liaisons.

Although reluctant to enter into marriage, Derek placed duty and honor above all things. Since he had assumed the title, it was his responsibility to provide an heir. He planned on doing that at the appropriate time, already deciding the qualities he would seek in a mate. She would be plain, but fair, young, no more than 18 years old, of a sweet temperament, and, he hoped, fertile.

Once the obligation of producing an heir had been fulfilled, Derek was fully prepared to conduct his life separately from his wife. He would always treat his wife with the utmost respect and dignity. She could retire to the family estate in the country, where he would make periodic obligatory visits. In his mind, the marriage was to be very proper and civilized. That he might be missing something essential in his life was not an idea Derek would consider. Experience had taught him the need to be prudent and avoid the unpredictable entanglements of love.

Derek felt Tristan's blue eyes upon him, and he cast his friend a measured glance. "I'm afraid I am becoming melancholy," he said mockingly. "Forgive me. You are right, of course, Tris. Charity is merely a name attached to an unfortunate incident in my past. And she should be treated accordingly. I need to focus my attentions on the mysterious Diana

Rutledge or whatever her real name is. Drink up, old boy. I've a sudden urge to have a chat with our little adventuress."

"What the devil are you doing in here?" A sharp female voice pulled Diana out of her blissful state of sleep, and she awoke groggily. She sat up in her chair, stretching her stiff, aching muscles.

"I am sorry," Diana replied in a small voice. "I must have fallen asleep when I stopped reading. Although I do enjoy Lord Byron's poetry, I must confess it generally does have this effect on me."

Caroline, sitting primly on the edge of her bed, narrowed her eyes suspiciously at Diana. "Do you mean to say that it was you reading to me this afternoon? Not my sister-in-law Alyssa?"

"I stayed with you today," Diana said, watching Caroline intently. "Mrs. Roget thought it best you were not left alone."

Caroline turned her head away. "I am perfectly fine now," she said briskly. "Thank you for your concern."

Diana acknowledged the other woman's remarks with a slight nod of her head. She had the uncanny sense that Tristan's wife was not at all the shrew she appeared to be, but it was obvious she was uncomfortable in Diana's company. Diana was spared from making any additional comments by a sudden knock on the door.

"Come," Caroline called out.

"Lord Tristan is home," the young maid said when she entered the room. "And he is requesting that madam join him in the front salon at once."

At the mention of Tristan, Caroline's entire face lit up, and she smiled a genuine smile. "Inform him that I shall be down directly, Gwen."

"Oh, no." The maid blushed with confusion. "Not you my lady." She lifted her finger and pointed directly at Diana. "The other madam."

Caroline's eyes widened in shock and she dropped her gaze dejectedly to her lap. Her hands shook visibly as she systematically ran her fingers over the wrinkles on the skirt of her gown.

"Leave us, Gwen," Caroline eventually whispered.

Once they were alone, Caroline turned to Diana. "You may inform my husband that I will not be down for dinner this evening," she stated in an icy tone.

"Nonsense," Diana insisted, determined to put an end to all the misunderstandings. For whatever reason, Caroline had decided that Diana represented a threat to her, and Diana wanted to dispose of that incorrect notion at once. She had no intention of allowing Caroline to spend the evening alone, brooding in her room. "You will come down to the front salon with me. Since your maid is off this afternoon, I shall be pleased to assist you in changing your gown."

Caroline stared hard at Diana. "Why are you being so kind to me?" she asked in a low voice.

"May I speak bluntly?" Diana asked, and before Caroline could respond, she said, "I am well aware that my presence here has caused a problem between you and your husband, and for that I am truly sorry. Tristan has been nothing but kind to me, and I would not want to repay that kindness by upsetting you. I have no idea why I have been summoned downstairs, but I see no reason why you cannot be present. In order to avoid any additional misunderstandings, I think it would be best if you accompany me. Don't you agree?"

Caroline showed her astonishment at Diana's remarks. "Tristan told me a wild tale about you last night," Caroline said. "I didn't believe a word of it."

"Neither would I, if I were in your place," Diana said, not in the least bit offended. "I am hoping your husband has uncovered some information that can help me sort out the mess my life has suddenly become."

Without further comment, Caroline rose from the bed. Diana breathed a sigh of relief, knowing she had won Caroline over, at least temporarily. With Diana's able assistance, Caroline changed her gown relatively quickly. After taking one last look in the mirror over her dressing table, Caroline left the bedchamber, Diana trailing behind.

Diana saw the surprise register on Tristan's face as she and Caroline entered the salon side by side. After a moment's hesitation, he strode across the room, meeting them halfway, an utterly charming smile on his handsome face. He brought his wife's hand to his lips in a soft, seductive manner, and Diana felt like an intruder as she witnessed his welcome. Caroline's breathing quickened noticeably when Tristan caressingly held her hand, but she greeted her husband cautiously.

Diana muttered a hasty and nearly incoherent greeting. She moved to the far side of the room to allow Tristan and Caroline a few moments of privacy. No matter what difficulties the couple faced, it was obvious that they loved each other deeply.

Self-consciously, Diana stepped away from the embracing couple, colliding directly with a large, unmovable object. At first Diana assumed she had backed into a piece of furniture, but when she turned around, she gasped loudly with surprise. Standing directly in front of her, with his magnificent cold, blue eyes sparkling down at her, was the Earl of Harrowby. And he was not smiling.

Chapter Five

The earl took a step forward, placing himself even closer to Diana. She felt her cheeks become warm, and she was instantly aware of a queer excitement charging the air. She favored the earl with a nervous smile and an almost inaudible greeting, unconsciously taking several steps back from him.

The earl's proximity was unnerving. Diana felt the power he exuded with his very stance, his every movement, and she found herself frightened by the intensity of her reaction to him. He fairly took her breath away, Diana admitted to herself. She did not remember him being so broad of shoulder, so lean and muscular. Of their own volition, her eyes drifted down the length of him, and she admired the way his golden buckskins tightly hugged his muscular legs. He smelled good, Diana realized with surprise, like leather and spices and fresh air.

The earl coughed and flecked a bit of imaginary

dust from his immaculate coat of navy-blue super-fine.

The earl's cough ended Diana's scrutiny. Stiffening her spine, she returned his stare boldly, refusing to be intimidated by his forbidding demeanor. He met her gaze directly, a mere hint of amusement lurking in the depth of his eyes.

"Good evening, madam," Derek said.

"My lord," Diana replied, dipping a graceful curtsy. For an instant, she thought he might take her hand, and she fought down a rising sense of panic at the idea of touching him. "I was not expecting to see you this evening."

"Oh," he responded, raising an eyebrow. "I hope you are not distressed by my presence, madam. We do have unfinished business that demands our attention."

Neither his tone nor his manner suggested he was overly concerned about Diana's feelings. She disliked his condescending attitude and felt no compulsion to hide that fact. She eyed him irritably.

"Then I sincerely hope, my lord," Diana stated, in a voice dripping with insincere sweetness, "that our business will be swiftly concluded, so you may take your leave. I would not, in any way, wish to inconvenience you."

She could see she had sparked his ire, but before he could answer her, Tristan intervened. "Would you prefer we left the two of you alone to conclude your business?"

Both Derek and Diana turned to Tristan at the same time, answering in unison, "No!"

Regaining her composure first, Diana responded in a calmer voice. "I would prefer that both you and Caroline stay, Tristan." She turned to the earl and said in a challenging tone, "That is unless you have any objections, my lord?"

"Of course I have no objection, Diana," Derek said in a smooth, charming voice.

Diana raised her chin disapprovingly at his caressing voice and familiar use of her given name, but she held her tongue.

"Come, let us all sit down and be comfortable," Caroline said. "Tristan, pour some drinks for everyone. Sherry for Diana and myself please."

Diana deliberately avoided the matching gold brocade love seats, heading directly for a small, gilt-edged chair near the fire. She folded her hands demurely in her lap, waiting soundlessly while Tristan poured and served the drinks. After completing his duties as host, Tristan sat on the settee next to Caroline. The earl, Diana noted with irritation, chose to remain standing.

"Let us begin," Derek said commandingly. The earl took a long sip of his drink and began talking. "As I have already informed Tristan, I spent the better part of last night and this morning searching through my cousin's papers. I found no reference to you, madam." He glared pointedly at Diana, and she unflinchingly met his stare.

"That is hardly surprising, my lord," Diana countered, "given the fact that we have now established Giles had two wives simultaneously. I strongly doubt he kept a copy of our marriage lines in an unsecured location."

"Perhaps," Derek conceded. "Would you be so kind as to tell me, Diana, the name of your London solicitor?"

Diana gave him a puzzled look and shrugged her shoulders. It seemed an odd question, but not one she was adverse to answering. "Mr. Thomas Bartlett handled all the affairs of my late father. I have not required the use of his services since my father's death. He would, however, be the man I would call upon if needed."

"What about Mr. Jonathan Marlow?" the earl inquired.

Diana paused for a few moments, trying to place the name. Shaking her head, she replied slowly, "I am not acquainted with a Mr. Marlow."

"Are you quite sure?"

"Yes, of course."

The earl paced back and forth in front of her, his handsome features filled with suspicion. Pulling a piece of paper from his inside breast coat pocket, he presented it to Diana with a flourish.

"It appears, madam," he said in a scornful tone, "that you have made your first and last mistake. The current owner of the Red Boar Inn conducted the purchase of the tavern with the solicitor of the previous owner. The solicitor in question was Jonathan Marlow. And the previous owner, if my eyes do not deceive me, was you, madam."

Diana reached for the paper silently, eyeing the earl dubiously. She quickly scanned the contents of the deed and read the signature. Her lips curled up slightly in a mocking grin. "'Tis a very interesting document, my lord," she remarked cynically. "But I am afraid I must inform you, it is not worth the paper it is written upon." Diana leaned back in her chair and took a dainty sip of her sherry.

"I received that document from the owner himself, madam. This property was among those you demanded the deeds for. As you can plainly see, I am merely fulfilling your request. I have produced the appropriate deed for you. The problem is, however, that you no longer own the establishment."

"That is not my signature," Diana stated in a flat, emotionless voice. "And I have never heard of Mr. Jonathan Marlow until this very moment."

When the earl threw up his hands in exasperation, Tristan intervened. Coming forward, he reached for the deed in Diana's outstretched hand. "May I?" he asked, and at her nod, he took the paper from her. "Are there any other documents available so we may compare the signatures?"

Diana turned her head up sharply at Tristan. The earl's mistrust was to be expected, but somehow she thought Tristan was on her side. He gave her an apologetic smile and said, "It is the only way we can exonerate you, Diana."

The earl reached into his breast coat pocket, pulling forth the rest of the papers Diana had given him yesterday. She heaved a sigh of relief when she saw he still had her marriage contract in his possession.

"Check the signature on the marriage contract," she said smugly.

Tristan brought the documents over to the Sheraton writing table in the corner of the room. He turned up the wick on the lamp, casting a bright light on the papers. The earl raised a skeptical eyebrow at Diana, who sat motionless in her chair; then he followed Tristan over to the desk.

Caroline also walked over to the desk, wanting to examine the evidence herself. Tristan cleared his throat twice and said in a voice filled with regret, "I am afraid, Diana, the signatures do appear to be one and the same."

Diana snorted in disgust and rose from her chair. She strode over to the desk and stood before her three adversaries, her hands on her hips. "Naturally the signatures appear the same. I imagine Giles

65

hired the very best forger he could find. And yet I am forced to conclude they were in a rush when this particular document was forged, since there is a discrepancy. Look closely at the names. Can you not see it?"

The three heads turned back to stare at the documents. "I've found it," Caroline called out excitedly. "There it is. The second name. On the deed for the tavern the name reads Diana Maria, but on the marriage contract it is signed Diana Marisa."

"Thank you, Caroline," Diana remarked in a stiff voice. "I am glad at least someone is willing to examine closely the evidence before passing judgment." She stared at the two men, waiting expectantly.

Tristan colored slightly, but apologized readily. "You are right, of course, Diana. We should not have been so hasty." He turned to the earl.

"I do hope you will accept my apology also, madam," Derek said, keeping his tone level and his expression impassive.

"I ask only that you treat me with a fair and open mind, my lord," Diana said gracefully.

"I feel it is appropriate to drop the subject for now," Caroline said. "I'm sure Cook has prepared a marvelous supper for us this evening. I insist you stay and dine with us, Derek. Or do you have other plans?"

"Nothing that cannot be changed, Caroline," he replied smoothly. "I would be honored to join you for dinner."

Diana gazed at the earl from beneath her lowered lids, annoyed with her heart's involuntary skip of pleasure when he consented to stay for dinner. She tried to convince herself she wanted him to stay only because she needed to know what his next move was to be. Yet as he gallantly extended his muscular arm to escort her into dinner, Diana knew she was not being completely honest with herself.

Dinner turned out to be a far more pleasant experience than Diana could have imagined. Caroline was an accomplished hostess, and she kept a lively flow of chatter going through each course and put everyone at ease. The food was as delicious as Caroline had predicted, from the cream of watercress soup to the roast leg of lamb with tarragon sauce and the rich hazelnut cake with chocolate sauce.

Diana had never before dined in such elegant surroundings. The table fairly sparkled with the fine cut of the crystal, heavy sterling silver flatware, and gold-edged china. Even the creamy white tablecloth was lovely, with its fine Venetian lace edge. The candles on the table and sideboard glowed romantically, casting an unreal atmosphere in the large, formal dining room. Liveried servants stood a discrete distance behind each diner, rushing forward unobtrusively to refill a wineglass or to offer up another tasty morsel of food. Although raised among considerable wealth, Diana was unaccustomed to such luxury, and she found that she enjoyed it tremendously.

The conversation during dinner centered on harmless bits of gossip and amusing wartime escapades of Tristan and the earl, watered down, Diana had no doubt, for her and Caroline's benefit. Diana listened mostly, relaxing amid the warmth and established comradery of the others, occasionally interjecting an astute comment or observation.

Diana's quick wit and agile tongue were not lost on Derek. Why was she so damn likable? he wondered. And stunning, he thought, absently tapping his fingers on his wineglass. Surely her hair had not been so golden yesterday, nor her skin so smooth and porcelain-like, with just a pale hint of roses brushing her high cheekbones. Despite her rather plain black mourning gown, Derek could still see and admire her full breasts and slender waist. He could only imagine how lovely she would look properly dressed with her creamy shoulders and breasts rising above the bodice of a low-cut evening dress.

"Don't you agree, Derek?" Tristan said, interrupting Derek's thoughts.

Shifting in his chair, Derek turned toward Tristan, uncomfortable at being caught unawares.

"Sorry, Tris," Derek apologized with an artful grin. "I'm afraid I didn't quite catch that."

"Help me out," Tristan said, raising his voice a bit. "Caroline is beginning another long discourse on Lord Byron's exalted talent, and Diana is clearly being too polite to disagree."

"I am certainly not being too polite, Tristan," Diana said, wagging her fork at him. "I find Byron's poetry to be stimulating, a bit fanciful, yet totally engaging. I derive a great deal of pleasure from his work."

Caroline spoke up before the men had an opportunity to comment. "You see, Tris. Diana agrees with me. We spent a perfectly delightful afternoon together, reading Byron's poetry." Caroline's eyes twinkled mischievously at Diana, who grinned directly at her.

Derek was aware of the current of conspiracy between the two women, and when he caught Diana's eye, she gave him a broad wink. He was momentarily caught off guard, but after a brief hesitation, he smiled at her.

"I believe, Caroline," Derek said in a soft drawl, "it is not so much your admiration for Byron's poetry that Tris and I take exception to, but your regard for him. He continually proves he is not a man worthy of such regard."

"Oh, really, Derek," Caroline retorted hotly. "Since when have you become such a prude? Byron is merely a man who craves excitement and pleasure. He enjoys amusing women and a few fellows around the decanter. What is so wrong with that?"

"Nothing at all, Caroline," Derek agreed, with a charming smile. "Except the excitement and pleasure is often perverse, the women usually married, and the decanter bought on credit."

"Well, I still find him amusing and I am proud to call him my friend," Caroline insisted.

"He should be honored, my dear lady," Derek responded with kindness, not wanting to upset Caroline. She had always been blind to Byron's faults, no matter what Tristan had told her over the years.

"Tell me, Caroline," Diana said, "are you also acquainted with Mary Shelley? I recently read her novel, *Frankenstein,* and found it most fascinating."

Caroline shook her head. "I am not familiar with either the author or her work. Have you read this book, Derek?" She grinned impishly at him, showing she held no anger toward him over his criticism of her beloved Byron.

"I also must confess I am unfamiliar with the work," Derek responded smoothly. "Tris?"

"I do believe I recall the story," Tristan said, sitting back in his chair and crossing his arms in front of his chest. "Is it not the tale of a man destroyed by the huge, unlovable, lonely creature he has created?"

"Yes," Diana whispered softly. "I found the story quite moving."

"Then I shall be certain to read it also," Caroline declared, rising to her feet. "And now if you gentlemen will excuse us, we will leave you to your port and cigars." She waited until Diana had also risen from her chair; then the two women swept regally out of the dining room.

Once alone in the drawing room, Diana and Caroline fell into a companionable silence.

"Would you care for anything to drink?" Caroline asked suddenly, walking over to the Pembroke table in the corner, where various decanters of cut crystal were filled with spirits.

"No, thank you," Diana replied, confused by the other woman's anxious tone of voice. Although Diana did not think she could lay claim to a friendship with Caroline, she did believe they had progressed beyond awkward politeness.

"I am sorry for the dreadful way I have been acting," Caroline blurted out, "both yesterday when you first arrived and today. My conduct was disgraceful. I can only offer in defense that I was . . . not quite myself."

Diana's eyes widened in surprise at Caroline's apology. "It really is not necessary to explain," Diana replied gently. "Mrs. Roget already informed me about your medication."

"But I must explain," Caroline insisted. "I was so jealous when I first saw you with Tristan yesterday. He was so kind and solicitous toward you, and when he told me that ridiculous story about Giles—well, I thought for sure he was lying to me." Caroline's voice became strained as she fought against the urge to cry. "I thought Tristan—well, that he might have an interest in you."

It took a few minutes for Diana to comprehend

Caroline's meaning. Tristan interested in her? The very notion was absurd!

"There is no cause for distress, Caroline," Diana said, too affected by the other woman's sadness to be insulted by her remarks. "Surely you cannot doubt Tristan's affection. Why, 'tis plain for anyone to see how dearly he loves you."

"I know," Caroline said, shaking her head. And then without warning, she burst into tears.

Diana walked over to Caroline and place a hand on her shoulder to comfort her, but Caroline sobbed louder. Diana fumbled in the pocket of her gown, pulling out a snowy-white handkerchief and handed it to Caroline.

After a few moments, Caroline regained control, and her sobbing slowed to short hiccups. "You must think me the greatest fool," Caroline said, wiping her face. "I am sorry to be such a watering pot. I just seem to be taking everything to heart these days."

Diana escorted her to the settee and they sat down. "You must not get so upset, Caroline," she said softly. "Tristan is a special and wonderful man. He loves you very much and would never do anything to hurt you."

"I know that he loves me," Caroline admitted as she patted her nose. "And I love him so—almost beyond reason, I'm afraid." Caroline sniffed loudly, and her eyes filled again with tears. "But I am so unhappy, Diana."

Caroline put her head in her hands and wept loudly. Uncertain how to react, Diana patted Caroline's hand gently, waiting for her to regain her composure.

Finally Caroline threw her head back against the settee. "I'll get you a drink," Diana said, hoping the other woman would be able to collect herself before the men joined them. She was sure Caroline would not want Tristan to see her so distraught, and the earl would most likely jump to the conclusion that Diana was the cause of Caroline's unhappiness. Caroline accepted the glass of brandy with a sniff and took a tentative sip.

"You must tell me what is wrong, Caroline," Diana said sympathetically. "Perhaps I can help you."

"If only you could," Caroline said wistfully. "It is all so dreadful." She hung her head and spoke in a low monotone. "I am barren, Diana." Caroline heaved a tremendous sigh, and continued speaking, her voice so low that Diana had to lean closer to hear her. "Tristan and I were married over five years ago. At the beginning of our marriage, I was relieved that I didn't become pregnant. I was present when my sister-in-law, Alyssa, gave birth several years ago, and it frightened me. But since that time, I've come to realize how much I want a baby, need a baby. And yet I cannot conceive."

"What does Tristan say?" Diana asked, finding it difficult to keep her expression impassive.

"Nothing," Caroline whispered. "He refuses to discuss the subject any longer, since it upsets me so much. Tristan claims it doesn't matter, but I don't believe him. I know how much he adores children. You should see him with his two nieces, Diana. He fairly dotes on them. And they think the sun rises and sets on their uncle Tris." Caroline blew her nose again and heaved another sigh. "How I long for a child of my own."

"I am so sorry," Diana said with genuine feeling. She was not unfamiliar with the longings of unfulfilled motherhood. "Have you spoken to a physician about this?"

"Yes," Caroline replied. She gave a small, hollow

laugh. "I've seen several doctors, for all the good it has done me. They are a bunch of charlatans, the lot of them. Even Baron Wells, Tristan's family physician, and a man I have great respect for, can come up with no particular reason for my problem. Baron Wells told me I must relax and not think about it so much, but I cannot help myself. I fear I'm becoming quite obsessed." Caroline shrugged her shoulders. "And it is beginning to affect my marriage."

"You must not allow that to happen, Caroline," Diana insisted.

"I know."

"Is there anything I can do?" Diana offered, touched by Caroline's raw anguish.

Caroline's face suddenly became very still. "I do know there are people who can mix potions for barren women, but the cures I have tried thus far have made me dizzy and sick to my stomach. I just know if I could find the person with the right knowledge I can give Tris a child. Will you help me find such a person?"

Diana eyed Caroline with trepidation, uncertain how to respond. Caroline had already tried the usual cures concocted for her problem with no success. At this point, she appeared desperate enough to do something dangerous, and Diana could not allow that to happen. But what could she do? Through her love of flowers and gardening she had gained some knowledge about the healing properties of plants and herbs, but she knew nothing about concocting a remedy for a barren woman. What possible assistance could she offer to Caroline? Diana racked her brain for a suitable reply, while Caroline continued to watch her with luminous eyes.

Finally, Diana said, "It is true, Caroline, that some healers will sell you a portion for your ills and know very little about the power of the herbs in it. These individuals are usually of an unsavory and dishonest nature. Oftentimes, the cure they sell you can be dangerous, sometimes fatal." Diana paused a moment to allow the importance of her words to sink in. "I do possess a rather small amount of knowledge about the healing properties of certain plants and herbs."

Caroline reacted instantly to her words, throwing her arms about her and hugging her tightly. "Oh, Diana," Caroline cried, her voice choked with emotion. "I feel as though my prayers have finally been answered. I shall be in your debt for the rest of my life."

"Wait a moment, Caroline," Diana cautioned. "I can make no promises. My knowledge is somewhat limited." And she was not precisely sure what she was doing when it came to creating potions for fertility, she concluded to herself silently.

"You are just being modest," Caroline insisted, tilting her chin upward. "I just know you shall be able to help me. You can make a list of the things you will need this evening. I shall send Lucy out to the apothecary first thing in the morning." Caroline turned anxiously toward Diana. "That is to say, if we can purchase everything at the apothecary. Do you think you will need any special sort of ingredients?"

"Special ingredients? Do you mean like the eye of a newt or ground spiderwebs," Diana teased, unable to help herself.

"Well," Caroline said, her voice trailing off.

Her expression clearly told Diana that she would have moved heaven and earth to find any item Diana requested, no matter how ridiculous. Diana knew, in that moment, she had made the correct decision in offering her assistance to Caroline. At the very least, she could be sure her potion would not harm the other woman. And perhaps it would even help.

Tristan and Derek entered the drawing room at that moment, and all further discussion between Caroline and Diana ceased. Tristan immediately strolled over to his wife's side, and Diana marveled at his devotion. The earl's voice startled Diana and she turned quickly toward him. She raised her face and met his gaze. His normally cold blue eyes softened as they gazed at her, and he broke into a charming grin.

"I must take my leave, madam," he said pleasantly. "I shall call on you tomorrow so we may discuss your future plans."

Unconsciously, he lifted Diana's hand to his lips. Diana drew in her breath sharply at his warm, intimate touch. Then she admonished herself to calm down as the earl's lips gently caressed her hand, soft and feather light.

"Until tomorrow," he said in a deep husky voice, his powerful eyes never leaving Diana's face.

"Now please don't call on us too early in the morning, Derek," Caroline instructed the earl, hooking her arm through his and walking him to the front door. "Diana and I will be busy for most of the morning. You may collect her directly after luncheon. Perhaps you could bring your new phaeton? I'm sure Diana would enjoy an outing in Regent's Park."

Belatedly, Diana followed them and she arrived in the entrance foyer just as the earl left the house. She stood at the bottom of the staircase, absently rubbing her hand, puzzled by his strange behavior. Tristan also came out of the drawing room and invited both the women back inside.

"I think I shall retire now," Diana said, deciding she needed some time alone. She was very confused and slightly suspicious about the earl's rather pleasant good-bye. He obviously had decided to change his tactics when dealing with her. Why?

"Good night, Tristan. Caroline," Diana called to the couple as she began the long climb up the central staircase.

"Sleep well, Diana," Caroline said. "I shall see you first thing in the morning."

Diana did not miss the anxious note in Caroline's voice, and she felt a pang of guilt. She sincerely hoped she could in some way aid Caroline. Even if she couldn't help Caroline become pregnant, she could at least prevent her from doing harm to herself.

Diana shook her head suddenly, laughing out loud at the irony. Caroline was so positive Diana would be able to assist her in having a baby. She wondered how strong Caroline's faith in her would be if Caroline knew the truth about her. When it came to the conception of a child, Diana had only a vague notion of how it actually was accomplished physically. Naturally, her ignorance put her at a great disadvantage, but after all, virgins usually were ignorant in those matters.

Chapter Six

Diana slept fitfully that night, awaking suddenly in the early morning hours, her body drenched in a cold sweat. She squirmed uncomfortably under the thick satin coverlet for a time, until she finally sat up in disgust and threw off the offending material. Running one trembling hand across her damp forehead, she pushed her hair away from her face and tried to slow her ragged breathing.

She squinted in the semidarkness, wondering what the hour was. No point in trying to gain any more sleep, she decided with a weary sigh. The demons haunting her dreams would surely return if she tried to close her eyes again.

The images in her dreams had been so real that she could still hear Giles laughing at her, still picture his evil, malicious grin. She shuddered at the memory, but refused to give in to the tears she felt stinging the back of her eyes. Giles was dead, and no matter what bizarre circumstance he had left her in—legally married or not, stolen property, stolen funds—it should not matter. It was time to finally let go of the pain and humiliation of her past.

Diana felt a knot of anxiety form in her stomach as she allowed the memories to surface one final time. Giles, gloomy and foreboding on the trip to Cornwall after the wedding ceremony. His loud contempt for her on their wedding night, mocking her maidenly curiosity about the intimacies between a husband and a wife, and rejecting her in no uncertain terms. His blatant refusal to consummate their marriage was merely the ominous beginning of the years of neglect to follow.

When Giles had first left her, Diana had been shocked and hurt, but her spirit remained optimistic. She had swallowed her pride and bewilderment and vowed to do whatever was necessary to become the kind of wife Giles would have been proud of. She studied all the genteel arts so prized among women of society: music, painting, needlework. She strived to turn Snowshill Manor into a beautiful home, a place of elegance, warmth, and comfort.

Her efforts were all for naught. When Giles returned to Cornwall after her father's death, he cared nothing for the lovely home she had worked so hard to create nor her personal achievements. Diana could recall with startling clarity the fury and spite in Giles's voice as he accused her of trying to cheat him out of his rightful monies. He took great delight in informing her that he had only married her for her fortune and that he had no interest in her. Diana's fragile confidence and sense of self-worth were shattered.

The veiled threats Giles had made against her had really not been necessary. She was defeated, lacking of both spirit and will. She signed whatever papers he brought her, never questioning his motives. She was merely thankful that, once she did as he demanded, he no longer took the time to remind her how deficient he found her as a wife and as a woman. And then he would leave, not to been seen again for months.

Left on her own, Diana found her instincts for survival emerging, and her fighting spirit and self-confidence slowly returned. However, her secret pain and humiliation had always resurfaced during Giles's rare visits to Cornwall, for he had always made it perfectly clear that he could barely stand the sight of her.

Giles's double life explained a great deal about the man Diana had mistakenly called husband. She always felt there was something dark and menacing in the back of Giles's mind, and she had always believed she was the cause of it. She knew now Giles must have projected onto her the anger and disgust he felt as a bigamist. With his perverse sense of logic, he had probably blamed her for the entire situation.

Diana felt the warm wetness on her hand, and brushing a silent tear aside, she vowed to lift from her heart the burden she carried about her inadequacies as a woman. It was her final link to Giles, and she was determined to break it.

Off in the distance, Diana heard the grandfather clock in the hall strike the hour. Nearly dawn, she mused. She decided to get up. No doubt Caroline would be knocking at her door soon, requesting her list for the apothecary. Diana lit the candle by her bedside, holding it high in her hand as she walked barefoot across the room. She searched among the drawers of the small writing desk for a paper and quill. Locating the items, Diana dipped the quill into fresh ink and began composing her list for the apothecary.

Chamomile flowers, lemon grass, blackberry leaves, orange blossoms, hawthorn berries, and rose hips. Diana read the list carefully, hoping she had remembered all the ingredients. She would instruct Caroline to brew the concoction carefully and to drink it twice daily for several weeks. It was nothing more than a soothing blend of flowers she often made for herself when her nerves were on edge. Perhaps it would help Caroline follow her doctors advice to relax. Diana surveyed the list again and then made another notation: passion flower leaves. She suspected Caroline would like that. Diana added the passion flower leaves purely for effect; she knew they had no mysterious power in determining whether or not Caroline would conceive a child. And yet if Caroline truly believed passion flower leaves contained some special power to help her, perhaps they would.

As Diana had predicted, she had barely finished writing before she heard a discreet knock at her door. She crossed the room soundlessly and opened the door quickly, not wanting to arouse the entire house. Caroline stood breathlessly in the door- way, clutching her silken wrapper together with one hand.

"I was on my way downstairs to the kitchen when I saw your light," Caroline said lamely, entering the room. "Tristan was sleeping so soundly, and I just couldn't keep my eyes closed, so I thought I'd get myself something warm to drink. Is everything all right?"

"Yes," Diana answered automatically, her mind puzzled at Caroline's statement. Sleeping with

Tristan? But they had separate bedchambers. She looked at Caroline with a bewildered expression.

"Tristan's brother, Morgan, and his wife also share a bed every night," Caroline explained in her defense. "And Morgan is a duke."

Diana nodded mutely, refusing to think too closely about it. She knew that, when husbands and wives were intimate, they took their clothes off and slept together in the same bed, but she had always thought it was something they did occasionally, perhaps once a month or so. If Tristan and Caroline had slept together every night for the last five years, and Caroline had not yet become pregnant, then she must indeed be correct about her problem. She was indeed barren.

"Caroline," Diana said, her voice tinged with regret. "I really don't think there is anything I can do to help you."

"Don't say that, Diana," Caroline cried. "You promised me."

Diana winced at the panic in Caroline's voice, the accusing note of disappointment. "I cannot perform miracles, Caroline. If you and Tristan are already together every night—" Her voice trailed off, her cheeks flushing with embarrassment.

"Good Lord, Diana," Caroline cried out. "You cannot possibly think that Tristan and I . . . every night! Good Lord!"

Diana's face grew even hotter, and Caroline giggled. She paused suddenly when she saw the paper on the writing desk. "For me?" Caroline asked hopefully.

"Yes," Diana reluctantly admitted. "'Tis a very special brew that is designed to calm your nerves and relax your body."

Caroline's eyes sparkled with excitement as she picked up the paper and read the contents. "How often shall I take it and when?" She turned expectantly toward Diana.

Caroline waited patiently for the specific instructions. Only by the light of the full moon, Diana wanted to say, but she did not. In her opinion, the entire situation had gotten completely out of hand, but she had come this far and could not abandon the woman now. "You must drink this twice daily, Caroline, in the morning and at night."

Caroline nodded enthusiastically, and Diana's mind raced furiously as she concocted instructions. She was firmly convinced that, the more Caroline believed the potion would help her, the greater the chance it actually might. "Now you must wait one full week before you start drinking the brew. And then take it each and every day for three consecutive weeks."

"Anything else?"

Diana chewed furiously on her lower lip, trying to properly phrase her next remark. "During those three weeks, you should probably—well, that is—at least once a day."

"Make love?" Caroline asked. She rubbed her chin thoughtfully. "Only once a day?"

Good God, Diana thought with alarm, her eyes widening with surprise. Did people actual do it more often? Diana was momentarily stymied by her ignorance. Since Caroline obviously had considerable experience on this subject, Diana decided it would be prudent for her to make the decision.

"What is your opinion?"

Caroline pondered the question for several moments. "Twice a day," she decided pertly and then

.gave a small laugh. "It will be as if we are newly married. I dare say, Tristan won't know what is going on." She laughed again. "I will, however, endeavor to make sure he is far too content to give it much thought."

"Fine," Diana agreed hastily, anxious to end the discussion. "Instruct Lucy to bring the herbs directly to me so I may blend the brew properly. I shall deliver it to you when it is ready."

Whispering a quiet thank you into Diana's ear, Caroline hugged her tightly before she left the room. Diana stood staring at the closed door for several minutes after Caroline had gone, offering a silent prayer, hoping she had not unwittingly made an already difficult situation worse.

"Are you warm enough, madam?" the earl inquired in a polite voice. "Perhaps you would like another blanket?"

"I am perfectly fine," Diana answered, tilting her face up to the sunshine. The air was crisp, but the sun's rays were warm and inviting. It felt glorious to be out-of-doors. She turned slightly in the phaeton, facing the earl. "I have never before ridden in an open carriage. Thank you for bringing it."

Derek merely smiled as he picked up the reins and expertly negotiated the carriage onto the main street. "Caroline suggested we drive up to Regent's Park," he said conversationally. "But I thought it might be best if we head in the opposite direction, toward St. James's. It tends to be less crowded at this time of day, and there are more interesting sights to see along the way."

"That would be lovely," Diana said smoothly. She was well aware that the earl would also run less of a risk of meeting up with members of the *ton* in St. James's Park, but that would also work to her advantage. She had no wish to be viewed with speculation by prying eyes and gossiping tongues. "It probably would be best if we avoid the crush."

They drove along at a sedate pace, and Diana was glad the earl did not feel compelled to engage her in mindless conversation. There was a considerable amount of traffic as they drove down Regent Street, and Diana admired the earl's skill with the whip as he guided the horses through the maze of coaches, wagons, and pedestrians.

Derek pointed out Carlton House, the prince regent's London residence, and she craned her neck to catch a glimpse as they drove by. "Is it truly as lavish as they say?" she asked.

"Overdone in the extreme, madam," the earl stated. "Lots of gilding on the ceiling designs, walls covered in French moire silk, shiny marble floors, countless pieces of new and antique furniture, and endless bits of artwork. It is truly an assault to the senses to wander the rooms of Carlton House." Derek leaned closer Diana, remarking in a conspicuous tone, "And I have heard that the regent's new pavilion at Brighton is even more excessive."

Diana digested this piece of gossip silently, wondering at the earl's congenial manner. When bidding her good night last evening he had been almost friendly, but Diana had eventually attributed his pleasant manner to the enjoyable dinner and quantity of wine consumed rather than a change in attitude toward her. She wondered if he had discovered any information this morning that might have influenced his belief of her story.

They turned down the tree-lined mall heading toward Buckingham Palace and veered off sharply to the left, onto a gravel drive as the carriage entered the park. The new spring grass smelled fresh and the sunlight filtered charmingly through the trees, shimmering off the small lake they circled. As the earl had predicted, there were few people about, and Diana saw only one other carriage and several lone gentlemen on horseback.

Derek pulled the phaeton off the path, settling it between two trees. Lithely, the earl jumped down from his seat and automatically reached up to assist her.

"Shall we stroll a bit, madam?" he asked, extending a gloved hand.

Diana hesitated momentarily, eyeing the considerable distance down, but then placed her hand into his much larger one. She jumped down from the carriage, fervently hoping she would not miss her footing and land in a heap at the earl's feet. His strong arm steadied her, and she landed without incident.

The earl tethered the horses to an enormous oak tree, and he and Diana ambled among the sparse trees and sloping hillside. She glanced covertly at the earl as they walked, admiring the fine figure he cut in his forest green greatcoat with its numerous capes. He was hatless on this fine afternoon, his hair curling in charming disarray just below the collar of his cravat. His leather breeches were fawn colored, and his black Hessian boots sported their customary high shine.

Seemingly unaware of her scrutiny, the earl casually removed his leather driving gloves and pocketed them. "I spoke with Mr. Bartlett this morning," he announced without preliminary.

"My father's solicitor?" Diana asked.

"Not your father's solicitor," the earl said. "Mr. Thomas Bartlett has since retired from the firm and

85

is no longer engaged in the practice of law. He now lives in Surrey. I spoke with his son, Mr. James Bartlett, today."

"What did you discover?" Diana asked, coming directly to the point. She had learned, during her brief acquaintance with the earl, he would not have brought this meeting up unless it was somehow significant.

"Shortly after your father's estate was settled, a letter requesting the transfer of all business papers pertaining to the estate was received by Mr. Bartlett."

"Who sent this letter?"

"Apparently, you did."

Diana frowned up at the earl, waiting for an accusation of some kind. When it was not forthcoming, she asked, "Did you, by any chance, happen to see this letter?"

"I did."

"Well," Diana said, a hint of sarcasm in her tone, "pray don't keep me in suspense any longer, my lord. Did I send the letter?"

"I think not," he replied strongly. "The new solicitor, to whom the documents were to be sent, was Mr. Jonathan Marlow. Mr. Marlow, according to Mr. Bartlett, is a man of somewhat dubious reputation among those members of the legal profession."

"Why do you believe I did not send this letter?" Diana asked, pleased but puzzled by the earl's lack of suspicion. "Was my middle name again incorrect on the signature?"

"No," Derek replied. "Only a middle initial was used, and the signature naturally resembles your own. Since you have previously stated you have no knowledge of Mr. Marlow, I am inclined to believe this letter is another forgery."

The earl reached up to grab a leaf off a tree, and as they walked past, he absently tore at it. "When Mr. Bartlett received the letter he reluctantly complied with the request and dutifully sent the papers on to Jonathan Marlow. As a precautionary measure, however, Mr. Bartlett kept in his possession a copy of those documents he thought were most significant. He still has, among other things, a copy of your father's will and a copy of your marriage contract."

Diana heaved a sigh. "So you now finally believe I was married to Giles?"

"Yes," the earl answered, without hesitation. "The marriage contract in Mr. Bartlett's possession exactly matches the copy you presented to me when you first arrived. Although the contract is not conclusive evidence the union actually took place, the intent was clearly there. I can think of no reason to doubt your story."

"What happens now?" Diana ceased walking and faced the earl directly.

He looked down at her. "I made some very discreet inquires about your situation to James Bartlett. The next step is to produce your marriage lines. If the document predates Giles's wedding to Henriette, which you have already stated it does, Mr. Bartlett can file a petition on your behalf."

Diana frowned. "For what?"

"So Giles's marriage to Henriette can be declared invalid and you may be recognized as his legal widow."

She looked at him, totally confused. "Why on earth would I want to do that?"

The earl raised an eyebrow. "Was that not your original intention?"

"Good Lord, no," she said, her eyes wide. "What have I done to leave you with that ludicrous impression?"

The earl took a deep breath. "Will you then please explain to me, madam," he said with annoyance, "precisely why I have spent the past two days mucking about this city, making all sorts of inquiries, following numerous dead ends, if not to have your claim as Giles's widow proven and announced to the world?"

Diana was astonished by his remarks. No wonder he usually scowled at her, she thought, if he truly believed she sought recognition as the Dowager Countess of Harrowby.

"I never asked you to intervene on my behalf, my lord," she proclaimed with emotion. "That, if I am not mistaken, was your own idea. I have never felt obligated to prove to anyone, yourself included, my true identity. I have merely been defending myself against your accusations for the past two days." She raised her chin and continued speaking. "I came to London to settle my late husband's affairs and reclaim the property my father bequeathed to me. In light of the shocking discovery I have made since my arrival in London, I think it is best for all concerned if the notion of being declared Giles's legal widow be forgotten. That was never my original intention anyway."

"Are you sure?" the earl asked, running his hand through his hair. "If you abandon this now, you will also be relinquishing any claim to the dowager countess's property and the widow's portion."

"I don't want it," Diana stated emphatically. "If I press the matter legally, I shall be subjecting innocent people, not to mention myself, to a very public and probably humiliating trial. What of Henriette

and young Rosalind? Shall I fight to have an innocent child proclaimed a bastard just so I may use
the title dowager countess? Surely you do not think
I am so vain and selfish?"

She turned and began walking back to the phaeton before the earl could utter a response. He followed quickly after her, reaching her side in three
great strides.

"I am sorry, Diana," he said softly. "I have judged
you most unfairly."

The earl's apology soothed her growing resent-
ment. "It's all right," she said wearily. "I know this
entire incident has not been easy for you either."

"No, it has not," the earl replied as they reached
the phaeton. He gazed off in the distance. "What do
you intend to do now?"

Diana shrugged her shoulders. "Return to Cornwall, I suppose. I still own Snowshill Manor, and
I have a small amount of capital invested locally
that provides me with a modest income. It will be
sufficient until I can gain control of the properties
my father left me." She gave a hollow laugh. "I don't
believe even Giles could have sold all of them."

"Will you allow me to assist you with the investigation of the deeds of ownership for the remaining
properties?"

"There really is no need for you to trouble yourself, my lord," Diana said quietly.

"If you prefer I not involve myself, naturally I will
comply, madam," the earl said in a stiff voice.

He turned to walk away, but Diana detected the
note of hurt in his voice, and she reached out to
stop him. He looked down at her hand holding his
coat lapel and then back up at her face. Her hand
grasped the fabric.

"You misunderstand my meaning, my lord," Diana

said gently. "It is simply that I have no wish to further inconvenience you. Since you have been generous to offer your assistance, however, I shall be most grateful for it."

Derek felt his throat go dry as he tried to formulate a reply to her gracious response. Diana stood so close to him, merely gazing at him, and her gentle touch made him feel warm, even through the layers of clothing. Transfixed by her gentle brown eyes, he slowly brought his gloveless hand over to brush against her cheek. Her skin was soft, smooth, and flawless, and it felt velvety to his touch.

Diana looked up at the earl's blue eyes twinkling down at her, and her breathing suddenly became very shallow. Her cheek felt warm where he caressed it, and she had the strangest feeling that he meant to kiss her. She licked her lips nervously, her pulse racing at the thought of their lips touching.

Derek succumbed to his desire and leaned down toward Diana, his lips gently caressing her mouth. He thought to give her only one chaste kiss, but as he touched her soft lips, he discovered he wanted more from her. He increased the pressure of his lips, his mouth opening slightly so his tongue could explore her sweetness.

Diana recoiled in astonishment at the first touch of his tongue. The earl was not deterred, and he deepened the kiss. Relaxing her guard, Diana allowed herself to truly experience the kiss—to enjoy the unique feel of him, the exotic taste of him, the hard strength of him. His kiss sent a wave of heat coursing through her body, and she heard herself moan with pleasure. Swept up in the moment, she clung to him with both hands, meeting his kisses with increasing ardor.

Suddenly, without warning, Diana felt herself

being hurled toward the ground. The earl hugged her tightly against his chest when they rolled on the grass, his muscular body cushioning hers as they fell. Diana felt the breath rush from her lungs when they hit the ground, but the earl's solid body took most of the impact from the fall, and she was miraculously uninjured. When Diana finally regained her breath, she was horrified to discover the earl flat on his back, with her indecently sprawled atop him.

Fear clutched Diana's heart at the earl's very unexpected move and she tried to disengage herself from his strong embrace. He would not allow it, and she began to panic when she realized her legs were straddling the earl's hips. She could feel the rigid proof of his desire through her gown, and her fear intensified. Would he attack her now? Had her wanton response to his kisses given him the mistaken impression she would allow him to take liberties with her?

She struggled again to straighten herself upright, giving a shriek of alarm when the earl grabbed her forcefully by the hips and pulled her back against his hard flesh.

"For God's sake, keep still, woman," he hissed in her ear. "Someone has just fired a shot at us and may very well be taking aim to fire another!"

Chapter Seven

"Are you injured?" Diana whispered, her voice breaking the eerie silence.

"No," the earl answered with a grimace as he struggled to shift his position. Diana tried awkwardly to wiggle off him, but he still held her tightly by the hips and her knee became wedged between his upper thighs.

He let out a groan, and Diana immediately ceased her movement. "Did I hurt you?"

"Will you kindly remain still, madam, before you succeed in causing me a most indelicate injury," he said through gritted teeth.

Diana flushed furiously when she caught the meaning of his words, and she stretched her offending leg out. She held her tongue for a few minutes, trying not to dwell on their acutely embarrassing position. She could feel every inch of the earl's hard body pressing intimately against her, his strong arms, his broad chest, his powerful thighs. As she tried to focus her thoughts on something else, anything else, besides the man pinned beneath her, Diana wondered if there had even been a pistol shot. She certainly had not heard anything. Of course, her senses had been focused rather intently on the earl's lips at the time.

"May I please get up now?" she whispered, her embarrassment mounting as she recalled her wanton response to his kisses.

"No," Derek stated forcefully. He took a deep breath, tightened his arms around her shoulders in a viselike grip, and rolled her on to her back. As they turned, he kept his body indecently close to hers in order to protect her.

Diana's embarrassment knew no bounds as the earl flattened his body against hers. It had been bad enough when she had been draped over him, but now he lay intimately on top of her. She shut her eyes in pure mortification and was about to deliver a scathing retort when she heard the noise of a powder blast and the zipping sound of a bullet. She turned her head instinctively toward the sound, trying to rise, but the earl shoved her back down.

Diana groaned as her head hit the grass, but she said nothing. She lay motionless, and after a few minutes of heart-stopping quiet, Derek cautiously rose to his knees. He searched the small cluster of trees where the shots had come from, but could see no movement. He squinted hard, looking for the telltale glint of sunlight on metal that would alert him to the location of someone holding a weapon.

Finally deciding whoever had shot at them was no longer in the area, Derek turned his attention to Diana. She was sprawled on her back beneath him, her wide eyes riveted to his face. Her bonnet had been knocked off, and wisps of golden hair fell artfully about her face. He saw a faint bruise on her throat just below her jawline, and he had a most perverse desire to kiss it with his lips and caress it with his tongue. Her left hand was unconsciously curled across his thigh, and his flesh was pulsing at her innocent touch. He cleared his throat loudly and turned his head away, not wanting her to see the unbridled lust in his eyes.

God's blood, he cursed silently to himself. They had just been shot at by an unknown assailant who at that very moment could still be lurking about waiting for a second chance, and all he could think about was how much he wanted to kiss Diana again.

"Is it safe now?" Diana asked timidly.

"I believe it is safe now, madam," Derek stated gruffly, rising to his feet. He reached down to lift Diana up, but kept his face averted, his eyes still scanning the area from which the bullets were fired.

Although Derek felt confident the immediate danger was past, he instinctively knew they would not be completely free of attack until they had escaped the park. He glanced quickly over at Diana as they walked to the carriage, trying to gage her condition. She was obviously badly shaken, but she retained her composure with surprising dignity. Thank God for that. The very last thing he needed in this situation was an hysterical female.

"I'm going to jump up into the carriage first," Derek said as he untied the horses and held tightly to the reins. "If I give you an arm up, do you think you can swing up next to me?"

Diana regarded him with huge eyes, and giving him a wan smile, she nodded.

"Good," he said succinctly. He was overwhelmingly glad she did not question his rather strange request. Valuable time would be wasted if he had to explain that, by entering the vehicle first, he would be deliberately making himself a target in case the attacker was still watching them.

He placed his hand on the side of the carriage and jumped into the phaeton. His eyes were moving constantly, alert to any possible danger.

"Ready?" the earl asked.

He held the carriage reins securely in his left hand, and without waiting for her to respond, he reached down with his right hand and hoisted her into the carriage. Despite her fear of heights and falling, it had been easier than she thought. All she had to do was hold on to his arm while he lifted her into the phaeton. He flicked the reins, and they took off at a rapid pace. Diana nearly fell off her seat, but with the earl's assistance, she straightened herself up and held on tightly. He did not slow the carriage until they were in the middle of traffic on Regent's Street.

Diana tried several times to begin a conversation, but she found her voice would not cooperate. Nervously she fussed with her hair, trying to pin back the loose strands falling forward onto her face. She felt the breeze on her head as the carriage drove down the street and realized her bonnet was missing. It was probably still lying in the grass back at the park, she decided, shivering with relief that she too was not back at the park on the ground.

The carriage came to a halt in front of Tristan and Caroline's home, and Diana at last found her voice. "Do you have any sort of explanation for what has just occurred, my lord?"

Derek turned to her slowly, giving her a devilish grin. "It appears, madam," he said in a voice laden with relief, "that in a public park, in the middle of the afternoon, someone, in an attempt to wound or perhaps even kill us, fired two pistol shots." His grin widened. "The question remains, however, as to which one of us was the intended target."

"Damn it! How I wish I had been there!" Tristan repeated for the third time.

Derek, Diana, Caroline, and Tristan were gathered in Tristan's private study. Diana and Derek were seated in matching leather wing-back chairs in front of Tristan's massive oak desk, while Caroline sat a bit off to the side in a smaller chair. Tristan paced energetically in front of them.

Caroline rolled her eyes at her husband's remarks. "Yes, we all have heard how very disappointed you are, Tris. I am sure the next time Diana and Derek endeavor to get shot at they will be sure to include you in the party."

Tristan gave his wife a quelling look, but she did not wither under his intense gaze. Giving her a broad smile, he turned back to Derek.

"Are you sure you didn't see anything?" Tristan inquired.

"Nothing, Tris," Derek informed his friend absently. Derek's attention was distracted from the conversation as his eyes wandered repeatedly to Diana. She sat stiffly in her chair, her untouched glass of brandy clutched tightly in her hands. Her face was nearly void of color, and she had been uncharacteristically silent since they had entered the study. He reached out, gently touching her arm.

"Would you like to go upstairs and rest?" he asked in a soft voice.

Diana looked up at him, her eyes wide and frightened. "I prefer not to be alone now."

It didn't make sense to her, but now that the

immediate danger had past, she could not stop her heart from racing nor her palms from sweating. She felt afraid and vulnerable, realizing how close they had come to being seriously injured. The earl had protected her life, and she needed the physical reassurance of his strong, masculine presence to fight the terror threatening to engulf her.

Diana saw the genuine concern in the earl's eyes and nearly lost her fragile composure. She looked away and unwittingly took a large sip from the glass she held. She immediately began coughing and sputtering as the fiery liquid burned all the way down to her stomach.

Tristan, standing next to Diana, reached over and patted her soundly on the back. "Packs a bit of a punch, doesn't it, Diana?"

She merely nodded and continued coughing, her eyes watering. When she finally regained her composure, the earl flashed her a sympathetic grin. "Try taking very small sips," he advised.

She would have preferred to have thrown the rest of the liquor into the potted plant in the corner of the room, but all eyes were upon her. She took a cautious sip, somehow managing to swallow the rest without coughing. She placed the empty glass on the edge of Tristan's desk, quivering slightly from the alcohol and her vivid memories of the afternoon.

"What is to be done now, Derek,?" Caroline asked. "Shall the authorities be summoned so this incident can be investigated?"

Tristan and Derek exchanged knowing glances. "I don't think it is necessary to inform the authorities at this time," Derek responded. "After all, we have no conclusive evidence to give them. Neither Diana nor I saw anyone."

"What will you do?" Diana asked quietly, knowing the earl would not simply drop the matter.

"I will allow Tristan to help me, of course," he answered with a smile as he stood up. "He is obviously very eager to get involved. Aren't you, Tris?"

"I shall organize a select group of men to begin making inquiries at once," Tristan promised. "And now I do believe, Diana, it would be best if you went upstairs and rested a while."

"Yes, of course," Diana agreed, feeling more tired than ever before. Caroline quickly stood up also, her intentions to accompany Diana upstairs clear to everyone.

"No, Caroline," the earl insisted in a deep voice. "I'll go with her."

Caroline raised her eyebrows in surprise, but made no comment.

The earl placed a comforting arm around Diana's shoulders and led her out of the study.

They had already begun climbing the center hall staircase before Diana realized how heavily she was leaning on the earl, and she tried to pull away. He tightened his grip and began lightly stroking her back, hoping to soothe her. When they reached her bedchamber, he turned the brass door latch and entered the room first, pulling her in by the hand. He left her in the center of the room and casually strolled about, his eyes scanning every inch of the beautifully appointed chamber.

"Is there anyone under the bed?" Diana quipped, trying to rid herself of the rising panic she felt knowing she would soon be alone.

Derek grinned and walked over to her. He stood for a few seconds directly in front of her, his rich, blue eyes boring into her. She gave a small, nearly inaudible cry and stumbled toward him.

His arms wrapped around her, offering her the comfort and security she so desperately sought. "You are safe, Diana. You are safe," he whispered gently over and over again into her ear, until she gradually felt calmness begin to replace her fear.

Diana swallowed convulsively, determined to keep herself from bursting into sobs. She lifted her face. "You must think I am the greatest fool," she whispered.

"Don't say that, Diana. I've seen men on the battlefield act with far less courage and intelligence than you have shown today."

Derek gazed down into her haunted eyes, feeling the control he was exerting on himself slip. He gave into his passionate need and leaned his head forward to claim Diana's lips, which he had ached to do since they had first arrived safely back at the house.

Diana responded to his kiss instantly, her arms reaching up to encircle his neck and press herself even closer to him. His lips moved against hers, teasing them open. His tongue slipped boldly into her sweet mouth, thrusting forward and then withdrawing. She met his probing tongue with her own.

Derek groaned aloud at her uninhibited, passionate response. He kissed her deeply again and again. His hands slid down her back and arms, caressing her, encouraging her to give into the fiery tremors of desire threatening to claim them. His lips traveled down to the base of her throat, kissing, nibbling, and biting at her neck. His hand moved lower, gently caressing her breasts. He could feel the furious pounding of her heart beneath his palm.

Derek reached up and pulled the pins from her hair, letting it fall to her hips in a golden wave. He buried his head in its rich softness, breathing in the sweet, clean scent of lavender. His senses were aflame. His chest was tight, his breathing labored, and his manhood heavy and stiff.

All he could focus on was the beautiful, passionate woman he held in his arms and the desperate ache of desire he felt for her. He wanted to see her lying naked on the bed, covered by nothing but her glorious tresses. He yearned to see and kiss every inch of Diana's exquisite body, to taste her flawless skin, to feast on her nipples. He wanted to feel her naked flesh moving against his own burning skin. He longed to hear her cry out in ecstasy as he thrust deep within her, taking them both higher and higher until everything exploded in the ultimate fulfillment. Derek wanted her with a fierce intensity he found almost frightening.

Greedily his fingers unfastened the buttons down the front of her gown, opening it to her waist. And then his mouth was on her nipples, and he was biting her gently through the soft fabric of her chemise, almost as if she were naked.

Diana responded mindlessly, arching her back and moaning deep in her throat. She had never imagined anything like this. She heard her own heartbeat pounding loudly in her ears, drowning out every bit of modesty, every bit of reason. All she could do was feel and experience the wondrous things the earl was doing to her. His lips traveled once more up to hers and he kissed her again, his tongue lightly exploring her mouth.

"Oh, God, how I want you, Diana," he whispered, his voice harsh with desire. His hands stroked down her back and cupped her buttocks, lifting her up and pressing her hard against his swollen manhood.

She gave a startled cry of fear at his words and actions, realizing for the first time how completely beyond herself these exciting new sensations made her react. What would happen now? Would they make love, as Caroline called it? Diana's confusion and ignorance caused her to pause, and she swallowed hard, unable to formulate a response either with her voice or with her body.

Derek felt the change in her immediately—the stiffening of her body, the pulling away of her arms. He tilted his head down, and when he saw the fear and uncertainty in her soft brown eyes, he felt like kicking himself for being such a damn fool. Randy goat. Insufferable cad. Diana had turned to him in pain and fear and he had nearly succeeded in taking advantage of her vulnerable state. He was appalled at his lack of control and absence of honor.

Gently, Derek loosened his hold on her and took a step backward. Diana swayed slightly, and for a moment, he was afraid she wouldn't be able to remain standing without his support, but she did. She held the bodice of her dress together with one hand, while pushing the heavy strands of loose hair away from her face with the other.

Shuddering with mortification, Diana fixed her stare on the rich Oriental carpet at her feet, unable to meet his eyes. She was certain he thought her a whore. She waited in trepidation for the insults to begin, barely able to imagine his anger at her sudden, abrupt change of heart.

"I do hope you will be able to forgive my disgraceful behavior, madam," Derek murmured in a low voice.

Diana moistened her lips with her tongue. Why was he being so kind? They both knew she too was responsible for what had occurred. It was not fair for him to shoulder all the burden of guilt. Yet her mind was a tumultuous jumble of feelings, emotions, and thoughts she did not understand and could not clearly articulate.

"I—I'm not quite sure what came over me," she muttered, her face flushed with embarrassment.

Derek gazed for a moment at her lovely face, struggling hard to look at him, and he turned away from her. His desire for Diana was too fresh and his need too overwhelming for him to remain so close to her and not again gather her into his arms. He strode purposefully to the door and opened it, but paused a moment, his back toward her as he spoke.

"It was my fault, Diana," he said in a strong voice, hoping to ease some of the guilt and confusion he saw on her face. "Please, forgive me." And then he was gone.

Diana's body went limp when the door closed, feeling strangely lost without the earl's strong presence. Methodically she fastened the buttons of her gown, refusing to dwell on how they had become undone in the first place. She wandered aimlessly about the room, picking up her silver-handled brush from the dressing table in the corner and absently brushing the tangles from her hair. She started to sit down on the low stool in front of the table, but stopped short as she saw her reflection in the mirror.

Her lips were red and slightly swollen from the earl's kisses, her cheeks flushed with color, her eyes still glowing with sensuality. Diana shuddered. She did not wish to be reminded of their lovemaking. She walked to a chair near the large window on the far side of the room, and she sat there staring sightlessly out at the garden below. She stroked the brush through her hair, deliberately shutting her mind to the questions and feelings swamping her, unwilling to confront them. She stayed there for several hours, long after the sun had set and darkness had fallen. But she was no closer to understanding her dilemma than when she had first sat down.

Chapter Eight

"Would you care for more tea, my lord?" Diana asked politely, holding aloft the floral-patterned Spode teapot.

"No, thank you," Derek replied blandly. He balanced the delicate porcelain teacup he held awkwardly in his large hand. Then he glanced again at the small clock on the drawing room mantel.

"What time did you say Tristan was returning home?" he asked.

"Tristan *is* at home, my lord. I am sure he will be down to join us momentarily. He must have been . . . detained . . . upstairs." Diana stammered slightly, her cheeks flaming.

"Tart?" Diana asked, holding out a scrumptious assortment of pastries, scones, and small sandwiches. Her hand shook slightly.

Derek looked down at the plate and then up to her carefully schooled features. Although Diana was outwardly appearing calm, he sensed she was anything but comfortable at finding herself alone in his company. In the week that had passed since their mishap in the park, she had successfully avoided all his attempts at getting her alone, yet he had persistently called every afternoon.

As hard as he tried, Derek had not been able to dismiss Diana from his mind. At that moment, his memory was vivid with the smooth feel of her lips, the lush curves of her body, and the burning heat of her passion. He felt his body hardening as he studied her lovely face.

Derek was confused and baffled by his reaction to Diana. Never before with any woman, even his beloved Charity, had he felt this intense ache, this need, deep within his soul. He had to discover the cause.

"We need to talk, Diana," Derek said quietly in a deep voice.

Diana's eyes widened in panic, and she squirmed noticeably in her chair. "Do try a pastry, my lord," she suggested, raising the plate higher. "The cream ones are a favorite of Caroline's. Cook makes them especially for her."

Derek scowled down at her, unable to form a civilized response. He finally had an opportunity alone with her and all she wanted to do was talk about tea and pastries. Pastries, for God's sake!

Derek placed his teacup none too gently on the mahogany table between them and stood. He walked about the room in agitation, finally halting before the fireplace, his back to Diana. He could feel her eyes boring into his back as he picked up the poker and rolled a fat log onto the flames.

"Have you discovered any new information about our difficulties in the park?" she said suddenly.

"Nothing," he replied with a heavy sigh, allowing her to direct the conversation for the time being. "Since no further attempts on my life have been made, the investigator Tristan hired is inclined to believe it was an isolated incident."

"What is your opinion?"

"I am not so easily convinced," he announced, shrugging his shoulders. "My judgment might be prejudiced, however, since I was one of the individuals being shot at."

"I am going home," Diana blurted out suddenly.

Derek whirled around at her statement. "What?"

"I said I am going home," she repeated, avoiding his eyes, "to Snowshill Manor in Cornwall. I decided this morning. I'll be leaving as soon as I can make the appropriate arrangements."

"I don't think that would be wise," Derek said slowly. He stared at her a long, silent minute, knowing he needed to choose his words carefully so as not to unduly frighten her. "I believe you should stay in London—at least until we can be certain you are no longer in any danger."

Diana wrinkled her brow. "You just told me the investigator has determined the incident in the park was an isolated case. And there have been no further attacks."

"Precisely," Derek said softly. While he had deliberately been jaunting about town, Diana had not ventured forth from the safety of Tristan and Caroline's house the entire week. He knew that the damning piece of evidence indicated Diana had most likely been the bullets' target.

Diana frowned in puzzlement for a moment until understanding suddenly lit her face. Her eyes flew to Derek's in alarm. "Do you mean to imply I was the intended victim, my lord?" She shook her head vehemently. "Surely, you are mistaken."

She picked up her teacup and nervously took a large sip, crying out when the hot brew burned her tongue. "Darn," she cursed softly, thrusting the cup down on the table.

Derek crossed the room and sat on the gold brocade settee next to Diana. She was so upset that she hardly seemed notice his movements.

"I did not mean to frighten you, my dear," he whispered in her ear.

"Well, you have," she snapped, turning to him. Her fingers flew to her throat and she fidgeted nervously with the high black lace collar of her dress.

"You must be mistaken," she said again, clasping her hand in her lap. "There cannot possibly be someone in London trying to harm me. The only people I am acquainted with in the entire city are Tristan and Caroline. And you, of course."

Derek saw the flicker of doubt in her eyes, and it wounded him. Did she really believe he was capable of such treachery? He then recalled her past experiences with Giles, and he could not fault her for a moment of mistrust.

"We are dealing with an unknown adversary, Diana. Anything can happen," Derek said softly.

"That settles it," Diana declared. "If you truly believe I am in danger, I must leave London at once."

"What!" Derek shouted, appalled at the idea. "Diana, have you not heard a word I've said?"

"I heard each and every word you uttered, my lord," she said, thrusting her chin up. "I also understand the most appropriate course of action. If there is danger in London, then I must leave—as soon as possible."

Derek shook his head and chuckled softly. Her

reasoning did have a ring of logic to it, even if it was convoluted in the extreme. The wonders of a woman's mind. He stretched out his long legs and folded his arms comfortably across his chest. There would be no fighting her on this. He could tell by the firm set of her chin and the rigid set of her back that she was poised for a confrontation.

"I don't suppose there is any possibility you will reconsider your decision?" Derek asked smoothly.

"I will not change my mind."

"Fine," he said simply.

"Fine," she repeated.

Derek saw several emotions cross her face and took heart at her obvious distress. Perhaps she would miss his company. "Naturally, I shall accompany you."

"Accompany me?" Diana said in astonishment.

"Really, madam," Derek said with a charming smile, "you did not actually believe I would allow you to leave here on your own?"

Diana gave him a wary look. "It is unnecessary for you to travel the entire distance to Cornwall. I would, however, appreciate an escort out of London."

"I shall accompany you all the way to Cornwall," he insisted. "And who knows how long I shall stay there once I arrive?"

Diana's mouth opened in shock, but before she could respond to him, the drawing room doors swung open and Tristan and Caroline strolled in.

"Sorry, we're late," Tristan called out cheerfully. "We had a bit of business to attend to, didn't we, Caroline?" He gave his wife a positively lecherous grin, and she blushed prettily.

"Tris," Caroline admonished in a silky voice. "Please behave. You are causing Diana to blush."

Derek looked at Diana's red face, and to spare her further embarrassment, he said quickly, "Diana and I have been making plans for our departure. You did say you wanted to leave tomorrow morning, didn't you?"

Diana merely nodded her head.

"Must you leave?" Caroline asked, sounding genuinely sorry at the idea of Diana's departure.

"Yes," Diana croaked. "I have already stayed far longer than I intended."

"We shall miss you," Tristan said as he accepted a cup of tea from his wife. "Perhaps you will come and stay with us the next time you are in London? Or better yet, come visit us at Westgate Manor, our country home in Hampshire."

"That is most kind of you, Tris. I cannot begin to thank you and Caroline for all your kindness during my stay. I am very grateful."

"I had best take my leave if I am to make all the arrangements for our departure tomorrow," Derek said.

Now that he had settled on a course of action, he was rather pleased with the way events had turned out. He especially enjoyed the look of total astonishment on Diana's face when he had informed her of his intentions to accompany her to Snowshill Manor. There would be numerous opportunities to discuss the unfinished personal business between them on the long ride to Cornwall. And there would be no interruptions. Derek would see to that.

"I shall be here at first light, madam. I expect you to be ready and waiting."

"Yes, of course, my lord," Diana answered readily.

Smiling smugly and bowing, the earl grasped Diana's hand and kissed it. It was the first intimate contact he had with her all week, and it felt wonderful to touch her velvety skin again. He heard her sharp intake of breath as his lips grazed her hand, and his heart soared, knowing she was affected by his touch.

"Until morning, my dear," he whispered softly, causing Diana to lean forward to catch his words, and she nearly collided head-on with him as he stood up. He made his good-byes to Tristan and Caroline and then flashed Diana a final smile before quitting the room.

True to his word, the earl presented himself at Tristan's door just as dawn was breaking. Diana was coming down the staircase when he arrived; a young footman carrying her small satchel preceded her. She exchanged pleasantries with the earl and bid a friendly good-bye to the small group of servants gathered in the hall to see her off.

"With Cook's compliment's, madam," Mrs. Roget said, handing Diana a large wicker hamper. "We hope you have a safe and pleasant journey."

"How very thoughtful!" Diana exclaimed. "Please convey my thanks to Cook and to the entire staff for their outstanding service during my visit. They do you proud, Mrs. Roget."

The earl watched Diana with growing admiration as she said good-bye to the other servants, calling each by name. It was amazing what a few minutes of sincere appreciation and thanks did for everyone's morale. By the time they left the marble-tiled hallway, everyone was beaming.

Derek watched Diana's face register surprise when she saw the large traveling coach, complete with liveried driver and coachmen. Derek opened the carriage door and handed her up.

"Your lunch, I presume," he teased, passing along the basket. He swung up into the coach and sat on the heavily padded seat across from her.

"I suggest you watch your step, my lord," Diana said flippantly, patting the hamper, "or I will not share my treats with you."

"In that case, I shall endeavor to behave," he replied. "I must confess I have a great curiosity to taste your treats, Diana."

Diana's eyes widened and he cast her a look of pure innocence. Resolutely, she turned to stare out the window.

"It won't work," he said conversationally.

"I beg your pardon," she replied haughtily.

"You have a very expressive face, my dear. It's often possible to read your thoughts."

"Oh really, my lord," Diana said sweetly, her eyes shooting daggers at him. "Can you actually read my thoughts? How very interesting."

He laughed heartily, enjoying her wit as she hastily averted her face.

"Ready, your lordship?" the driver yelled down.

"Proceed, Langston," Derek shouted, his eyes never leaving Diana's beautiful face.

At the earl's command, the carriage took off down the deserted street at a clipping pace. Diana shifted uncomfortably under the earl's scrutiny, spreading her skirts out on the seat and fidgeting nervously with the latch on the wicker hamper. For pity sake, was he going to stare at her all the way to Cornwall?

"Am I making you uncomfortable, Diana?" he asked with a devilish grin.

"Of course not, my lord," she responded primly. "I enjoy being stared at in such close quarters. In fact, I was just wondering if you were going to be staring at me for the entire journey."

"That sounds most pleasant," he declared.

She felt uneasy and needed to reassure herself that she had acted with sound judgment when she'd agreed to the earl's escort. She was completely under his control now, riding alone with him in his coach. He could do whatever he wanted and she would be powerless to prevent it. She supposed she ought to be afraid of him. The last time she had ridden alone in a coach with a man had also been on a journey to Cornwall; Giles and she had traveled there after her wedding. She shuddered at that memory, but quickly shut it off from her mind. The present earl was nothing like his cousin. He was a man of honor. She was not afraid of him.

"It is a long way to Cornwall, my lord," Diana said softly. "I believe you will quickly grow tired of my company."

"You are only partially correct, Diana. 'Tis a long way to Cornwall." Derek settled back on the plush burgundy leather bench and covered his eyes with his hat. He stretched his legs out until they were touching the edge of her seat, then crossed them at the ankles. And he announced in a pleasant voice, "I am going to try to sleep for a bit. I suggest you do the same."

Within minutes he was breathing evenly, and Diana was shocked to realize he had indeed fallen asleep. In slumber his features relaxed and softened, giving him the appearance of being younger than his 35 years. The earl's piercing blue eyes—which were, to Diana's way of thinking, the most forbidding aspect of his character—were hidden under his hat. He was, without question, the most handsome man she had ever seen, and her heart pounded when she remembered how he had held her in his arms and kissed her.

Diana watched him for several miles, then shifted her stiff body into various positions, trying to find one that was comfortable. The coach was larger than any she had ever been in before, and it was a far cry from the cramped mail coach she had ridden in on her way to London. A bit of teasing from the earl was a small price to pay for the luxury of a private coach.

A sudden, loud tapping noise on the top of the carriage drew Diana's attention to the ceiling of the vehicle. "Finchely Common, my lord," the driver yelled down.

The earl came instantly awake. He threw his hat into the corner of the coach and slid his hand into his cloak. Diana gasped loudly as he drew out a silver-cased pistol and checked the barrel.

"Expecting someone, my lord?" she asked.

"Never hurts to be prepared," he answered cheerfully. "This particular stretch of road, while not actually very far from London, is a special favorite of several notorious highwaymen. They tend to be attracted to open, lonely places like this when deciding upon a vehicle to stop and rob."

They waited for several tense miles; then the driver sounded the all clear. Derek poked his head out the open carriage window to assess the situation for himself and, apparently satisfied with what he saw, put the pistol beneath his cloak.

He gave Diana a roguish smile and asked, "Shall we open your hamper and see what wonderful delights Tristan's cook has prepared for us?"

Diana shook her head in wonder, amazed at his ease with potential danger, his total lack of fear. She knew she would never come to any harm while he was protecting her. The only real danger she faced was of her own doing. If she wasn't very, very careful, she would fall in love with the earl. And that would have been, by far, the most dangerous thing she could possibly have done.

Chapter Nine

The aroma of fresh-baked bread instantly assaulted Diana's senses when she opened the wicker basket. "My goodness," she exclaimed with delight. "There is enough food in here to feed Wellington's army."

The earl gave a small chuckle as he bit into the thick ham sandwich she handed him. "I spent several years with the good duke," he remarked. "And believe me, we did not always dine on such excellent fare."

"It was very kind of Cook to prepare all of this," Diana said, daintily chewing on a chicken leg. "I shall be sure to mention it to Caroline and Tristan when I write to them."

"Will you miss Caroline and Tris?"

"Yes," Diana said. "They were very kind to me. And I did enjoy their company. It was harder saying good-bye to them last night than I anticipated. Poor

Tristan. I'm afraid Caroline and I became rather emotional."

"You two did seem to get on well together."

"Surprisingly, we did," Diana agreed, cutting a hunk of cheddar cheese and passing it to the earl. "After we got over an initial misunderstanding, we became most friendly. I must confess, however, both Caroline and Tris were nothing like I imagined members of the *haut ton* would be."

"How so?"

"For one thing, they were very accepting of me, despite my rather bizarre situation. They weren't snobby or pretentious or self-important. They have a deep and genuine love for each other, and they're not afraid to express it. They are two rather extra-ordinary people." Diana struggled awkwardly with the wine bottle, trying unsuccessfully to remove the cork.

"You sound surprised," the earl said, reaching over and taking the bottle from her.

"They are gentry," Diana said simply, shrugging her shoulders. "I had no notion of what to expect."

"And what of me, Diana? Am I what you expected?"

"You, my lord," Diana lied, "are precisely as arrogant, overbearing, and autocratic as I anticipated."

Gleefully, she let him mull her comment over as she held out her empty glass. Derek filled it automatically, and she took a cautious sip, her eyes watching his astonished expression over the rim of her glass.

Diana searched again through the basket. Pulling out two freshly baked apple tarts, she handed the earl one. They continued eating in companionable silence as the coach lurched and swayed on the road. When they had sufficiently stuffed themselves,

Diana put aside three generous portions of food, carefully wrapping them in separate linen napkins. She then insisted the earl pass the food out to his driver and coachmen.

"You want me to what?" he shouted, surprise ringing in his voice.

"I am sure your men are hungry, my lord," Diana said. "There is plenty of food here. 'Tis only fair they receive a portion of it."

"You are going to spoil them," the earl grumbled, but he complied with her wishes. "I've never before met a lady so concerned about servants' feelings."

"It is hardly spoiling someone to offer him food," Diana said. "I learned a long time ago a little kindness and consideration can do much for a person's morale and self-esteem, no matter what his position in a household."

"I cannot fathom that my cousin ever treated any of his household servants with kindness or consideration," the earl stated. "And yet the staff continues to act as though they are still loyal to Giles instead of me."

"I cannot imagine Giles being kind to any servant," Diana said quietly. "During his brief visits to Cornwall he was most demanding of the staff, almost abusive at times." His behavior had probably been a reflection of his feeling toward her, Diana amended to herself. She tilted her head and studied the earl. "If your household servants are surly with you, it is probably because they are wary. Demonstrate to them you are not like their former employer and they will come around."

"Prove my good intentions to a group of servants?" Derek asked in an amazed tone.

"You misunderstand me," Diana said. "Show them you are a fair man who can be trusted. Loyalty is earned, my lord, not purchased."

Derek snorted. "You sound like an army officer." Yet her observations made sense. He knew from experience that earning loyalty was the first and most important step he took when establishing a relationship with the soldiers who had served under him. Would it work with servants? "I don't have much experience handling domestic matters."

"What you really need is a wife, my lord," Diana responded instantly. Almost without thinking she added, "Why have you not yet married?"

He raised an eyebrow at her. Diana averted her eyes at his critical stare, suddenly becoming fascinated with the buttons of her wool traveling cloak. What ever had possessed her to ask him such an intimate question? She felt her cheeks flush with color as she waited for his response, not sure what she wanted most: for the earl to drop the matter entirely or to answer her question.

"I almost did marry several years ago." He gave a deep, self-mocking laugh. "The lady in question preferred another."

"I can't believe that," Diana said softly.

Derek stared hard at her, wondering briefly if she was scoffing at him. "I can assure you it is quite true. He had a title. I did not."

"I am sorry," Diana said tentatively, her eyes fastened upon his face. "It was not my intention to cause you any distress by recalling unhappy memories."

An expression of grief briefly crossed the earl's handsome features, but it vanished so quickly Diana was not certain she had seen it. Derek gave her a philosophical smile.

"Never fear, Diana," he said matter-of-factly. "That incident is all in the past and long since forgotten.

I am fully prepared to fulfill my obligations to my noble lineage and the earldom. Naturally, I shall marry and produce an heir. I intend to start searching for a suitable applicant this coming Season."

"Applicant," Diana said faintly. "You sound as though you are hiring a servant."

"Nonsense," Derek insisted. "One must be practical when approaching the Marriage Mart. I will merely allow the information that I am in need of a bride to circulate among several well-connected matrons. After that, all I have to do is attend a few select social functions in order to meet all the eligible young misses. Once I find one who meets my requirements, I shall make an honorable offer of marriage to her father or guardian."

"It sounds positively barbaric," Diana whispered in horror. "So cold and calculating. Surely you are jesting?"

"I am quite serious," he responded calmly. "That's how it is done. I think the worst part of it will be attending the balls and parties. They can be excessively boring. And lemonade and stale cookies at Almack's is a trial. Can't be helped, however."

"You really are serious," Diana said in amazement. Unable to stop herself, she added, "What precisely, if you don't mind my asking, are your requirements for a wife?"

"No more than eighteen years of age, docile, biddable, reasonably intelligent, with a trim figure and a pleasing face, and if at all possible, unspoiled. I simply can't abide tantrums."

Diana shuddered involuntarily at the open expression on his face. He sounded as though he were listing the salient points of an item he wished to purchase, not a woman he wanted to marry. She realized he was being completely honest, and she was truly stunned by his attitude.

Diana give Derek a disdainful look. "What about her family background? And her dowry? Shouldn't she have a large dowry?" Diana asked, her voice dripping with sarcasm.

"Minor considerations," he declared, with a wave of his hand. "I have no need to marry for money, and a respectable birth is all I require."

"What about her teeth? Shouldn't she have sound teeth?"

Derek shot Diana a quelling look, but did not respond.

"It seems as though you have given this a great deal of thought, my lord," Diana stated in a deceptively calm voice.

"Precisely," he murmured, ignoring the harsh way she was staring at him. "I have decided it is best to approach these matters with a clear plan of action already devised. Therefore, I have created a list of the characteristics I find suitable in a wife. It will make the search much simpler."

"Humph!" He sounded so damned smug. Diana felt her temper flaring.

"You appear a bit agitated, madam. I hope I have not said anything to distress you."

Diana was silent for a moment as she fought to control her anger. "Agitated?" she retorted sharply. "Agitated? Yes, well—no, no, I am . . . disappointed. Utterly disappointed. I just cannot believe that you can be so cold . . . and arrogant . . . so smug and conceited."

"I hardly think you are qualified to give me marital advice, madame," he declared coldly.

Diana gasped loudly at the insult, overwhelmed with rage. "How dare you?" she said indignantly. "I know a great deal more about marriage than you

120

think, sir. I know firsthand how awful . . . how painful and humiliating it can be when you are wed to the wrong person." She was shouting at him now.

"There is no need to get so upset," Derek bellowed back. "Marriages of convenience are an everyday occurrence."

"You are not talking about a marriage of convenience, my lord," Diana said emphatically. "People marry for money, for power, for position, and, yes, in rare cases, for love. You are glibly spouting nonsense about searching for an applicant who meets your requirements as if you need only the temporary convenience of a wife until you can beget your heir. A wife, my lord, is also a woman with a mind and feelings of her own. She ought to be valued for the person she is in her own right, not treated as chattel or some kind of subservient creature to your passing whims."

"Are you quite finished?" Derek grumbled.

"I had thought better of you," Diana muttered sourly. "Truly, I had thought better of you."

Silence invaded the coach for several long minutes. Finally the earl spoke. "I am sorry I have distressed you."

"What?" Diana exploded, still too upset to listen.

"I said I was sorry," Derek yelled loudly.

"Oh," Diana murmured, starting to feel a little embarrassed over her tirade. "Yes, well, I didn't mean to get so . . . well . . . so—"

"Loud?" Derek asked.

"Emotional," Diana said with a pointed look, her temper again flaring. "You reminded me a great deal of Giles just now," she continued in a calmer voice. "You frightened me."

The earl blanched visibly at her comment. "I think you may have picked up too many romantic notions living with Tristan and Caroline this past week."

"The very last thing a woman in my circumstances can afford to do is to cherish foolish romantic dreams," she told him with sober eyes. "That is one lesson I have learned very well." She sighed deeply. "You, however, are more fortunate, my lord. Don't be so hasty to throw away your opportunity for happiness with such a narrow-minded vision of women and marriage. It will be a mistake you will be forced to live with for the rest of your days."

Diana turned her face to the window, effectively ending the discussion. Listening to the earl speak so coldly about finding a wife had shaken her. She was overwhelmed with sadness, thinking back on her own unhappy marriage, and her future looked no brighter. She would return to the security of her home in Cornwall and probably live out the remainder of her life there, alone. Her prospects for marriage were almost nonexistent, and her horrible experience with Giles left her unable and unwilling to open her mind to it, even if there had been suitors to consider.

Diana breathed a heavy sigh of regret and tried to shake off her gloomy thoughts. She curled up on her side, cushioned her head with her hands, and closed her eyes. Amazingly, she was able to fall asleep in a relatively short time.

As the coach pulled into a deserted innyard, Diana awakened and straightened up in her seat, stretching out her legs.

"We are stopping to water and feed the team," Derek informed her, running his fingers through his rumpled hair. "Would you like to walk about for a moment?"

Diana nodded, and when the carriage came to

a halt, Derek opened the door and swung down. Reaching up for Diana, he caught her at the waist and set her on her feet, enjoying the sensation of holding her tightly. She gave him a weary smile, but backed away from him as soon as her soft leather slippers hit the soil. They strolled leisurely about the deserted innyard, before Derek suggested they go inside for refreshments.

"How may we serve you this afternoon, milord?" the innkeeper asked, greeting them at the door.

Derek grasped Diana's elbow, leading her into the inn. The taproom was deserted except for two laborers sharing a pint of ale together in one corner. Derek noted the general cleanliness and pleasant aroma of the room, and he decided the lack of customers was due to the hour, not the quality of service.

"I require a room for her ladyship to refresh herself and a private parlor, if you have one, where we can take some refreshment," Derek announced in an authoritative voice.

"Oh, yes, milord," the landlord replied as he bowed to them both. "We have a private parlor at the back of the inn. I'll just light the fire to warm the room while my sister shows the lady upstairs."

Turning away from the earl and Diana, the landlord bellowed loudly for his sister. She appeared shortly, a young, slender girl with a crisp white apron tied about her waist. She stood at the edge of the heavy oak bar, her hands on her hips. "How am I ever going to get my stew in the pot if you keep screaming for me, Harry?"

"Hush now, Gladys," the innkeeper fretted. "We have guests. Show her ladyship to the room at the top of the hall, and then bring her up fresh water. Hurry up now!"

Gladys frowned at her brother, but followed his orders without further complaint.

Diana gathered up her skirts and followed Gladys up the stairs, where she was directed to a small but clean room. It was a far sight better than the conditions of the ten separate inns she had stopped in on her way to London, and Diana appreciated the neat surroundings.

She removed her cloak and smoothed out the wrinkles of her black gown. She was heartily sick of the garment, having worn it and her one other mourning dress exclusively for the past few weeks because she had been forced to abandon her traveling trunk in Salisbury with her broken-down carriage. Unfortunately Diana had brought no extra funds for purchasing new dresses while in London, so she was reduced to wearing these two garments continually.

Diana felt better after washing her hands and face and brushing out her hair. She deftly rolled her blond locks into a tight chignon, securing it at the nape of her neck. She went back downstairs and stood uncertainly in the taproom until Harry spotted her and rushed over.

The innkeeper nearly tripped over a chair in his haste to reach her, and then he bowed and scraped his way toward the back of the room leading her to the private parlor. Diana brought her hand up to her mouth and coughed loudly to hide her grin. She noticed Harry had tied a freshly laundered white apron around his paunchy middle, no doubt to impress his wealthy guests. Diana decided she liked Harry. He might be a bit obvious in his desire to ingratiate himself, but clearly he was no fool.

As Diana entered the private parlor the earl's back was to her, but apparently he heard her enter because he turned immediately. The innkeeper rushed away quickly to fetch their food.

"Harry is most eager to please. I fear he might fall flat on his face in his enthusiasm to prove his worth," Diana said with a slight smile.

Then her breath caught in her throat as she took in the full measure of the earl's appearance. He too had removed his traveling cloak, and the rich burgundy color of his waistcoat set off his coloring most attractively. His cravat was simply, though faultlessly tied, and his golden buckskin breeches were tightly fitted, with his powerful leg muscles bulging through the material. He was absolutely magnificent, she decided.

"Do you mind?" Derek inquired politely, holding up a smoldering cheroot.

For an instant Diana thought he was chastising her for staring so rudely at him, but when she noticed the cheroot, she sighed with relief. "I don't mind at all if you smoke."

The earl paced the room calmly, puffing on the cheroot. Then the innkeeper knocked sharply on the parlor door. Without waiting for a reply, he entered, Gladys following close behind him. Harry carried a tray laden with numerous plates of food. He waited impatiently while Gladys laid down a fresh tablecloth, plates, cutlery, and glasses; then he swiftly arranged the food in the center of the table.

"Would you prefer wine or ale with your meal, milord?" Gladys asked, her empty tray dangling down at her side.

"Wine, of course," her brother hissed in annoyance. "I shall bring it at once, your lordship." Harry shoved Gladys out of the room and returned with the wine. He hovered expectantly around the table until the earl dismissed him.

"And, Harry," Derek called out as the innkeeper was leaving, "please be sure my men are fed as well."

Harry's chest puffed with importance, and he left the room beaming. Diana smiled in amusement. Taking the seat opposite the earl, she folded her napkin in her lap and watched him.

Derek cut a thick slice of beef and put it on her plate. "I hope you are hungry, Diana," he said conversationally. "I don't intend to stop again until morning, and even then I cannot guarantee we will find such a well-kept establishment."

"Or such an accommodating innkeeper," Diana said with a laugh.

Derek gave her a charming smile and helped himself to the pickled vegetables. Diana sliced the crisp bread and filled her plate with a section of squab, a slice of pork pie, and vegetables. After eating every crumb on her plate, she indulged in a generous serving of fruit compote and a wedge of fruitcake with rum sauce.

Derek watched her eat in pure fascination, wondering where such a small, slender woman put such a great quantity of food. As she swallowed her last bite of cake, he told her just that.

Diana thrust up her chin at his remark. "You just told me I should eat heartily, my lord."

"Just so, Diana," Derek said soothingly. "I was merely speculating as to where all the food goes. You are quite thin, except for your—" He stopped abruptly, as his eyes traveled to her breasts.

"My lord," Diana said in a censuring tone, but he interrupted her.

"You must cease addressing me so formally, Diana. It reminds me too much of Harry." He flashed her what he hoped was his most engaging grin.

After drinking the last of the wine, they left the

parlor, and took another stroll about the innyard in the afternoon sunshine. Derek left her standing outside the coach under the watchful eye of his driver, Langston, while he went back inside to pay Harry. When he left the inn to join Diana in the carriage, the innkeeper called his thanks as he followed Derek out of the inn and halfway across the yard.

Derek, who was rushing away from the overly grateful innkeeper, immediately noticed Harry's chattering had stopped abruptly as Derek swung up inside the carriage. Once settled in the seat across from Diana, he turned to look back at the innkeeper, who was now staring bug-eyed at the coach pulling out of the yard.

"What did you do?" Derek inquired, observing the smirk on Diana's face.

"Just bidding Harry farewell, my lord," she replied.

"Derek," he corrected absently.

"Very well, Derek."

"What did you do?"

"I merely winked at the good innkeeper, that's all," Diana said nonchalantly. "He acted most surprised."

"I should say," Derek blurted out. "He probably thought you were flirting with him."

"No. Do you really think so?" Diana asked, her eyes shining with mischief.

"Poor Harry," the earl chuckled. "It's a wonder he didn't have apoplexy. Well, at least you got him to keep quiet for a few moments."

They both shared a quiet laugh. The coach pulled out on to the main road and the journey resumed. The coach made good time, despite the disgraceful condition of the road in certain places, and Derek and Diana spent a pleasant afternoon alternating between congenial conversation and light sleep.

As nightfall approached, Diana grew apprehensive, staring out the carriage window into the inky blackness. The earl had mentioned he intended to travel through the night, and she wondered if it would be safe. Hadn't he already informed her an elegantly equipped carriage barreling down a lonely stretch of road was the perfect invitation for a robbery?

"Hungry, Diana?" The earl's deep voice called to her from the darkness.

"No, my lor—no, Derek."

"Frightened?"

"Apprehensive, perhaps."

"Don't be," he told her soothingly. "This particular stretch of road is well-known to my men. We are perfectly safe."

Derek spoke with such assurance that she knew he was telling the truth. Diana slowly released the breath she was holding. She curled up in the corner of the coach, allowing the swaying motion of the carriage to gently lull her to sleep. Her final conscious thoughts before succumbing to slumber were of her impossibly handsome traveling companion, and she slept deeply through the night with a wistful smile on her lips.

Chapter Ten

Derek watched the sun rise gradually over the trees while the coach rolled down the road. He stretched out his stiff arms and shoulders, debating whether or not to again ride up top. He had spent several enjoyable hours in the box the previous night driving the coach, as much to give Langston a rest as to escape the confines of the carriage.

With morning fast approaching, Derek was loath to leave the coach, however, on the chance Diana would suddenly awaken and find herself alone. Of course, she would not mind his relieving Langston of the ribbons. Knowing Diana as he did, he felt certain she would applaud his efforts to assist his servant.

What a truly unusual woman she was. The more time he spent in her company, the greater he was intrigued by her plainspoken manner and unique charm. As the morning light gently illuminated the carriage, Derek was able to observe her at his leisure. She appeared much younger in sleep and her lovely features took on a vulnerable quality. The haunted look that so often dominated her soft brown eyes was gone. Her long, thick black eyelashes made her porcelain skin look even creamier, and they contrasted sharply with the wisps of golden-blonde hair framing her face.

Almost as if by intuition, Diana became aware of Derek's scrutiny and opened her eyes. She blinked several times, still sleepy and disoriented. She shifted her position until she was sitting upright and gave the earl a crooked smile.

"Good morning, my lord," she said groggily. At the earl's answering frown she hastily corrected herself. "Derek."

"Did you sleep well?" he inquired.

"Yes, surprisingly well, as a matter of fact. Your carriage is quite comfortable. I've never been inside such a luxurious vehicle."

"This is the first time I've ridden in it also. Giles commissioned its construction last year," Derek said.

"I see," Diana remarked softly, looking about the interior of the coach. Knowing Giles had also ridden in the vehicle instantly took away some of her pleasure. She twisted her hands nervously in her lap, unsure how to respond.

"I shouldn't have said that," Derek said, his deep voice breaking the awkward silence.

"It's all right," Diana assured him.

"No, it isn't all right, Diana. God's blood, woman, it was probably your money that paid for all this luxury." Derek reached over and grasped her hands in his much larger ones. "I'll make it up to you, Diana. I swear it."

A lump formed in Diana's throat as she gazed into his handsome face. He really was a good man. "That is not necessary, Derek," she said mistily, fighting back her tears. His sincere kindness touched her heart, but she felt no compulsion to have him pay for another man's mistreatment of her. "The money is not important. Truly. I am grateful to be finally free of Giles. I want only to forget."

At that moment, the carriage halted so suddenly that Diana was thrown across the seats and into Derek. He caught her easily and pulled her onto his lap, cradling her gently against him. She could feel the solidness of his chest and the strength of his arms as he held her, and she discovered she did not want to draw away from him.

She lifted her head. Mere inches separated them, and she could feel his warm breath on her cheek. He was going to kiss me, Diana thought, leaning forward to encourage him.

A smile tugged at the corner of his mouth, and then his lips brushed against hers softly, sweetly. She shivered at the intimate contact. His tongue nudged her lips apart, slipping inside her mouth. She gave a deep sigh of contentment and wrapped her arms around his neck, pressing herself against his hard body.

Derek kissed her gently at first, then more forcefully. His fingers caressed her back, his strong hands cupping her hips and holding her intimately against his hardness. She returned his kisses ardently, her heart fluttering wildly as the blood pounded in her temples. She felt helpless to stop herself, reveling in the delicious warmth that invaded her each time their tongues met.

They were interrupted suddenly by a banging noise on the top of the coach. Langston yelled out,

"I've stopped at an inn, my lord. Do you want to get out and have your breakfast?"

Derek reluctantly tore his mouth away from Diana's, muttering an oath under his breath. He regretfully called out, "Yes, we'll stay."

Derek turned his attention back to Diana, who was still sitting on his lap. Her face was blushing a becoming shade of pink, and she was struggling to remove herself from his embrace. She pushed forcefully against Derek's chest, and when he let go of her so suddenly, she fell to the carriage floor.

"Don't," she screamed indignantly when he reached down to help her. "I can manage." Grabbing on to the edge of the leather seat, she lifted herself up, but the coach lurched, and instead of landing on her side of the compartment, she was once again sprawled across the earl's lap.

"I could have done that, my dear," he murmured softly in her ear as she struggled to right herself.

Diana managed to scramble off Derek's lap and sit down on the seat next to him, just as Langston opened the carriage door. Her face was flushed from her exertions and embarrassment, and her breathing was unsteady.

Langston's expression was unreadable as he held the door open for them. Derek swung down unassisted. He reached up to grab Diana, and she pressed her hands on his broad shoulders to steady herself. Once on her feet, she moved out of his reach and began walking toward the inn.

"Do you think we will be able to get a room where I can refresh myself?" Diana asked, still struggling to calm her ragged breathing.

Derek nodded, then instructed Langston to go inside to make all the necessary arrangements. By the time they reached the doorway of the establishment, Langston had secured a room for Diana and ordered breakfast for all of them.

Once alone in her room, Diana soaked the small washrag in a basin of cool water and held it up to her face. She felt confused and bewildered, and a trifle embarrassed over her display in the coach earlier. Lord only knew what might have happened if Langston had not interrupted them! As much as she tried to, Diana was hard pressed to come up with any reasonable explanation for her behavior toward Derek. One heart-melting smile from him and her heart lurched in reaction. One touch of his lips to hers and she completely lost all sense of reason, all sense of caution.

Methodically Diana completed her toilet while pondering her problem, discarding several possible solutions in rapid succession. She finally abandoned the notion of trying to figure out why she was acting so unlike herself where the earl was concerned. Clearly, the only sensible thing to do was to remain a discrete distance from Derek at all times, therefore avoiding the difficulty of having to maintain her composure in the first place.

True, it would hardly be easy to stay at a distance when traveling cooped up inside a carriage with the man, but it was not impossible. She would just have to find a way. Resolved on her new course of action, Diana left the room to join Derek for breakfast.

A private parlor was unavailable in this more crowded inn, but Langston was able to obtain a secluded corner table for Derek and Diana. Derek rose immediately to his feet when she approached the table, and they began their meal in silence.

Pursuant to her new plan, Diana limited the breakfast conversation to safe, mundane topics, such as the excellent weather and tasty food. If

Derek thought her overbearing manner a bit odd, he did not comment, and he appeared to be content to follow her lead.

Derek enjoyed watching Diana as she ate her meal. He could tell she was still flustered by their earlier encounter in the carriage because she deliberately tried to monopolize the conversation. She daintily buttered a muffin, and Derek felt the blood rush to his head as he observed her long, slender fingers with lustful regard, imagining them boldly caressing his hot, naked flesh.

As the meal progressed, Derek's thoughts seemed to run away from him, becoming more and more lustful. By the time breakfast was concluded, his body was so heated, his manhood so swollen, he could not leave the concealment of the table because his tight-fitting breeches would immediately reveal his lecherous intentions.

Diana ate the remaining bite of sausage on her plate and congratulated herself on successfully accomplishing her mission. She had just shared a perfectly pleasant and very impersonal meal with the earl. Pleased with her success, she made a motion to rise from the table, but at Derek's strained grin, she returned to her seat.

"Are you feeling all right, Derek?" she asked, trying to keep her tone mildly curious.

"Fine," he responded with a grimace. "Please do stay and have another cup of chocolate, Diana."

Not wanting to appear rude, Diana complied with his request, forcing herself to drink another cup of chocolate, while he stared about the crowded taproom taking deep, even breaths.

Finally, breakfast was completed and they stood up simultaneously from the table. Diana hesitated only slightly before she took hold of the arm Derek offered her; then they stepped outside into the sunshine. Neither one spoke as they took their customary stroll about the innyard to exercise their cramped muscles.

After circling the yard three times, Derek announced it was time to leave. They reentered the coach and the journey resumed. They conversed pleasantly for an hour until Diana announced her desire to rest. She curled up in her corner of the coach, closed her eyes, and feigned sleep.

Derek was puzzled by her actions, but not unduly disturbed. For some unknown reason, Diana had decided to keep a polite distance, and he respected her wishes. He too was disturbed by the rampant desire consuming him each time they kissed and the strange possessiveness he felt toward her. Perhaps a bit of distance between them would help him once again regain command of his senses.

Later that afternoon, Derek took the ribbons from Langston, and Diana breathed a sigh of relief. She was having difficulty pretending to sleep all the time, and she was not quite sure how to keep herself constantly aloof when engaging in conversation with Derek.

The coach pulled into another inn as dusk approached, and this time, Derek calmly informed Diana that they were going to spend the night. As she entered the inn on Derek's arm, Diana was momentarily timorous, certain every eye must be trained upon them. She knew they must look odd, traveling with neither maid nor valet, but Derek handled the innkeeper with his usual style and grace and had no difficulty in securing the remaining two adjoining rooms for them.

As they entered their second week on the road, their traveling days took on a similar pattern, with little altering except the quality of the inns and the changing landscape. Diana's nerves were stretched taut with the strain of keeping up an impersonal, yet polite facade, and Derek had grown gloomy at her withdrawal. He repeatedly asked her if something was wrong, and she continued to insist everything was perfectly fine. Her response, she knew, only served to further his anger. Derek spent more and more of his time riding on the outside of the coach with his men, rather than inside with her, and Diana tried valiantly to convince herself she was glad to be spared his company.

As Diana gazed out her window now, the upland pastures and moorlands of wild desolate beauty told her they had driven far into Devon and would soon be entering Cornwall. If the weather held, she might even reach home by nightfall of the next day.

She gave a heavy sigh at the thought. The coach pulled into a small village, and not even the picturesque row of fishermen's cottages hugging the hillside—with their thick whitewashed stone walls, slate roofs, and distinctive chimney pots—could dispel her gloom.

Derek instructed his driver to escort Diana into the inn. They were met by the innkeeper's wife, who directed Diana to a small corner table that afforded her some privacy from the curious eyes of the crowded taproom. Diana ordered a meal for herself and the earl, also requesting the earl's men be served whatever they wished. Derek joined her soon after that, and she was at first glad of his company, for it discouraged the bolder stares she had been receiving.

A pretty young barmaid brought their supper, favoring the earl with a broad wink when she set down the plates of hot food. Diana unconsciously ground her teeth together, excessively annoyed at the maid's familiar manner. Derek, his eyes trained on Diana's face, barely noticed the maid, assuming he was the cause of Diana's ire.

Dinner was a strained affair. Diana remained lethargic and depressed throughout, eating very little of the excellently prepared meal, even forgoing the delicious Cornish pastry, with its chunks of beef, potato, onion, and turnip baked to perfection inside a light, flaky crust.

Derek also did not eat with his usual enjoyment, and Diana frowned slightly when he signaled the barmaid to bring him a second bottle of wine. Diana excused herself soon after, wearily following the innkeeper's wife to the top of the stairs, where her bedchamber was located.

Although the room was rather small, Diana was pleased to note it was clean. The bed, though not overly large, had a soft mattress and fresh linen. Diana accepted the lit candle from the innkeeper's wife with thanks and, once alone, began to mechanically undress. She sponged off her travel dirt in the small copper basin, thinking longingly of a proper bath and vowing to burn her two black mourning gowns upon her arrival home.

After putting on her nightgown, Diana sat on the edge of the bed, brushing out her hair. The rhythmic stroking helped ease the tension in her head, and Diana laid back against the covers. Perhaps once she was home at Snowshill Manor she would be able to forget about Derek and the unsettling effect he had on her. Grimacing with honesty, she forced herself to admit doing so was unlikely.

Although the earl aptly demonstrated his desire for her, and she had unwittingly encouraged him,

Diana doubted she was the kind of female he would be interested in for any length of time. She remembered well his rather antiquated requirements for a wife. And she did not fill his requirements—not that she would ever be interested in becoming his wife. Being married to one Earl of Harrowby was enough to last a lifetime. Wasn't it?

Feeling confused and unhappy, Diana sank into the soft mattress and pulled up the covers. Despite her sadness, she was exhausted and quickly fell asleep.

A sharp knock woke Diana abruptly. Alarmed, she sat up quickly, thinking she somehow had overslept. She looked through the partially opened shutters into the blackness of the night and realized it was not yet morning. The room was in near darkness, the faint glow of the almost extinguished candle casting unreal shadows about the room. For a moment Diana thought she might have been dreaming, but there came a second, louder knock.

Diana rose from the bed and walked barefoot across the cold, hardwood floor. She hesitated briefly in front of her chamber door. The earl's voice boomed loudly in the quiet night.

" 'Tis me, Diana. Pray, open the door."

Diana never thought to object, but simply turned the key in the lock and swung the heavy oak door open to admit the earl.

He stood in the doorway, his left shoulder braced nonchalantly against the doorjamb. He had removed his coat and it was carelessly slung over his right shoulder. His silver waistcoat was unbuttoned and his snowy-white cravat was untied, dangling limply around his neck. His plain ivory shirt was open at the throat, and Diana could see a tiny curl of chest hair peeking up from the exposed area. Their eyes met, and Derek flashed her a positively wicked grin. Diana swallowed hard.

"Did I wake you?" Derek asked lazily from his slouch. Without waiting for her response, he straightened up and strode past her into the room.

Without glancing at her, Derek walked to the chair in the corner of the chamber and flung his coat across it. He then removed his waistcoat and wilted cravat and began calmly undoing the shirt studs at his wrists.

"Do close the door, Diana," he said conversationally, his back toward her. "I believe I am beginning to feel a draft."

Diana stood in the same spot, her feet rooted to the floor, her hand tightly clutching the latch of the open bedchamber door.

"What precisely are you doing, Derek?" Diana whispered when she at last found her voice.

He twirled around to face her, and for a long moment he simply stared at her. "I should think it is obvious," he announced with amusement. "I am getting undressed."

Diana felt a prickle of fear when she heard the slight slurring in his voice. "You're drunk," she accused in a horrified whispered.

"A bit foxed perhaps, madam," he replied, his tone indicating how insulted he was by her remark. "I can assure you, however, I am not completely under the hatches."

Diana continued to stand by the open door, wondering what to do. Whenever Giles had become drunk, he used to fly into the most terrible rages. Dubiously, she eyed Derek, uncertain of his mood. He appeared congenial enough. Perhaps he was merely confused about where his bedchamber was located.

She wiped her damp palms against the soft flannel of her nightgown and faced the earl bravely. "Derek," she said in a gentle voice, "I fear you are a trifle confused tonight. This is my bedchamber."

Derek gave an exaggerated sigh and ran his hand through his rumpled hair. Crossing the room rapidly, he stopped when he reached her side. He grinned crookedly down at her, and Diana's heart starting pounding as she looked up into his uncommonly handsome face.

"I believe, Diana, you are, in truth, the one who is confused," Derek said with a wicked grin. "You see, my dear, this also happens to be my bedchamber."

With that said, he reached out a powerful arm and swung the chamber door closed with a resounding bang.

Chapter Eleven

"I cannot possibly share a bedchamber with you!" Diana exclaimed.

Derek raised an eyebrow, but gave no response. He casually strolled back to the chair in the corner of the room and sat down. Crossing his ankle over his knee, he began to tug laboriously at his left boot. When he was unsuccessful in dislodging it, he raised his head. "Would you mind?" he asked, stretching out his leg toward her.

It took every ounce of Diana's self-control not to shout from the depths of her constricted lungs. "Yes, as a matter of fact, I do mind," she hissed through clenched teeth.

Derek shrugged and went back to tugging on his boot. At last it gave way and he waved the black Hessian triumphantly, before dropping it carelessly to the floor and focusing his attention on its mate.

The sound of the second boot hitting the floor cata-pulted Diana into action.

She strode purposefully across the room to con-front Derek. He was still seated and she took full advantage of the rare opportunity to tower above him. She planted her legs and stood with her hands on her hips, glaring menacingly at him.

"Derek, we simply cannot share a bedchamber," Diana snapped, her tone unyielding.

"Why not?"

"Why not? Why not?" Diana sputtered, clearly stunned by his simple question. "Because it just isn't proper. That is why not."

Derek cocked his head and gave her boyish grin, which infuriated her.

"You will leave this room at once," she com-manded, stomping her foot in frustration.

His grin quickly faded. He too stood up, scowling down at her. "I am sorry you find my company so distasteful, Diana," he told her in a clipped voice. "This is, in case you haven't noticed, a very small establishment, and I was able to secure only this one room tonight."

"Fine," she snapped. "You may stay here. I'll go outside and sleep in the coach."

She turned to leave, but he grabbed her arm. "Stop being so bloody ridiculous, Diana," he yelled. "You're acting like a spoiled child."

Her back stiffened, and she twisted free of his grasp and moved beyond his reach. But he moved to her side again.

"We cannot share this chamber. I cannot possibly sleep in the same room with you," she whispered, her voice clouded with emotion. "And if you have to ask me why I cannot do so, you do not deserve to know the answer."

Derek watched the shadow of pain cross her expressive face and he felt like an utter cad. He shook his head briskly, trying to clear his mind from the effects of the wine he had consumed. Pushing his own bewilderment and hurt at her distant behavior of the last few days aside, he focused instead on her suffering.

"You must know I would never harm you, Diana," he said softly. "I would give my very life to keep you safe."

The tenderness in his voice was her undoing. She gazed up at him, saw the genuine concern in his expressive blue eyes, and wilted inside. Choking back a sob, Diana turned to Derek in her misery, burying her face in his broad shoulder. Her hands tightly clutched the front of his half-open shirt, and she sobbed loudly, finally allowing the tension and uncertainty of the past week to claim her.

Understanding only that she needed his comfort, Derek enfolded her in his arms. Pulling Diana close against his heart, he gently kneaded her shoulders through the shimmering hair hanging freely down her back.

After a moment she became quiet, and Derek became acutely aware of every curve of her body. Her breasts were pressing against his chest and he could feel her nipples through the soft material of her nightgown. His pulse was racing and he felt his manhood stiffen in response to her proximity. Muttering an oath under his breath, he loosened his hold on her slightly and shifted his feet backward. He knew he had to pull away from her, as erotic images of her invaded his mind, playing havoc with his already aroused senses.

Diana was also conscious of the change in his body, and she could feel the heat against her own skin where their bodies touched. She dropped her arms and backed away from him. Yet, unable to stop herself, Diana stared in rapt fascination at Derek's naked chest behind his unbuttoned shirt. It was so broad and muscular, the dark, curling hair glistening in the moonlit room. She felt her cheeks grow hot.

They stood there for several long moments until Derek could no longer bear not touching her. He captured her chin in his hand and ran his fingertips lightly along her jaw line. When she lifted her face, his mouth covered hers. His kiss was filled with raw emotion. He felt her tremble and heard her deep throaty moan.

Her response fired his passions and his hands roamed freely down her luscious curves in a sensuous, searching caress. His tongue probed the sweetness of her mouth, seeking and then finding her tongue.

Derek's hand cupped her breast lovingly, his thumb rubbing insistently through the fabric until her nipple grew taut and hard. She shivered with delight, giving herself over to the blinding pleasure he was creating with an abandonment that shocked and dismayed her. As his kiss deepened, Diana became frightened, and with a small cry of anguish, she turned away from Derek's kisses and stiffened in his arms.

Mutely she stared up at him. She was breathless and shaken. Her legs felt weak and her heart was pounding. All she could think of was how wonderful it felt when he kissed and stroked her body.

As she stared into Derek's intense blue eyes, Diana realized she could no longer deny the love she felt for him. A single tear rolled down her cheek. She shuddered in fear of the feelings he could so quickly arouse in her. She trembled with uncertainty over the intense passion between them—passion she did not fully understand and was helpless to control.

Derek lifted his hand and gently brushed against her cheek, his fingers catching her tear. "Why do you cry, Diana?"

She refused to answer; instead she turned her face into his hand, rubbing back and forth against the strength of his fingers. She attempted to reconcile the torment of her heart and spirit, but his touch was distracting. How she reveled in his touch! The strength and roughness of his hands contrasted sharply with the softness of his caress. She felt her heart turn wildly in her breast, and she could not stop herself from pressing a hot, probing kiss on his palm.

A jolt of desire shot though Derek at the touch of her searing lips. He marveled anew at the intensity of his reaction to her. She was by far the most perplexing woman he had ever known, yet he burned with his need to possess her. He wanted to kiss and caress every inch of her supple body. He wanted her wild and wanton, her body hungering for him. He wanted to drink his fill of the exquisite, responsive passion he had merely tasted thus far. Passion, he strongly suspected, no man had yet truly discovered.

"I am afraid," Diana whispered suddenly, her face cradled in his hand.

"Of me?" he said, sounding surprised.

"Of us," she answered helplessly, turning her head away. His eyes were too sharp, too keen. She felt as though they could look into her very soul and instantly know all her secrets.

"You feel it too, don't you, Diana?" he murmured huskily. "The searing flame, the intense attraction, the nearly uncontrollable excitement between us."

Diana kept her eyes downcast. She felt very unsure. She was naive and inexperienced in the ways of love and did not know how to respond.

"I don't understand," she confessed. "You make me shiver and tingle and ache for something—I don't even know what." She stared at him. "What are you doing to me?"

"Desire, my sweet," he told her, with a smile of triumph at her admission. He knew he wasn't being completely honest with her. He had felt desire for many women in his life, but it was never like the intense need he felt for Diana. That he could not explain, but he did understand desire. "I have awakened your long dormant passions and given you a mere hint of the exquisite pleasure that awaits us."

Her eyes grew even wider at his words. Heat flushed her face and her breathing quickened. Good Lord, she thought with wonder and dismay, even his voice affected her.

Derek saw her reaction, and the tightening in his loins sent him to the very edge of his self-control. He grabbed her around the waist and lifted her high in the air. Then slowly, tantalizingly, he slid her down the front of his body, feeling her respond instantly as she made contact with his hardened flesh. He wanted her to feel his excitement for her, wanted her to know that she too possessed the power to drive him to mindless passion.

"Lord, how I want you, Diana," he breathed in her ear. "Do you want me also, my love? Will you come to me now? Will you spread your silken thighs for me, so I can appease this hunger that burns deeply within both of us?"

Diana groaned softly at his words, her mind barely coherent. She squeezed his shoulders hard in response, but then disengaged herself from his embrace. Her breathing was ragged as she looked into his beautiful blue eyes. Her ignorance compelled her to speak her fears.

"I am frightened, Derek," she whispered hesitantly. "Will you hurt me?"

Derek felt his throat tighten at her words. He should have known Giles would have treated her roughly, perhaps even brutally. It explained much about her hesitation and her seemingly innocent and inexperienced response to his advances. He trapped her in his arms and pulled her head close to his until their noses touched.

"I won't hurt you, sweetheart," he declared softly. He lightly kissed the tip of her nose and then began trailing kisses from her temple, to her ear, to her neck, and finally to her lips, emphasizing his promise.

Diana allowed herself to be persuaded. She glanced up at Derek's handsome face and her last vestiges of fear and doubt were finally dispatched. Her heart ached with the knowledge that she loved him, and she knew, more than anything else, she wanted to belong to this man.

Derek saw the fear and doubt leave her eyes, and he felt victorious. Not only for himself, but for Diana as well. Even though she had been married, he now knew she had not achieved much pleasure from that union. Tonight, he was going to change all that. Tonight, he was going to show her the true magic that could exist between a man and a woman.

Starring hypnotically into her eyes, Derek reached out, swiftly undoing the buttons down the front of Diana's nightgown. He eased the garment away from her shoulders and the soft flannel fell away from her body, puddling at her feet.

Diana could see the muscle of Derek's jaw flexing and hear his rapid, uneven breathing. She blushed furiously, averting her eyes. No man had ever seen her naked before. Her hands moved up instinctively to shield her body, but Derek caught her by the wrists.

"Don't be shy, Diana," he coaxed. "You are so very beautiful."

Her blush deepened, and Derek gathered her into his arms. He knew she was embarrassed, and he tried to distract her. He dipped his head and gave her a slow, wet kiss. As he kissed her, his mind filled with the lovely vision of her unclothed flesh: her skin so white and flawless, her breasts round and firm, her nipples dusky rose. Her tiny waist emphasized her slender hips and sleek legs, and the soft curls between her thighs were golden and delicate. To Derek, she was sheer perfection.

"I'm naked," she murmured when he ceased his kiss.

"I know." Derek flashed her a wicked grin.

She met his eyes with a confidence she did not feel. "Why do you still have your clothes on?"

"I won't for long, sweetheart." He laughed huskily.

He leaned down and nuzzled her neck, then scooped her up in his arms. He strode across the room and lowered her to the bed, kissing her continuously. Groaning, he finally broke away and stood up, a bit unsteady. With his back to her, he removed his shirt and breeches and then turned to face her. Diana, reclining against the pillows, widened her eyes in shock, as she got her first frontal view of a naked man.

Words failed her. He was so magnificently beautiful. Without his garments, he looked enormous to her, with his broad shoulders and massive chest.

Her eyes drifted down the length of him, following the dark curls of hair that began on his chest, to his flat stomach and then to his manhood, which was thrusting outward, thick and swollen.

Diana swallowed hard. She drew a deep, steadying breath, trying to calm her nerves. She fervently wished she wasn't so ignorant. She had a general idea of how things went between a man and a woman, but she was not entirely clear about what happened. Would Derek be disappointed in her lack of experience? Would he be able to tell?

Ignorant of her fears, Derek eagerly joined her on the bed. Stretching out on his side, he faced her, his head resting casually on his angled arm. He gently placed her hand on his chest and Diana no longer had time to ponder her ignorance. His flesh was warm beneath her touch and she was enthralled by it. His chest felt hard and muscular and the hair covering it was soft and springy. Fascinated, she ran her fingers through the hair, massaging the muscles underneath. She discovered his flat nipples, so like hers and yet so different. She rubbed her thumbs roughly over them, just as he had done to her. To her surprise and delight, they tightened and hardened.

Her lovely face was a wonder for Derek to behold. Her eyes were glittering with excitement and it heated his blood to see her so curious, so guileless in her quest to discover his secrets. He was barely breathing, yet he somehow managed to remain perfectly still while Diana innocently explored his body. He wanted her to know the feel of him so when they finally came together she would be familiar with him.

Diana's hand moved down his chest, stroking his stomach in slow circles. She hesitated when she

149

reached the thick nest of curls at his groin, but Derek, feeling her intention, reached down and lifted her hand, placing it over his swelling arousal. "Touch me, Diana."

"Oh, my God," she whispered brokenly, curling her fingers around him.

Derek let out a loud groan at her innocent touch, and she instantly jerked her hand away.

"Did I hurt you?" she asked, her eyes wide with concern.

He gave a small laugh that sounded more like a moan. "If you hurt me anymore, I shall disgrace myself, sweetheart."

Diana giggled nervously, not completely understanding his remark. She snuggled close to him, rubbing her cheek against the fine hair on his chest. He was being so patient with her, so gentle and loving. Her heart swelled with emotion.

She lifted her chin so he could kiss her mouth, and he willingly complied. She could feel the change in him as he kissed her. His mouth was hot and demanding, while his hands were bolder, more insistent, as they swept her body.

His mouth burned a path down her throat to her breasts and his lips fastened hungrily on her nipple. He suckled gently, kneading and stroking with his tongue until her nipple was hard and erect. Then he turned his attention to her other breast, while his hand traveled down her soft belly to the delicate triangle of blonde curls between her thighs.

She stiffened instinctively and tried to clamp her legs together. She had no idea he would want to touch her *there*.

"Derek, please, no . . . no . . . I—"

"It's all right, sweetheart," he murmured soothingly. "I won't hurt you. Just relax."

He pressed soft kisses along her cheek and murmured sweet endearments against her ear. Diana listened to his beloved voice and gradually overcame her trepidation. His fingers returned to her thighs, gently probing, until he found her. She was slick and hot, and he skillfully slipped his forefinger inside.

A bolt of pure sensation speared her body at his touch. She moaned loudly, arching her back at the explosive warmth in her belly. Diana felt overpowered by the intense sensations claiming her. She had never imagined anything could be so incredibly pleasurable. What was he doing to her? She lifted her wide and questioning eyes to Derek's face, needing to know if he too felt this intense heat and tension gathering deep within his own body.

Derek looked down at her, his eyes glazed with desire. He could barely control himself. She was so sweet, so trusting. His fingers stroked her rhythmically, and he could feel her stretching to admit him. She was very small. He sucked in his breath. She felt hot, moist, and incredibly tight. He could wait no longer.

"I am going to come inside you now," he whispered hoarsely.

Diana trembled at his words, hovering on the edge of her own passion, and she willingly opened herself to receive him. Derek covered her body with his own and Diana welcomed his weight. She felt his manhood probing her; then he reached down and parted her softness. He entered her forcefully, thrusting deeply into her dampness.

When he surged into her shivering body, he heard Diana's strangled cry of pain as he ripped through a strong, thick membrane. Derek instantly froze. It was her maidenhead.

She was a virgin! But that wasn't possible. She had

been married for more than three years. His eyes flew to her face, the questions flooding his mind.

Diana's head was back against the pillows and her eyes were shut tight. Her lips were pressed together in a thin white line, and he could see she was in pain. All questions quickly vanished as his thoughts turned to her.

He carefully brought himself up on his elbows. He felt himself throbbing deep within her, but he forced himself to ignore his own passion.

"I hurt you," he said in a quiet voice.

Diana blinked up at him, but didn't answer. She felt oddly apart from herself and more a part of him since their bodies were joined together. The stinging pain she first felt was fading, replaced by a throbbing discomfort. He was so very large that she could feel her body stretching to hold him. She had been startled, especially after he'd said he would not hurt her, but the pain was lessening. She wanted more of him.

"The pain is not so bad now," she assured him, involuntarily squeezing the muscles that held him so firmly inside her.

"Christ!" Derek groaned loudly at her action, his control slipping.

Diana could feel him shuddering as he fought to regain control of himself. She lightly stroked his back, feeling the need to comfort him. "Please don't stop now, Derek," she pleaded, in a raspy voice.

He could not resist her. Derek withdrew slightly, then plunged deeply into her, trying to go slowly, but she was so small and tight he was nearly beside himself. He heard her groan, and he immediately stopped, thinking he was hurting her. He waited tensely for her reaction; then she experimentally moved her hips up to meet him. His rod swelled even larger, and he began thrusting powerfully inside her warm, moist sheath.

Diana answered his thrusts by moving her body in unison with his. With her acceptance of his flesh, the pace of Derek's lovemaking increased. Diana clutched her fingers frantically about his shoulders, as the tempo quickened and the twisting, tightening feeling deep within her lower body grew more intense.

Derek's eyes never left Diana's face as he felt the frantic tension within her cresting, and she moaned his name in a bewildered voice. He was conscious of nothing except her as she shuddered and quivered in fulfillment. Her sweet pleasure brought him to his own release, and he held her tightly, arching his back in primitive surrender, pouring his hot seed deep inside her.

Everything went blank for an instant; then Derek collapsed on top of Diana, his breathing still ragged, his brow damp with sweat. He was embedded deep inside her, his body still enjoying the insensible pleasure she had given him. He nuzzled her neck and sighed with contentment.

Diana answered him with an affectionate squeeze, still too dazed and satisfied to understand what had happened to her. She hadn't known what to expect and could never, even in her wildest dreams, have imagined anything so shattering, so consuming, so complete. She snuggled closer to Derek's hard, damp body.

"I love you." The words were out before Diana was even aware she had spoken them.

Her declaration was met with total silence. Derek allowed himself only a brief moment to experience the warmth and joy her simple statement brought his long protected heart before consigning it to the back of his mind. Uppermost in his thoughts was the nagging fact that she lied to him, probably from the very first.

She had been a virgin! That fact led him immediately to the conclusion Diana had never been married and was not, as she claimed, his cousin's widow. But who was she? And what was the true purpose of this elaborate hoax? Silently, he cursed himself for being such a fool to be taken in so easily by her beauty and guile.

Diana shifted slightly under him, reminding him sharply that he was still sheathed within the warmth of her body. He could feel himself begin to grow hard inside her, his body hungering again for her sweetness.

Angrily, Derek jerked his hips up, separating himself from her. Rolling over onto his back, he stared gloomily up at the ceiling, trying not to touch her as she lay beside him. Confusion and frustration washed over him, and he spoke at last, his voice cold and sarcastic.

"Perhaps now that we have shared this intimate moment together, you will be kind enough to explain to me, madam, precisely who the hell you are?"

Chapter Twelve

Diana felt suspended in time. She heard Derek's voice, but did not comprehend his words. Her mind and body were still floating on the sensations and pleasures of their lovemaking, and she felt sleepy and deliriously happy.

Sighing contentedly, she turned to Derek, burrowing her face into his shoulder. She missed his warmth, the feel of his strong arms. She threw her arm across his chest and twined her legs through his, moving even closer.

"I'm cold, Derek," she whimpered when he did not wrap his arms around her.

"Then I suggest you pull up the coverlet." His voice was flat, emotionless.

Diana lifted her head, suddenly becoming aware of his rigid expression. She felt a prickle of fear clutch her heart.

"Is something wrong, Derek?"

"I asked you a question, madam," he snapped. "I am waiting for your response."

Diana shrank away from his coldness, her inside tightening. Something was wrong, very wrong. His beautiful blue eyes, moments before filled with passion and tenderness, were narrow with anger and mistrust. She moved to the far corner of the bed and sat up, pulling the linens to her chest to hide her nakedness.

"I'm sorry," she said slowly, trying to keep the rising sense of panic from her voice. "I didn't hear your question."

"I asked who you were," he responded. "And no more lies, please. I've grown weary of your little masquerade."

Diana stared at him for several stunned minutes, completely bewildered. Was he jesting? A covert glance at his harsh expression confirmed that he was not. But what did he mean? Tell him who she was? He knew perfectly well who she was.

Diana shook her head in confusion. "I'm sorry, Derek. I don't understand what you want me to say."

"Telling me the truth would be a refreshing change," he snapped. "That is, if you think you are capable of it."

Diana's fear and bewilderment turned to anger at the accusing note in his voice. She might not understand his absurd questions, but she certainly understood he was calling her liar.

"You are being maddeningly cryptic, Derek," she retorted. "I refuse to be spoken to as if I were a dim-witted child."

"You refuse! You refuse!" he shouted, rolling suddenly across the bed and grasping her wrist tightly.

Her eyes widened in terror, but she would not be

cowered by his brutality. She met his angry eyes squarely, her voice steady.

"Now that you have proven to us both how very strong you are, you may release my arm—unless, of course, you would prefer to break it."

Derek flushed slightly, suddenly aware of his cruelty. He dropped her hand, as if it burned him, and leaped from the bed. Their conversation was going nowhere. He walked over to where his clothes lay scattered on the floor and pulled on his breeches and shirt. Giving himself additional time to calm down, he reached over and lit a hand of candles. Deciding to try another tact, he turned again to question her.

Diana clutched the covers to her breast, her wrist throbbing with pain where he had grabbed her. She felt at an even greater disadvantage, since he was partially clothed while she was still naked. Her unbound hair was falling forward and she distractedly reached up to push it off her face.

As she lifted her arm, Derek caught a glimpse of her naked breast, the soft, pale skin glistening in the candlelight. He felt his traitorous body harden in response. Using iron will to repress his overactive passions, Derek forced himself to view her with contempt.

"Let us begin again, shall we? To start with, I know you were never married to my cousin—or anyone else for that matter."

"What?"

"You were a virgin, Diana," he said evenly, vowing to keep his temper. "Married women are not virgins."

"How did you know?" she asked.

"The pain you felt at our coupling was caused by your maidenhead, Diana," he answered. "And this is the final proof." His hand snaked out, wrenching the covers from the bottom of the bed and exposing bed linen along with a good portion of Diana's shapely legs. The candlelight illuminated the spots of bright blood, mixed with his seed, on the sheet.

Diana yanked the covers back down and scrambled toward the center of the bed, away from him. Her mind was racing as she tried to formulate an answer. How could she possibly explain her relationship with her husband?

"Giles never wanted me," she said finally, warmth flooding her face.

"Really?" Derek remarked, raising a disbelieving eyebrow.

Diana looked away, unable to meet his eyes. "It's the truth. On our wedding night Giles became quite drunk and very insulting. He took great delight in telling me he married me only for my fortune and had no intention of being intimate with me. I slept alone that night."

"That was only one night," Derek said. "You claim to have been married for several years. I know you stated Giles did not live at your home in Cornwall, but you admit he visited. There were other opportunities."

Diana lifted her head. Her voice trembled, but she said, "Giles was most adamant in his rejection of me. During those few years that never changed. He reminded me, each time I saw him, how lacking he found me in all the genteel qualities he so admired in a woman. He pronounced me common and physically unappealing."

Diana closed her eyes, fighting back the tears at her bitter memories, the pain and humiliation of her past consuming her with a vengeance.

Derek felt a sharp twinge of guilt at being the catalyst for her pain, yet he could not credit her story.

No man in his right mind could possibly look at her and find her wanting. Derek knew his cousin. Giles did not possess the will to resist such a beautiful female. She had to be lying.

"Tell me the truth, Diana," Derek said softly. "Who put you up to this ridiculous charade? Was it Marlow?"

"No. No, it was not Jonathan Marlow," she whispered brokenly. "It wasn't anyone, Derek. I am telling you the truth about my marriage to Giles."

She turned her pale face up to him, studying him in an attempt to gauge his reaction. His face was set in grim lines; his expression was one of disbelief. She felt her heart turn over. Could this be the same man who had just made love to her, who had initiated her into womanhood with such tenderness and sweetness? No, this cold-eyed stranger was not that man. This cold-eyed stranger was someone she did not know.

"You don't believe me," she said dully, her voice a mixture of pain and regret. "I don't know what else to do, what else to say. I have told you the truth, yet you refuse to believe me."

He walked away from the bed, then picked up the remainder of his clothes slowly. He opened the door, hesitating only a brief second before walking through it and slamming it hard behind him.

Diana flinched at the noise. She felt cold and dead inside. The man she loved with all of her heart, the man she had given herself to freely, joyfully, had just called her a liar and could no longer bear the sight of her. But why? Why? What had she done that was so very wrong?

Diana sunk down into the bed, burying herself deeper into the covers. There was no way she could force Derek to believe her. She would simply have to wait until they reached her home and she could produce her marriage lines for the earl. Perhaps then he would finally acknowledge she spoke the truth.

Diana turned her face to the pillow, weeping softly. He didn't trust or believe her. She shifted her hips and felt the soreness between her legs. It was a vivid reminder of what they had shared together, something Diana had felt was perfect and beautiful. Until now.

Diana painfully admitted to herself that, despite her shock and hurt at Derek's behavior toward her, she still loved him. That was one emotion she could not so easily dismiss. But any dreams she might have cherished for a future with him were gone. How could she even consider sharing her life with a man who clearly did not trust her?

Of course, she had no reason to believe Derek would have ever contemplated sharing his life with her. But she had dared to dream and hope. And he had called her a liar and rejected her in no uncertain terms.

Eventually, she would prove to Derek she was telling the truth about her marriage to Giles. Would it make a difference? Not as far as Diana was concerned. Love could not survive without trust. And Derek did not trust her. She could not spend the rest of her life tied to a man who continually doubted her honesty.

Diana felt an overwhelming sense of helplessness and loss. For a brief, glorious moment, she and Derek had captured and held something rare and beautiful. But the moment was gone. Coldness flooded her heart when she thought of what she had lost. Tears fell softly, and as the streaks of light brought forth the dawn, Diana dully contemplated the long, lonely years stretching ahead of her.

* * *

Diana awoke late, feeling empty and sad. She ate her breakfast alone, dutifully chewing and swallowing each bite, although she tasted almost nothing of it.

"The carriage awaits you, milady," the innkeeper's wife said to Diana.

"Thank you," Diana replied graciously. She finished the last of her meal and wiped her fingers on her napkin. Diana walked out of the inn, keeping her eyes fixed straight ahead. Langston stood by the carriage, waiting to assist her inside. She assumed Derek was already seated inside since he was not on top of the coach. She took a deep breath and gathered up her skirts, but stopped short when she saw the coach was unoccupied.

Diana turned questioning eyes to Langston. "The earl?"

"How flattering that you missed me, madam." Derek's mocking voice sliced through the quiet morning air.

She forced herself to raise her eyes to the sound. Derek was mounted on a large gray stallion she hadn't seen before. His face was unshaven, his hair rumpled, and his clothes, the same from last night, looked as though he slept in them. He was as handsome as ever. Diana's heart skipped a beat as she met his cold blue eyes, but she refused to cower before him.

"Good morning, my lord," Diana said evenly.

The sight of her standing there so proud and beautiful unnerved him. Her face was very pale, and she had dark smudges under her eyes, attesting to her lack of sleep, but Derek thought she looked as lovely as always.

"I trust you slept well last night," Derek taunted her, unable to help himself.

He heard her suck in her breath sharply, but she refused to be baited. "How very kind of you to inquire, my lord," she responded sweetly. "Unfortunately, I did not rest well early in the evening. A constant gnawing sound kept me awake for a considerable length of time."

"A gnawing sound?"

"Yes," she continued, her eyes glittering. "I believe it was a rat. Thankfully, it left my bedchamber early and I slept most soundly after that."

Her barb effectively delivered, Diana flashed a dazzling smile at the earl. She held tightly to Langston's hand and jumped into the carriage.

Derek stared at the closed carriage door, admiring her courage. The only consistent thing about Diana was the fact that she could continually surprise him. He drew alongside the carriage, but Diana pulled the shade down, and he could not see inside. He guided his mount to the road, and the coach dutifully followed his lead.

Diana spent the morning vacillating between self-pity and anger. Seeing Derek again rattled her more than she cared to admit, and she was more determined than ever to exonerate herself. Her pride could not bear the idea that he thought her to be a deceitful woman.

They made a brief stop in the early afternoon for lunch. Diana stepped from the carriage, and she knew instantly she was once again back in Cornwall. Everywhere, the countryside was permeated by the sea. The remoteness and inaccessibility of the area always had something of an otherworldly atmosphere clinging to it, and Diana could feel the very essence of the Cornish coast when she gazed out at the rugged shoreline.

Diana again ate a solitary lunch, but she did not mind. She was only a few hours from home and that knowledge lifted her spirits. After she reentered the carriage Derek opened the door and stuck his head inside.

"There are no road markers ahead. Can you tell us which road to take?"

He moved aside so she could lean out the carriage door to see the road up ahead. She deliberately avoided touching him, not trusting her own reaction.

"The fork to the left," she informed him. "Tell Langston to have care. The road from St. Ives undulates through bare and rock-strewn moorlands and can be difficult to negotiate for someone who doesn't know it."

Derek gave his driver the instructions, then joined her inside the coach. Diana was surprised and a bit alarmed, but kept her expression cooly impersonal.

"We will be there soon?"

"Yes," Diana replied.

"Have you missed your home?"

"Yes, I have. It will be good to return."

"I want to discuss what happened last night."

Diana whipped her head around. "I think you have already said enough, my lord. I know you doubt my word. The very first thing I shall do when we reach the manor is produce my marriage lines. Will that convince you?"

Derek grimaced slightly, but made no comment.

"It won't convince you," she responded slowly, correctly reading his expression.

"Forgeries are not uncommon."

"I see," she stated in her most haughty tone. "Then I suppose you should next travel to Chippenham so you may read the church register and speak with the vicar. That is, unless you think I have also arranged for the chapel records to be forged and enticed the vicar to lie for me."

Derek did not respond, his silence increasing the already volatile tension in the carriage. Diana starred stonily out of her window, wanting to weep over the torment his mistrust was causing.

"Do you know how Giles died?"

"I beg your pardon?" The question caught her unawares, as he intended.

"I asked you what you know of Giles's death."

She gave him a disgruntled glare. "I know only what you have told me. Giles died very suddenly."

"He was murdered," Derek explained softly.

"What!"

"Giles was found with his throat slit in a rather unsavory section of London. Despite all my efforts, his killer has not yet been located."

Diana's eyes widened in fear. "Why did you not tell me this before?"

"I didn't think it was necessary," Derek answered, his tone deliberately mild.

"Why is it now necessary?"

"You are very adept at deception, madam. Perhaps with the proper encouragement you will provide the missing details that will solve my cousin's death."

Diana raised her hand and swung at Derek. Her palm hit his cheek with surprising accuracy and the sound of her slap echoed through the closed carriage with a resounding crack. Her eyes were huge in her colorless face, and her trembling hands betrayed her intense agitation as she faced him squarely.

"First you call me a liar, and now you accuse me of murder!"

Derek lifted his hand to his stinging cheek, staring at her in surprise. But she looked so stricken that he felt his own anger evaporate, knowing he had pushed her too far.

"I have been the Earl of Harrowby for over three months, but not until your arrival in London was I shot at," Derek said, more to himself than to her. "I had to wonder if there was a connection."

A displeased frown settled over Diana's face. "What have you concluded?" she sneered. "Pray, don't keep me in suspense any longer, my lord. Is there indeed a connection?"

"I sincerely hope not." His voice was a rough murmur, but his eyes studied her, searching desperately for the truth.

"You don't really expect me to dignify that remark with an answer, do you?" Diana snarled at him. "And what of my situation? I arrive in London to reclaim the property my dead husband tried to steal from me, only to discover he has another wife and a child. When I press my suit to the current earl, I am shot at in a public park. Only three people know of my existence in the city, and the only one who would stand to gain anything by my demise is you, sir. If I were removed, you could recover the deeds of my properties and keep the wealth. There would be no one to stop you."

"You can't be serious," Derek roared.

"How does it feel, my lord," she taunted, "to be accused of such evil intent?"

Derek leaned across the coach. "Believe me, Diana. If I wanted you dead, it would be so," he said, his voice flat, and cold.

"If your aim is to frighten me, my lord," she whispered, "you certainly have succeeded." She closed her eyes.

"Perhaps now you will finally be honest with me." Derek watched her as she pressed her body against the back of the seat.

"I have been honest with you, but you refuse to believe me. You will simply have to wait until I can prove my case. And then you can take your leave, and I hope to God I never again lay eyes on you."

Tears gathered in her eyes as she turned her head away and stared out the carriage window, attempting to ignore him. After a few minutes she recognized the rough terrain and realized they were only a few short miles from her home. Determined not to address the earl again, Diana instead tapped on the roof of the carriage to gain the driver's attention. When the carriage slowed down, she leaned out the open window and called out to Langston.

"Keep a sharp eye out for the black wrought-iron gate up ahead. It will be on your right, Langston. Those are the gates that mark the drive to Snowshill Manor."

Langston followed Diana's instructions without mishap, and before long, the coach turned down the appropriate drive. Diana watched the numerous oak trees that lined the drive whirl past her, and her confidence began to renew itself. She was finally home! Her excitement increased with each turn of the wheel as they came closer and closer to the manor house.

There was an eerie quiet as the coach crunched down the gravel drive and pulled up in front of the house. Diana squirmed about impatiently in her corner of the coach, annoyed that Derek was blocking her view. She could not yet see her beloved home.

All was still when Derek stepped down from the coach. He stepped back, preventing her exit. She shoved Derek hard, and when he did not budge, she pressed herself indecently close to him and lowered herself to the ground, sliding against his rigid form.

This intimate contact, the first since last night, left her breathless and a bit shaken. It took a few moments before she regained her composure.

Diana's senses were immediately assaulted by a strange, pungent odor. Charred, burned wood and the acrid smell of smoke attacked her nostrils. She lifted her head slowly and gazed in shock at the crumbled and gutted building before her. Her stomach clenched tightly in agony. It had been such a lovely house.

Diana observed with almost detached emotion that amazingly the east facade of the house, with its mullioned windows and five alternating gables, still possessed a look of solid serenity despite the charred and blackened stones.

Her eyes drifted to the great window on the left side of the entrance porch, its more than 500 panes of glass broken and shattered. She leaned against the carriage for support, her mind whirling, her brain refusing to credit what her eyes told her.

She felt light-headed, and her breathing was rapid. She sensed, rather than saw, Derek move closer to her and she was grateful. Her knees were starting to buckle, and she allowed herself to succumb to the darkness that was threatening to overtake her. Her mind was filled with the images of her ravaged home and her final conscious thought was of her house. Snowshill Manor, her beautiful Tudor home, her safe haven from the cruelties of the world, had been gutted and burned beyond recognition.

Chapter Thirteen

As Diana swooned, Derek caught her by reaching out a strong arm to support her back and prevent her from hitting the hard ground. He felt conflicting emotions while cradling her still form close to his heart.

"Lady Diana! Lady Diana!" Derek turned his head and saw an elderly man hurrying toward them. The man was dressed entirely in black, except for his white cravat, and his undignified run contrasted sharply with his formal attire. Derek deduced he was Diana's butler.

"Is she hurt?" the man asked without any preliminaries.

"No, she has just fainted," Derek responded.

Diana came awake suddenly and blinked several times.

"Simpson, is it really you?"

"Oh, Lady Diana," the old man cried. "Thank God, you have finally come home!"

Diana demanded that Derek put her down, and when he did, she took a step away from him, accepting the older man's arm with gratitude.

"What has happened, Simpson?" she whispered in horror, her eyes sweeping over the charred ruins of the manor house.

"It was positively dreadful, milady," Simpson said. "The fire started four days ago and it took us nearly two full days to extinguish it."

"Two days!"

"It was horrible," Simpson said. "Almost all the men from the village came to help. They said the smoke could be seen for miles. Despite everyone's valiant efforts, we were unable to save anything." The man lowered his gaze to the ground.

Diana patted Simpson soothingly on the shoulder. "It's all right, Simpson. I am sure you did everything humanly possible. Was anyone injured?"

"There were a few minor burns and lung pains from the smoke. Nothing serious."

"Thank God for that," Diana muttered.

"How did the fire start?" Derek asked.

Both Diana and Simpson turned to look at him, clearly annoyed at his interrupting their conversation.

"Simpson, the new Earl of Harrowby. My lord, my butler, Simpson," Diana said by way of introductions.

"Milord." Simpson made a stiff formal bow to Derek.

"How did the fire start?" Derek repeated.

"We don't know," Simpson said, eyeing him distrustfully.

Derek scowled at the butler. Simpson met his gaze

steadily, giving no outward sign of being intimidated. Derek grunted, unwillingly admiring the butler's loyalty to Diana and his protectiveness of her. The earl thought of his own London household staff and realized, with regret, they would never show him the same devotion.

"It's all right, Simpson," Diana said. "You have my leave to speak freely in front of his lordship."

Simpson gave Derek a final distrustful glance before saying, "We believe the fires were deliberately set, Lady Diana. As best we can determine there were three separate fires set simultaneously in different sections of the house. Whoever decided to burn the house knew what they were doing. It was a most thorough job."

"It's a miracle no one was killed," Derek mused, surveying the burnt remains.

"The entire staff was having supper in the kitchen at the back of the house," Simpson said. "By the time the flames were discovered, the blaze was already beyond our control."

Diana walked slowly toward the front entrance. The once beautiful oak doors were gone, two charred hunks of wood hanging precariously in their place. The stunning brass fixtures, blackened from smoke and heat, were barely distinguishable. Even the elaborate stone carvings over the entrance arch, so painstakingly cleaned and restored by a craftsman from Devon, were damaged. Diana felt like weeping.

"Don't get too close, Lady Diana," Simpson said. "The interior beams were badly damaged. The entire structure is most unsound."

Obediently, Diana backed away. "I shall rebuild," she said with determination, swallowing her unshed tears. "We can organize a work crew to begin the cleanup tomorrow morning. Who should we put in charge, Simpson?"

The butler gave her question a good deal of thought before he said, "Colins, the groundskeeper, is best suited for the job. His family has lived in these parts for generations, and he is familiar with the people. Our local men are too busy on their farms this time of year to spend the daylight hours working away from their fields. I have heard, however, of a tin mine at Land's End that shut down last year. Colins will have his pick of good men who will be grateful for the work."

"Fine," Diana said approvingly. "I shall speak to Colins myself. Is he about the property?"

"Tomorrow," Derek said, interrupting her. "It is fast becoming dark, Diana. We had best ride out to the village and secure lodgings for the night." He turned to the butler. "Where have you been sleeping, Simpson?"

"In the old caretaker's cottage," Simpson answered.

"Oh, Simpson," Diana cried with dismay, "that old place hasn't been used for decades."

"It isn't all that bad, Lady Diana," Simpson hastily assured her. "With some major housecleaning and minor roof repairs, the dwelling was made livable. Fortunately, the remainder of the staff are local folks with family living in the community. I sent them all home. I hope that meets with your approval, milady?"

"Of course," Diana said instantly. She felt riddled with guilt for not being there when she was most needed. "I'm so very sorry this has all fallen to you, Simpson. You have done an admirable job as always. I cannot begin to express my gratitude."

"I am very glad you are home," Simpson whispered. "I have been beside myself with worry."

Diana fixed her stare on the butler's gray hair, afraid if she looked into his eyes her tears would give way. They had been through a lot together these past few years, and it felt good to know someone truly cared about her well-being.

"Thank you, my friend," Diana whispered back to Simpson. "I will ride out at first light tomorrow. Are you certain you will be all right out here?"

"I shall be perfectly fine," Simpson said.

With one last look at the blackened shell that had once been her beloved home, Diana climbed up into the carriage. She gave a deep sigh as Derek followed her inside. She had hoped he would ride his gray stallion to the village and leave her in peace.

They spoke not a word until the carriage entered the village. Derek glanced curiously out the window, impressed with the remoteness and rugged grandeur of the land. The village was made up of scattered granite cottages and farmsteads, with the church and inn standing side by side as the focal points at the end of the main street. As his eyes scanned the horizon, Derek could just distinguish the small fields marked out by stone hedges and, in the background, the pounding sea.

"Do you wish to stay here at the Rose and Crown?" Derek asked when the carriage stopped in front of the inn.

"'Tis the only establishment within twenty miles," Diana said dully. "It is small, but I am sure we can obtain two rooms."

The pain in her voice touched his heart. "Diana," he said, reaching out his hand.

"Don't!" she screeched, moving farther back into

her corner of the coach. "For God's sake, can't you just leave me alone?"

"I only want to help, Diana," Derek said soothingly.

"Help. You want to help me?" She laughed, her voice rising with hysteria. Then she shook her head, the mocking laughter rising in her throat. "That's rich."

Derek clenched his jaw, keeping his growing anger in check. Diana was perilously close to losing all control. If he shouted at her, she would probably crack.

"I will see to our accommodations," Derek grumbled, jerking open the door.

His statement stopped Diana's laughter. "I can see to my own accommodations, my lord," she yelled. "Our agreement was for you to escort me to Cornwall and you have done just that. There is absolutely no need for you to concern yourself about me any longer."

"You are spouting nonsense, Diana," Derek said patiently, turning to face her. "We shall discuss this later, after you have had a chance to rest."

"We most certainly will not discuss this later," Diana retorted. She scrambled down from the carriage after him when he ignored her outburst and began walking away from her. "In case you have forgotten, my house is now in cinders. There are countless things I must attend to at once. I do not have any time for you, my lord."

Derek continued walking toward the inn, acting as though he hadn't heard her, which was impossible because she was shouting. Picking up her skirts, Diana trudged after him, but she was waylaid by several townsfolk who recognized her and were anxious to speak of the fire. By the time she joined

Derek, he was already eating a second serving of the delectable roast lamb, buttery new potatoes, and fresh greens he had ordered for dinner.

"You are very popular," Derek said dryly, popping a warm roll into his mouth.

"Don't be ridiculous," Diana said, taking the chair opposite him. "They are merely being polite."

As Diana began to launch into a lengthy discourse about why Derek had to leave Cornwall the next morning, she was interrupted by a steady stream of individuals offering her their condolences and showing their support.

Derek watched these exchanges with interest and eventually decided it was not merely politeness that motivated the people of this village to speak to her. Most of them seemed genuinely fond of her and distressed over her tragedy.

Diana greeted the people with deference, calling most by name and accepting their sympathy with genuine warmth. She refused to allow pity to enter into the conversation and again reiterated her determination to rebuild her ruined home.

By meal's end, Derek was forced to admit he had been guilty of misjudging Diana. She must have told him the truth about Giles and her life in Cornwall. A woman so well respected, so admired, by so many people, could not be guilty of the deceit he had accused her of.

Derek wanted to tell her just that, but it seemed unlikely he would get the chance to be alone with her. As the hour grew late, Mrs. Potter, the innkeeper's wife, descended on the table. Waving a beefy arm, she shooed away the three men clustered around Diana.

"Be off with you, lads," Mrs. Potter clucked. "Can't you see Lady Diana's weary to the bone? She needs to be resting now, not listening to the likes of you three carry on."

After much shuffling of feet and lazy nods, the three men took their leave. Mrs. Potter grumbled her approval and then turned her attention to Diana.

"I've had the boys fill up the copper tub for your bath, milady," she said. "'Tis a good thing your old traveling coach broke down again just outside of town. The Sutters were only too happy to take in your maid, Amy, and her poor husband, Richards. Thank God they were still at the farm when the fire broke out at the manor house. My Joe's gone down to the Sutters to pick up your traveling trunk. At least you'll have a few fresh changes of clothes."

"You are a wonder, Mrs. Potter!" Diana exclaimed. "How can I ever thank you?"

"No thanks are needed," Mrs. Potter said, blushing at Diana's gratitude. "We both know I owe you far more than I can ever repay."

Derek, watching the exchange with pure fascination, was startled to see Diana leap to her feet and give Mrs. Potter a small hug. "I shall find my own way upstairs, Mrs. Potter," Diana said. "With Joe gone, you are quite shorthanded. Best see to your customers. I can manage by myself."

Then Diana turned to Derek, and the warmth and tenderness left her eyes. "I think it would be best if I bid you farewell tonight, my lord," she said in a cool voice. "I doubt I will be seeing you in the morning since I will be gone very early. I presume any future correspondence between us will be done through our solicitors. Thank you for accompanying me home. I wish you Godspeed on your return journey to London."

Dismissing him with a curt nod of her head, Diana turned and bolted from the room before giving Derek a chance to reply. Derek reluctantly allowed Diana to leave, knowing he could not very well have a scene with her in a public taproom—especially a taproom where she was surrounded by dozens of loyal villagers. They would probably lynch him if they thought he was upsetting her.

A burly man carrying a sizable traveling trunk entered the inn and spoke with Mrs. Potter. Derek decided he must be Joe, who had been sent to fetch Diana's clothes. He watched the man climb the short staircase with the trunk and waited expectantly for his return.

When Joe came back down the stairs, Derek signaled him, requesting a bottle of brandy with two glasses. After Joe placed them on the table Derek filled both glasses and pushed one toward the other man.

"Would you care to join me, Mr.—"

"Potter, Joe Potter," he said, hesitating briefly before picking up the glass.

"Ah, Mr. Potter. You must be the owner of this fine establishment," Derek said in his most charming voice. He quickly refilled Joe's glass and indicated that he should sit down.

"Just for a moment," Joe said reluctantly after determining Mrs. Potter had the rest of the taproom well supplied with food and drink.

"I am Derek Rutledge," the earl stated.

"I know who you are, milord," Joe said with barely concealed distaste. "Word travels fast in a small village."

Derek could not help but compare Joe's attitude with that of the fawning innkeeper, Harry. Joe, it appeared, was not so easily impressed with money and a title.

"Is Lady Diana all right?" Derek asked.

The innkeeper shrugged his shoulders noncommittally. "I didn't see her," he answered. "She told me to leave her trunk outside her door. Guess she was taking her bath."

Derek's body immediately heated at the notion of Diana naked in the tub, her full breasts rising provocatively above the water. He shook his head and took a large gulp of brandy, attempting to banish his erotic thoughts.

"Your wife seems very fond of Lady Diana," Derek said, stretching out his long legs.

"Everyone is partial to her," Joe said simply, "and with good reason. Lady Diana isn't like most other gentry we have around here."

Joe leaned forward in his chair warming to the subject. "The majority of the land around here is owned by the Duke of Hereford, but the family is seldom in residence. Now, normally I would say that an absentee landlord is not the best kind, but in this case we all prefer it. Last time the old duke came down to visit, two of them London dandies who came with his grandson had a carriage race right through the center of town. Knocked over everyone in their path who couldn't get out of the way fast enough. Blacksmith's four-year-old son was killed."

Derek grimaced at the callousness of his peers as Joe continued with the story.

"Soon as Lady Diana found out, she was spitting mad. Marched right up to the castle, she did, and read them the riot act. 'Course, the family had already left, but she browbeat the steward into paying the damages for the property that was destroyed, not to mention the little boy's funeral. There's not many who would go against their own kind for a laborer's child."

"No, I don't suppose there are," Derek agreed.

"'Course, Lady Diana's helped in all sorts of ways around here. She's given a job to just about anyone who's needed it, and she will always come to help when there is sickness about. She has a talent for healing, she does, and she's generous with her skill and time. That's how come my misses is so grateful to her."

"What happened?" Derek said, knowing Joe was waiting to be asked before he spoke.

"My boys took powerful sick a few years back," Joe said, his voice wavering. "I traveled all the way to St. Ives to bring the doctor, much good it did the poor lads. All he did was bleed them and tell us to pray. Mrs. Potter was practically dead on her feet, what with staying up all night trying to care for them and worrying so much.

"On the third day, Lady Diana arrived. First, she brewed this awful-smelling concoction from the bag of herbs she brought and fed it to the boys every few hours. Then she sent Mrs. Potter off to bed and sat up the whole night caring for my lads. Imagine that, a countess caring for an innkeeper's lads." Joe wiped a tear away at the memory. "That's a pure lady."

"What about her husband, the earl? What was he like?" Derek asked after Joe had taken a sip of his drink.

"Never set eyes on him myself," Joe said. "Heard tell he was a mean one though. It was common knowledge most of the maids working up at the house were scared to death of him, and I heard the earl used to upset Lady Diana something fierce whenever he came home." Joe regarded Derek sheepishly, suddenly aware of whom he was speaking with. "Was he your brother?"

"Cousin," Derek said absently. Noticing the innkeeper's wary look, he added, "I always thought he

178

was something of a bully myself, Joe. I have to confess I never much liked him."

Joe seemed to relax after Derek's admission and accepted a third glass of brandy. Mrs. Potter came up to the table, casting a deep frown at her husband.

"We need another keg of ale brought up from the cellar, Joe," she told him. "And best bring up some more cider. Had a lot of women in this evening to see Lady Diana, and the cider's nearly all gone."

Joe drained his glass and stood up. "I can show you to your room when you're ready, milord," the innkeeper said.

"His lordship will be taking the front room at the end of the hall," Mrs. Potter informed her husband.

"Is that next to Lady Diana's?" Derek asked casually, suspecting it was not.

"No," Mrs. Potter stated firmly. "She is sleeping at the other end of the hall. Her room is directly below our bedchamber."

Derek swallowed his amusement and faced Mrs. Potter with what he hoped was a sincere countenance. She stood with her hands on her hips, looking down at him like a mother hen defending her young.

"I should like the room next to her ladyship. Would you be so kind as to arrange it, Mrs. Potter?"

"No," she replied flatly.

"Mavis," Joe Potter cried out. "I am sure you can accommodate the earl."

"Lady Diana told me to put him in the room farthest away from hers, and that's just what I aim to do." Mrs. Potter's tone brooked no argument.

"I am her closest male relative," Derek said in his most commanding tone. "I must see to her safety."

"I don't care if you're the bloody Prince of Wales,"

Mrs. Potter snorted derisively. "I take my orders from Lady Diana. Besides, she is quite safe here. No harm will come to her while she is under my roof."

Derek silently appealed to Joe, but the innkeeper shook his head. "I'll not go against Lady Diana's wishes."

Derek cursed to himself. Were they all bewitched by her? Lady Diana this, Lady Diana that.

Sullenly Derek refilled his glass, and the Potters went back to their work. He gave them a disgruntled look, but they were too busy to notice.

Resigned, Derek decided not to make a fuss. He would sleep in the chamber they assigned him tonight. Let Diana have her small victory. She might have thought she had dismissed him, but in his mind the contest of wills between them was far from over. And he had every intention of winning.

Chapter Fourteen

It began as such a pleasant dream. Diana was strolling leisurely along the path in her formal rose garden, the intoxicating fragrance of the perfect blooms lifting her spirits. She paused beneath an arched trellis clustered with climbing rosebushes, admiring the brilliance of the scarlet dew-drenched blooms. Her gardener had surpassed himself with his efforts this season, she acknowledged, and made a mental note to inform him of her delight.

She reached up and plucked a single perfect rose from the vine, rubbing the flower's velvet petals across her face. She cupped the flower in her hands, cradling the single blossom within her palms, mesmerized by the rose's fiery glow.

Suddenly the flower burst into flames, and Diana cried out in alarm as her hands were scorched by the heat. She pulled her hands apart, dropping the rose, and immediately the ground beneath her feet became engulfed in flames.

The flames smoldered and crackled, and Diana felt a hard knot of fear deep within her stomach while she watched the fire grow. It ran rampant, igniting everything in its path and heading in a straight line directly toward her house.

"Dear God, not my home," she screamed in panic. She tried to beat down the flames with her feet, but the fire spread too quickly. Her heart pounding with fear, she started sprinting toward the house, trying desperately to reach the manor before the flames.

Diana could smell the smoke in her nostrils and feel the heat of the fire on her skin, but she kept running toward the house. Tears streaked down her face and her lungs felt as if they would burst, but she kept on running, crying out desperately for help.

The air was filled with thick black smoke and Diana could no longer see what was in front of her. Debris was falling around her, and showers of sparks rained down on her as she stumbled in the darkness.

"Help me," she sobbed in fear and frustration. "Dear God, won't somebody help me."

"Diana, I'm here," a man's voice called through the darkness. "Diana, wake up!"

"Derek," she cried out in relief, reaching out through the thick black soot. The air suddenly cleared and she could see a tall male figure racing toward her. It had to be Derek. He had come at last.

She ran forward to meet the man, but as he came closer the raging inferno ignited again, and Giles's cruel face came into focus. She screamed hysterically, her mind lost to all reason.

"Wake up, Diana! Wake up!"

Diana felt a stinging slap on her cheek and abruptly opened her eyes. Her body was drenched in sweat and she was visibly trembling. Derek sat on the edge of her bed, his handsome face lined with worry. She looked beyond him and saw Mavis and Joe Potter staring at her with open curiosity.

"Diana, can you hear me?" Derek asked. His voice was firm but gentle.

She nodded her head and tried to swallow the lump of fear in her throat. It had all been so frighteningly real. "I had a nightmare," she said unnecessarily. "I'm sorry if I woke you."

"Lord, woman, you nearly woke the dead with your screams," Derek said.

Diana shuddered at his reference to the dead, and Giles's distorted face immediately came into her mind's eye. "I am fine now," she hastily assured them all. "Pray don't let me disturb your sleep any longer. Please go back to bed."

"Well, if you're sure you're all right now," Mavis said skeptically.

"I'll sit with her until she falls asleep again," Derek said.

Mavis gave a grunt, but at Diana's nod of approval, she quit the room with her husband. As soon as the Potters left, Diana threw herself into his arms, nearly knocking him off the bed. He felt her body shiver, and instantly his protective nature was aroused. She had endured so much. If anyone had a right to nightmares, it was Diana.

She clung to him frantically, pressing herself close to him, as if she wanted to crawl inside his skin. Diana began muttering incoherently, her dialogue a rambling jumble of words, emotions, and fear.

"The flames were everywhere—and smoke, lots of thick black smoke. I tried to reach the house, but I couldn't see anything. And then I heard your voice calling me, and I thought I was safe, but it wasn't you. It was Giles."

Derek held her close, feeling the strength of her fear. "It's all right now," he said soothingly, his hand stroking her hair. "I am here with you, Diana. Nothing will harm you, I promise."

She burrowed even closer to him and he rocked her back and forth like a small child. He felt her breathe in deeply.

"Forgive me for being such a weak, helpless fool," Diana muttered.

"You're not a fool, Diana," Derek insisted. "And as for helpless"—he paused and chuckled—"you, my dear, are about as helpless as His Majesty's Navy."

She answered his jest with a wan smile, then took another trembling breath. It felt good to be held in the circle of his strong, protective arms. Too good. It was impossible for her to disregard Derek's cruel accusations of the previous night, but basking in the warmth of his embrace allowed her to forget his mistrust for a while. Derek's allure was too irresistible, her love for him too impossible, to abandon in her time of need. She needed him. Tomorrow would be soon enough to begin the healing process and forget him.

Derek carefully disengaged himself from her embrace and walked over to the small dressing table. He kept a sharp eye on Diana as he lit several candles. Her head was bent low, her long blonde hair effectively hiding her expression. He could see her shoulders tremble slightly as she fought to conquer the remaining vestiges of her fear.

Derek could feel himself reaching out to her, his heart, his very soul, longing to shield and protect her from any danger, real or imagined. He shook his head over the irony. In many ways she was as much a mystery to him as she had been the first day she entered his London town home. Yet despite his various misgivings about her, Derek knew the inexplicable bond that drew him to her was forged in steel. Even if his mind dared not accept how much he had come to care for her, his heart was determined to force him to face the truth.

Diana lifted her head at Derek's blustering sigh. She might think he was the most contrary, irrational man she had known, but underneath it all she knew he was, in truth, a good and kind man. That was why she loved him so—and wanted him so.

He gazed at her exquisite loveliness in the candle glow, and the open trust he saw in her eyes nearly brought him to his knees. He would not betray that trust, he vowed, approaching the bed. He stood so close to her he could smell the sweet lavender scent in her hair. His body tightened with desire.

"Are you feeling better now, sweetheart?" he asked gently. "Perhaps you would like me to fetch you something to drink—a glass of wine or some brandy?"

Diana shook her head. "I am not sure my stomach would stand for it." She hesitated, then wrapped her arms around his waist. She cuddled up against him, her cheek resting against his stomach. "Please stay with me tonight, Derek." Her voice was a mere whisper.

He smiled in the darkness. "Ah, so now you are back to calling me Derek."

"I have been very angry with you."

"I know. I was feeling a bit of anger myself."

"You realize, of course, since my house and all my possessions are now in ashes, I cannot prove to you I was telling the truth," Diana said in a soft voice.

"About being married to Giles, that is."

"I now believe you were being honest with me," he assured her, his voice equally as soft. "Besides, everyone in the village addresses you as Lady Diana. They all know you are the Countess of Harrowby."

Diana squeezed her arms tighter around him. "That proves nothing. The people of this community know only what I've told them. I could have said I was Lady Godiva, and they would have called me that."

Derek's attention was momentarily diverted by the provocative image of Diana riding stark naked upon a horse with nothing but her golden blonde hair to conceal her charms. Her restless movement brought him abruptly out of his pleasant daydreams.

She threw her head back and strained her neck to look up at him. His skin glowed bronze in the candlelight and Diana felt her passions rise as she imagined his mouth covering hers in a deep, provocative kiss. She raised her arms to his chest, her hands fingering the lush velvet of his midnight-blue dressing gown. Her hands froze when she realized he wore nothing underneath the robe.

Disappointed she had ceased her explorations, Derek eased himself down on the bed next to her. He covered her small hand with his larger one and placed them over his racing heart. Gazing with rapture at her lovely face, he thought how warm and giving her lips looked. He leaned forward and kissed her. Just a small taste, he promised himself.

Diana welcomed his kiss hungrily, her tongue meeting his with the fierceness of her need. One kiss turned into two—and three and four and more. Derek lost count as each kiss became more intimate, more demanding.

Diana rubbed her breasts against his chest brazenly. The belt of Derek's dressing gown had loosened, and she could feel the thick hair on his chest through her nightgown. It made her wild. Diana became almost frantic with her need to touch him, to feel his hardened strength against her. His kisses aroused her flesh, but her soul cried out for his love. She wanted desperately to release the love she held for him deep within her heart by worshiping him with her body.

Diana's hand slid provocatively down Derek's chest to his lap. She found the split in his robe, and her exploring fingertips could not resist slipping beneath the fabric and brushing the tip of his enlarged manhood.

Derek gave a loud growl of sensual excitement. He wanted to rip the nightgown from her succulent body and bury himself deep within her womanhood, but he somehow managed to catch himself before he ravaged her. He wanted to go slow and easy this night. He wanted to enjoy each and every facet of their lovemaking. If only Diana would cooperate!

"Slow down, love," he whispered huskily, trailing kisses down her throat. "Else it shall be over before we've even begun."

"Oh, Derek," she said in his ear, "I shall go out of my mind if you do not touch me soon."

He eagerly complied with her wishes. The little erotic whimpers she made as he caressed her firm breasts did nothing to aid his resolve to be languid in their coupling. Diana backed away from him with a sensual look of delight and excitement in her brown eyes. He watched, mesmerized, as she undid the small buttons of her nightgown and lifted it up and over her head. Tossing the garment aside, she challenged him with her eyes to do the same.

Derek took off his robe, and Diana felt her mouth go dry with desire. She openly appraised his naked flesh, and Derek grew even larger. He was nearly shaking with need when he finally stretched out next to her on the bed. Diana immediately rolled over, pressing herself against his hot flesh. Within minutes, they were both ready to explode with excitement.

"Open your eyes, Diana," Derek commanded, pushing her shoulders against the pillows and covering her body with his own. "I want to see your eyes glow with pleasure as I make you mine again."

Diana obeyed him. Her gentle brown eyes were dark with passion and love. Grasping his hips firmly, she pulled him toward her. He entered her with one firm thrust, and a cry of pleasure burst from Diana's lips as he filled her.

She could feel him pulsing inside her and it made her wild. Wantonly she met his hips thrust for thrust, urging him on, begging him to bring her to the ultimate release.

Derek was smoldering with barely controllable lust. He whispered tender words of love and erotic words of sensuality to her as he pumped in and out of her burning sheath. He felt her legs stiffen and knew she was about to climax. Her cries of pleasure pushed him beyond his control and he spilled his hot seed inside her just as she peaked.

He collapsed on top of her, his mind floating away from his body, the pleasure so intense and the connection so complete that he was stunned.

"My God, I love you, Diana," he blurted out. He was so astounded by the revelation that he spoke without thinking.

The room remained silent. He raised himself up

on his elbows and gazed down at his beloved. He saw the steady rise and fall of her chest and heard her even breathing. She had fallen asleep! Derek wasn't sure if he should be amused or insulted.

He couldn't believe it. He had finally opened his heart to her, and she had slept through it. Derek chuckled in the darkness, the absurd humor of the situation not wasted on him.

Gently, seeking not to disturb her, he withdrew himself from her body. He rolled onto his back and crossed his arms behind his head, trying not to dwell overlong on this most astonishing revelation. He was in love with Diana. He wondered how she would react to the news. Tomorrow morning would be soon enough to explore these strange new feelings of love, he decided, relaxing against the pillows.

He would awaken Diana with soft, featherlike kisses and arouse her senses to a fever pitch. And as they coupled, he would proclaim his love for her and watch her eyes grow misty with contentment.

Totally satisfied with his plans, Derek settled down into the mattress and pulled up the thick coverlet. He gathered Diana into his arms and held her close, savoring her warmth. He fell asleep that way, holding her next to his heart, his mind filled with the hope and promise of the wonderful life they would share together.

When Derek woke in the morning, Diana was gone. He didn't panic at first. He simply assumed Diana had risen early and was embarrassed to face him after her rather uninhibited behavior last night.

After taking stock of the room, however, he was forced to revise his original opinion. All of Diana's belongings were gone—her clothes, her shoes, her cloak, her hairbrushes and other personal items. Even the traveling trunk Joe had brought last night with Diana's clothes was missing. A feeling of dread encased him when he realized she was truly gone. She had left without waking him. More important than his own hurt feelings was the real possibility that she could be in danger.

He bolted from the bed, barely shrugging into his robe before bellowing for Joe. The innkeeper met Derek halfway up the stairs, his face registering his shock at encountering an angry and half-naked Derek at this hour of the morning.

"Where is she?" Derek roared.

Mrs. Potter crept up behind her husband. She took in Derek's disheveled appearance with a jaundice eye and answered his question. "Lady Diana has left for Snowshill Manor."

Derek scowled at the pair. Not that he was surprised. Diana had stated several times she would leave for the estate at first light.

"When I awoke I noticed all her clothing and personal effects were gone from the room," Derek stated flatly, not in the least concerned with revealing the fact he had spent the night with Diana.

"Lady Diana asked me to move her things to another room," Mrs. Potter said, her face flushing slightly. "She said the other one gave her nightmares."

Derek merely grunted. "Who escorted her out to the manor?" he snapped.

"Escorted?" Joe asked with a puzzled frown.

Derek rolled his eyes skyward, trying valiantly to keep his temper in check. "Don't tell me that you let her ride all that way by herself. Are you daft, man?"

"Now there is no need for you to be calling my Joe

names, milord," Mavis said, pushing her husband aside and planting herself firmly in front of Derek. "Lady Diana was anxious to ride out this morning. And why should she be needing an escort? She never has before."

"Her house has never been deliberately set afire before, Mrs. Potter," Derek said sarcastically. He heaved a heavy sigh. "How long ago did she leave?"

"About two hours," Joe said, his face masked with worry.

"Do you think she could be in danger?" Mrs. Potter asked, understanding Derek's agitation.

"I sincerely hope not," Derek said. He ran his fingers through his disheveled hair. "Tell my driver to have my horse saddled and ready to leave in twenty minutes."

Derek turned and started back up the stairs, willing himself to remain calm. There was no reason to get into a panic, not at this stage. Diana was just being headstrong. It was unlikely she would encounter any danger.

Derek washed quickly. He had just begun shaving when Joe brought in a steaming tray of hot food. "Mrs. Potter thought you might be hungry," Joe said lamely, setting down the tray. Joe lingered a few minutes, but Derek was in no mood for conversation.

Derek ate the tempting food quickly while he dressed. His mind kept recounting Simpson's words about the fire being deliberately set. The arsonist had done a most thorough job, true, but was his task complete? Had he achieved what he had intended? Or was the main task yet ahead of him?

Chapter Fifteen

It took Derek longer to reach the manor house than he'd hoped, due to his unfamiliarity with the rugged coastal terrain. Joe Potter's directions could only be described as minimal, but fortunately Derek possessed a keen sense of direction and an excellent memory. He recognized several key landmarks on the road, and in the end, the lack of proper signposts did not hamper him in reaching his destination.

When he turned his gray stallion down the tree-lined drive, Derek could not believe the changes already underway. The eerie silence of yesterday afternoon was gone, replaced by the hum of activity as workmen, carts, horses, and supplies clogged the drive.

He quickly scanned the crowd of burly workmen until he located Diana. She was standing in the middle of what appeared to be a command post. An old, battered wooden table served as her desk, upon which various papers were strewn. Derek noted with amusement several rocks being used as paperweights to keep the documents from scattering about the lawn in the gusting wind.

A large group of men were clustered around the table, all apparently trying to give Diana advice simultaneously. Simpson stood next to his mistress, trying to maintain some kind of order. He was not very successful. Everyone was talking and shouting at once.

Derek tethered his mount to a tree and approached Diana cautiously, uncertain of his reception. She was engaged in earnest conversation with two members of her work crew and unaware of his presence for several moments. Some sixth sense must have alerted her to his nearness, because she paused suddenly in midsentence to turn her head in his direction.

Her eyes widened in surprise, but she did not acknowledge him. Instead, she returned her full attention to the men before her. Within minutes she somehow brought order to the boisterous crowd, and the men disbursed to begin carrying out her orders.

Derek noticed Simpson was still hovering about Diana, but she spoke to the butler in a low voice and soon he too was gone. Then she turned back to Derek, waiting for his approach with her chin held high.

Derek's heart was pounding loudly in his chest as he strode toward her. He could not yet decide how he wanted to greet her. Should he kiss her senseless or throttle her lovely neck for putting herself in possible jeopardy and scaring him half to death?

"Good morning, my lord," Diana's voice rang out. "How very nice to see you this morning."

"Back to my lording me again," Derek said with a wry grin. "I got the distinct impression last night you were going to call me by my given name from now on. Was I mistaken?"

"Of course not, Derek," Diana said slowly, placing great emphasis on his name. Insufferable man! How could he remind her of last night? And what on earth was he doing there? Diana demanded her heart cease its ridiculous pattering and vowed to disregard the exciting effect Derek was having on her. He most likely had come to say good-bye. She refused to allow herself to hope for more. "It was most kind of you to travel so far out of your way before beginning your journey back to London."

Derek towered above her, standing so close she could feel the warmth of his body. "I don't understand why you keep insisting I am leaving this morning, Diana," he said with a twinkle in his eye. "I can't imagine what I have said or done that has led you to that false conclusion."

Diana's heart skipped another beat at his words. "You have fulfilled your obligation to return me safely home, Derek," she replied evenly, meeting his eyes. "Naturally, I assumed you would return to London."

"Not without you," he said softly.

"I beg your pardon?" Diana asked, startled.

"You heard me correctly," Derek said, taking yet another step closer to her. "Do you honestly think I am so lacking of honor that I would leave you behind with the threat of danger still here? It is very possible the culprits who torched your house are still lurking about in the district. I want you with me until this mystery is solved. It is the only way I can be assured of your safety."

His honor. Of course. Derek's words sliced

through the burgeoning hope that Diana did not even realize she had cherished until this moment. How very foolish of her to even entertain the notion he had stayed because he cared for her— or even because, God forgive her for hoping, he had somehow fallen in love with her.

"There is no need for you to remain here, Derek," she stated firmly, glad her voice did not betray her inner sorrow. "I am among my own people now. I will be perfectly fine."

Derek gave her an angry scowl. "Damn it, Diana, don't fight me on this," he said. "You are my responsibility and I intend to take care of you, whether you want me to or not."

"There is no need to shout at me," Diana yelled back at him, her heart sinking anew at his words. "I can hear you well enough. For pity's sake, Derek, you are close enough to be standing on my toes."

Derek shot her a murderous look, then glanced around. There was enough hammering, sawing, and banging noises among the work crew to prevent their shouting from attracting an audience for the moment. Impulsively, Derek grabbed her arm in a grip that was gentle, yet unshakable, and dragged her farther away from the ruined ashes of the house to the privacy of the rose garden.

"We are going to discuss this, Diana, in a calm and rational manner," Derek said grimly.

"There is nothing to discuss," she gritted through her teeth. "I release you from all your responsibilities, obligations, or whatever else you want to call them. You may return to London with a clear conscious, content in the knowledge you have admirably performed your duties toward me."

"Are you quite finished?"

"No." Diana took a deep breath. "I do want you to

send out one of your investigators to Chippenham so my marriage to Giles can be substantiated. Even though the estate room has not yet been cleared of debris, I am certain all the documents I kept there have been destroyed, including the only copy I possessed of my marriage lines."

"There is no need for that, Diana," Derek said.

"But there is, Derek," Diana said. "The rebuilding of my home will nearly deplete me of my funds. I'm afraid I will have to ask you to repay some of the monies Giles stole from me. I cannot do that unless I prove to you he was, indeed, my husband."

"I told you before I believe your story about your marriage to Giles. You do not have to prove anything to me, Diana," Derek repeated wearily. "I will gladly give you anything you desire."

Diana looked at him, surprised. "What has prompted this sudden change of heart?"

"Last night," he whispered huskily.

Diana gave a small cry and turned away from him. Her face flushed with heat as she remembered her wanton abandonment in his arms. "I was not myself last night."

"Oh, I think you were," Derek said with a wicked grin. "In my opinion, you were your most delightful self last night."

"I had a nightmare," Diana stated emphatically. "I was afraid and you offered me comfort. You were just being kind. That's all."

"I am seldom kind," Derek said. He pulled her reluctant body toward him. "You have the basic facts concerning last night correct, my love, but you have neglected a few rather salient points. Shall I refresh your memory?" He bent his head down and trailed small kisses along her neck.

"Stop that!" Diana exclaimed, trying to elude

him. She slapped her hands ineffectually against his broad shoulders. She could barely speak, let alone think, when he held her thus. He allowed her to escape from his embrace, and Diana quickly walked away from him, retreating farther into the garden.

Diana heard Derek following her, and she increased her speed, but stopped suddenly under a flowering rose trellis. Her body began to shake uncontrollably as she realized where she stood. This was the exact spot where her nightmare had begun last night.

"What's wrong? Are you cold?" he asked and she knew he had noticed her trembling.

"No, I'm not cold," she stammered. When he reached for her this time, she welcomed his arms. "This is where my nightmare began last night."

"Oh, Diana," he whispered with genuine concern. "You must never be afraid when I am near you."

"It's strange, but I don't feel afraid when you are with me," she said, not understanding how that could be true, but knowing it was.

"Then I shall endeavor to stay by your side as much as possible," Derek told her in a charming voice.

Diana shook her head sadly, pulling away from him. "You must return to London, Derek—without me."

"I don't want to be without you," Derek said, his voice rich with emotion. "Marry me, Diana."

Diana blinked her eyes twice and looked at him as though he had just sprouted wings. She began to berate him for his cruel jest, but the scathing retort died on her lips when she realized he was being serious.

"Good Lord, Derek, have you taken leave of your senses?"

Derek threw up his arms in mock despair. "You are a true romantic, my sweet!" he said with a wry grin. He held his arms open, beckoning her. "Enough of this foolishness, Diana. Come here and give your future husband a proper kiss."

Diana's eyes narrowed in suspicion. Derek was acting with supreme confidence, and it rankled her. What did he expect her to do? Fall into his arms in gratitude and start blubbering like an idiot, just because he had asked her to marry him? Diana straightened her spine and glared up at him.

"I don't seem to recall agreeing to your ridiculous proposal, Derek," she said in a haughty voice.

"Oh, but you will, my dear," he said, advancing upon her.

Diana backed away from him, her heart thundering furiously in her chest. She could feel the panic rising in her throat. To marry Derek might have been her secret dream from the moment she'd realized she loved him, but faced with the reality of the situation, Diana was having serious doubts.

Her marriage to Giles had been such a cruel mockery. It had taken her a long time to get over the pain and despair. If she failed as Derek's wife, it would be all the more painful because she loved Derek with a depth of feeling she had never felt for Giles. If she married Derek and their relationship fell apart, it would crush the very life from her. Diana shuddered at the thought.

"I never thought I'd marry again," she whispered. "Ever."

"It will be different this time, Diana."

"How?"

"I will sleep by your side every night," he said earnestly.

"There is more to marriage than intimacy, Derek," she said with a huff.

"I know, Diana," he said with a smile. "There is love. And you love me."

Diana lifted an eyebrow, truly annoyed at his smug smile—and livid because he was speaking the truth. "Oh, really," she replied sarcastically. "And just how did you come by that interesting bit of fiction?"

"You told me," he said lightly. "The first time we made love."

She frowned. "And you called me a liar that night," she whispered, her voice cracking with pain at the memory still vivid in her heart.

"I was an idiot," Derek said sincerely. "I hope you can forgive me."

" 'Tis not a question of forgiveness, Derek," she responded earnestly. "It is a matter of trust." She turned her back on him and gave a slight shrug. "Do you know I spent the entire carriage ride from my house to the village yesterday waiting for you to accuse me of setting the fire at my own house? It merely seemed the next logical step, after you first accused me of lying about my marriage to your cousin and then implied I might have knowledge of his murder."

"I have wrongly accused you far too many times, Diana," he said with regret. "I can only promise you I shall never do so again."

Diana closed her eyes to conceal the wave of pain that washed over her. How she wished things were different! "It won't work, Derek," she said in a flat, emotionless voice. "You don't trust me, and no amount of one-sided love can compensate for that."

"You are wrong, Diana," he shouted. He grasped her shoulders, turning her around to face him. "I do trust you. And the love in this relationship is not one-sided. I happen to love you also. Very much."

Diana's knees buckled. For one horrible moment she thought she was going to fall, but Derek's strong arms prevented her from hitting the ground.

"What did you say?" Diana asked, shaken.

Derek gave her a heart-melting smile. "I thought you said your hearing was sound, my love," he teased. "But if you want me to, I shall be happy to shout it again. I love you." He leaned forward and kissed the tip of her nose. "And I want you to be my wife."

"Good Lord, I must be dreaming," Diana muttered to herself.

She staggered to a garden bench and sat down with a loud thud. Derek followed her at a leisurely pace, the maddening grin never leaving his handsome features. He looked perfectly delighted with the morning's turn of events. She felt ill.

"You know, Diana," he said in a conversational voice, "I was rather hoping you would be a bit more enthusiastic over the prospect of becoming my wife."

She lifted her hand and rubbed her forehead furiously. She was having difficulty concentrating, and Derek's unshakable good humor was rattling her even more. He loved her! He wanted to marry her! Why wasn't she leaping with joy? Why didn't she throw her arms around him, loudly proclaim her love and devotion, and express her boundless happiness at the idea of belonging to him throughout this life and into eternity?

"I'm not sure I would make you a proper wife, Derek," she said softly, voicing her innermost fears. She met his eyes boldly.

"You will be a perfect wife, Diana," he said reassuring her.

She turned her head aside, knowing she would not be able to gaze into his eyes without losing complete control of her magnified emotions.

"I am very confused, Derek," she said honestly. "And scared."

Derek leaned over and whispered in her ear. "I know, my love." He gathered her up in his arms and held her close. "I know only this, Diana. I love you, and I will have you for my wife."

Diana smiled despite the gravity of the situation. "You sound very confident, my lord."

Confident, he thought. Perhaps determined was a better word. Derek sat quietly holding her, trying to think of a way to break through her defenses. The strange thing was he understood her reluctance all too well. He too had vowed never again to risk his heart. But he could no more stop the tide of love he felt for Diana than he could hold back the wild, pounding sea. And he told her just that.

"We were meant to be together, Diana," he said. "Once you come to accept that, we will be able to begin our wonderful life together."

"I need some time, Derek," she whispered.

"Naturally," he agreed, pleased she was no longer refusing him outright. "If you decide quickly, however, we can be married at that charming little church in the village before we leave for Chippenham."

"Chippenham? Why on earth do you want to go there?"

"For legal purposes," he explained vaguely.

"I see," Diana muttered softly. Her gentle brown eyes had grown as big as saucers.

"Since we must leave here for a while, I rather like

the idea of traveling together as man and wife. Don't you agree?"

"Derek," she screeched, jumping up from her perch. "You just promised to give me some time to think about all of this."

"I am giving you time," he replied with false innocence.

She wrinkled her brow at him. "How can I possibly consider leaving here soon?" she exclaimed. "I have only just arrived. And there are countless matters that demand my immediate attention."

He looked down at her. True, he had agreed to give her time to make her decision, and he had every intention of honoring his promise. Yet it was essential Diana understand he was still in control of the situation.

"The danger is very real here, Diana. You must remain under my protection until I have determined you are no longer at risk. We need to travel to Chippenham to obtain a copy of your marriage lines to Giles to establish a legal claim to your properties. I will not leave here without you." Derek gave her a concerned look, trying to gauge her reaction. "We shall set out in a fortnight. That should give you sufficient time to organize your affairs and set the plans in motion for the rebuilding of Snowshill Manor."

With that said, Derek reached down, kissed her long and hard, then turned away.

Diana stared breathlessly at his retreating back, her mind whirling. "I will have you know that I don't much care for your exceedingly arrogant manner, my lord," she shouted at him, her lips still tingling from his kiss. "I will also remind you, sir, I have not yet agreed to any of this."

"A fortnight, Diana," he bellowed as he walked

away, not once glancing back at her. "We can return to Cornwall as soon as our business is concluded." And then to her total chagrin, she heard him start to whistle a bawdy tune just as he vanished from her field of vision.

Chapter Sixteen

They were, by far, the longest two weeks of Diana's life. Derek treated her with total kindness and infinite patience, which only served to heighten her confusion. He also proceeded to charm each and every one of the members of the tightly knit community he came in contact with. By the end of the second week even Mavis Potter, who had been the most wary of the lot, thought he was a perfect gentleman and the ideal husband for Lady Diana.

The more everyone grew to like him, the more suspicious Diana became. Giles too had been charming before they were married. What would prevent Derek from turning into a monster once they were wed? Diana would lie awake in bed at night, her mind running rampant imaging all sorts of horrors occurring if she were Derek's wife and under his control. Only until she was perched on the very edge of sanity did Diana catch herself, and then she would spend her final waking hours desperately trying to clear her mind of those ridiculous thoughts.

Derek was nothing like Giles. Derek loved her. Derek cared about her. He protected her. And she loved him maddeningly. Yet that was the rub. Diana was too insecure to trust her own instincts and too much in love with Derek to believe her heart could be objective.

On the day prior to their departure for Chippenham, Diana left her dressmaker's shop in haste. She was scheduled to meet the architect from St. Ives at the Rose and Crown Inn at two o'clock and it was already half past one. If she hurried to the inn, she might be able to gobble down a quick luncheon before the meeting.

Diana was annoyed at having to waste a part of her last day in town having new garments fitted, but it could not be avoided. Her only surviving gowns were black mourning dresses. She had no clear notion of how long she would be gone from the village and Diana was determined to bring along a variety of gowns. She had no intention of ever again being reduced to wearing only two black gowns for days on end.

In defiance of convention, Diana instructed Mrs. Lowell, the seamstress, to sew several new gowns for her in soft pastels. Diana still wore her mourning black while in the village, but she decided to forsake her widow's weeds once she left town. It would serve no purpose to continue with the hypocrisy of wearing black in honor of her dead husband. Giles had shown her neither honor nor respect during his lifetime. She owed nothing to his memory.

As Diana crossed the quiet street, she spied a boisterous group of men leaving the Rose and Crown.

She did not at first recognize Derek, but when she heard his distinctive laugh clearly, her heart raced. She wondered frantically if he had seen her. She simply wasn't up to another one of his charming assaults on her senses. He was methodically wearing down her resistance, and these days only a few minutes spent in his company were sufficient to rattle her.

Today, however, Diana needed to be in full possession of her wits for her upcoming meeting at two o'clock. The architect had reluctantly agreed to take on the redesigning of her new house, and he had to travel a fair distance to see her. The very least she owed the man was a clear mind and her undivided attention.

Despite the fact that she was appalled at her lack of courage, Diana slipped down a narrow alley and practically ran to the side entrance of the nearby church. She opened the door and slid inside, wondering gloomily how long she would have to hide in there.

"Have you come to post banns today?" a familiar male voice whispered in her ear.

Diana let out a startled cry and whirled around to confront Derek. She shot him a scathing look, but did not respond to his question.

Derek took her silence in good humor. Nothing much seemed to bother him these days. Diana had not totally accepted the idea of becoming his wife, but the earl knew it was only a matter of time. He was a patient man, confident in the eventual outcome of the matter, and to his mind, Diana was a prize well worth waiting for.

Standing beside her in the church, Derek noticed at once that Diana was dressed in a new frock, and although it was the customary black, it flattered her coloring and figure. The tightly fitted bodice outlined the lovely curves of her bosom, and the lacy, high-ruffled collar accented her graceful neck. He resisted a strong impulse to lean down and kiss her soft lips, knowing it would only make her wary and confused.

Derek turned his attention from Diana and surveyed the interior of the church with distracted interest. It seemed to him everything he encountered in Cornwall during his visit was ancient and mysterious and had a story or legend attached to it. This lovely medieval church was no exception, he decided, as his eyes came to rest on an unusual carving on the side of a chair.

"What is that?" he asked, pointing to the chair, on the side of which was a carved figure of a mermaid looking into a mirror while combing her long hair.

"That is the mermaid chair," Diana said in a hushed whisper. "According to legend, a beautiful woman used to sit at the back of this church each Sunday, captivated by the voice of the squire's son as he led the congregation in hymns. Eventually, she enticed him to accompany her to the sea, and the pair set off to Pendour Cove, which many locals refer to as Mermaid's Cove. Anyway, they were never seen again, although 'tis said that on warm summer evenings they can be heard singing a ghostly duet."

"What a haunting tale," Derek said softly.

He gave Diana a hungry look, and she swayed unconsciously toward him, but caught herself before melting in his arms.

"I thought you were going to spend the afternoon at the manor house," Diana snapped at him, irritated by her lack of self-control.

Derek had been spending the majority of his days

working at the manor. Diana felt both shocked and proud when she left the safety of the rose garden the morning he proposed and encountered him, stripped down to his fine cambric shirt, working side by side with her laborers clearing away the debris from the fire.

That gesture had gone a long way in endearing him to the men of the village. When it was later discovered Derek had been an army officer and had fought the French under Wellington's command, his status among the men rose to near sainthood.

"I thought I might join your meeting with the architect this afternoon," Derek said. "Elizabethan design has always been something of a hobby of mine." When she frowned, he tactfully added, "That is, unless you have any objections?"

"How do you know about my meeting?" Diana asked, suspicious of him again.

"Simpson informed me," Derek responded casually. "He thought I might be interested in hearing about the design plans for my future home."

Not Simpson too, Diana thought with a groan. Why was it that everyone, except her, had so readily accepted her marriage to Derek? Diana forced herself to remain calm when she spoke again.

"It is not your house, Derek. It is my house. Besides, even if I did marry you, I cannot believe you would want to live out here in such a remote area," Diana muttered peevishly. "Don't you have other residences?"

"Several," Derek said. "I inherited them along with the earldom. The Harrowby ancestral manor is a rambling old castle. Even as a boy I remember thinking it was dank, drafty, and cold. Parts of the original structure are still standing, reputed to have been constructed during the reign of William the Conqueror. I've never much cared for the old mausoleum."

"There must be other places?"

"Two country houses, a cottage in Brighton, and of course the London town home, which you have already seen," Derek said.

"I am sure you would prefer living in those houses rather than out here in Cornwall," Diana said.

"That all depends," Derek said.

"On what?"

"Where you want to live," Derek said simply. "You see, my dear, I would even be content staying at the old caretaker's cottage if that would make you happy."

Diana gave an audible sigh at his sincerity. He was unshakable in his determination to win her. Why could she not just accept her good fortune gracefully?

"I could be your mistress, Derek," she said without thinking.

Diana clutched at the lapels of his navy blue jacket and spoke quickly, almost desperately, before she lost her nerve. Even the darkening scowl on his face did not deter her. "No, please listen to me, Derek. There is no need for us to marry. When you return to London, you can locate a suitable place for me to live. I'll stay in London with you until the manor is rebuilt, and then we can travel to Cornwall together. When you decide you have had enough of the rustic Cornish life, I'll follow you away from here, no matter where you go. I promise I'll stay with you, Derek. That is, for as long as you want me."

Derek gazed down at her. "Cornwall is not a very convenient place to keep a mistress, love," he said lightly.

Diana turned her head away, her cheeks warm.

My God, what had come over her? She had just made a most indecent proposal to the man she loved. Inside a church, for pity's sake. She was so confused.

"It is going to be all right," he told her gently. "I love you, Diana."

"We're going to be married, aren't we, Derek?" she whispered, her voice quavering as tears trickled down her face.

"Yes, we are."

"I'm very frightened of that." She sniffed loudly, and then whispered fearfully, "You will wait, won't you, Derek? You will wait until I am ready?"

"I will wait, love," he said with infinite kindness. "No matter how long it takes."

Three days later Diana stood in front of St. Michael's Church in Chippenham. Her eyes scanned the tall pinnacle towers and projecting gargoyles as her mind searched for a clear memory of the building. She couldn't forget that this was the church where she had said her wedding vows with Giles, and she began to tremble.

"There is no need to go through with this, Diana," Derek said. "I can escort you back to the inn and return alone later to speak with the vicar."

She shook her head. "I must do this, Derek," she said, starting up the stone steps before losing her nerve. He followed quickly on her heels.

They were greeted at the door by the vicar, who was donning his hat in preparation for leaving the church. He was much younger than the vicar who had married her, and Diana knew immediately this man was not the same man who had presided over her vows with Giles. She was momentarily deflated at not being able to locate an eyewitness to the event, yet she was astute enough to realize even if it were the same vicar, it was possible he would not remember her wedding ceremony. That would be even more distressing.

Given that fact, Diana felt their arrival at the church couldn't have been timed better. The vicar was obviously in a rush and would not have time to question the unusual request of two strangers too closely. However, now that she was faced with the task, Diana was hard pressed to put her request into words. She could hardly tell the vicar the true circumstances of her visit, and yet she loathed the idea of lying to him.

Derek saved her from having to make a choice by suddenly intervening.

"Good afternoon," Derek said pleasantly. "I am Derek Rutledge, Earl of Harrowby, and this is Lady Diana." Derek shook hands enthusiastically with the vicar. "We have traveled here today on a most urgent and confidential matter concerning a member of our family. We were hoping, sir, you would be able to assist us."

Both Derek's title and conspiring tone caught the vicar's immediate attention.

"I am Reverend Brenton," the vicar replied pleasantly. "I shall be pleased to help you, if I can, my lord."

"Splendid!" Derek exclaimed. Then Diana and he followed the vicar into the vestibule, which afforded them some measure of privacy. "Four years ago, Reverend Brenton, my cousin was married in a private service at this church. His unexpected death has caused our family innumerable difficulties, since his personal papers were left in total disarray and are scattered in various locations. Somehow, in all the confusion, his marriage lines have been misplaced.

211

I was hoping it would be possible for us to see the church register so we may copy down all the necessary details."

"The register," the vicar repeated, clearly disappointed. "Naturally you may read the register, my lord."

Reverend Brenton swiftly located the appropriate book and waited impatiently while Diana began leafing through the pages.

Derek noted the clergyman's restlessness. "Please don't let us keep you from your business, sir," he said, hoping the vicar would seize the opportunity and leave them alone.

Reverend Brenton hesitated. "If you are sure that I can be of no further assistance, my lord?"

"You have been most helpful, sir," Derek said, escorting him down the center aisle of the church. "We are indebted to you for your kindness this afternoon."

The vicar left and Derek returned to Diana's side. She continued with her task, her hands trembling as she turned each page in the book. He stepped back, allowing her to read through the register in privacy.

"Derek?" she called out faintly.

"Have you found it?" he demanded, moving close to her side.

"No," she whispered. "I must have missed it. Please will you look?"

He leaned over the large leather-bound book and began reading. "What was the date again?"

"September 3, 1814." Several long minutes past. Then Diana said bleakly, "It isn't there, is it?"

"No, it isn't, sweetheart," Derek replied in a calm voice. "And I'm afraid I know the reason why."

Diana closed her eyes and waited several horrible

seconds for Derek to call her a liar. At this point he certainly would be justified since she was unable to prove the existence of her marriage.

"There is a page missing from the book."

Diana's eyes flew open. "What?"

"Someone has torn a page from the register, Diana!" Derek exclaimed. "If you look closely along the binding, you can see where it has been ripped out."

Her eyes followed his fingertips along the spine of the book, and she gasped when she saw the small remnants of a torn page. "Giles?" she asked breathlessly, not sure if she felt angry or relieved.

Derek shrugged his shoulders. "Perhaps. Tell me truthfully, Diana. What did you intend to do with the page when we located it?"

"Remove it from the register," she said, heat filling her face. "And when I was certain we no longer needed it, I was going to destroy it."

Derek grinned. "My thoughts exactly." He closed the book with a loud bang. "I am inclined to believe Giles is responsible for this. He probably removed the page soon after your wedding ceremony, when he decided to go through with his second marriage to Henriette. This way, it would be extremely difficult to prove in a court of law he was a bigamist. Giles could continue to easily steal the remainder of your money and property, since you believed you were his wife. Even if you ever found out about Henriette, you would have been hard pressed to prove Giles was ever married to you. With no church records to back up your story, your own wedding papers would have been of little value. Giles could have claimed that they were a forgery and that you made up the entire wild tale for your own personal gain. It would have been his word against yours."

"I don't doubt who would have won," Diana remarked, shuddering.

Derek's answering frown indicated he agreed with her. Taking her arm, he escorted her outside the church into the fading sunlight. They walked the short distance back to their accommodations at the Lord Nelson Inn in reflective silence.

They were both so absorbed in private thought that Derek was startled when he glanced up just in time to avoid colliding with a gentleman alighting from his phaeton.

"I say, Rutledge, I thought that was you," the stranger said in a tone of false joviality. He leaned forward and practically leered at Diana. "I suppose you were too intent on other matters to notice me. Can't say I blame you." He waited expectantly for Derek to make the introductions.

"Bennington." Derek swore under his breath. Of all the bad luck! This was hardly the opportune moment to run into Henriette's brother. Yet Derek knew he was neatly trapped, so he attempted to make the best of it.

"Lord Bennington, may I present Lady Diana . . . Crawford," Derek said reluctantly, relieved he had remembered Diana's maiden name.

"I am charmed to make your acquaintance, Lady Diana," Lord Bennington drawled. He broke into an easy grin, and taking Diana's gloved hand, he lifted it to his lips.

For an instant Diana simply stared at the sandy-blond head bent low over her hand, but when she caught Lord Bennington slyly watching her, she snatched her hand back in annoyance. His strange pale green eyes were appraising her person far too boldly. Diana took a small, unconscious step toward Derek, answering Bennington's slick, assured smile

214

with a positively frigid one of her own.

"Lord Bennington." Diana acknowledged the introduction with an aloof nod of her head.

"Lady Diana is my fiancee," Derek said in a tight, hard voice.

"Oh, really," Lord Bennington said with a raised eyebrow. He regarded them speculatively. "I had no idea you were betrothed, Rutledge. I assume it happened recently?"

"Very," Diana said. She considered the sandy-haired man standing before her. He was an ordinary-looking man in his middle forties, expensively dressed and neatly groomed, yet there was something about him that gave Diana a physical chill. Perhaps it was the way his eyes glinted between half-closed lids when he regarded her, or maybe she was just reacting to the tension she could sense from Derek.

"If you'll excuse us, Bennington," Derek said in a deceptively pleasant voice, "we'll be on our way. We are late for an appointment. Good afternoon."

Derek placed his hand possessively in the small of her back and neatly steered her around Lord Bennington before the other man had a chance to utter another word.

"I don't think I like Lord Bennington," she said.

"I don't happen to like him very much at this moment either," Derek said. "His rather inopportune appearance has complicated our lives."

"Don't look so glum, Derek," Diana said encouragingly. "I thought you handled him rather well."

"I am afraid you are missing the point, Diana. Do you know who he is?"

"Lord Bennington?" Diana felt a shiver of forboding. "Was he a friend of Giles?"

"Not exactly," he answered glumly. "Bennington

215

is Henriette's eldest brother."

"What! Oh, no," she groaned. "Of all the rotten luck."

"Indeed," Derek said. "Now that Bennington knows you are my intended we cannot travel back to Cornwall together. Under the circumstances, I think our best course of action is to return to London."

"London?" Diana's mind went blank at his statement.

"We will have to announce our betrothal as soon as possible," Derek said forcefully. "Before Bennington has an opportunity to relate our little encounter this afternoon to anyone."

"Yes, of course," Diana replied in a suddenly small voice. "The activities at the manor can progress without our supervision. The architect informed me it will take several weeks for him to draw up new plans for the house." A wave of pure panic washed over Diana when she realized the danger of agreeing to return to London, but she remained outwardly composed. Turning her face deliberately away from Derek's, Diana fixed her gazed straight ahead and they continued down the street.

Derek's thoughts were grim when they entered the Lord Nelson Inn. Earlier he had felt lucky securing lodgings at this particular coaching inn, since it served the Bristol-Chippenham-London stage and was usually very busy. Derek had only managed to get one bedchamber for the night, but he realized that it would be a blessing. The last thing Diana needed in her current frame of mind was to sleep alone in an unfamiliar room.

Diana didn't even question him when he ordered a hearty meal sent up to the privacy of their bedchamber. He wondered briefly if she even realized

Notorious Deception

they would be sharing the room for the night.

After dinner, Diana moved behind the screen to change into her nightclothes. She felt weary to the bone and was hoping the morning light would bring a more cheerful mood to her sagging spirits. She twisted and turned awkwardly for a time, trying to undue the buttons down the back of her gown. Usually the innkeeper's wife or a serving maid preformed this small task for her, but tonight she had no help.

"I need your assistance, Derek," she called out wearily. "The fastenings of my dress are down the entire length of my back and I am unable to reach them all."

Derek followed the sound of her voice, stepping behind the screen. She had already turned her back toward him, and the first thing he noticed was the flawless white skin of her bare shoulders. He gallantly resisted the temptation to caress her, but his fingers shook from the effort as he fumbled with the small fabric-covered buttons.

Diana's softly murmured thank you broke through his lustful thoughts of carrying her to the bed and seducing her. He hurried out from behind the screen, debating whether or not to leave the room while she completed her toilet, but he wasn't sure if she would need any further assistance from him.

"All done," Diana said.

He turned from his position by the half-opened window to see her standing in the middle of the room, facing him. Her white silk nightgown was enchanting. It was so sheer that the light from the fireplace illuminated every curve of her beautiful body. She smiled shyly.

He felt his mouth go dry at the sight of her. "You are exquisite, my dear," he said softly.

Adrienne Basso

"I do love you, Derek," she declared solemnly, advancing toward him. She wrapped her arms around his waist and pressed her face against his shoulder.

Derek sighed. Any noble promises he had previously made to himself about waiting until she agreed to marry him before they again made love vanished. He could feel his body's automatic response to her nearness. He was already fully aroused, swollen and heavy with his need. Derek began kissing her. Once he started, he could not stop. He couldn't help himself. She was warm and sweet, and he couldn't get enough of her.

It was exactly what Diana wanted. She returned his kisses with restless moans, pressing herself closer and closer to his hardened strength. She felt his hands stroke down her back to her hips, and they both trembled with excitement.

Somehow, they ended up on the bed, with Derek's jacket off, his cravat untied, and his shirt unbuttoned. Diana's nightgown was gathered up around her thighs, and her fingers were frantically tugging at his clothes.

"Please," she whispered, moving her body wildly against his. She was almost beyond herself. The hair on his chest brushed against her breast, making her nipples hard. She thrust her tongue into his mouth, and he moaned.

"I ache to be inside you, love," he said hoarsely. Rolling onto his back, he lifted her hips and placed her astride him.

"Derek, I'm not sure I understand," she murmured as he gripped her flanks and carefully eased himself inside her.

"Then I will show you, my love," he said. Sweat beaded on his forehead.

"Oh, my," Diana whimpered with bewilderment, feeling her body stretching to receive his fullness.

"Easy sweetheart," he groaned when she pushed up against him.

"Isn't that how you do it, Derek?"

He nearly spilled his seed at her sultry banter. Reaching down, he moved his hand between their bodies seeking her softness and caressing her. His stroking fingers helped her find the natural mating rhythm. He moved his hips forcefully, meeting her thrusts, until they were both lost to the insensible ecstasy of their love.

Diana bit her lip hard to keep from screaming as she found her release. Watching her lovely face contort with pleasure brought his own release, and Derek let go, spilling his hot seed so deeply inside her that he nearly touched her womb.

Slowly, Derek's limbs relaxed beneath her. He felt consumed with contentment. It was as if their very souls had mated, not merely their bodies. He stroked her back gently, savoring the deep feelings of satisfaction and commitment he felt for her.

She stretched forward until she lay flat on top of him, her silken hair covering them both. Her face rested on his chest.

"Will it always be this good between us, Derek?" she asked, her breathing still erratic.

"If I can somehow manage to survive," Derek said with a teasing groan.

Diana hit his shoulder with her clenched fist. "I'm being serious," she said.

"Ouch," he yelped. "So am I, my love."

Diana merely grunted loudly, a fair imitation of him. Derek burst into laughter and hugged her tightly. Their bodies were slick with sweat, and breathing in the salty, sexy fragrance of her skin made him harden inside her again. Idly, he wondered if she was aware of it. When she pressed light kisses along his throat and shifted her position on top of him, he knew she was.

"It is too soon, sweetheart," he implored, trying to stop the rampant desire from overtaking him. "You are too tender." He ceased his protest when she playfully bit his neck.

Lord, she was going to be sore in the morning, he thought. Expertly, he rolled her onto her back, balancing himself above her on his elbows. Smiling wickedly, he slowly began making love to her again.

"Shall we see if it can be as good as before, my sweet," he whispered seductively.

"We shall make it even better," she said with a delighted laugh. "But only if you think you can survive, my lord."

Chapter Seventeen

When Diana and Derek arrived in London two days later, it was raining. As the carriage traveled down Regent Street, Derek suggested Diana accompany him to his town home before preceding to Tristan and Caroline's house. Diana adamantly refused. A message had already been sent from Chippenham informing Tristan and Caroline of Diana's arrival. They would be expecting her sometime today. Besides, it would hardly be proper for Diana to accompany Derek to his home unchaperoned, even if she was announced as his betrothed. And even though the possibility was remote, Henriette might still be in residence. Diana did not relish meeting her again. There was also the question of Derek's servants. Diana had no wish to subject herself to their curious eyes either.

After pointing out these facts to Derek, he was forced to concede the logic of her arguments and brought her directly to Tristan's home. They were informed by Sutton, the butler, that the Ashtons were at the opera, but the staff had been told of Diana's impending arrival. She was warmly greeted by the staff. Both Sutton and Mrs. Roget, the housekeeper, made a special fuss over her. Being once again in such a comfortable and friendly atmosphere reinforced Diana's belief that she was right to accept Tris and Caroline's standing offer of hospitality.

Diana slept until noon the following morning. Tristan and Caroline had returned quite late the night before, and Diana hoped they too had slept in.

After enjoying a delicious breakfast in her room, Diana dressed with care. Her new pale yellow gown's low-cut neckline showcased her ample bosom and the puff sleeves gave her a carefree air she did not usually display. Diana hurried down to the front salon, hoping to find Tristan and Caroline. Diana was looking forward to seeing her friends again and catching them up on all the extraordinary developments of the past few weeks.

There were no servants in the main hall, so Diana strolled unannounced into the front salon. She stopped short when she discovered a couple seated upon the settee locked in a passionate embrace. At first glance Diana believed she had stumbled upon Tristan and Caroline, yet upon closer inspection, she noticed the color of the woman's hair was a distinct shade of auburn, instead of Caroline's golden blonde.

Horribly embarrassed, Diana hesitated in the doorway, wondering if she had been observed. She began to slowly retreat, but her movement caught the eye of the gentleman, and he broke away rather reluctantly from his partner.

A pair of steely-gray eyes regarded Diana with open hostility. No, it was not Tristan, but the glowering stranger's resemblance to Tris was marked, and Diana knew he must be a relative. The man continued to stare rudely at her and Diana felt a shiver run down her spine.

"Was there something you wanted?" he barked loudly.

At the man's bellowing question, the lady on the settee turned around to face the doorway. She colored slightly when she saw Diana, but her face took on a pleasant expression.

"I do beg your pardon," Diana said, stammering out a hasty apology, and she started backing out of the room. "I did not know anyone was in here."

"No, wait," the woman called out in a melodic voice. "Please don't leave." She disengaged herself from the possessive hold the gentleman still had on her arm and rose elegantly from her seat. Walking toward Diana, the woman extended her hand in greeting.

"You must be Lady Diana. Tris and Caroline told us at the opera last evening you were expected. It is lovely to finally meet you. I am Tristan's sister-in-law, Alyssa. And this is my husband, Morgan."

Bewildered, Diana took Alyssa's outstretched hand. Alyssa was several inches taller than Diana, with a willowy figure and unusual green eyes. Diana thought she was lovely. "How very nice to make your acquaintance," Diana muttered absently.

Morgan also stood up, and Diana felt instantly overpowered by his presence. He was by far the most overwhelming man she had ever encountered. He was exceedingly tall and broad of shoulder, yet it was not only his physical dominance, but the aura of power and arrogance he exuded that affected Diana. This was clearly not a man to trifle with.

Alyssa turned around to look at her husband. "Good Lord, stop scowling so Morgan," Alyssa berated him. "You are frightening Lady Diana."

Morgan grimaced at his wife, but schooled his exceptionally handsome face into a more relaxed expression. Diana favored him with a small smile, wondering how two brothers could be so very different. Tristan was so boyish and carefree, while his brother appeared intense and somber.

Tristan's brother! This must be the duke and duchess that Caroline was always talking so enthusiastically about. She rolled her eyes in mortification as she realized her mistake.

"Your Graces," she muttered faintly, dipping a low curtsy.

"There is no need for all of that!" Morgan exclaimed in a deep voice, startling Diana anew.

"Oh, yes," Alyssa said, agreeing with her husband. "There is no cause for such formality among friends, Diana. May I call you Diana?" At Diana's confused nod, Alyssa continued. "Please come in and sit down with us. We were going to ring for Sutton to bring our tea, but the bell appears to be broken. Then we got—um—distracted."

"I can certainly tell you are related to Tristan," Diana said to Morgan, remembering the passionate embrace she had interrupted.

Both Morgan and Alyssa laughed at her remark and Diana flushed, appalled at her cheek. Thankfully, she was saved from making yet another awkward apology by the loud banging of the salon doors as they were unexpectedly thrust open.

The walls fairly shook as the doors swung back

and forth on their hinges, and a young child came racing into the room.

"Katherine!" the duke bellowed sternly.

The child immediately froze in place, lifting two solemn eyes at Morgan. "Yes, Father," she whispered.

"Leave this room at once, young lady" he said firmly.

Crestfallen, the little girl complied. Diana had to bite her tongue to keep from commenting while she watched the child drag her feet out of the room in a forlorn manner. The child's obvious distress tore at her heart. How could the duke be so cruel to such a tenderhearted little girl?

There were a few moments of strained silence as Katherine closed the salon doors softly behind her. Then there was a loud knock at the door. Morgan crossed the room swiftly, yanking open the door. Katherine stood demurely in the doorway, an angelic expression on her face.

"May I please come in, Father?"

"I should be delighted to have your company, Puss," Morgan said with a slight bow to his daughter. He held out his hand, and Katherine confidently slipped her delicate, small hand into her father's large palm. Hand in hand they walked into the room, stopping in front of Diana.

"Lady Diana, may I present—" Morgan began, but he was interrupted by a high-pitched squeal.

"Papa! Papa!" A chubby little toddler came bounding into the room, literally flinging herself at the duke. Wrapping her arms around Morgan's leg, she held on tightly, shrieking with delight.

With a rueful grin, the duke carefully pried the child lose from his leg and bent down on one knee to greet her at eye level.

"And exactly how did you get up here, little miss?" Morgan asked the toddler.

The little girl brought her face forward, resting nose to nose with her imposing father. "Papa," she said happily, giving him a sloppy kiss.

"I brought her upstairs, Father," young Katherine said. "Did you know she can climb the stairs by herself if you hold onto her hand?"

"Is that right?" Morgan replied, clearly impressed with his daughter's accomplishments.

"Katherine," Alyssa said addressing her older daughter in a reprimanding tone. "I thought you and your sister were going to stay in the kitchen with Mrs. Roget and Cook for a while."

"We were down there for a very long time, Mother," Katherine said, "and I wanted to come upstairs to see Uncle Tris and Aunt Caroline. When I left the kitchen, Juliet followed me."

Just then a very harried-looking Mrs. Roget entered the room. "Thank goodness!" the housekeeper exclaimed when she saw the children. "I told Cook they would be here."

"Katherine," the duke said sternly. "Didn't you ask Mrs. Roget's permission to come up here first?"

"I'm sorry, Mrs. Roget," Katherine said instantly.

"No harm done," Mrs. Roget said, before either parent had a chance to scold the child.

"Thank you, Mrs. Roget," Alyssa said. "I hope the girls were not too much trouble."

"No trouble at all," the housekeeper responded sincerely. "We always enjoy it when the children come to visit." She smiled affectionately at the girls. "Would you like me to have some tea sent up?"

"That would be lovely, Mrs. Roget," Alyssa answered.

"I'll have a footman bring it in as soon as it is

ready, Your Grace," Mrs. Roget said. Dipping a small curtsy, the housekeeper left the room.

"We already had our tea," Katherine told her parents. "And Cook let us have some strawberry tarts. They were very good. I had one and Juliet ate two."

All eyes turned to the chubby toddler, and she grinned charmingly at everyone. Diana coughed softly, bringing her hand to her lips to hide her smile.

"Now for the introductions," Morgan declared. Taking each of his girls in hand, he brought them in front of Diana. "As you undoubtedly have realized, Lady Diana, these two little scamps are my daughters, Katherine and Juliet."

Katherine made a surprisingly dainty curtsy. Juliet, suddenly feeling shy, hid behind Morgan's leg, peering out occasionally to see if Diana was still watching her.

"I am honored to meet you, ladies," Diana said, nodding her head in greeting. She thought the girls were positively adorable. Katherine was the very image of her father, with her raven-black hair and smoky-gray eyes, while little Juliet was all blonde curls and sweet blue eyes. Turning to Alyssa, Diana said, "They are both so beautiful."

"Thank you," Alyssa said with motherly pride. "Naturally we feel they are exceptional, even though they can be a handful at times." She leaned over and whispered to Diana, "I'm afraid Morgan spoils them terribly."

Diana eyes widened at that comment. The duke certainly did not appear to be the sort of man who would tolerate, much less spoil, two young girls. Diana turned her head sharply toward the duke, considering Alyssa's words.

Morgan was lounging comfortably on the settee

with Katherine perched next to him rhythmically swinging her legs. Juliet was clamoring to sit with them also, so he reached down with one arm and lifted the child onto his lap. The toddler squirmed for several moments until she found an acceptable position. Cuddling close to her father, she clutched the velvet lapel of his jacket with one hand and then popped the thumb of her other hand into her mouth.

The momentary peace was shattered with the arrival of Tristan and Caroline.

"Uncle Tris," Katherine yelled, jumping up from the settee and nearly knocking over a porcelain vase in the process. Juliet, not to be outdone by her sister, scrambled down from her father's lap and ran to Tris also.

Delighted, Tristan bent down to embrace them. Scooping them both up simultaneously, he held a child in each arm as he said, "And how are my charming little nieces today?" Tris began kissing and tickling them and they burst into joyful giggles and screams.

Diana glanced at Caroline. She was watching her husband intently as he played lovingly with the girls. Diana felt her throat tighten with emotion. Suddenly, she understood Caroline's desperate need to give Tristan a child of their own. Caroline was right—he would make a wonderful father. Diana offered up a silent prayer, hoping it would soon come to pass.

Still giggling with excitement, the girls next greeted Caroline with equal enthusiasm. Sutton and two footmen arrived with the tea, and eventually everyone was served refreshments. After some rather intense pleading by Tristan and Katherine, and several warnings about not spilling anything on the carpets, it was decided the girls could stay for tea. Diana was surprised to realize she was glad Morgan allowed it.

Diana's experience with children was limited to the youngsters of her village, and they were no doubt on their very best behavior when in her presence. It was fun being with Tristan's nieces, even if they were a bit rambunctious.

"'Tis exceptionally tolerant of Tristan and Caroline to allow us to bring the girls over without their nurse," Alyssa declared. "The poor woman has come down with a dreadful cold, and she will be confined to bed for several days."

"We take great delight in the girls' visits," Tristan said, wiping strawberry jam from Juliet's mouth. "They always liven up the place. And they are so very much like their uncle Tris, aren't they, Caroline? Perfectly well-behaved little angels."

"The girls are perfect of course," Caroline said in a teasing voice. "I am not certain the same can be said of you, Tristan."

Young Katherine's infectious laughter caught on, and soon everyone was enjoying the jest. The Earl of Harrowby was announced in the midst of all the laughter.

Derek greeted Diana and the other adults warmly, clearly delighted to be among his friends again. Juliet toddled boldly up to him, and after giving her a kind smile, Derek reached down and ruffled the baby's soft blonde curls. Then he turned his undivided attention to Katherine.

Katherine's eyes widened with excitement as Derek approached her. She was obviously well acquainted with him, but she did not greet him with the same unreserved excitement she used with her uncle. Instead, Katherine curtsied to Derek, and her eyes were wide as saucers when he addressed her as Lady Katherine and returned her greeting with a formal bow and a gentle kiss to her hand.

"Just look at Morgan grind his teeth," Tristan said. Diana and the other two women focused their attention on the duke, who was watching his oldest daughter with a decidedly possessive gleam in his eye.

"I hope Derek has not offended the duke," Diana said in a worried voice. She had the utmost confidence in Derek's ability to protect and defend himself, but she did not want to see Derek pitted against so formidable an opponent as Morgan.

"Oh, Morgan isn't offended, Diana," Alyssa said. "He is obsessively protective of the girls, especially Katherine."

"I don't believe he is even aware of what he is doing," Caroline said in amazement.

"He isn't." Alyssa shook her head and said with good humor, "God only knows how we will manage when the girls are grown and become interested in the opposite sex."

"Ah, then we shall see my brother's true protective instincts emerge," Tristan said with a boyish grin. "'Tis merely poetic justice a rake like Morgan should have the responsibilities of raising daughters."

"Tristan!" Caroline said.

"Oh, sorry, Alyssa," Tristan said sheepishly. "Reformed rake."

Alyssa smiled mischievously at her brother-in-law, then crossed the room to stand by her husband. Diana could see Morgan instantly relax when his wife touched his arm, and he absently stroked her hand while she spoke quietly to him.

"I do believe I have some serious competition for your affections, Derek," Diana whispered to him when he sat down next to her.

They both turned toward Katherine, who was still standing in the same spot, her pretty face openly curious.

"Katherine likes me because I treat her like a grown lady," Derek said. "And because I gave her a new pony for her fifth birthday this past December."

"I think she is very fond of you, Derek," Diana said. "You must be certain not to inadvertently hurt her feelings."

"Ah, 'tis a curse I carry," Derek said mockingly. "To be adored by women of all ages."

Diana jabbed him in the ribs and called to Katherine. "Come and sit with us. Derek was just telling me about your new pony. I should like to hear all about it."

Katherine enthusiastically complied and wedged herself between Derek and Diana. She was soon chattering away, and Diana was impressed by the quickness of her mind. Katherine was certain to grow into a much admired young lady someday. Then Morgan truly would have his hands full.

Juliet snuggled in Tristan's lap, her face buried against his broad shoulder, and her thumb once again in her mouth. Her eyelids were drooping, and it seemed to be only a matter of time before the child succumbed to sleep.

Morgan was also keeping a close watch on his youngest daughter. Diana saw the duke walk over and say something to his brother. Then he reached down and gathered the sleeping child in his arms.

As the duke left the room, Alyssa told Katherine to follow her father upstairs so she could join her sister in a nap. Katherine's lower lips instantly jutted out in rebellion, but she did not protest.

Adrienne Basso

"I would be happy to accompany you upstairs, Katherine," Diana said, feeling the child's disappointment at having to leave.

Katherine immediately brightened at the suggestion. "And the earl too?"

Derek flashed her a charming smile. "I should be honored, Lady Katherine."

"That is most kind of you both," Alyssa said thankfully. She bent down and gave the little girl a kiss on her cheek before they left.

Once in the hallway, Diana was waylaid by Sutton, who handed her a parcel that had arrived earlier in the day. As Diana held the package in her hands, Katherine began fidgeting, so Diana instructed Derek to bring the little girl upstairs without her, explaining she would follow after she opened her package.

The parcel was a hatbox, with the address of a fashionable London millinery discretely printed in gold-leaf lettering on the top. She wondered if it was a mistake that the box had been sent to her. Although she had heard of the shop, she had never before patronized that particular establishment.

Curious, she untied the yellow ribbon around the box and then smiled to herself. Thinking she had solved the mystery, she decided Derek had ordered a surprise gift for her. Anxiously she lifted the lid—and caught her breath sharply when she looked inside.

She would have screamed, but she was so shocked that her voice failed her. She instantly dropped the box and it fell to the floor, the contents spilling out. The room actually swam before her eyes for a few seconds and then a feeling of cold dread washed over her.

Endless questions raced through her mind as she stood there, her gaze transfixed on the marble floor.

Lying at her feet was a crushed black bonnet she remembered all too well. She had lost it several weeks ago, in St. James's Park, during the confusion that had ensued when an unknown adversary had fired two pistol shots at her and Derek.

Chapter Eighteen

"Is something amiss, Diana?" Morgan asked.

The duke's gentle voice startled her and she jumped. Morgan's overwhelming presence, coupled with her shock at discovering the bonnet, caused her to become speechless. She simply stared up at him dumbstruck while he repeated the question. Scrupulously avoiding the duke's piercing gray eyes, Diana shook her head.

But Morgan planted himself firmly in front of her, saying he would not move until Diana either spoke to him or Derek arrived to deal with the situation. Diana was very pale and nervous, and her fists clenched and unclenched her gown.

"I should like to help you, Diana, if you would only allow it."

She raised her head slightly, but she still refused to meet Morgan's gaze. Her eyes came to rest instead on the duke's snowy-white cravat. She saw a red stain marring the perfection of the garment and realized it was a bit of strawberry jam, no doubt from Juliet's sticky little fingers. Despite her fear, Diana smiled. Perhaps she had been too quick to judge the duke. Any man who was so loving with his children must have a kind heart, no matter how arrogant his exterior. And he had offered his help.

"This came for me today," Diana said in a shaky voice, bending low to retrieve the hatbox and bonnet.

Morgan stretched his powerful frame down, picking up both the box and the hat before Diana could. Grimacing, he held up the crushed bonnet.

"It isn't very attractive, I'll grant you that," the duke said wryly. "I am sure the establishment you purchased it from will take it back."

Diana shot him a look of pure exasperation. "Good Lord, you think I am this upset because I don't like the stupid thing?"

Morgan lifted a dark eyebrow. "Exactly why are you so upset, Diana?"

"The bonnet," she said passionately, pulling it out of his hands. "It is my bonnet. At least it was my bonnet." She put her hand to her head and rubbed her temples. Morgan continued to stare at her. "I was wearing this bonnet when Derek took me for a carriage ride in St. James's Park a few weeks ago. Someone fired two pistol shots at us that afternoon, and in all the confusion, my bonnet was lost."

"Are you absolutely certain this is the same bonnet?"

"Yes."

At her answer, Morgan asked, "Who delivered this package? Is there a note inside?" He began firing questions at Diana, but she could only shake her head, not knowing the answers.

"Tristan!" the duke shouted.

Diana winced. She had never heard anyone shout with such a loud, booming voice.

Tristan strolled into the hallway after a few moments. He was clearly accustomed to his brother's yelling and didn't seem to think anything was unusual. Morgan unceremoniously thrust the empty hatbox into Tristan's hand.

"Find out which one of your servants accepted this package today," the duke said. "Then find out everything you can about it. What time the box was delivered, what precisely was said when it was left, a complete description of the person who delivered it, and so forth."

Tristan's demeanor changed radically at his brother's request. "What is the trouble?"

"I'll tell you after you bring me the information I need," Morgan said, dismissing his brother.

Diana thought Tristan might protest the duke's high-handed manner, but he didn't. After Tristan left, the duke once again spoke to Diana. "Do you want me to have Derek summoned?"

"No," she replied softly. "He will be down soon enough."

"Fine. We shall rejoin Alyssa and Caroline," Morgan said.

The conversation between Alyssa and Caroline halted abruptly after Diana and Morgan entered the room and the two women saw Diana's pale face and Morgan's grim expression.

"What has happened?" Alyssa asked directly.

"Diana received a most disturbing package," Morgan told his wife. "We hope to know more about it when Tristan returns."

Diana could see both women were exceedingly curious, but they did not ask any further questions, and she was grateful. The minutes seemed to drag by as they waited anxiously for Tristan and Derek to arrive. Caroline, the most socially adept of the group, kept up an endless stream of soothing chatter, and Diana appreciated her attempts to keep the mood light.

Derek and Tristan entered the room together, their expressions solemn.

"Well?" Morgan demanded without preamble.

"Not much, I'm afraid," Tristan replied. "One of the underfootmen, Robins, took the parcel. He said it was delivered by a young boy dressed in unkempt and none-too-clean clothes. The lad practically threw the box at my footman and then ran away. The boy said the package was for Lady Diana Rutledge.

"Oh, God," Diana said. "He used my married name."

Derek placed a comforting arm around her. "It is all right, love," he said soothingly. "We will get to the bottom of this mystery."

"Mystery!" Diana echoed, her voice rising with panic. "It is hardly a mystery, Derek. First I am shot at. Then my house is burned. Now my missing bonnet suddenly appears. It is obvious someone is watching me very closely. But why?"

All three men exchanged concerned glances.

"Giles," Derek finally whispered softly. "This has to be tied to him in some way. There might even be a connection to his murder."

Caroline gasped loudly at Derek's comment. Diana backed away from him and began pacing the room in agitation, coming finally to rest in front of a large overstuffed chair in the corner of the salon. As she faced everyone, her fingers gripped the fabric back of the chair.

"How is it possible the boy was told to use my married name?" Diana asked. "Aside from my servants in Cornwall, and you, no one else knows of my marriage to Giles. My home was burned and along with it my marriage lines, and Derek and I discovered only a few days ago that no record exists of the wedding in the church where the vows took place."

"We don't know who set fire to the Manor, but we assumed Giles removed the information from the church register himself," Derek said. "Perhaps we were mistaken."

"Whoever is behind all of this is someone who knew Giles well," Morgan said. "What was the name of the solicitor you wanted to question, Derek? The one who disappeared so suddenly."

"Jonathan Marlow," Tristan and Derek said at the same time.

"Have your men had any success in locating him, Tristan?"

"Not yet," Tristan replied. "They have managed to discover a few things about him, however. None of them very flattering, I might add." He cast a questioning eye toward Caroline and Alyssa. "Shall I get the files from my study, Morgan?"

"Well, you certainly can't expect us to leave now," Alyssa huffed, correctly interpreting her brother-in-law's look.

"We will not leave unless Diana requests it," Caroline readily agreed.

Everyone waited for Diana to speak. She felt torn. She certainly could use the moral support, but she did not want Caroline and Alyssa upset by what might be revealed. In the end, Diana figured the women would probably eventually wheedle the information out of their husbands anyway, so she asked them to remain.

"I would appreciate if you both stayed," Diana said gratefully. "That is, if your husbands don't object."

"It is not their place to object," Alyssa said immediately. Her ready response brought a frown to Morgan's face, but his wife ignored it.

Soon everyone was reading through the papers Tristan brought out and commenting on various unsavory facets of Jonathan Marlow's character. Although the documents contained a wealth of information about Mr. Marlow, there was actually very little that would shed any light on Diana's problem.

"I think we all agree Jonathan Marlow is a dangerous man," Diana said, placing the papers she had been reading on the tea table. Everyone nodded in accordance. "If Marlow is, as we believe, the man behind all this nonsense, then I fear I have placed Tristan and Caroline in grave danger by living here with them. I'm going upstairs to begin my packing. I should be completed within the hour."

The room erupted in pandemonium as everyone began talking and shouting at once.

"We just won't hear of it, Diana." Tristan exclaimed loudly. "I am sure you are safe here with us, but if you are worried, I shall have men posted round the clock to ensure your safety."

"It is not my safety that worries me so much, Tris," Diana said. "I am more concerned about you and Caroline."

"Well, I am concerned about your well-being, Diana," Derek said. "Either you remain here with Caroline and Tris, or you return home with me."

"Derek!" Caroline exclaimed in horror. "Diana cannot possibly reside at your house without a proper chaperon. What would people think?"

"For pity's sake, Caroline," Derek replied. "Who is

going to know about it? We will hardly be receiving social calls, nor attending any of the few functions taking place at this time of year."

"I seriously doubt you can keep Diana's living with you a secret," Tristan said. "Even if you kept her a virtual prisoner in the house."

"There are also the servants to consider, Derek," Morgan said.

"Yes," Alyssa agreed, "servants do gossip—within the household and among friends who are in service at other houses. Even among the most loyal staff, it would be difficult to keep this confidential."

"And your staff is hardly a loyal group, Derek," Diana said sarcastically.

"Besides," Tristan said, "there is always the possibility Henriette might suddenly descend on you."

The mention of Henriette brought an abrupt halt to the debate.

"If Henriette ever found out you two were living in the same house, it would be common knowledge among the *ton* within hours," Caroline said with authority. "Diana's reputation would be ruined beyond repair."

"Diana could stay with us," Morgan said.

"No," Diana replied, shaking her head. "It is very kind of you to offer Morgan, but I must refuse. I would not only worry about the risk to you and Alyssa, but also to the girls. If anything ever happened to Katherine and Juliet, I wouldn't be able to live with myself."

"If you insist on leaving, we could try to find someone suitable to chaperon you while you were at Derek's house," Alyssa said. Then shaking her head, she added, "Of course, that plan does have the potential of putting another innocent person at risk."

"You are back to your original decision, Diana," Derek declared. "Stay here, or leave with me."

"That is not a solution," Diana said.

"Now, wait just a moment," Caroline said, interrupting. "It would be proper for Diana to stay with Derek if they were married."

Diana blanched visibly at the suggestion, and Derek felt a twinge of hurt at her reaction.

"I don't think that is a plausible solution, Caroline," Derek said hastily. He knew Diana was not yet ready to fully trust him and still needed more time to accept marrying him. Pushing aside his own bruised ego, Derek vowed to give Diana the time he promised her, despite his own great desire to have her for his wife.

"But, Derek, you don't actually have to get married," Caroline said. "You could just pretend to be married."

"What!" everyone shouted simultaneously.

Caroline held up her hand. "Hear me out first," she said, then took a deep breath. "It would be improper for Diana to inhabit Derek's house as an unchaperoned, unattached female, but it would be perfectly proper for her to be there if she were Derek's wife. The servants might gossip about the sudden nuptials, and Henriette might even find out, but it wouldn't create a scandal. Diana might even be able to uncover some clues while living in the house."

"And what happens to Derek's pretend wife when this mystery is solved, Caroline?" Morgan said. "Does Diana succumb to some fatal disease or just suddenly disappear one morning, never to be seen again?"

"Well," Caroline said, hedging.

"I was going to marry Derek anyway," Diana said

suddenly. "In fact, he has already told Lord Bennington we are betrothed. That is the main reason we have returned to London: to announce our engagement."

"Bennington?" Morgan asked. "Why would you tell Henriette's brother about your impending nuptials?"

"It certainly wasn't by design," Derek replied, actually forgetting about the meeting in all the ensuing confusion. "We ran into him quite by accident in Chippenham."

"Personally I think it is splendid news," Tristan cried with delight. "There is no need for a pretend wedding at all. We shall have the real thing."

"No," Derek said. Above all, he did not want Diana to feel she was being forced into the marriage. "We will wait until all this mess is cleared up before we actually marry."

"Yes," Diana quickly agreed, biting her lip.

"All right, that solves one problem," Morgan stated. "Now what about Diana's background? She can hardly be introduced into society as Giles's widow." Turning to Derek, Morgan asked, "How did you introduce her to Bennington?"

"I used her maiden name and introduced her as Lady Diana Crawford." Derek's eyes narrowed in concern. "You are right about Diana's background, Morgan. We must create a plausible lineage for her, as well as an opportunity for us to have met."

Silence prevailed as everyone pondered the newest point in question. "You certainly have a talent for finding fault, Morgan," Caroline said grumpily.

"I am merely being cautious, Caroline," Morgan replied, giving her a charming smile.

"I know!" Tristan shouted excitedly. "Since Diana's

true identity must forever remain unknown, we shall claim Diana is related to us."

Morgan stroked his chin as he considered his brother's idea. "That just might work."

"Actually, that would be an excellent solution," Derek said. "When Diana first appeared at my house, she naturally instructed the butler to announce her as the Dowager Countess of Harrowby. Later I told him, and the footman who also heard her state her name, Tristan was playing a rather humorless prank on me."

"You never told me that before, Derek!" Tristan exclaimed.

Derek shrugged his shoulders and smiled at his friend.

"It certainly sounds like the kind of mischief that would appeal to you, Tris," Alyssa said with a grin.

"Not you too, Alyssa," Tristan protested with exaggerated drama and everyone laughed.

"I'm afraid you've been found out, little brother," Morgan told him. "Your suggestion about Diana has merit, however. We shall claim her as a distant cousin."

"Henriette also saw Diana on that first afternoon," Derek said, suddenly remembering. Turning toward Diana, he asked, "How were you introduced to her?"

"I wasn't," Diana said, smiling. "Henriette never stopped talking long enough for me to be properly introduced."

"Then it is settled," Tristan said cheerfully. "You shall be our cousin, Diana."

"Are you certain you want to claim me for a relative?" Diana asked skeptically. "This will be a falsehood you will have to adhere to for a very long time."

"Speaking as the head of our family, we would

be delighted to welcome you as one of our own," Morgan said sincerely.

"My father was in trade," Diana said.

"And from what I gather, very successful at it," Alyssa said calmly. "You should be proud of that, Diana. My own father was a viscount. He was also a gambler, a drunkard, and a coward."

"Thankfully his daughter inherited none of those characteristics," Morgan said with a gentle smile at his wife. "And she, in turn, possessed the good sense to marry me."

"Ha," Alyssa said with a straight face. "As I recall, Morgan, I wasn't given much of a choice."

Diana wasn't certain, but she actually thought she saw Morgan blush.

"If you are sure that you want me," Diana said with emotion, "I would be honored to be known as your cousin."

"Splendid!" Caroline exclaimed with true delight. "Now we must plan the wedding. I suppose it will have to take place this evening."

"Is all that really necessary?" Diana asked. "Can't we just tell everyone we ran off to Gretna Green to get married?"

"Gretna Green!" Caroline looked positively scandalized. "The entire point of this charade is to lend an air of respectability to your marriage, Diana. I hardly think Gretna Green qualifies."

"Since Diana is now an Ashton cousin, she should be married from our house," Alyssa said kindly. "Morgan is the head of the family."

"Yes, that is true," Caroline reluctantly agreed. "I rather had hoped we could have the wedding here"—Caroline turned to the duke with a pleading look—"if Morgan has no objections?"

"It would probably be easiest," Morgan said.

"What do you think, Derek?"

"Fine," he replied absently. "Morgan, Tris, and I have business to attend to this afternoon. We shall leave the wedding details in your capable hands, ladies.

"Good," Caroline said, "I do need one of you to locate someone to play the vicar."

"I'll do it," Tristan said. "I am certain I can engage a Drury Lane actor who would be pleased to earn some extra coin. Paid adequately, he should hold his tongue about this entire hoax." Tristan rose to his feet and turned to his wife. "Anything else?"

"I don't think so," Caroline said. She stood up and practically chased the men from the room. "We will all meet here this evening at, shall we say, seven o'clock?"

Everyone nodded in agreement. After brief good-byes, the men quit the room.

"Now," Caroline said, clapping her hands together with glee, "where shall we begin, ladies?"

Chapter Nineteen

Two hours later, Diana stood in the middle of Caroline's bedchamber while the renowned modiste, Madame La Belle, refitted Caroline's wedding gown on Diana. Caroline had insisted that Diana wear the lovely dress, and Madame La Belle, along with three of her most talented needlewomen, had been summoned to make the necessary alterations.

"I have recut the neckline to accommodate Lady Diana's amble bosom, Your Grace," the dressmaker explained to Alyssa as Diana modeled the gown for them. "All we have to do is take up the hem a bit and the dress will be ready."

"It looks lovely, Madame La Belle," Alyssa said.

The antique white dress did indeed look beautiful, Diana thought. It was an elaborate ensemble of satin and lace, aglow with dozens of tiny seed pearls. The newly designed low-cut neckline enhanced the romance of the dress, accenting the tightly fitted lace bodice and the graceful sweep of the full satin skirt.

"I have finished sewing the fresh roses on the headdress, madame," one of the assistants told Madame La Belle, handing her employer the veil.

Madame La Belle inspected the headpiece with a critical eye before placing it on Diana's head. The two layered tulle bridal veil was gathered in a tight circle at the crown, under a floral headdress made of fresh pink and white roses. The dressmaker adjusted the headpiece and fluffed out the cascading veil of tulle.

"You look just like a princess," a small voice called from the doorway.

"Katherine," Alyssa said as the little girl ran into the room. "What are you doing here? I thought you and Juliet were taking a nap."

"We were, Mama," Katherine replied, nearly colliding with Madame La Belle in her excitement to reach Diana. "Juliet is still sleeping, but I woke up."

Katherine reached out a tentative hand to touch the glimmering satin of the skirt. "Why are you all dressed up, Lady Diana? Are you going to a party?"

"Not precisely, Katherine," Diana said, noting Madame La Belle's annoyance as she stepped off the small stool she was standing on and bent down to speak to the little girl.

"I am going to marry the earl tonight," Diana said, not sure how Katherine would react to the news.

"Really?" Katherine said, clearly impressed. She moved closer to Diana, whispering conspiratorily in her ear, "When I get older, I'm going to marry the earl too."

Diana smiled at the child's sincerity and nodded in agreement. "I am sure Derek would like that very much, Katherine."

"Will I be getting a new dress, Mama?" Katherine asked.

"Katherine," Alyssa said, but Diana interrupted.

"I'm afraid there won't be time for a new dress to be sewn," Diana told the little girl. "But I am sure Madame La Belle can create a crown of pink and white roses for you, just like mine. We shall ask her to sew long satin ribbons that will hang down your back. Would you like that?"

"Oh, yes!" Katherine exclaimed. "I shall go and tell Mrs. Roget and Cook at once." And before Diana or Alyssa could stop her, Katherine bounded out of the room.

"I hope you don't mind my interference, Alyssa," Diana said. "I know Katherine is very fond of Derek, and I didn't want her to feel left out."

"It was very sweet of you to be so considerate of Katherine," Alyssa replied. "Juliet is too young to attend the ceremony, but I suppose it will be acceptable for Katherine to be present—unless Morgan objects."

Diana and Alyssa smiled, knowing it would be highly unlikely the duke would refuse his oldest daughter anything.

"If you are ready, my lady," Madame La Belle interrupted, her voice still tinged with annoyance. "We do not have much time."

"Yes, of course," Diana said, obediently stepping back up on the stool. "I can't begin to tell you how grateful I am that you were able to do this work on such short notice, Madame La Belle. Both Caroline and Alyssa agreed you were the only person capable of correctly altering my wedding gown."

Her mouth full of pins, the modiste smiled up at Diana. She appeared somewhat placated by Diana's flattering comments and swiftly completed the task of pinning up the hem of the satin skirt.

With the assistance of Madame La Belle and Alyssa the heavy gown was then gently lifted off Diana. As she stood on the small stool, clad only in her embroidered chemise, Diana could feel Madame La Belle's sharp eyes on her stomach. Diana knew the modiste was searching for her own explanation for the suddenness of the wedding.

But Diana's flat stomach revealed nothing. With a slight shrug the dressmaker brought the lovely gown over to the window, so the hem could be sewn by her assistants in the late afternoon sunlight.

"It seems as though madame has formed her own opinions about the reason for this hasty ceremony," Diana whispered to Alyssa.

"Her eagle eyes miss nothing," Alyssa whispered back. "Caroline was certainly right about selecting Madame La Belle for this little task. Not only is she an excellent seamstress, but she is known for her extraordinary supply of gossip. The tradesmen of Bond Street will know of your marriage by the close of business tomorrow."

"Oh, God," Diana groaned, feeling very unsure of herself. "I must confess, I am beginning to have my doubts about this whole business, Alyssa."

Alyssa regarded Diana kindly. "Don't worry about it, Diana. No one is forcing you to do anything. There is still plenty of time to change your mind."

Diana shrugged into her wrapper, tying the sash tightly. "I think I will go to my room and rest for a while."

"Fine. I promised Caroline I would arrange the flowers in the drawing room. Please don't hesitate to send a servant for me if you need anything."

"Thank you," Diana said.

After Diana explained to Madame La Belle where

she could be reached if she was needed, she and Alyssa left the room together. Alyssa turned from her in the hallway, and she called to the duchess.

"If you come across Katherine downstairs, will you send her up to me? I think I would enjoy her company just now."

Alyssa smiled and nodded her head. Diana walked slowly down the long hallway to her room, hoping young Katherine would come up to her bedchamber soon and provide the distraction she so desperately needed.

Caroline cast a jaundiced eye around the drawing room as Sutton finished lighting the last of the candles. He turned to his mistress, awaiting further instructions, and was rewarded with a brilliant smile.

"It looks splendid, doesn't it, Sutton?" Caroline remarked, pleased with what she beheld. The room sparkled with the glow of hundreds of candles, and the sweet heady aroma of fresh flowers permeated the air.

"The duchess has done an admirable job arranging all the blossoms," Sutton agreed, hardly believing the transformation that had taken place in only a few short hours.

"Alyssa always has had a talent with flowers," Caroline said, gently fingering a cream-colored rose. "I want you to make sure the drawing room doors remain open throughout the ceremony, Sutton. This way any of the servants who wish to may see and hear the entire service from the hall."

"I am certain all the female staff will be present, madam," Sutton said wryly. "There has been a tremendous amount of excitement belowstairs ever since we learned of this evening's nuptials."

"Excellent," Caroline said with delight. With a final parting glance at the exquisite room, she left. Caroline crossed the large entrance hall and encountered Derek and Tristan entering the house. They were accompanied by a third man, who she assumed was the actor Tristan had engaged to play the part of the vicar.

"Good evening, gentlemen," Caroline called gaily to the trio. She took a brief moment to admire Tristan and Derek, handsome and elegant in their formal black-and-white evening attire. Then she focused her attention on the third man.

"This is Reverend Penley, Caroline," Tristan said.

"Oh, Tristan," Caroline admonished with apparent disappointment. Rudely she circled Reverend Penley, clucking her tongue and shaking her head as she walked. "He is not at all what I had in mind. Not at all. I really don't know if he will due."

"I beg your pardon, madam." The reverend spoke with censure in his tone.

"No offense meant, sir," Caroline hastily added, realizing her ill manners, "but you are far too young and well turned out to play the part of the minister."

Turning to her husband, Caroline continued her complaint. "I realize you were restricted by time limitations, Tris, but I do think you could have found someone more convincing. He hardly looks like a man of the cloth. Don't you agree, Derek?"

"Hm," Derek murmured. He was not paying the least bit of attention to her. His gaze was riveted instead to the second-floor landing. He was seriously contemplating the merits of charging up the stairs to speak with Diana. Derek had been having second thoughts about the whole idea of a mock wedding all afternoon. He wanted a few minutes alone with Diana to discuss it, but he hesitated, not wanting to further upset her.

"Derek." Tristan's voice beckoned him away from his thoughts. "Caroline insists that my man here does not look the part of a vicar. What is your opinion?"

He turned his attention to the man in question, intently scrutinizing him.

"I suppose I must agree with Caroline," Derek answered. "He doesn't much resemble a reverend."

"Well, I never—" the Reverend Penley began, his face coloring with righteous indignation.

"Please excuse us, sir," Tristan quickly interjected. "I'll have our butler show you into the drawing room and bring refreshments. We will be in shortly for the ceremony."

The reverend was reluctantly led away by Sutton. Caroline noted her husband's growing ire and prudently decided to placate him.

"I suppose he isn't all that bad, Tris," Caroline said with a sigh. "I am sure he will make a credible reverend, as long as no one notices how young he is."

The scowl on Tristan's face deepened. "I hate to disillusion you, Caroline, but the Reverend Penley is not an actor. He is a true vicar of the Anglican Church."

"What!" Derek cried out, not sure he heard Tristan's remark correctly.

Tristan grinned sheepishly at his friend. "It was going to be a surprise for you, Derek. Call it a wedding gift, if you will."

"Oh really, Tris," Derek answered cooly, his eyebrows raised in disbelief. "And precisely when were you going to inform me of this little surprise? Before or after the ceremony?"

"Before, of course," Tristan said indignantly.

Alyssa entered the hallway holding Katherine by the hand. Their untimely arrival instantly halted the discussion. "Morgan has informed me he will escort Diana downstairs in five minutes, unless he is instructed otherwise. Is everything ready?"

"Not exactly," Derek said. "Tristan and I have a few things to discuss first. We will join you shortly." Derek gave the women a stiff bow and then practically dragged Tristan from the room.

"Now what?" Alyssa asked her sister-in-law. Caroline explained as they walked into the drawing room, her face flushing red when they encountered the Reverend Penley.

"The duke will be escorting the bride downstairs momentarily," Caroline told the minister in a rush.

Tristan, sitting calmly in a comfortable chair in his private study, listened without interruption as Derek vented his anger and frustration.

"I have thought this entire idea of pretending to be married was ludicrous from the start, Tris."

"Exactly."

"And now you expect me to trap an unsuspecting Diana into a binding marriage by substituting a real vicar, when she believes the man is only an actor, playing a part."

"Precisely."

"I can't do that to her, Tris. Diana will be my wife one day, of that I am certain. But I won't deceive her like this. It just isn't right."

"She doesn't have to know, Derek."

"You are crazy."

Tristan smiled at his friend, not at all offended. "The reason I found a real vicar was for Diana's safety, Derek," Tristan said. "If anyone ever discovered you are only pretending to be married, it would be a disaster. I'm not certain either of you would ever recover from the scandal. Since Diana admitted she planned on marrying you sometime in the future, I decided it would be a wiser choice to go ahead and do it now."

"And how am I supposed to explain this to Diana?"

"You don't have to. When Diana is finally ready to become your wife, you can tell her the truth." Tristan leaned back in his chair and crossed his arms over his chest. "Or you can have another wedding ceremony. You can decide when the time comes which course of action is best. The main point is, Diana will legally be your wife. Now. You can protect her, Derek. Isn't that what you want?"

"Yes," Derek answered slowly, still not convinced he was doing the correct thing.

"I have managed, with a great deal of difficulty, I might add, to obtain a special license." Tristan patted his breast coat pocket. "It is your decision whether or not to use it."

It took Derek only a few moments to decide. More than anything he wanted Diana for his wife. He knew it was wrong to deceive her, but as Tristan so aptly pointed out, Diana need never know of it. Longing and love overshadowed the guilt twisting in the pit of his stomach.

Grinning, Derek remarked lightly, "Come along, Tris. I don't want to keep my lovely bride waiting."

Lovely she certainly was. Derek could hear the audible sighs of admiration and squeals of excitement from the servants as Diana descended the long staircase. She was led into the drawing room tightly clutching Morgan's arm, the tension in her small frame obvious with each step she took.

The growing trepidation Diana had been feeling all afternoon was building with each unsteady step she made toward Derek. He regarded her with an unwavering intensity, and Diana felt the tension inside her twist into an even tighter knot.

The only thing Diana truly wanted to do was shout her objections and race from the room, but her throat was so closed with emotion that she doubted if she could even utter a sound.

Instead she stood trembling next to Derek, facing the pretend reverend as he began the pretend ceremony, hoping her panic would not give way to full blown hysteria. Out of the corner of her eye, Diana saw Caroline take a purposeful stride forward as the reverend began speaking, but Tristan grasped his wife tightly around her waist and hauled her back to his side.

"Who giveth this woman in marriage?"

"I do." Morgan's deep voice startled Diana, and then panic set in as she felt the duke release his strong grip on her arm and place her right hand over Derek's.

The minute Derek felt Diana's cold hand touch his own, he knew he had made a mistake. He loved this woman. She had endured enough suffering at the hands of Rutledge men in the past. He could not, in good conscience, be party to another marital deception toward her. He had no right to deceive her, no matter how noble his intentions.

The Reverend Penley finally ceased speaking and there was a taut silence in the room. Everyone was waiting for Derek to repeat his vows.

"Would you kindly excuse us for a moment," Derek said to the room in general. And then, he abruptly left the drawing room, dragging a dazed Diana behind him.

Derek negotiated his way quickly through the crowd of muttering servants in the hallway. He didn't stop until he'd reached Tristan's private study. Only after he had shut the door firmly behind him did he finally release Diana's hand.

"I can't go through with this, Diana."

"Thank God." Diana sank down slowly into a nearby chair. She felt dazed and shaken and immensely relieved. "I don't know what possessed me to agree to such a ridiculous charade, Derek. I am merely thankful you had the courage to put an end to it."

"There is something I must explain to you, Diana," he said in a grim tone.

Diana distractedly pushed her veil off her shoulders and lifted her face. "Yes, Derek."

"About the Reverend Penley—"

"Reverend Penley? Who is that?" Diana asked.

Derek sighed. "Reverend Penley is the minister who is waiting to marry us in the drawing room, no doubt extremely curious as to why I stopped the wedding in the middle of the ceremony."

"Oh."

"He isn't an actor, Diana. Reverend Penley, that is."

"He isn't," Diana repeated vaguely, not at all certain why Derek was carrying on about this man.

"No."

Diana shot him a scathing glance. "I presume there is a point to all of this, Derek. Kindly make it before my head explodes."

"Reverend Penley is an ordained vicar, Diana."

Diana went very still. "Are you saying he was going to marry us? Really marry us? Legally?"

"Yes."

Diana's eyes squeezed shut. "You weren't going to tell me, were you?"

"No."

Diana slowly exhaled the breath she had been holding. "Then why did you stop the ceremony, Derek?"

"I could not bring myself to deceive you," he said simply. Sighing audibly, he crossed the room and gently pulled her to her feet. He regarded her solemnly. "I take full responsibility for everything, Diana. I discovered the truth about Reverend Penley a few minutes before you came downstairs. Tristan felt he was protecting you by arranging for a legal wedding, and I agreed with him. I know now it was wrong. I only hope you can forgive me."

Diana smiled fleetingly. Lord, what a mess. "Why does this have to be so damn complicated, Derek?"

He frowned slightly at her uncustomary use of profanity, and then he smiled down at her. "Let us make it very simple, shall we?" Gallantly, he dropped to his left knee in front of her. Holding her hand over his heart, he said quietly, "I love you, Diana, with all my heart, and I shall try my hardest to be a good husband to you. I shall endeavor to be a solid provider, a strong protector, a faithful companion, and a most willing lover. Will you do me the great honor of becoming my wife?"

Diana was silent for several heart skipping minutes. "Since I am already dressed for the occasion, my lord," she finally said, breaking into a smile. "Why not?"

Chapter Twenty

It was a lovely wedding ceremony, despite the vicar's barely concealed irritation. Diana stood next to
Derek, confident and relaxed, repeating her vows in
a firm voice. Her previous doubts about his lack of
trust in her had been banished. Derek had proven
the ultimate confidence in her judgment by telling
her the truth about Reverend Penley. And he had
proven his own sense of honor by not being able to
deceive her. It was, Diana believed, a good beginning.

"My lord, you may kiss your bride."

Diana smiled as she heard a loud sniffle and
saw Tristan roll his eyes heavenward, before
good-naturedly stuffing a linen handkerchief into
Caroline's hand.

Derek smiled also as he gathered his bride firmly
into the circle of his arms and covered her mouth
with a searing, passionate kiss. Reverend Penley,

whose sense of propriety had been stretched past the breaking point, coughed loud and hard. Derek reluctantly released Diana, but the look he bestowed upon her was so filled with love and rampant desire, Diana noted that Reverend Penley colored visibly.

Fortunately, there was no opportunity for the minister to make a comment. The family enthusiastically moved in on her and Derek to offer their congratulations, and Diana embraced a tearful Caroline.

"I only hope you will be as happy as Tris and I have been," Caroline said, sniffing and dabbing at her eyes with her soggy handkerchief.

"I hope so too, Caroline," Diana whispered, feeling on the verge of tears herself.

Diana next hugged Alyssa and Katherine, but hesitated as she stood before Morgan. He regarded her with serious eyes.

"I have always believed Derek was an honorable man," Morgan stated firmly, and Diana nodded her head. "Never the less, if you should ever find yourself in need of help, Diana, for any reason, you can always come to me."

Diana's throat tightened with emotion. "Thank you, Morgan," she replied simply, putting her arms around the duke in gratitude.

"Hey, what about me? Don't I get to kiss the bride?"

Diana turned around to face a grinning Tristan. "By all rights I should be furious with you, Tris," Diana said as she allowed him to kiss her cheek.

Tristan had the grace to look embarrassed. "You have forgiven me though, haven't you, Diana?" He actually sounded worried.

"I went through with the wedding, didn't I?" Diana said with a soft laugh, hugging Tristan tightly, clearly demonstrating she harbored no ill feelings toward him.

Derek stood nearby, his gaze directed on his bride as she embraced his friend. His wife! The words sounded immensely pleasing to Derek's ears. He waited until she moved away from Tristan before he approached her.

"Happy, sweetheart?" Derek whispered, his lips softly grazing her temples.

Diana placed her arms around his neck and smiled up at him. "I didn't think it was possible to feel this much bliss, Derek."

"Just wait until tonight, my love," he replied with a sensual grin.

Diana blushed prettily and was spared further teasing by Sutton's announcing dinner.

"May I go to dinner too, Father?" Katherine asked, her gray eyes sparkling as she hopped from one foot to the other in restless excitement.

"It is late," the duke replied. "Besides, you have already eaten your dinner, Puss. 'Tis high time you joined your sister upstairs. Juliet is most likely asleep."

"But Juliet is a baby," Katherine protested vigorously. Wrapping her delicate fingers around her father's strong hands she said beseechingly, "Oh, please can't I stay up."

Morgan sighed heavily. "If you promise to go to bed without a fuss, I shall save you a piece of the wedding cake."

"May I eat the cake for breakfast?"

Tristan's deep laugh rang out clearly. Morgan scowled at his younger brother before bending low and whispering in his daughter's ear, "You may eat your cake for breakfast if you promise not to tell your mother."

"I promise," Katherine responded immediately. Gripping the duke's neck tightly, she pressed her small head to his chest. "Good night, Father. I love you." With a parting hug, she quickly dashed across the room toward the young maid waiting to escort her upstairs.

Swallowing hard, Morgan straightened up and joined the celebration in the dinning room. Reverend Penley declined an invitation to dine and bid a hasty good-bye to all.

Alyssa shook her head as he left. "I am certain he thinks we all are candidates for Bedlam," she remarked, smiling.

"Yes," Morgan agreed dryly. "I doubt he will soon forget this wedding ceremony."

The Reverend Penley was soon forgotten as everyone settled in to enjoy the marvelous dinner Cook prepared. Striving for a more informal atmosphere, Caroline dismissed the servants after they placed a large assortment of culinary delights on the dining room sideboard.

"Since the ladies have spent an exhausting afternoon preparing for this evening's celebration," Caroline said, "I think it is only fitting our husbands serve us our dinner."

"Here, here," Alyssa said, with a mischievous wink at Morgan.

Diana tapped her wineglass with her silver fork in clamoring agreement.

The three husbands exchanged pained glances before Tristan jumped up from his chair. "It shall be our pleasure, ladies."

With a minimal amount of grumbling, Derek and Morgan soon followed.

Caroline gave Tristan a catlike grin of satisfaction as he set a filled plate for her, then returned to the buffet for his own dinner. Caroline's grin faded quickly.

"Tristan, you didn't put any chicken crepes on my dish," Caroline said, enviously eyeing Diana's plate. "Nor any lobster and oyster pie, or fish pate or roast beef. And there is a very meager portion of honeyed carrots and spinach souffle."

"Oh really, my pet," Tristan said, swirling his glazed roast pork loin into the apple brandy sauce before taking a bite. "I am sorry. After you have finished eating what I have brought you, I shall be pleased to fix you another plate."

Giving Tristan a suspicious look, Caroline lifted her fork, but she held it suspended above her dish.

"Touche, my dear, for serving me my least favorite foods," Caroline muttered under her breath, swallowing her creamed turnips.

Tristan gave her a bold stare and promptly got up from his dinner to arrange a second plate of food for his wife. He poured wine into everyone's goblets and made a toast to the health and future happiness of Diana and her groom.

After dinner, Diana and the other women again defied convention by sitting at the table with the men as they indulged in their port. Then Caroline abruptly scraped back her chair and rose to her feet.

"I believe it is time for us to adjourn to the drawing room."

"Will you play for us tonight, Caroline?" Tristan asked, pulling out his wife's chair.

"I would be delighted."

Diana and Derek followed the two couples into the drawing room. Caroline sat in front of the pianoforte and sorted through her music sheets. Tristan lifted a branch of candles from the mantelpiece and thrust it into Derek's hand.

"I am sure you are both tired from today's excitement," Tristan said with a straight face. "Mrs. Roget has prepared the corner suite for you. I believe you know the way, Diana. We will see you both in the morning."

"Late morning," Derek said firmly, and Diana felt her cheeks grow warm. "Good night, everyone. Many thanks to you all for sharing this rather unusual but very special day with us."

Diana lowered her head, suddenly feeling quite shy, and she murmured her thanks and good night. She placed her hand into Derek's and they walked side by side up the stairs.

When they reached the suite at the end of the long corridor, Diana found her eyes riveted on Derek's strong, capable hands as he opened the bedchamber door. She shivered slightly, imagining how it would feel to have those wondrous hands on her body again, caressing and stroking her.

"Are you cold?" Derek asked. He held Diana's hand as they walked into the room.

"No," Diana said, turning to face him.

"Nervous?" Derek shut the heavy mahogany door and leaned back against it.

Diana moved toward him very slowly. She reached up and stroked his jawline. "Impatient, my lord," she said in a husky, sensual tone. "I am most impatient."

Derek gave a throaty laugh and claimed her lips with an intoxicating kiss. Diana pressed against him and she felt his already swollen manhood against her belly.

"I feel as though I have waited a lifetime to have you near me like this," Derek murmured.

"It has only been a few days, Derek."

"A few days? It seems much longer." He caught

her fingers in his hand and began nibbling on the tips. "Besides, it is different now, Diana. You are my wife."

He said wife with such love and passion, Diana felt her stomach knot with emotion. Derek's hands slid around her waist, reaching automatically for the small buttons at the back of her dress. Diana heard him curse softly as he succeeded in unfastening only one of the buttons while ripping out three.

"Have a care, Derek," Diana said, reproaching him, when she heard the buttons hit the floor. "This is Caroline's dress and I'll not have it ruined."

"Oh, all right," he grumbled. "Turn around so I can properly unhook the damn thing."

Obediently, Diana presented her back to him and lifted up her unbound hair.

Finally, he succeeded in separating all the fastenings and his hands touched her bare back and shoulders as the lovely dress fell to the floor. Derek leaned in closer, brushing his lips against her earlobes.

"Are the petticoats and chemise you're wearing also borrowed from Caroline?"

"No."

"Good."

Diana heard a loud rendering sound, but not until she felt the cool air on her posterior and legs, did she realize Derek had torn off all her underclothes.

"Derek!"

"Sorry, love. But I am afraid I have reached the limits of my endurance. Too many damn buttons."

Diana shook her head and turned around to face him. He had somehow managed to remove his jacket, waistcoat and cravat, and they lay in a heap on the floor next to her gown. She glided her hands sensually up his chest, reaching for the studs on his shirt. With a wicked grin, she gripped the edges of the soft linen tightly, wrenching it apart.

The fine pearl studs fell to the floor in a shower of light. Derek's eyes gleamed as he looked into her eyes. "I truly am the most fortunate of men, to be so blessed with a wife whose lack of patience rivals my own."

Diana giggled and danced away from him toward the bed. A large fire roared in the hearth and the room felt deliciously warm on her unclothed body.

Derek shrugged out of his breeches, tossing them casually on the floor. Quietly, he moved toward his unsuspecting bride as she stood near the bed, her back to him.

"I love you, Derek," she said.

Derek smiled slowly. He did not answer her with words, but instead reached around her waist. He rubbed her soft belly; then his hands drifted up to cup her breasts, his thumbs teasing the sensitive buds of her nipples. Diana moaned softly and pushed back against him.

"You drive me beyond thought, Derek."

"As you do me, my love."

He gently pushed her onto the bed and rolled her on her back. His hand slipped between her thighs, just as his lips descended on her mouth.

"You are so sweet, my love," he whispered thickly as her felt her thighs relax and her legs part. He eased a finger into her damp heat.

"Oh, Derek."

He moved his body down the length of her, kissing her breasts, her ribs, her flat stomach, and the silky skin of her upper thighs. Her fingers clenched his scalp as he lowered his mouth to intimately caress her inner softness.

"My God!" she exclaimed, truly shocked at his actions. "Derek, you musn't—"

Diana's voice trailed off as the excruciatingly sweet pleasure inside her tightened. She could barely breathe as he gently sucked on her sensitive flesh. Derek continued his intimate caress and she arched her back in savage surrender to him when the searing climax overtook her.

Diana groaned and drew him deeper into her body, her legs hugging him, her hands frantically clutching the solid muscles of his upper arms.

Derek moved inside her with slow, even strokes, and when her body begin to convulse, he increased the pace. He let out a loud, uninhibited shout as his shuddering climax broke, filling her with his seed. Fully sated, he collapsed on top of her and several minutes passed before he stirred.

"Am I crushing you?"

"No," she lied, still too filled with languid delight and contentment to care.

Derek rolled onto his side and gathered her close against him. She immediately placed her leg over his and cuddled up to his chest.

Diana sighed. "I do believe this is the most wondrous part of making love, Derek."

"Now? After it is all over?" She felt, rather than saw, his questioning frown. "Pray, go on, Diana."

She struggled to sit up so she could see his face and better explain. He allowed her to lift herself up, but he shifted her body so she was pinned atop his chest, their chins nearly touching. Derek's expression was unreadable.

"You know, Derek, in some ways, what comes after can be even more intimate than the act of love itself," she said solemnly.

He cocked an eyebrow at her. "How so?"

"I firmly believe, in these special moments

together, we form the true bonds of love and devotion."

"We do?"

"Yes."

Derek gazed into her eyes. "This time we now share together is the merging of our hearts, Diana."

"Yes, my love," she whispered, her eyes filling with tears at his understanding. "And our souls, Derek. Our very souls."

"Caroline, you really must try to get hold of yourself, dear," Tristan told his wife. He gently stroked her shoulder and rubbed her back, trying to soothe her. "You will make yourself ill with all this weeping."

"I know, Tris," Caroline said with a sniff. She stood next to her husband in the front hallway, bidding farewell to Derek and Diana. It was late afternoon, and the newlyweds were finally ready to depart. Their leave-taking had begun very amicably until, without warning, Caroline burst into tears.

"Caroline, our house is only a few short blocks away," Derek said softly, feeling very inadequate. He glanced nervously over at Diana. "We intend to see a great deal of you and Tristan."

"Of course," Caroline said, waving her damp handkerchief. "Please forgive me. I don't know what came over me." She took a deep steadying breath and smiled bravely. "I have been so highly emotional these past few days. I don't know why. Sometimes I feel as though I can't control myself."

Diana's eyes narrowed speculatively at her friend. Could it be possible? Lack of emotional control was an early sign of pregnancy. "Anything else unusual affecting you, Caroline?" Diana asked, injecting a lightness into her tone.

"Not really. I have been feeling a bit more tired, but we have been keeping rather late hours this past week." Caroline regarded Diana with a puzzled expression. Then her eyes widened.

"Well?" Diana said, not needing to ask Caroline anything else.

"I'm not sure," Caroline answered, her eyes barely concealing her excitement and wonder. "It is possible, though. Very possible."

"Oh, Caroline." Diana moved forward to embrace her friend, and Caroline burst into another round of noisy sobs.

Tristan looked over the two women's heads at Derek. "I don't imagine you have any idea what this is all about?"

Derek shook his head ruefully. "Not a clue, Tris."

Tristan shrugged his shoulders philosophically and waited for his wife to regain control. After several minutes of conspiratorial whispers, Diana moved out of Caroline's arms.

"We shall allow you one day of total privacy," Tristan informed Derek. "Then Morgan and I will come calling."

"Be sure to bring Alyssa and Caroline when you visit us," Diana said as the young footman held open the door. "And let Alyssa know the girls are also welcome. I'm sorry we did not have a chance to bid them all farewell today."

"My brother has often joked about his daughters' sleeping habits," Tristan said with a grin. "I always thought his stories were prone to exaggeration, yet it is my understanding little Juliet even beat the sun up this morning."

At the mention of Juliet, Caroline again began to snivel, and Derek seized the opportunity to beat a hasty retreat. With a quick nod of farewell, he firmly guided Diana out the door, down the front steps, and into his waiting carriage.

"Was it really necessary to bring the coach, Derek?" Diana asked breathlessly as her husband motioned to his driver to leave. " 'Tis only a short walk to your house and the weather is very pleasant this afternoon."

"I informed my staff last night to expect my bride today, Diana. It is fitting that the newest countess arrive in grand style at her London home."

Diana sat silently during the short ride. She experienced a myriad of emotions when the carriage halted in front of the familiar house. She could not help but remember the disaster that had befallen her the first time she had walked through those doors.

Derek jumped lithely down from the coach and held out his hand. "Ready?"

Diana placed her hand in his firm grip and gave him a solid smile. His strong presence gave her the boost of confidence she badly needed.

Before they even began the short climb up the steps, the front door was opened by the butler, Dobbs. He bowed stiffly, signaling a footman to come forward to assist Derek and his bride with their outer garments, while another footman assisted the driver with their traveling trunks.

"Good afternoon, Dobbs," Derek said curtly, unbuttoning his midnight-blue greatcoat. "I see you have assembled the staff, as I requested."

"Yes, my lord," the butler answered formally.

A middle-aged woman, her black bombazine skirts rustling noisily, stepped nervously forward. "Mrs. Standen, my housekeeper," Derek said, his tone a bit less harsh as he introduced the woman.

The housekeeper bobbed a small curtsy, and Diana automatically extended her hand in greeting. "So nice to meet you, Mrs. Standen. I am Lady Diana."

The housekeeper appeared taken aback at her friendly greeting, but after a slight hesitation, Mrs. Standen accepted Diana's hand and dipped another curtsy.

"Welcome, your ladyship," Mrs. Standen said. She cleared her throat apprehensively. "On behalf of the entire staff, I should like to take the liberty of congratulating you on your marriage."

"How very kind of you, Mrs. Standen," Diana replied graciously. She strolled casually into the large entrance hall, turning her attention to the dozen openly curious faces regarding her. "Would you do the honors please?"

Breaking into a genuine smile, Mrs. Standen took her place importantly at Diana's side and went down the rows of servants, introducing each one. Diana shook hands with all of them and spent a brief moment questioning them on their duties in the household.

By the time she was finished, Derek could see by the staff's amazed expressions that Diana had clearly made a favorable impression.

With a haughty wave, Dobbs dismissed the staff, but Diana asked Mrs. Standen to remain for a moment. "My maid was unable to make the journey from Cornwall, Mrs. Standen, so I shall need your assistance in selecting a lady's maid to serve me while I am in residence."

Mrs. Standen bit her lip thoughtfully. "We don't have anyone who has been trained for the position, my lady. But Molly does have some skill with hair."

"Molly shall suit me just fine, Mrs. Standen."

"Excellent," Derek said, approaching his wife. "You can inform Molly she may begin her duties tomorrow morning, Mrs. Standen."

His dismissive tone sent the housekeeper retreating to the servants' quarters. Derek turned to Diana, smiling. "I am most anxious to give you a personally guided tour of your new home, my dear. Shall we being with the upstairs bedchambers?"

Chapter Twenty-one

The house tour Derek initiated progressed no farther than the upstairs chambers. He began the tour by first showing Diana his bedchamber, which was also, he wickedly pointed out, her room. After reassuring her this was not the same chamber Giles had occupied, Derek successfully persuaded her to join him in the large four-poster bed for the remainder of the afternoon. They didn't even bother to dress for dinner. Derek ordered a sumptuous meal to be prepared and served in their bedchamber. They ate casually, Derek clad only in his dressing gown, loosely belted at the waist, while Diana wore her blue silk robe.

The following morning while Diana and Derek shared a hearty breakfast in their bedchamber, Diana met her new maid Molly. There was not, however, much for the maid to do, since Derek firmly insisted to the young girl that the countess would be spending the day abed. At first confused, the girl merely stared at them, but the gleam in Derek's eyes conveyed his meaning, and the maid turned a bright shade of red. She mumbled something incoherent and fled swiftly from the room.

Diana groaned loudly. "Derek, how could you! No doubt Molly will run directly to pass this little tidbit along to the rest of the staff. How shall I ever face them?"

"For heaven's sake, Diana, we are newly married." Derek leaned back in his chair and bit forcefully into a piece of toast. "Not to mention master and mistress of this household. It is hardly our concern what the servants will think if we choose to spend the day locked away in the privacy of our bedchamber."

"I suppose you are right," Diana muttered, not entirely convinced.

She strolled passed his chair and Derek's arm snaked out, pulling her into his lap. He nuzzled her neck, and she closed her eyes and turned her face into the hollow of his shoulder. His arms tightened comfortingly around her and she pushed aside her earlier misgivings. Being cradled so lovingly in Derek's arms brought a feeling of closeness and love that overshadowed everything else.

Diana came awake slowly, the forceful knocking on the door pulling her reluctantly away from her peaceful slumber. Why on earth was someone pounding so relentlessly on their bedchamber door? Diana sat up suddenly, fear clutching her heart. There must be danger!

She poked Derek none too gently in the ribs. He rolled over, then sat up abruptly when he too heard the noise.

"What the bloody hell is going on?" he growled, jumping up naked from the bed. He shrugged into his brocade dressing gown and stalked barefoot to the door. "Someone is going to lose his job over this," Derek muttered, ferociously yanking open the door.

Diana hastily sat up in the bed, pulling the sheet to her chin. She could hear Derek's angry growl as he spoke to whoever it was that so rudely woke them. And then her eyes flew open wide as she heard a loud female voice answer her husband.

"You must not blame Dobbs for any of this, Derek," the female voice said. "I have been waiting all morning to speak with you, but there was no sign you would be arising anytime soon. Then one of the maids let it slip that you didn't leave your room at all yesterday. I just knew I had to take some action."

"Oh, really?" Derek's voice was dangerously cold.

"Um, yes."

Diana squirmed forward in the bed, trying to catch a glimpse of the mysterious woman who was speaking to her husband. The voice sounded oddly familiar, but she could not yet place it.

"Let me assure you, Henriette, there is no possible explanation you can give that will excuse your rude behavior today."

"Derek, you don't understand. I have just come from my modiste, Madame La Belle, and she told me the most shocking tale. I simply could not credit it."

"I presume you are referring to my recent marriage, Henriette," Derek stated softly.

There was a dramatic pause. "So it is true."

"Yes," Derek said. "And I can assure you I have no intentions of discussing it with you while you are standing in the hallway outside of my bedchamber. If you are still here this afternoon, I would be delighted to present my bride to you. Downstairs. In the front salon, if you please, Henriette. Like civilized people."

And without a further word, Derek slammed the door shut on Henriette's sputtering comments of protest. "Four o'clock, Henriette," he barked, striding away from the door toward the bed.

"That was Henriette." He threw off his robe and climbed into the bed.

"I gathered as much." Diana felt the corners of her mouth tug into a smile.

"Apparently she was at the dressmaker's this morning and learned of our marriage."

"Caroline told me she selected Madame La Belle because of her reputation for gossip," Diana said as she fluffed the pillows for her husband.

"I am sure even Caroline did not think Henriette would find out about our marriage this quickly," Derek grumbled, stretching back on the pillows.

"No, I'm sure she did not," Diana said. When Derek was comfortably situated on the bed, she pushed back the covers and stood up.

"Where do you think you are going?"

Diana smiled at the tone of Derek's voice. He sounded like a young boy who had just had his favorite toy taken away. "I am going to ring for Molly."

"Why?"

"For one thing, I could use a nice, hot bath," she said patiently.

"Mm, that sounds inviting."

"I shall be pleased to order one for you also, my lord."

"Why can't I share your bath, sweetheart?"

Her eyes lightened with humor. "I do believe that would defeat the very purpose of a bath."

Mumbling, Derek lifted his arms up and folded them back behind his head. Relaxing against the pillows, he took great delight in watching his naked wife walk about the bedchamber searching for her wrapper. Finally giving up on the task, she instead picked up his discarded dressing gown and put that on.

A very timid knock at the door brought Molly into the room. By her quick response, Diana knew the maid must have been close enough to hear Derek's encounter with Henriette.

"Good morning, Molly," Diana said to the girl in a pleasant voice. The maid dutifully bobbed an awkward curtsy, her eyes wide at the sight of Diana in the earl's robe. "Please instruct one of the footmen to have a bath set up for me in here. Then I shall need your assistance in unpacking and selecting a gown. I am sure it will need to be pressed." Diana glanced speculatively around the room. "Do you happen to know where my luggage has gotten to?"

Molly nodded her head enthusiastically. "Dobbs had it brought to the other suite, milady. The one down the hall that connects to the master bedchamber."

The mention of the master bedchamber brought an unintentional reminder of Giles, and Diana shuddered. She was glad Derek had never occupied the master's suite, knowing she would never be able to enter the room without thinking of Giles and an endless array of unpleasant memories.

"I don't think I shall be moving into that room presently, Molly. Please see that my things are brought in here at once. We can unpack what

I need for today now and have another armoire brought in for the other gowns later."

"Yes, milady." Molly dipped another small curtsy and bustled out of the room.

In a relatively short time, the large copper tub was brought in and filled with steaming hot water. Diana's trunk was located and the necessary items removed. Derek watched the proceedings from his comfortable perch on the bed. Due to the vastness of the room's size, his presence was not yet known by the army of servants parading in and out of the chamber. With a military eye, Derek admired the precise, methodical way his wife organized and directed the servants. He conceded she certainly had a talent for dealing efficiently with the staff.

The final item dragged into the bedchamber was a tall dressing screen. When Derek heard Molly instruct the footman to set it up in front of the copper tub, he finally spoke.

"Remove the screen."

Molly jumped and whirled around. "Your lordship?" she asked in a squeaky voice.

Noticing how nervous the maid became upon discovering Derek's presence, Diana quickly intervened. "You may place the folded screen in the corner," Diana said to the footman. After he left, Diana dismissed her maid. "I can see to my own bath, Molly. I shall ring for you when I am ready to have my hair done." With a darting glance in the direction of the bed and a grateful look at Diana, Molly left.

The door had barely closed behind her when Derek rose from the bed. "You are going to have to do something about Molly, my love," Derek said, trailing his hand through the bathwater, testing the temperature. "She is very skittish."

"Only around you, Derek," Diana said with a rueful grin. "You must try not to be so intimidating."

"Diana—"

"Well, so authoritative then. Molly is young and a bit timid, but I would really like to give her a chance to prove herself in this position. 'Tis only fair, Derek."

"Whatever you say, my sweet." As his beautiful wife slipped off her robe and sank into the warm bathwater, Derek's thoughts were no longer on the young maid. "Whatever you say."

Punctually at four o'clock, Derek entered the front salon, Diana anxiously clutching his arm. Henriette was already in the room, restlessly pacing about. And she was not alone. Perched delicately on the edge of a fragile rosewood chair was Mr. George Rotherby, whom Derek remembered as Henriette's favorite escort during her marriage as well as now.

Henriette ceased her pacing. Her eyes narrowed speculatively on Diana, as if she had a fleeting recollection of her, but could not place the face with a name.

"Henriette, I am honored to present my wife, Diana," Derek said evenly. "Diana, this is Henriette, recent widow of my cousin, Giles."

"Haven't we met before?" Henriette asked curiously.

"I don't believe so," Diana said slowly. "To my recollection we have never been formally introduced."

Henriette appeared to carefully consider the matter as Derek led his wife toward George Rotherby.

"Mr. Rotherby, may I present my countess, Lady Diana," the earl said with a trace of pride in his voice.

Mr. Rotherby immediately stood. "I am truly

honored, Lady Diana," he said. With a decidedly exaggerated air, he gingerly took Diana's hand and raised it to his lips.

She politely hid a smile. Rotherby, a man Diana judged to be in his mid-thirties, was without question a true dandy. He was dressed in the height of fashion, in the brightest shades of yellow and green Diana had ever seen anyone wear, man or woman. Before resuming his chair, Rotherby meticulously brushed a small piece of lint from the cuff of his green velvet jacket and then turned to smile at Diana with a look of avid curiosity.

"Shall we have some tea?" Derek asked casually, eyeing the silver service and plates of pastries on the table.

Diana as well as Henriette automatically reached for the silver teapot, their hands colliding in the process. Mr. Rotherby giggled nervously, obviously anticipating a scene. Diana was the first to recover and, with a flash of insight, decided her best course of action would be to defer to Henriette. While it was not essential, it was preferable, having the other woman as a supporter, rather than an adversary. "Would you do the honors please, Henriette?"

Henriette nodded her head approvingly and made a great show of pouring the tea into the delicate porcelain cups. She continued to gaze at Diana, her lips pursed in a thin line. Derek could not remember a time when Henriette had ever been so quiet. It was a refreshing change. He wondered idly if Henriette would be able to successfully place Diana in her memory.

After the tea was served, the conversation became forced and awkward. The mounting tension was broken by the arrival of Dobbs.

"The Duke and Duchess of Gillingham have called,

my lord," the butler said, his face expressionless. "Are you receiving callers this afternoon?"

"No, we are not, Dobbs," Derek said to the stone-faced butler. "However, we shall naturally make an exception in the case of the duke and duchess, since they are my wife's relations. Show them in at once."

Henriette sat up in surprise at that little snippet of information and looked to Rotherby. He raised his eyebrows in exaggerated wonder and they exchanged cryptic glances.

"I know we should have waited before we called," Alyssa said with a bright voice as she greeted Derek. "But Morgan insisted we stop in to see how Diana was adjusting to her new home. You know how protective he can be." Alyssa stopped in the center of the room and turned to Henriette, acknowledging her for the first time. "Lady Henriette, how very nice to see you. I had no idea you would be visiting today also."

"Lady Alyssa," Henriette replied in a thin voice. "You are related to Derek's new wife?"

Alyssa frowned. "Only by marriage. Diana is Morgan's cousin."

"Oh," Henriette said in a disbelieving tone.

Morgan moved next to his wife and stood directly in front of her. "Lady Henriette," he said in a deep voice.

"Good afternoon, Your Grace," Henriette said, her teacup rattling in her hands.

The awkward moment was broken by Mr. Rotherby as he rushed forward to greet the duke and duchess. He fairly beamed with delight as he made a great show of relinquishing his chair to the duchess.

Dobbs soon made another appearance, this time to announce the arrival of Tristan and Caroline.

When Diana and Tristan were standing side by side, Diana saw Henriette's expression of recognition and the duke's piercing eyes warning the woman not to speak.

Diana rang for more tea and cups and everyone settled in for a visit. The conversation reverted to safe, mundane topics, such as the unusually warm weather. Very little was said about her and Derek's sudden marriage, except that it had been a love match, heartily approved of by Diana's Ashton cousins.

After an hour, Diana finally began to relax. It appeared they would manage to get through Henriette's entire visit without a single mishap. She had been most anxious about spending any amount of time in the woman's company. Diana felt no personal animosity toward her, knowing she was innocent of the wrongs Giles had wrought on Diana, but the unpleasant memories surfaced all the same. At least Henriette was ignorant of them and Diana was certain Derek would do everything in his power to make sure it remained that way.

"Where are you staying while you are in town, Henriette?" Caroline asked, accepting a second cup of tea from Diana.

"Well, I suppose I shall stay with my mother," Henriette said, floundering.

Sitting close to his wife, Derek could feel Diana reacting to Henriette's sudden distress and he squeezed her hand tightly. It would be just like his softhearted wife to extend an invitation to Henriette to stay with them. Previously he had allowed her to treat the London house as her own, since he was seldom in residence, but since he was married, all that was going to change. Considering all the other complications facing them, the very last thing Derek needed was to have Henriette underfoot.

Tristan jumped into the conversation trying to cover the strained silence, but Henriette rose to her feet. Holding herself stiffly erect, she sailed across the room, muttering her excuses and a hasty farewell.

"Come along, George," she said in a frosty voice.

Mr. Rotherby cast a soulful look of regret at them, but dutifully rose to his feet and followed Henriette.

"Henriette, wait," Diana called, catching up to her before she reached the door. "There is something we would like to discuss with you." The stony expression on Henriette's face made Diana feel inexplicably guilty. She was so deliciously happy, and Henriette was obviously miserable. Reacting purely on instinct, she said, "Since you no longer have a London residence, Derek and I have decided to give this house to you."

"What!" Henriette said.

"My goodness," Mr. Rotherby squeaked.

Committed now, Diana rushed on. "Well, I am sure it means a great deal to you. I recently learned from Mrs. Standen that your husband purchased this house when you were first married. Derek and I don't intend to spend a great deal of time in town and we have little need for a London home. Actually, we regard this house more as yours than ours. We thought you might like to own it." Turning beseechingly to her husband, Diana added, "Isn't that right, Derek?"

Derek scowled, but did not reply. Nor did he contradict her offer.

"I don't know what to say," Henriette said, the lines of tension starting to ease from her face. " 'Tis true though, foolish as it may sound, that I have always adored this house."

"Then you should own it," Derek said with a sigh, walking across the room to join them.

"It is a very generous offer, Derek," Henriette said, as if she had not yet agreed to the idea.

"You will accept?" Derek asked.

"Thank you, I will." Henriette broke into a sincere smile. "Naturally I wouldn't even consider moving back here until my full year of mourning has been observed."

"That is your choice, of course," Diana said. "Derek and I will be in town for only a short time, a few weeks at most. Once we leave, you may do as you see fit."

"I plan on staying in town until the end of the week. May I call on you again before I leave?" Henriette asked.

"We would like that, Henriette," Diana said, but Derek remained silent.

When the door shut behind Henriette and Rotherby, Diana placed her hand over Derek's. They both were still facing the door, their backs to the others.

"I hope you are not angry with me, Derek," she whispered.

"It is a little late to be concerned about that now, Diana," he said dryly.

"I don't know what came over me," she said "Henriette looked so forlorn and defeated."

"I agree Henriette was obviously distressed, but was it truly necessary to give her a house to cheer her up?" He shook his head. "You realize of course, Giles probably used your money to buy this house."

She nodded. "I know. It doesn't really matter, though. I don't think I will ever be comfortable living here, Derek, and I strongly suspect you feel the same. I also believe I shall always feel this way, no matter how much time passes. By giving

Henriette the house we succeed in making her happy and relieve ourselves of the burden of living in Giles's shadow."

"That might very well be the case, but I do think you should have at least discussed this with me first."

"I know. I am sorry."

"Is everything all right?" Tristan asked, interrupting their intimate conference.

Derek turned around and walked back into the room, pulling Diana along with him. "Everything is fine, Tris. My impulsive wife has just agreed to consult with me in the future before giving away any more of my houses."

Diana grinned sheepishly at everyone, marveling that was all Derek was going to say about the matter.

"Fine," Caroline said, seemingly nonplussed by the entire incident. "Perhaps we can get on to more important business. It appears that gossip about your marriage is running rampant. Alyssa and I have discussed this matter at great length, and we have decided the only way to squelch this nasty gossip is for you to appear in public together. Lord and Lady Harrington are giving their annual spring gala Thursday night. It would be the perfect affair."

"No," Derek said in a firm voice. "It isn't safe for Diana."

"Oh really, Derek," Caroline said. "What could possibly happen to Diana in a ballroom filled with members of the *ton*?"

"I'm not sure," Derek replied. "But I have no intention of finding out."

"Tris," Caroline said, appealing to her husband.

"Now, Caroline, if Derek thinks it would be best

284

not to attend, we have to honor his wishes," Tristan said gently.

"The gossip could prove to be far more damaging, however," Morgan said. "Not that we are a family to succumb to the tabbies of the *ton*, as grandmother would say. But I would not want to jeopardize Diana's position in society. It is essential we contrive to escape the potential scandal. If an appearance at the Harrington's gala will do that, then it must be considered."

"True, we have all gone to a great deal of trouble to avoid a scandal," Derek said reluctantly. "It would be ridiculous to ruin that now." He saw Diana's eyes widen with both excitement and anxiety. "I suppose, if I keep unfashionably attached to my wife all evening, she will be safe. What do you think, Tris?"

"Sounds reasonable. Naturally, Morgan and I will be in attendance to offer our assistance," Tristan said with a smile as his older brother stifled a groan. "Come now, Morgan, it won't be all that bad. After all, if it weren't for Alyssa, you would never attend any parties."

"We might as well bring grandmother along," Morgan said gracefully. "She traveled up from Portsmouth yesterday, and she is anxious to meet our newest cousin."

"Wonderful!" Caroline exclaimed. "Alyssa and I will call for you at noon tomorrow, Diana. We will visit Madame La Belle so she can create a spectacular new gown for your debut into society. I feel certain it shall prove to be a memorable affair."

Chapter Twenty-two

Diana tugged nervously on the bodice of her evening gown, trying to stretch the scant material upward, in a fruitless effort to cover the top of her nearly exposed breasts.

"You look so beautiful, milady," Molly said in genuine awe, ignoring Diana's squirming. The young maid expertly pinned the final strand of blonde hair into place and stepped back to admire her handiwork. "None of the gentlemen will be able to take his eyes off you tonight, and the women will be green with envy."

Diana cast her maid a dubious look, then rose from the dressing table to survey herself in the full-length glass. She gasped slightly as she took in her reflection in the mirror.

The violet moire taffeta of her dress shimmered seductively in the candlelight, the richness of the material and the deep hue of the gown setting off her coloring gloriously. The style of the dress was exceedingly simple. It was high waisted, with a widely cut heart-shaped neckline and tight-fitting bodice, displaying not only the crevice between her breasts, but a portion of them as well. The tiny puffs of sleeves were off her shoulders, and the long skirt was full and flowing. Her hair, artfully arranged with twisting curls pinned atop her head, exposed her neck. Long, snugly fitted, elbow-length white kid gloves covered her arms, and matching violet slippers encased her feet.

"I feel positively naked," Diana muttered, trying again to raise the neckline of the gown, convinced she was showing far too much neck, throat, and bosom. The gown had not looked so deeply cut when she and Alyssa had selected it from the dress plate at Madame La Belle's. She couldn't even begin to imagine what Derek would think of her attire.

A soft knock at the bedchamber door distracted her and she sighed with relief when Alyssa entered the room.

"You are stunning," Alyssa said. "I predict you will be an instant success. Derek will have his hands full keeping all the eager young bucks at bay tonight."

Alyssa's words did not comfort her. "Are you sure about this dress, Alyssa?" Diana asked anxiously. "I feel absolutely indecent in the thing."

" 'Tis the very height of fashion, Diana," Alyssa said soothingly. "The color looks splendid and you certainly have the figure to carry the style of the gown."

Diana sighed. "I always thought you were supposed to wear something plain and white for your debut into society," she mumbled.

"Young virginal misses straight from the schoolroom wear white," Alyssa said. "You, my dear, are

287

a countess. Besides, with all the gossip circulating about your sudden marriage, it is important to make a dramatic entrance tonight."

Diana grimaced at her friend, not sure if she wanted her entrance into society to be quite so dramatic. Then with a critical eye, she shifted her attention to Alyssa's evening attire.

The gold-patterned raw silk gown the duchess wore was similar in style, but not as revealing as Diana's dress. Alyssa's sleeves were on her shoulders, and the neckline was not as plunging. It was, however, the necklace around Alyssa's throat that immediately captured Diana's attention. It was double chained, with alternating emeralds and diamonds and the centerpiece stone was a single pendant: the largest, richest-colored-green emerald Diana had ever seen.

"My bridal gift from Morgan," Alyssa said quietly when she noticed Diana staring.

"It is magnificent."

Alyssa turned to study the gem in the mirror. "It is a bit ostentatious for my tastes, but it pleases Morgan when I wear it." She turned back to Diana. "We must proceed downstairs at once, Diana. Morgan's grandmother has arrived. She is waiting in the front salon to speak with you before the ball tonight."

"Is there a problem?" Diana asked as they swept out into the hallway and quickly trod down the steps of the long, curved staircase.

"Don't worry. Everything is fine. Since you are to be introduced into society as an Ashton cousin, as well as the Countess of Harrowby, the dowager duchess thought it prudent that she speak with you before we arrive at the ball."

Alyssa abruptly stopped when they reached the

landing, her breathing rapid and uneven. "Wait a minute please, Diana," she said.

Diana paused in midstride and turned back to the duchess. Alyssa's face was very pale and she was taking deep, gulping breaths as she clutched the polished mahogany banister.

"Good heavens, Alyssa. Are you all right?"

"Yes, I think so," Alyssa said, straightening up. "I just became a bit light-headed for a moment. It has passed now. It is not unusual though. I am generally affected this way in my first few months."

"Alyssa! My goodness, are you increasing?"

"Oh, dear." Alyssa's cheeks flamed. "I didn't intend to blurt out my news in this manner." Flustered, she wiped her damp brow. "You must promise me that you will not tell anyone about this, Diana. Especially Caroline. Morgan and I have not yet told the family about the baby, and even though Caroline has never said anything, I know how distressed she is that she and Tristan have not yet had a child of their own."

Diana favored the duchess with a smug smile. Just wait until she heard Caroline's news. Imagine, both Alyssa and Caroline pregnant at the same time! She wasn't sure who would be more surprised, the women or their husbands.

"Naturally, I shall leave it to you to relate your good news to Caroline. Don't wait too long though, Alyssa. I think you might be pleasantly surprised at her reaction."

Alyssa recovered her breath, and gathering up their skirts, they proceeded at a slower pace to the front salon. The dowager duchess was alone as they entered the room. She was sitting regally on the brocade settee, a half-empty glass of sherry resting leisurely in her left hand.

Diana moved in front of the older woman and

made a deep, low curtsy before her, while Alyssa made the appropriate introductions.

"You did that very prettily," the dowager duchess said approvingly. "Managed to sink down and rise up quite gracefully, without falling out of your dress. Most impressive."

Diana's cheeks flamed at the mention of her gown, uncertain how to interpret the remark. She was very nervous knowing she must meet with the dowager duchess's approval if the charade of her claiming to be an Ashton cousin was to succeed. Tentatively, she raised her head to look at the dowager.

Two warm gray eyes greeted her. They were the identical shade of Morgan's eyes. Diana felt the tight knot in her stomach ease a bit.

"Do you think my gown too daring, Your Grace? Alyssa assures me it is most fashionable, but I would appreciate your opinion."

The dowager duchess took a long swallow of her drink. "The gown is daring, my dear," she replied regally. "And most provocative. But you look splendid in it. I approve."

"Thank you, Your Grace."

"No need to stand on ceremony with me, Diana. My grandsons have informed me you are to be introduced as an Ashton cousin."

"Only if that meets with your approval, madam. I would not want you to be forced into it," Diana said definitely.

The older woman smiled. "I might be considered a doting grandmother by some, but I can assure you, Diana, I make up my own mind about things. I dare say, neither my grandsons, nor anyone else for that matter, can force me to do something I do not wish to."

"Oh, madam. I certainly did not mean to imply—"

"I know," the dowager said gently. She finished the last of her sherry before she spoke. "I've always been very fond of Derek, ever since he and Tris were boys at Eaton together. I'd be happy to lend him my assistance in this matter."

"Thank you."

"Tell me, why did you marry Derek?" the dowager duchess asked bluntly.

Diana blinked in surprise, but she answered the question readily. "I love him."

The dowager's gray eyes softened. "I am pleased to hear it. Derek deserves a loving wife, especially after that disaster with the Worthington chit a few years back. Damn foolish girl to prefer Lord Winchester over Derek." The duchess scanned Diana's face. "That is all in the past. I do believe you will be a credit to the Ashton family, my dear. Now, I must determine exactly how you shall fit in."

"I beg your pardon, madam?"

The duchess ignored Diana and tapped her fingers rhythmically on the arm of the settee while she concentrated. Diana could just picture the wheels turning under the soft gray turban that adorned the dowager's head.

"My great-niece," the elder women finally said. "Granddaughter of my only sister Charlotte. What was your mother's name, Diana?"

"Anne."

"And your father?"

"My father was Gerald Crawford."

"Fine. My sister was Charlotte. We shall say Anne was her only child and my sister foolishly turned her back on her daughter when she married Gerald Crawford because he was in trade. Your relation to our family was only recently discovered during the settling of your late father's estate. Naturally, we have welcomed you into the family. Since Derek is such a close friend of Tristan's, it is logical to assume Tristan and Caroline introduced you to the earl, and Derek was instantly smitten. Yours is, without question, a love match."

The dowager duchess paused when she noticed Diana's stricken expression. "It really will be best if we stick to the truth as much as possible, Diana. My sister left England and married a Scotsman the year Morgan was born. She died young and childless, so there will be no one to refute our story. And I hardly need add it is best if no one ever discovers how you actually met Derek."

Diana felt her cheeks color. Of course the duchess would have been informed of her marriage to Giles. The story the dowager had concocted was an interesting blend of truth and fiction. It should stand up to scrutiny.

After a brief hesitation, Diana nodded. She had barely known her mother and knew nothing about her grandparents. She felt no disloyalty to them by agreeing. "I shall be Anne's daughter and Charlotte's granddaughter."

"Splendid." The dowager duchess turned to Alyssa. "Please inform the others what we have decided so everyone's story will be in accord." She rose lithely from the settee, displaying agility in her slight frame despite her advanced years. "I have something here I want you to wear tonight, Diana." The dowager withdrew a flat jewel case from her gray reticule and handed it to Diana.

Obediently Diana took the box and opened it. She gasped loudly. "My goodness!" Diana exclaimed, gingerly lifting the sparkling necklace.

"The Norwood diamonds," the dowager duchess said with some pride. "They have been in my family for six generations. The gems are special, because they are always passed through the females of the family, instead of the males. They will belong to my great-granddaughter Katherine someday." Reaching out for the heavy necklace, the older woman fastened it around Diana's neck. "By wearing the necklace tonight, you will proclaim both your relation to me and my approval of your marriage."

"They are dazzling," Alyssa said. "And the perfect compliment for your gown, Diana."

Diana clutched her throat, feeling the coolness of the many faceted stones. "Thank you for trusting them to me this evening, Your Grace. I promise I shall be exceedingly careful."

"Call me Aunt Katherine," the dowager duchess prompted. "I confess, I shall enjoy hearing your husband address me as aunt." She smiled broadly. " 'Tis time to depart for the ball. It is sure to be a crush and I wish to arrive before it becomes overly crowded."

Respectfully, Diana and Alyssa followed the dowager duchess out of the room and into the vast entrance foyer.

"The earl and his guests are in the drawing room," a young footman informed them. "Shall I summon them, my lady?"

"Yes, Rogers," Diana said.

"Do you have a long cape, Diana?" the dowager duchess asked suddenly as the footman rushed off.

"Yes," Diana said, puzzled. "I had a velvet cloak sewn in a similar shade of violet to match my gown, but I thought it too warm for this evening. I was going to wear a light silk shawl instead."

"Have a servant fetch the cloak, Diana," the dowager duchess said with a twinkle in her silvery eyes. "If I know Derek as well as I think I do, he will put up quite a fuss when he sees you in that dress."

*   *   *

The dowager duchess's prediction about the crowd at the Harringtons' proved to be correct. The normally short carriage ride took twice as long because of the traffic in the streets. Diana did not mind the extra delay, especially since the dowager had accepted Derek's invitation to ride in their coach. The three occupants spent the time reviewing Ashton family history and conversing pleasantly. By the time the coach drew up to the residence, Diana felt quite calm.

After jumping down from the coach, Derek first assisted the dowager duchess from the carriage, then Diana.

"Have I told you yet how strikingly beautiful you look tonight, my love," Derek whispered into Diana's ear as he swung her down from the vehicle.

"I wanted to look well so you would be proud of me, Derek," she said.

"Are we all here?" the dowager duchess inquired in a strong voice when Morgan, Alyssa, Tristan, and Caroline joined them.

"We are ready, Grandmother," Tristan said. "Lead on."

"Feels as if we are back with the regiment, doesn't it, Tris?" Derek said.

"With grandmother as our commander, we are assured of victory," Tristan declared with an answering grin.

The party made their way swiftly up the front steps, which were clogged with people. The crowd seemed to miraculously part as the dowager duchess sailed up the stairs, her slight frame held stiffly erect. Diana could hear mumbled whispers and comments following them as they were ushered inside the mansion.

Politely, Derek lifted the velvet cloak from Diana's shoulders, intending to hand it to the waiting footman. He took one look at all the creamy white skin revealed by the plunging neckline of Diana's lovely gown and immediately placed the cloak back on his wife's shoulders.

The dowager duchess witnessed the exchange and quickly intervened, hoping to avoid a display of Derek's temper. "Come along now, Derek. Everyone is very anxious to see your new bride and I wish to introduce Diana to Lord and Lady Harrington myself."

"I too am anxious to present my wife," Derek said, flashing the dowager duchess a berating look, correctly surmising that the older woman knew about the dress. "I merely prefer, madam, that everyone not see so very much of my new bride."

Derek noticed the sudden glow of masculine approval in both Morgan and Tristan's eyes, and he knew without looking that Diana had taken off her cloak. He groaned in frustration.

"I think Diana looks stunning," Morgan said mildly.

"I agree," Derek said tightly. "I shall count myself fortunate, however, if I am not forced to draw my pistol in the middle of the ballroom tonight to fend off the unwanted advances every hot-blooded buck in attendance is bound to make toward my wife."

Diana placed her hand gently on his arm. "If you are that distressed, we shall leave at once, Derek." Her large brown eyes mirrored her concern and love for him.

She was so breathlessly beautiful. Her blonde hair gleamed in the light of the chandelier, and the magnificent diamond necklace around her throat glistened brilliantly. Diamond necklace! Where in the hell had she gotten that expensive piece of jewelry? Derek wondered.

"I asked Diana to wear the Norwood diamonds tonight, Derek," the dowager duchess informed him. "I hope you don't mind."

Derek gave the older woman a withering look, but her keen gray eyes softened in understanding.

Derek felt like a fool. He was behaving childishly, and he knew it. He had certainly seen women in far more revealing gowns than Diana's. The problem was, he had never been in love with any of those women.

"Derek?" Diana said softly.

Mastering the remnants of his ire, he grasped his wife's arm firmly. "You will stay near me at all times this evening—is that clear? You will not partner any man in a dance unless I first approve of him—is that understood?" Diana meekly nodded her head. "Good. Now come along. Your Aunt Katherine wishes to present you to Lord and Lady Harrington."

Chapter Twenty-three

The calmness Diana had achieved during the carriage ride to the ball deserted her the moment she heard the footman announce in a loud, clear voice, "Her Grace, the Dowager Duchess of Gillingham." Diana's feelings hovered between extreme terror and total panic as she watched the dowager duchess stand proudly atop the three-step landing, regally surveying the crowded ballroom below. The dowager waited until Tristan and Caroline were also announced, then firmly held onto her grandson's arm, and descended to the ballroom floor.

Few of the dancing guests paid much attention when the dowager duchess or Caroline and Tristan were announced. Diana noted several heads did turn, however, when the butler next shouted, "The Duke and Duchess of Gillingham."

Derek and Diana immediately took up the vacated position at the edge of the landing and watched

Morgan and Alyssa glide down the steps. Diana took several shallow breaths attempting to master her nerves.

Derek possessively tucked her fingers in the crook of his arm while they waited to make their grand entrance. Diana could hear the low murmur of excitement among the guests as everyone began to focus their attention on them.

"We certainly are the main attraction this evening," Derek whispered, leaning close to Diana.

"Aptly put, my lord," Diana countered, the frozen smile never leaving her face. "It does seem as though every person in the room is gawking at us."

"The Earl of Harrowby, and his bride, Lady Diana," the butler shouted.

Derek held Diana atop the landing for a full minute, affording everyone a good long look at his countess. He stared nonchalantly down at the throng of elegantly dressed people as they looked up, scrutinizing him and his new bride. Then Derek and Diana leisurely descended.

Morgan, Alyssa, Tristan, Caroline, and the dowager duchess all rushed forward and Derek and Diana were quickly surrounded by a mob of curious well-wishers. After a time, Derek politely broke away from the crowd, steering Diana on a slow tour of the enormous room.

As they strolled, Derek occasionally introduced her to a select few and offered a congenial greeting to others. By the time they completed the circuit around the ballroom, Diana felt the color rising in her cheeks. She had never before been subjected to such intense scrutiny.

Her nerves were no longer stretched to the breaking point, and she felt surprisingly calm beneath the open appraisals of the men and the chilling stares of the women. She was, in fact, too much in awe of her husband's social graces to be concerned about her own nerves. Derek handled the openly curious members of the *ton* with the ease and skill of a well-seasoned diplomat. It was an aspect of his character she had not seen before, and it intrigued her.

The musicians struck up the first waltz of the evening, and Derek whirled her into his arms and joined in the dance, guiding her expertly across the polished floor, in perfect time to the beautiful music.

He held her improperly close to his lean body, but Diana was so enjoying the comfort and strength of his embrace that she chose to ignore the matrons raising their eyebrows. Sighing contentedly, Diana rested her head against his broad, muscular shoulder and allowed the lovely music to soothe and relax her.

Diana gazed lazily up at her husband, meeting his twinkling blue eyes. He looked devastatingly handsome in his starkly elegant black-and-white evening clothes. He was by far the most attractive man in the room. And he belonged to her. Diana could hardly believe her good fortune.

"Thank goodness, you know how to waltz," Derek said softly into her ear. "I was so anxious to avoid the crush I thoughtlessly forgot to ask you before we began the dance."

"I have a feeling it really would not matter if I knew the steps or not," she told him with an impish smile. "You guide me so expertly about the floor, all I really need to do is follow your lead. Truly, my lord, you dance divinely."

"For God's sakes, don't let Morgan or Tristan hear you say something like that." Derek groaned, rolling his eyes heavenward. "They shall derive endless amusement by parroting that remark to me at every opportunity."

Diana responded by tugging lightly on the soft, brown curls that hung over the collar of his white cravat and they both laughed. His broad smile quickly vanished, however, when he looked down at her.

"When I hold you this close, I can easily see down the front of your dress!" he exclaimed with ill humor. "For God's sake woman, I can practically see your nipples."

"If it upsets you so much, Derek, you shouldn't be looking down my dress."

Derek nearly missed a step at her flippant response. "Trust me, Diana," Derek muttered. "You won't be acting so coy if one of the more aggressive rakes begins making suggestive remarks to you."

Diana was not alarmed. "You are here to protect me, Derek," she replied mildly. "Besides, I am newly married. How could any man have the gall to approach me with an indecent remark?"

"The very fact that you are newly married makes you such an appealing target," Derek said patiently, trying desperately to take his wife's advice and not look down the front of her gown. He failed. Her fair, unblemished skin glowed creamy white under the brilliant candlelight. He swallowed hard and tried to concentrate on the steps of the dance. "You represent a true challenge to the more jaded rakes in attendance, Diana. I imagine the wager book at White's will be filled tonight with countless bets on when you shall take your first lover and who that lucky fellow shall be."

Diana cast him a skeptical look. "You forget, Derek, ours is a love match. Anyway, it doesn't matter what ridiculous wagers are made. There is only one man in this room who has the power to entice me into his bed. And he is holding me in his arms this very minute," Diana whispered seductively.

Derek favored her with a positively lecherous grin that brought a sparkling giggle to Diana's lips. When the last notes of the waltz were played, he led her from the dance floor toward a small alcove. Once there, he settled her comfortably on an empty red velvet chair, between the dowager duchess and Alyssa.

As soon as Diana sat down, she was immediately besieged by a dozen eager young admirers. They begged for an introduction, pleaded for the pleasure of a dance, and even vied for the honor of procuring a glass of lemonade to quench her thirst.

Diana was truly overwhelmed. The dowager duchess was smugly pleased over Diana's triumph while Alyssa seemed amused. Derek rudely glowered at all of the eager bucks, but only a handful were chased away by his scowls.

"Lady Diana has promised this set to me, gentlemen," Morgan informed them all in a cool voice.

Grateful for his interceding, Diana accepted the duke's outstretched hand and rose to her feet. She cast her group of admirers a hapless smile and left.

The evening progressed on much the same note. Diana only accepted an invitation to dance after her husband gave his silent nod of approval. With the exception of Morgan and Tristan, her partners were, by and large, men near in age to the dowager duchess, but Diana didn't mind. Surprisingly, she was having a wonderful time. This was her first ball and Lady Harrington's ballroom looked spectacular, with its glittering chandeliers, fanciful decorations of flowers and ribbons, crush of sophisticated, elegantly dressed people, and beautiful music.

"I know you are merely being protective of her, Derek," the dowager duchess said as Lord Harrington led Diana out onto the dance floor. "But I don't believe Diana has danced with anyone under the age of sixty all evening."

"Nonsense, Aunt Katherine," Derek replied baldly. "She has danced both waltzes with me and a set with Morgan and Tris."

The dowager duchess tapped her fan lightly on Derek's wrist. "That is not what I mean and you know it, young man," she said. "Everyone is beginning to comment on how possessive you are. It looks as though you don't trust your own wife, Derek. For heaven's sake, just choose one of the younger bucks to partner Diana in a country dance."

And thus, as the next tune began, Diana found herself being led out on the floor by George Rotherby.

"It is truly *marvelous* to see you again, countess," Rotherby gushed. "I could barely believe my good fortune when the earl suggested I partner you for this quadrille."

Diana smiled pleasantly at Rotherby and gracefully took hold of his outstretched arm. As they strolled out to the dance floor, she could not help but compare the obvious strength and masculinity of her husband to the quaint, effeminate manner of George Rotherby.

Tonight, Mr. Rotherby was dressed in a scarlet velvet evening jacket and a vividly patterned waistcoat of gold-and-scarlet brocade. The starch of his cream-colored cravat and collar points were so long and stiff his head was kept firmly facing straight ahead. As the dance began, he executed a faultless bow and Diana wondered how he managed it.

There was not much opportunity for conversation during the spirited dance, but the small spurts of conversation Rotherby engaged Diana in were centered primarily around clothing. His, hers, and the ensembles of various individuals as they came into view were each critically commented on. Mr. Rotherby had very definite opinions on styles, colors, and fabrics, and he was eager to express them.

Although there was very little touching involved in the dance, Diana was surprised when their hands met. She found the strength of Rotherby's fingers in direct contrast with the wiry thinness of his body and the foppish manner of his demeanor.

When the dance ended, Diana and Rotherby were on the far side of the ballroom. They had just begun making their way across the polished floor when a tall, broad-shouldered man stepped deliberately in front of them. Startled, Diana looked up to find a dramatically good-looking man with coal-black hair and even darker black eyes staring intently down at her.

"Introduce us, Rotherby," the stranger said.

"Lord Hampton," Rotherby said, clearly intimated by the request. "I'm not really sure—"

"I am Hampton," the stranger said silkily, ignoring the flustered Rotherby. "Forgive me for introducing myself, but I have been most anxious to meet you, Lady Diana."

"Really?" Diana replied coolly, hoping to put him off. "Well, now you have been granted your wish. Good evening, Lord Hampton."

Hampton laughed and moved in closer. "Meeting you was only a small part of my desire, Lady Diana." He gave her a sleepy, seductive smile. "Dance with me," he whispered softly.

For an instant Diana swayed unconsciously

toward Lord Hampton, hypnotized by the dark liquid pools of his eyes. His stare was provocative, the sensual power of his presence nearly overwhelming. Regaining her wits, Diana blinked several times and forced herself to look away from him. She could almost feel the danger lurking beneath his polished charm.

Not waiting for her acquiescence, Hampton placed his hand possessively on her arm. When he felt Diana's resistance, he said, "Of course if you prefer to forgo our dance, I would be delighted to show you the conservatory."

"Oh, dear!" Rotherby exclaimed in genuine distress. He made a move to grab Diana's other arm, but Hampton cast him a savage look. Rotherby visibly withered under the stare, and in the blink of an eye, he faded into the crowd. Hampton returned his dark gaze to Diana.

Several couples had taken their positions around them and were waiting for the music to begin. Diana knew she was neatly trapped. The last thing she wanted to do was draw attention to herself, and she was astute enough to realize Hampton would not relinquish his hold on her without a struggle. With perceptible effort Diana kept her voice calm and ordinary. "I will dance with you, my lord," she said finally.

"Splendid," Hampton replied, and he swept Diana regally into his strong arms.

Too late she realized the dance was a waltz. She closed her eyes momentarily, hoping the dance would be of short duration. When she opened them again, Lord Hampton was staring down at her. She stubbornly refused to meet his eyes.

"You are a very beautiful woman, Diana, but I suspect you are already aware of your unique charm."

Hampton's gaze lingered for several minutes on the glittering diamonds around her throat, then dropped lower.

Diana was not really surprised at his bold appraisal. She had sensed he was a dangerous man the moment she'd met him. His actions were merely proving her instincts correct.

"Enjoying the view, my lord?" Diana asked with bitter sarcasm. She felt her temper rising, but she was determined to put this rakish devil in his place.

"The view is extraordinary," Hampton murmured. "Your skin is flawless, Diana. And your breasts, why, your breasts are truly glorious. I think you will prove to be one lover who will not easily bore me."

His shocking statement caused her to stop dead in her tracks. Hampton tried to swing her around, but her feet held firm. It was one thing to coyly flirt and quite another to make such a personal, suggestive remark. A slow burning rage took possession of her.

"You, my lord, are a pig," she said in a clear, strong voice, pulling herself out of his grasp. "And if you ever dare to so much as speak to me again, Lord Hampton, I shall take great pleasure in slapping your conceited, arrogant face."

Turning swiftly on her heel, Diana stalked off, leaving Hampton standing alone in the mist of the dancing couples.

Diana made her way through the crowd without further incident and took a seat next to Caroline. None of the men were anywhere in sight and Diana was grateful. She was certain the agitation she felt was evident on her face and she had no wish to relate the incident to anyone, especially Derek.

"Were you just dancing with Lord Hampton?" Caroline asked. At Diana's curt nod, Caroline said,

Adrienne Basso

"You had best be careful around him, Diana. Hampton's the most notorious rake in London and probably the most dangerous."

"I don't doubt it," Diana said sincerely, feeling relieved she had escaped him.

"It really is a pity his striking good looks hide such a ruthless and dark soul," Caroline said as she viciously fanned herself.

Diana shuddered involuntarily and glanced over at her friend. She momentarily forgot her ire over Lord Hampton when she saw Caroline's ashen features. "Are you feeling unwell, Caroline?"

"I am feeling rather warm," Caroline said breathlessly. She continued to rapidly move her ivory fan.

Diana anxiously searched the crowded room. Tristan danced past them holding Alyssa in his arms. Morgan next whirled by with the dowager duchess, who was smiling with genuine delight while she danced with her eldest grandson. Finally, Diana saw Derek.

He was engaged in earnest conversation with several individuals, but he lifted his head the moment Diana fixed her stare on him. Derek quickly excused himself from the group and strode purposefully toward her.

"Caroline needs some fresh air," Diana said the moment he reached them.

"It would be my pleasure, ladies" Derek said, gallantly offering them each an arm. He led the way, and they pushed passed the crowds milling about the French doors and stepped out into the clear starry night.

"I just had to get away for a few minutes." Caroline sighed, breathing in great gulps of air. "It was so stuffy my head was spinning."

They decided to walk along the outer balcony and

enjoy the warm breeze. They conversed pleasantly until Caroline suddenly clutched her middle in extreme distress.

"I think I am going to be sick!" she exclaimed in true horror. Turning her head aside, she gripped the wrought-iron balustrade for support, leaned far over the railing, and threw up.

Derek was completely alarmed, but Diana firmly held Caroline by the waist and waited until she was finished. Keeping her face averted, Caroline whispered to Diana, "I am so embarrassed. Please send Derek away."

Diana instantly turned to her bewildered and worried husband. "Please go find Tristan," she said. "Caroline needs to go home at once."

Derek hesitated a few moments, not wanting to leave the women alone in this secluded section of the balcony. He quickly lost his reluctance, however, when Caroline groaned loudly, thrust her head back over the railing, and began retching again. He muttered a few words about returning as soon as possible and left to search for Tristan.

Diana fumbled in the pocket of her gown for a handkerchief and wiped Caroline's damp brow. Caroline accepted her assistance, then began weeping.

"I feel like the veriest fool, Diana," Caroline said, sobbing. "All I have done for months and months is complain about not being able to conceive a child. How desperately I longed for a baby! And now that my greatest wish has finally come true, I am a total disaster."

"Oh, Caroline, you are not a disaster," Diana said soothingly.

"But I am, Diana," Caroline said with a sniff. "Just look at me. I look awful. My complexion is pale and sallow. I feel light-headed and dizzy for a good part of the day, and I start weeping at the drop of a hat. And now, in the middle of this lovely ball, I have gotten violently ill in Lady Harrington's shrubbery. It is pitiful."

"It isn't pitiful."

"Oh, it is so. You are just trying to be kind." Caroline wiped her face with the handkerchief. "I certainly never suspected having a baby was going to involve all of this, Diana. I feel totally unprepared."

"You are going to be fine, Caroline. The symptoms you have just described are all normal. You must not worry so much. The nausea and dizziness will pass after a time, and you still have many months to prepare yourself for motherhood." Deliberately changing the subject, Diana asked, "Have you told Tristan yet?"

Caroline smiled slightly. "No. I just had to be certain I truly was pregnant before I mentioned it to Tris. I couldn't bear his disappointment if I were wrong."

"I think it is safe to inform him, Caroline," Diana said, smiling. "You know he will be thrilled with the news. And it is important for you to discuss these fears and concerns with someone. Who better than Tristan?"

"Who better than Tristan for what?" a familiar voice said.

"Tris!" Caroline's voice rang out with relief as she embraced her husband.

"Did Derek find you?" Diana asked.

"No," Tristan said, his arms automatically encircling his wife. "I finished my dance with Alyssa and came searching for Caroline. Lord Hampton said he noticed Caroline strolling on the balcony with you and Derek. Is everything all right?"

"Yes," Caroline said. "Everything is fine. I do feel rather tired, Tris. I should like to go home."

"Of course, sweetheart. I shall make our excuses to Lord and Lady Harrington." Tristan tried to break away, but his wife refused to relinquish her tight hold on his waist. "We rode to the ball with Morgan, so I will have to take his carriage and driver. I'll send the coach back for Morgan, Alyssa, and Grandmother later. Grandmother will be riding home with them since she is staying at their London house. I know my brother was ready to make his departure hours ago, but Alyssa and Grandmother are enjoying themselves too much. He will just have to wait until they are ready to leave."

Caroline nodded in agreement, but even in the dim outdoor lighting, Diana noticed the absence of color in her face. She was afraid Caroline was going to start retching again and then become completely distraught over her queasy stomach.

"I shall be happy to explain about the coach to Morgan, as well as make your excuses to Lord and Lady Harrington, Tris," Diana said. "I think it is best that you take Caroline home right away. She really isn't feeling well."

Tristan was immediately solicitous of his wife. "You are right, Diana. She is very pale." Tenderly he brushed back an errant wisp of hair from Caroline's forehead. Then he turned his attention to Diana.

"I don't want you staying out here alone, Diana. Promise me you will return immediately to the ballroom," Tristan said, sweeping his wife up into his arms. Caroline protested weakly that she could walk, but he ignored her and she clasped her hands around his neck.

"I shall go back inside now, Tris," Diana said. "I will call on you tomorrow afternoon, Caroline."

With a small wave, the pair disappeared into the darkness, Tristan electing to carry his wife around the outside balcony rather than through the crowded ballroom. Diana took a last breath of clean air and turned to leave. The moment she took a small step forward, a large gray shadow blocked her path. Alarmed, she looked up, but the figure remained in the shadows, and in the darkness of the night, she could not discern the features of the person standing before her.

"Leaving so soon, Countess," the stranger said in a low voice. "Now that I have finally succeeded in getting you alone, I was so hoping we could have a long, private conversation. It is vastly overdue."

Diana felt a chill ride up her spine. "You have me at a disadvantage, sir. Knowing my name when I am unaware of yours," she said, forcing a calmness into her voice she did not feel.

"I prefer to keep it that way, Countess," the stranger insisted. "For your safety, as well as my own."

"And I prefer not to have conversations with mysterious strangers," Diana said haughtily in her best imitation of the dowager duchess. "If you will kindly excuse me, sir." Shaken, but determined, she took a step forward. The stranger again blocked her way, but still remained in the darkness.

"I regret that I cannot excuse you, Countess," the stranger said. "I have no wish for our remarks to be overheard nor I suspect, will you."

"That is not my concern," Diana said, trying yet again to move past the man. She was in a relatively secluded section of the balcony and was uncertain if she could scream loud enough to bring attention to herself if necessary. Thus far, the man had made no threatening gestures toward her, but his detaining her, along with his refusal to reveal his identity, bespoke of the possible danger.

Diana strained her eyes in the darkness to see him, but could only briefly make out his silhouette and not his facial features. Her heart began to beat more rapidly in her chest.

"I often told Giles you appeared to be a woman of more intelligence than he credited you with," the man said in a silky voice. "Please don't do anything foolish to belie my confidence in you, Lady Diana."

Diana gasped at the mention of Giles. "Who are you?" she whispered in horror.

"Ah, I see I have finally succeeded in capturing your attention, Countess," the stranger said mockingly. "Have you changed your mind about leaving?"

Despite the dryness of her mouth and the thudding of her heart, Diana was able to keep her voice steady when she asked, "What do you want of me?"

"Very direct and to the point. I like that in a person, especially in a woman. It is such a rare quality. Giles was a fool to prefer Henriette to you. But I digress." Diana could not be sure, but she thought the man smiled in the darkness. "Giles stole something from me of extreme importance. And I want it back. Unfortunately, he met with his rather tragic and untimely death before he was able to reveal precisely where he was keeping my property."

Diana lifted her hand in confusion. "What does this have to do with me?"

"The item in question is of a sensitive nature. I am certain it is hidden somewhere in the London house you are now occupying. I expect you to find my property, Lady Diana, and return it to me."

In spite of the absurdity of the situation, Diana's curiosity was piqued. "What exactly is this item?"

"It is a small, leather-bound book containing the names of various members of the peerage. I assure you it has little value to anyone but myself."

"It sounds as if it might have great value, sir, if you are so very anxious to retrieve it," Diana said, feeling a bit less anxious. "Why should I assist you in finding this book?"

"Because I have in my possession a page from the church register from St. Michael's in Chippenham. This particular page verifies the marriage of Giles Rutledge, Earl of Harrowby, to one Diana Crawford. It is dated several months prior to the earl's marriage to Henriette. Now that Giles is dead, the charge of bigamy no longer applies, but I strongly suspect you would prefer this marriage not be made public. If you don't cooperate with me, I shall be forced to send the evidence of your previous marriage to the newspapers. British society feeds on scandals such as this one. I am sure the *Times* readership will find yours a fascinating story."

Diana felt the knot in her stomach tighten. This man knew everything. Her mind raced ahead, trying to formulate some sort of response. Then like a bolt of lightning, it hit her.

"Jonathan Marlow." Diana was so surprised by the revelation, she did not realize she had spoken aloud until she heard Marlow's voice.

"Ah, so you have guessed my secret, Lady Diana." Marlow clicked his tongue in admiration. "I am pleased. It proves to me what a very clever young woman you really are. Clever enough to locate what I want."

"If you know as much as you claim to about me, Mr. Marlow, then you are certainly aware I have no knowledge of where Giles kept any of his personal papers."

"Yes, it was rather shocking the way your husband treated you, Lady Diana." Marlow almost sounded sympathetic. "I confess, I was a party to some of his more lucrative transactions involving your inheritance. However in this case, it should not be too difficult for you to find my property. You are currently living in the house."

"And if I refuse?"

"That would be unnecessarily foolish. Make no mistake, Lady Diana. I will make your marriage to Giles public knowledge."

Diana did not doubt his intentions. She squinted in the darkness, hoping to catch a glimpse of his features. Even though she had correctly guessed his identity, Marlow still remained in the shadows. She could easily meet him again in the light of day and not know him.

"Despite what you have said, Mr. Marlow, I know this book must be of extreme value. If I find it for you, what will you give me for it?"

Marlow laughed. "You sound almost eager, Countess. I propose we make a fair exchange. You find the book for me, and I will give the church register page to you."

Diana nodded her head in agreement. She had no idea what she would do if she was able to locate this mysterious book, but she was not about to infuriate Marlow by refusing him outright. For now, it was best to agree to his demands and remove herself from his secluded company.

"How shall I contact you when I find your property?"

"There will be no need for that, Lady Diana. I shall be in touch with you."

"All right." Diana stepped forward, hoping he would let her pass since their business was concluded.

"Two days."

"I beg your pardon?"

"You have two days to find the book, Countess. And I must insist you not tell you husband about our little arrangement."

"If you wish."

"I have kept a close eye on you, Lady Diana, from the moment you set foot in London. The shots fired at you in St. James's Park were intended to instill doubts about the earl, and the disastrous fire at Snowshill Manor was necessary to assure your return to London. But I sent your crushed bonnet to Ashton's house to convince you of the vast network of people I command. If you try to cross me, Countess, I shall know of it. And if your husband interferes in any way, I will have him killed."

Chapter Twenty-four

Diana had no clear recollection of returning to the ballroom. It was odd, but after she had escaped from Marlow's menacing presence, she felt trapped and helpless. Derek was across the room, still searching for the already departed Tristan, and she suppressed an almost overwhelming desire to rush to him. It was all she could do not to burst into sobs. She felt a flood of fierce protectiveness toward Derek, sensing Jonathan Marlow also returned to the ballroom and was most likely observing them both at this very moment.

Only the knowledge that Marlow could be watching prevented Diana from running to her husband's side. Derek would immediately notice her agitation, and she was too frightened and unsteady not to tell him what had just occurred. She did not doubt for a moment Marlow's intent or his ability to carry out his threat to kill Derek, if she informed her husband of her distressing meeting.

No. She wouldn't tell Derek. Not yet. That discussion could only take place in absolute privacy. Reluctantly, Diana tore her eyes away from her husband. Schooling her features into a bland expression, she rejoined the dowager duchess in their corner of the ballroom.

Unfortunately, the older woman was not alone. Hovering next to her was Lord Bennington, Henriette's older brother.

"Lord Bennington informs me you are already acquainted," the dowager duchess said, as Diana sat down.

"We have met," Diana said noncommittally. She could hardly forget the chance meeting with Henriette's brother in Chippenham only a few days before.

"I am flattered you remembered me, Lady Diana," Lord Bennington replied with a smug grin. "I do hope you will be free for a dance."

"Perhaps later," Diana said, and Lord Bennington settled himself on an unoccupied chair and stared rather boldly at Diana.

She sighed loudly and attempted to ignore him. He was the least of her problems. The enjoyment she'd experienced at the start of the evening was gone. She sat silently next to the dowager duchess while the older woman engaged in idle chatter with Lord Bennington. Diana felt skittish and preoccupied as she kept a vigilant watch on Derek's every move, her eyes uncontrollably drawn to her husband's broad, muscular shoulders.

"I assume Tristan was successful in locating Caroline?"

Diana jumped guiltily when the dowager duchess

spoke to her. She was so absorbed in her worries over Derek's safety she had forgotten the promise she'd made to Tristan to explain their early departure to the members of his family and their host.

"I am sorry. I forgot to tell you," Diana muttered hastily. "Caroline was not feeling well, so Tristan decided to take her home. I told him I would make their excuses to Lord and Lady Harrington."

"Poor Caroline," the dowager duchess said, a hint of worry evident in her voice. "I hope it is nothing serious."

"I do not believe Caroline's illness is serious," Diana said distractedly.

The dowager duchess leaned closer to Diana and whispered gently in her ear, "Has anything happened to distress you, my dear?"

Diana's eyes flew wide open in alarm. "No," she said vehemently. "No, of course not, everything is fine."

The dowager duchess was not convinced, but she dropped the matter. She did note, however, the unconscious wringing of Diana's hands, which ceased the moment Derek's eyes met hers and he began crossing the room toward them.

Derek's physical presence calmed Diana, but obviously made Lord Bennington uncomfortable because he quickly took his leave.

"Has Caroline recovered?" Derek asked.

"She is feeling a little better," Diana said evenly, pleased to feel her breathing finally begin to slow down. "Tristan has taken her home."

"Good. Perhaps we can take our leave also?"

"No!" Diana said desperately. Both the dowager duchess and the earl stared at her. "I should like to stay until supper is served, Derek. Everyone has been talking all evening about the fabulous table

Lady Harrington sets. And her new French chef is touted as a culinary genius of unequaled skill. We certainly would not want to miss this meal."

Diana knew she must sound like a half-wit, babbling on about the soon-to-be-served supper, but she could not stop herself. Terrifying images of Derek broken and bleeding filled her mind. At all costs she wanted to avoid a hasty retreat, thinking Marlow would suspect her intentions to inform the earl of his demands.

Derek reluctantly consented to his wife's wishes, but sitting next to Diana during the sumptuous meal, he noticed her thoughts were anywhere but on the food. She spoke very little and ate even less. Mostly, Diana pushed the food around her plate in an abstract, brooding manner.

Derek waited patiently for another hour before insisting they leave. The dowager duchess, Morgan, and Alyssa also decided to depart, and after amiable good-byes were exchanged, the group split up for the journey to their respective homes. Derek was anxious to question his wife in the seclusion of their carriage, but the streets were not crowded at this hour of the night, and they quickly reached their residence.

Once inside the house, Derek suggested they adjourn to the drawing room for a drink. Diana declined the offer of a brandy, but followed him dutifully into the drawing room. He poured himself a generous portion of the fragrant amber liquid and waited with quiet calm for his wife to tell him what was bothering her.

Diana stood in front of the large fireplace, the crackling glow of the embers heating her already warm skin. Now that the moment was at hand, she felt her courage begin to falter. She had been so preoccupied with her fears for Derek's safety she failed to take into account her husband's occasionally volatile temper. She had already provoked him once this evening, albeit unintentionally, with her low-cut evening gown. That incident would surly pale in comparison to the news she would soon impart.

She observed Derek idly swirling the fine French brandy in his glass. She offered up a silent prayer, hoping Derek would find the strength to control his anger when she related her conversation with Jonathan Marlow. Mustering her courage, she plunged ahead.

"I met Jonathan Marlow this evening." Her voice was low and soft. She did not wait for Derek's reaction as she quickly continued. "He knows everything about me, including all the sordid details of my marriage to Giles."

"Jonathan Marlow! What are you talking about, Diana? Are you saying Marlow was at the ball this evening?" Derek spoke to her in a tight, unnaturally calm voice. Diana did not take that as a good sign.

"Please don't be angry with me, Derek," she whispered. "I honestly don't think I could bear it."

Her eyes were luminous in her pale face, and Derek could feel her anxiety. Her obvious distress aided him in keeping a tight rein on his explosive anger. Marlow with Diana—it was nearly unthinkable. Derek slapped down his brandy snifter, fearing the increasing pressure of his grip would shatter the fragile glass. He took a deep breath, swearing colorfully underneath it, and turned to confront his wife.

"Why did you not tell me this sooner, Diana?" Derek asked slowly, trying valiantly to maintain his self-control.

"Marlow threatened to kill you Derek, if I told you about my meeting him."

Derek scowled, not the least bit intimidated by the threat. "I am not all that easy to dispose of, madam." Derek's scowl turned into a questioning frown. "Do you think I am incapable of defending myself, Diana?"

In spite of her distress, Diana smiled. Derek sounded almost insulted. She stared intently at her husband, the man she loved with every fiber of her being, and her fears began to slowly diminish. Even at this distance she could feel the controlled strength in his broad, powerful frame. The directness of his piercing blue eyes bespoke his intelligence. Derek was clearly a formidable opponent, a man not easily bested in a fight, no matter how unfairly challenged.

"Marlow is not an honorable adversary, Derek," Diana said softly.

"I suspect Marlow is indeed a man devoid of honor. That is why he is so very dangerous," Derek said very slowly. "He could have hurt you, my love. And I would have been unaware of it and unable to protect you." His eyes were filled with pain. "I could never live with myself, Diana, knowing I had failed to keep you safe."

"Oh, God, Derek!" The sight of his obvious pain caused her to lose her fortitude completely. She flew across the room, her stomach in tight knots. Derek caught her up in his arms, and she clutched him tightly around the neck and buried her face in his broad shoulder.

"It's been Marlow from the very beginning, Derek. He hired the men who shot at us in the park and he is responsible for burning down Snowshill Manor. He even sent my crushed black bonnet to Tris and

Caroline's so I would know he was watching me. He seems to be everywhere, know everything. He makes me feel so helpless, so powerless. Marlow is toying with me, Derek, and enjoying himself while he does it."

"He will never harm you, my love," Derek said with determination. "Not while there is a breath within my body."

His words comforted her. But there was more to tell him. "I believe Marlow may have been responsible for Giles's death," Diana whispered in quiet horror.

"I have long suspected Marlow's involvement in Giles's murder," Derek said. "Something must have happened between the two men for Marlow to suddenly turn against Giles. Apparently they had several profitable and illegal business dealings together until something went wrong." Derek's face was shadowed. "Were you able to discover anything that might explain a feud between them?"

"Yes." Diana nodded her head enthusiastically. "Giles stole something from Marlow. A book. That is the reason Marlow contacted me this evening. He expects me to find and return this book to him."

Derek frowned in puzzlement. "What sort of book?"

Diana shrugged her shoulders. "I don't really know. He said I would know the book when I found it by the list of names written inside, some of them members of the *ton*. Marlow claims the book is of no value to anyone but himself."

Derek rubbed his chin thoughtfully. "I doubt this book is a social listing. It is most likely connected to some devious scheme of Marlow's—perhaps even a blackmail plot."

Diana gave an unladylike snort at her husband's

comments. "Oh, yes, Marlow harbors a proven talent for blackmail. He claims to have in his possession the missing church register page we sought in Chippenham—the page verifying my marriage to Giles. Marlow threatened to publicly disgrace us by sending the page to the newspapers for publication if I don't find this book of his and return it."

Derek's rigid expression softened slightly, and he gently smoothed back her hair. "You still have not explained how you met Marlow, Diana."

Diana pulled back out of his arms and gazed with trepidation into his brilliant blue eyes. "I did not exactly meet Marlow, Derek."

He slid his strong fingertips down the length of her arms and they came to rest on her hips. His big hands flexed carefully around her waist in a show of comfort and support.

"What happened, sweetheart?"

"As I said before, Derek, I did not formally meet Marlow. He waylaid me outside when I was alone on the balcony after Tristan and Caroline had departed. He seemed to materialize out of nowhere. He did not identify himself at first, and in the shadowy darkness I was unable to clearly see his face. When I attempted to leave, he blocked my path."

Derek's powerful grip on her waist tightened noticeably. "Did he touch you, Diana? Did he harm you in any way?"

"He did not harm me." Diana struggled and failed to release herself from her husband's crushing grip. "Derek, please, you are crushing the very breath from me."

"Sorry." He instantly relaxed his hands. "When I think of the danger you were in, it makes my head spin. If that bastard had hurt you—" Derek's voice, tight with fury, trailed off.

Diana leaned forward earnestly, hoping to reassure him. "Marlow will not harm me, Derek. I am too valuable to him, at least for the time being. He needs me to find this mysterious book of his."

Derek arched his brows in sudden understanding. "And he threatened to kill me if you did not comply with his demands?"

"Not precisely," Diana said. "He threatened to make public my marriage to Giles if I did not cooperate. He said he would kill you if I told you about meeting with him."

"Not a very likable chap, our Mr. Marlow." Derek's attempt at lightness eased a bit of the tension.

Diana made a noise that was half laugh, half groan. "He is a very unusual man. He actually seemed pleased when I deduced his identity. But what frightens me the most is that I never saw his face. He was very, very careful to make sure I did not get a clear view of his features. It forces me to conclude Jonathan Marlow might be someone who is already known to me, or perhaps someone I might have an opportunity to meet in the future. He obviously was a guest at the ball, so he is someone accepted in society, I presume under a different name."

"No wonder Mr. Marlow is so difficult to locate," Derek said in amazement. "He is leading a double life."

"Yet another charming facet of Marlow's character he shared with Giles," Diana murmured.

"Tell me, Diana, was there anything even remotely familiar about the man?"

Diana thought long and hard before answering. "Nothing," she replied, shaking her head in dismay. "I am ashamed to admit I could very well have spoken with him again before we left Lord and Lady

Harrington's party and not known it was he."

"This does put us at a decided disadvantage," Derek said.

"Marlow has allotted me two days to find his property." Diana looked searchingly into Derek's handsome face. "What are we going to do?"

There was a short pause while he pondered the best approach to combat their enemy. "I suspect we shall spend the next two days tearing this damn house apart, floorboard by floorboard if necessary, to find the book. After we discover exactly what it contains, we will know what Marlow is so anxious to retrieve. Once we have a better understanding of our adversary, I shall formulate a plan to effectively dispose of him." Tight-lipped, Derek gave Diana a meaningful stare. "Permanently."

The following morning Diana stood in the middle of the master bedchamber, trying to control her involuntary shivering and silently chastising herself. It is only a room, you ninny, she told herself. It has no magical powers over you. But it was Giles's room, a wicked voice within her said. His bedchamber. The room where he slept, he dressed, he lived. She shut her eyes tightly, trying to close out the sound of the voices and regain her equilibrium.

She was concentrating so hard she did not hear Derek enter the room. "Diana?"

She jerked her hand up over her mouth, effectively stifling the scream lodged in her throat. She turned and looked, terrified, toward the door.

Derek stood in the open doorway, his handsome face a combination of bewilderment and concern. "I am sorry, Diana," he said in a soothing voice. "I did not mean to startle you. Are you all right?"

She nodded her head viciously and responded in

a none-too-steady voice. "I am fine, Derek. You surprised me—that's all." She gave her husband a wan smile to prove her words. "I thought you were down in your study, talking with the investigator. Is the meeting over?"

"Yes." Derek strode across the room and stood before her. He reached down and clasped her trembling hands. "Are you cold, Diana? Your hands feel like ice."

Diana bit down hard on her lower lip, determined to overcome her anxiety. "I must confess I am a bit out of sorts," Diana admitted. Her eyes darted nervously about the bedchamber. "I know it is foolish, but this room reminds me so very much of Giles. It is most unsettling."

Derek glanced around the room. "I feel it too," he said. "I remember now it was the primary reason I decided not to occupy this chamber."

She relaxed visibly at her husband's remarks, comforted by his confession. If Derek reacted the same way she did, at least she knew she was not going crazy, she told herself with relief.

"I have already searched the other bedchamber on this floor, so I decided it was time to look in here," Diana said. "'Tis a reasonable assumption Giles would hide the book somewhere in his bedchamber."

Derek snorted. "You forget, Diana, my cousin was not a reasonable man. Besides, I already made a detailed search of this room when you first arrived, seeking evidence of your marriage to Giles. I found nothing."

Diana sighed, disappointed the bedchamber was yet another dead end, but relieved at having the excuse to leave. "Then there is no point in our searching again."

Once back in their bedchamber, Derek was pleased to note the color returning to Diana's face. His mouth curved up in an ironic grin when he remembered his wife's reasoning for impulsively giving this house to Henriette. Diana was right. They would never be comfortable living there.

"Tell me about your meeting this morning," Diana said.

Derek shrugged out of his forest-green jacket and loosened his stiffly tied cravat. Then he settled himself comfortably in a large, overstuffed chair near the lit fireplace. Casting his wife a decidedly lecherous glance, he patted his knees invitingly. "Come over here and sit with me, sweetheart. I shall tell you everything."

Diana smiled at him. Once she was situated in the his lap, he related his earlier conversation with Charles Ramsey, the Bow Street runner hired to investigate Giles's death.

"Ramsey has had limited success with the investigation," Derek said. "He was able to track down a man named John Wickers, who was at the scene of Giles's murder, but this individual is not able to provide any significant details about the murder itself."

"How did Ramsey locate Mr. Wickers?"

"Apparently, Wickers found Giles after he had been attacked. Wickers moved in on him, intending to relieve Giles of his purse and any other valuables he could find. Ramsey was able to trace Wickers through the pawnbroker who bought Giles's watch from Wickers."

"Isn't it possible Wickers killed Giles?"

"Precisely the question I put to Ramsey." He shifted his legs and pulled Diana closer to his chest. "Despite his rather sordid reputation as a pickpocket and a thief, Wickers is not considered a killer. He vehemently denies stabbing Giles, claiming he happened upon Giles after he had been knifed. Ramsey believes Wickers is telling the truth, and I am inclined to trust Ramsey's judgment in this matter."

Diana threaded her arms around his neck and sighed loudly. "Then we actually have learned nothing from Mr. Ramsey's investigation."

"No, there is an odd twist to the story," he said. "Although Giles was mortally wounded when Wickers discovered him, he was still alive and miraculously conscious for a few moments."

"What!"

"Giles even spoke to Wickers, yet his words make little sense."

"What did Giles say?"

"Wickers says it was all rather garbled and muddled, but he distinctly recalls Giles saying, 'Look to the foxes.'"

"Look to the foxes," Diana said slowly. "What in the world is that supposed to mean, Derek?"

He shook his head ruefully. "I haven't the foggiest notion. Ramsey thinks it might be a clue to the identity of Giles's murderer, yet I still believe Jonathan Marlow either hired someone to dispose of Giles or did so himself."

Diana snuggled closer to him. "Perhaps the fox is a reference to Marlow. A code name Giles used, or the name of a tavern or inn where he met with Marlow to conduct business, or even a clue to the name Marlow uses in society."

Derek shrugged. "Any or all of those explanations are quite plausible, Diana. But frankly, it is not my primary concern at this time. Our focus must be on Marlow and finding his black book. We only have a day and a half left."

"I know," Diana said quietly. "We still have a large portion of the house to search, but I am certain we will find it."

Derek smiled at the note of optimism in her voice. "I have given the entire staff the rest of the day off and instructed them to leave the house. Morgan and Tris will be here at one o'clock to help us search the servants quarters."

Diana's expression betrayed her dismay. "Is that absolutely necessary, Derek?"

"Yes," he said without hesitation. "The entire house must be searched, including the servants' floor."

"Giles could have hidden the book in the servants' quarters without their knowledge," Diana said.

"I am very aware of the fact," Derek said. "No matter what we discover, I promise I will not automatically accuse any of the staff of any wrongdoing until they have an opportunity to offer an explanation." Unless Dobbs proved to be in possession of the book, Derek said silently to himself. Then he would take great pleasure in dealing with the haughty butler swiftly and decisively.

"There is one thing we have learned with certainty," Diana said sadly. "Giles was capable of just about anything."

Chapter Twenty-five

The house was eerily silent as Derek, Diana, Morgan, and Tristan quickly, yet thoroughly, hunted through the servants' quarters.

"That was the last room," Tristan said in a discouraged voice as he stepped into the hallway to join the others. "Any luck?"

Everyone dejectedly grumbled their negative answers.

"What is next?" Morgan asked.

Derek paused a moment, scratching his head. "The kitchens. We have a few hours before everyone returns and we must complete our search of the servants' area today while they are gone. We can concentrate our efforts on the remaining rooms of the house tomorrow."

"Fine," Morgan said. "Tristan and I can begin in the pantry. Perhaps we will have greater success if we work in pairs."

The exhaustive search yielded nothing. The four of them probed numerous nooks and crannies, moved furniture around, and even pried up loose floorboards and bricks, but the result was always the same. Nothing was found.

"I must confess, I'm stumped," Morgan said.

He sprawled out on a drawing room chair and nodded his head slightly in thanks when Derek placed a glass of wine in his hand. Derek, Morgan, and Tristan were alone in the drawing room discussing tactics, while Diana was mucking about in the kitchen preparing tea for everyone.

"One thing is certain," Derek said with conviction. "I shall meet with Marlow in Diana's place, whether or not the book has been found."

"Of course," Tristan said immediately. "It would be to our advantage if we could locate that book, however. It might provide us with a better understanding of Marlow's motives."

"I am pleased to see you haven't forgotten the first rule of battle, Tris," Derek said with a slight smile. "Know thy enemy."

"Marlow certainly knows a lot about you and Diana," Morgan said. "What could possibly be in this mysterious book Marlow is so desperate to retrieve?"

Derek thoughtfully rested his chin on his clasped hands before saying, "I believe the book contains a record of Marlow's blackmailing activities. It would explain why Marlow kept only one copy of this book and why he told Diana she would recognize it by the names listed inside."

"Sounds plausible," Morgan said. "How the devil did Giles get his hands on this valuable book?"

"Hell, Marlow was probably blackmailing Giles," Derek answered ruefully. He moved in front of the fireplace and jabbed aggressively at the burning logs. "Lord knows Giles had enough secrets to entice the interest of a man of Marlow's character. We know Giles had other business dealings with Marlow, since Marlow admitted to Diana he aided Giles in selling some of her properties. Giles must have somehow stumbled upon Marlow's book and acting out of greed, or perhaps even self-preservation, stole the book. When Giles refused to return the book, Marlow either killed him or had him killed."

"But Marlow's plan backfired," Morgan said. "Apparently Giles died before Marlow was able to discover where the book was hidden. And now he has involved Diana in his search."

"Well, I plan to uninvolve Diana in the search and effectively destroy any future plans Marlow might be harboring that could threaten my wife," Derek said forcefully.

"What about this Ramsey fellow you hired, Derek?" Tristan asked. "Was he able to provide any critical information?"

Derek sighed with regret. "The shortened version of Mr. Ramsey's report reveals only that Giles uttered a cryptic and probably unconnected sentence before he died. The man who was in the process of robbing Giles at the time only remembers the phrase, 'Look to the foxes.'"

"What the devil does that mean?" Morgan asked.

Derek shook his head. "Your guess is as good as mine, Morgan. Diana thinks it might be a reference to Marlow, perhaps a clue to the name he uses in society, but we have no way of knowing."

The discussion came to an abrupt halt as Diana entered the room. Derek immediately sprang forward to relieve his wife of the heavily ladened silver tray she was awkwardly balancing in her arms.

"Thank you, Derek," Diana said breathlessly. "I did not realize it was such a long distance from here to the kitchens. The tray became heavier with each step. I almost dropped it twice in the foyer."

"You should have called for one of us to help you," Tristan said, filling his plate with several sandwiches.

"I did not want to disturb you," Diana said, pouring out the fragrant hot tea. "I suspected you would be discussing things you preferred I not hear."

Derek flushed guiltily under his wife's pointed glance. "It is not as though I wish to deliberately exclude you, Diana."

Diana's thoughtful brown eyes swept their faces. Tristan squirmed uncomfortably in his chair. Even Morgan would not directly meet her gaze. Diana tilted her head down to hide her smile.

"Of course you are not deliberately excluding me, Derek," Diana said, lifting her head. She stared at him with wide, innocent eyes.

Diana's ready agreement and open trust made Derek even more nervous. "Good Lord, Diana, don't tell me you expect to accompany me when I meet Marlow."

"Whatever would make you think such a thing?" she asked in a light voice. She smiled broadly at him as she held out a cup of hot tea toward him.

He was instantly suspicious. "You are being entirely too accommodating and reasonable," he said, snatching the cup from her hand.

"What a strange comment. Precisely what do you mean?"

"Yes, what do you mean?" Tristan said, biting into his second sandwich.

Derek shot his friend a withering look before addressing his wife. "I will deal with Marlow, Diana," he said in a commanding voice. He knew he sounded annoyingly superior, but it could not be helped. At all costs, Diana had to be protected. "This need not concern you."

"It already concerns me, Derek." Diana calmly sipped her tea. "Despite what you may be thinking, I am not foolish enough to want to take on Marlow myself," she said softly. "I gladly leave him to you." At Derek's triumphant smile, she quickly continued. "But I do take exception to being treated like a dim-witted child. I believe I have earned the right to be told of your plans. After all, I shall be left behind to worry about you."

Diana gazed expectantly at him, as did Morgan and Tristan. Derek smiled grimly, knowing he had been neatly outmaneuvered.

"I am certainly glad to know you are on my side," he said quietly. "I believe you can hold your own matching wits against Marlow, my dear. However, I would never allow you to be placed in such jeopardy. When Marlow contacts you, I shall finalize my plans." He bowed his head graciously. "And naturally I shall enlighten you."

"That is most considerate, Derek," Diana said, holding aloft a large platter of sandwiches she had made. "Now, gentlemen, is anyone else besides Tristan hungry?"

Derek and Diana spent the majority of the next day closeted together in various rooms of the house. They received several queer looks from the servants, but no one was bold enough to make a comment. Diana supposed the staff was becoming used to the eccentric behavior of the earl and his new bride. Their tireless searching was again an exercise in frustration. The mysterious book was not located.

Diana began to have serious doubts if Giles had ever possessed the book, but she knew Marlow would not be interested in hearing her opinion on the matter. He would demand results.

"It is still early, Derek. Do you think we should go out tonight?" She asked while they finished their dinner.

Derek frowned. "Was there some affair you specifically wished to attend, Diana?"

"Oh, no. But Marlow said he would contact me in two days to arrange a meeting. I haven't left the house since the ball. How will Marlow get a message to me if I don't appear in public?"

Derek grimaced. "I do not wish to make things any easier for Marlow, Diana. Truthfully, I would prefer it if he was unable to contact you. We could certainly use the extra time."

"For what?" Diana asked. "We have combed this house for two entire days and found nothing. I would prefer getting the whole mess over with as soon as possible."

Derek did not argue, but they did not go out that evening either. In the end, it made no difference. While Diana sat at her dressing table brushing her hair before retiring that night she noticed a folded note next to her hairpins. Her stomach felt decidedly queasy as she stared down at the bright white paper. With shaking fingers she picked up the offending note and quickly scanned it.

The King's Arms Tavern, on York Street. Ten o'clock, tomorrow morning. Come alone.

The note was unsigned, but there was hardly need for a signature. Diana knew very well the message was from Marlow. A small chill went through her. Somehow Marlow managed to invade her bedchamber, the most private and intimate part of the household, to deliver his message.

Derek came up silently behind her. He did not notice the small scrap of paper she clutched in her tightly closed fist. She saw his handsome reflection in the mirror and she relaxed when his strong fingers closed around her shoulders. He bent low, trailing a delicate line of soft kisses just below her ear. "Ready for bed?" His voice was deeply sensual.

Diana closed her eyes and leaned her head back. The urge to succumb to his seductive kisses was strong, yet she knew she must tell him about the note.

She turned in her chair to face her husband. The words she was struggling to speak were instantly forgotten as she took a full, long look at him. "You're naked," she said, feeling her cheeks flush.

Derek grinned broadly at her, and he lifted his hand, tracing with his finger the lines of her flushed cheekbones. "I always sleep naked, Diana. I thought you were becoming use to it by now."

Diana paused, unable to put her thoughts into words. It was one thing to cuddle naked against Derek's hard strength in their bed, but quite another to watch him wander casually about the room without his clothing. She did not think she would ever become used to that.

She swallowed hard. The sight of her husband's taut, sensual male body was having its usual devastating effect on her senses. Her breathing quickened and her pulses raced, and she felt the tingling desire deep in her belly. She longed to reach over and embrace his warm masculine form.

He leaned forward and began kissing her throat.

"Derek," she said weakly, holding up the fist containing the crumbled note.

"Mmm," he replied, his hand closing over her breast. Diana moved her head back so he could not kiss her lips and she waved her clenched fist at him.

Wordlessly, he reached for her hand and she relinquished her hold on the paper.

"Where was this?"

"On my dressing table."

"Bloody hell," he said softly. "That bastard must have one of the house servants working for him."

"I know. Only a member of our household could have placed the note there without drawing attention to himself," Diana said grimly. It pained her greatly to think one of the staff was disloyal to Derek. "What are you going to do?"

"Forget about it for now." He threw the note to the floor. Then he pulled Diana into his arms. "What am I going to do, my love?" he said hypnotically, sensually into her ear. "I am going to strip my beautiful wife of her clothing and carry her over to our bed, where I can hold her sweet, naked body in my arms. Then I am going to kiss her senseless and stroke and caress her until she is moist and burning hot and I can feel her body quiver with need. And then I will enter her warm sweetness. Fill her. Possess her. And I am going to feel her cling to me and listen to her moan and whimper for more as I drive her to mindless excitement. And when she is finally sated and totally relaxed, I am going to start all over again."

"Oh, Derek." Diana felt the flames of his words and the rigid trembling of his passion. She totally forgot about the note, about Marlow, about everything.

"There is one slight flaw in your plan my lord," she said as her body arched toward his tender stroking caresses.

"Problem?" Derek murmured, taking her nipple carefully between his teeth.

"I don't believe I can wait until you carry me all the way across the room to our bed," she said with a teasing growl. Reaching down, she glided her hand over his broad, naked chest and then lightly caressed the tip of his fully aroused manhood.

Derek groaned and thrust himself back against her hand. "Don't fret, my love. I am a man who has learned to appease his wife in all things." Laughing, he pulled her onto the soft carpeted floor.

Afterward, Derek held Diana in his arms, listening to her shifting restlessly in her sleep. Slumber eluded him. His mind was focused on the events of the upcoming morning. He assumed Marlow would have someone watching the house, but Derek needed to contact Tristan and Morgan. He decided to send a footman to bring Ramsey to the house to guard Diana. Since she would be left behind, she would need the extra protection the Bow Street runner could provide. Given the ease in which Marlow's note had been delivered, Derek felt justified in taking the extra precautions to guard his wife.

He did not doubt his own ability to effectively dispose of Marlow, but faint lingering doubts about Diana's safety haunted him. He loved and cherished his beautiful wife, and he was uneasy about leaving her. He knew if any harm came to her, he would probably kill Marlow with his bare hands.

Diana muttered something in her sleep and cuddled closer to him. He slid his leg lazily along hers until he felt her calm and relax. Vowing to keep her safe at all costs, he finally relaxed and fell asleep.

*   *   *

Diana awoke shortly after dawn, feeling heavy headed and uneasy. She sat up quickly, alone in the large four-poster bed. "Derek," she called out softly in the near darkness.

He appeared instantly at her side, and she noted with alarm he was already dressed. "You are leaving so early?"

"I am going to Tristan's house. He and Morgan must be told about the meeting with Marlow. I am also going to arrange for Ramsey to come to the house to stay with you while I am gone." Derek leaned over and kissed the top of her head. "Try to go back to sleep, sweetheart. I'll see you later."

"Don't forget you promised to tell me your plans, Derek," she said as he slipped quietly out the door.

Feeling restless and abandoned, Diana sank back against the pillows. She tried to take Derek's advice, but it was impossible to return to sleep. Giving up on that idea, she rose from the bed and leisurely dressed. She was waiting anxiously in the drawing room when Derek returned later with Morgan and Tristan by his side.

The men declined her polite offering of breakfast and immediately began an intense and occasionally heated discussion about how best to trap Marlow. When the final plan was agreed to, Diana was not sure she should have insisted on knowing all the details. It sounded far too dangerous.

"Is it really necessary for you to go yourselves?" she asked warily.

"We won't be alone," Derek said soothingly. "Over the past few years Tristan has found employment on his estate for several soldiers who served under our command during the war. They have agreed to help. We will be taking ten seasoned war veterans with us, all of whom are crack shots."

"You will take every precaution," she said, not knowing what else to say. She was feeling apprehensive and exceedingly powerless. "All of you."

"I can assure you, Diana," Morgan said, "none of us has any desire to get hurt."

Diana knew the duke spoke the truth, yet in spite of the apparent danger, she could see the men were excited about finally confronting their adversary. They seemed to actually be looking forward to the adventure.

"Ramsey is down in the kitchen eating his breakfast. He has been assigned the task of guarding you while I am gone, Diana," Derek said. "You will do precisely as he says. And stay inside the house until I return."

Diana nodded her head and watched with growing alarm as Derek loaded two pistols. He placed one in the breast pocket of his jacket and the other inside the waistband of his leather breeches. Diana glanced speculatively at Morgan and Tristan, wondering if they were equally well armed. She hoped so.

"Be on guard," she whispered softly to Derek. He nodded solemnly and gave her a hard, fast kiss of farewell.

Once alone, Diana nervously paced the drawing room floor for over an hour. Feeling tired, she sank down on the settee. Automatically her eyes scanned the room and came to rest on the large oil painting hanging over the fireplace.

She frowned in true annoyance as she stared at the likeness of Giles sitting triumphantly upon his horse, his face a mixture of pride and excitement while he displayed the bloody kill of the hunt. Diana turned her head away in disgust—of both the man and his obvious enjoyment of the blood sport. Killing a poor defenseless animal and then insisting the moment be forever captured on canvas—it was disgusting. The poor little fox looked so small and fragile. Little fox!

Diana whipped her head around and stared again at the picture. Yes, it was definitely a fox. Giles was holding a fox. Excited, she jumped up from the sofa and ran across the room.

Giles had uttered, "Look to the foxes," as he lay dying. Was it to this painting he was referring?

Diana intently examined the painting. Perhaps the clue was in the picture. Maybe she could recognize something in the background—a person, a landmark, anything that might reveal where the book was hidden.

Gingerly she traced her fingertips over the trees and falling leaves of the autumn countryside. Nothing looked familiar. In fact, just the opposite was true. The backdrop was merely a forest scene; there were no distinguishing features about it. It could have been any forest in England.

Disappointed, but not yet discouraged, she removed the painting from the wall. Even though both she and Derek had carefully searched this room, she almost expected to see a tiny wall safe hidden behind the painting. There was none.

Diana turned the painting over, carefully examining the back. There was nothing unusual about the paper backing protecting the picture. She burrowed her finger through an edge of the paper, gently tearing the lining away. She had ripped more than half of it off when a small black leather book dropped out and a sheet of paper floated slowly after it.

Diana almost screamed aloud in her exhilaration. She had found it! She had actually found Marlow's book! Eagerly she snatched up the book and quickly scanned the pages. As Marlow had told her there were lists of names, with various notations, numbers, and dates written by each entry. However, Marlow had been right. She could not make any sense of the entries.

She started running from the room, but stopped suddenly when she unintentionally stepped on the piece of paper. In all the excitement, she had completely forgotten about it. She picked it up, glancing down at it with uninterest. But the words Chippenham and Rutledge immediately grabbed her attention. Squinting hard, she read the page.

Diana gasped out loud in disbelief. She was holding the missing church register page validating her marriage to Giles. Derek had been correct all along. Giles must have stolen the page. Marlow had been bluffing when he'd said he'd it and threatened to send it to the newspapers as proof of her marriage.

Her temper flared at Marlow's deceit. What an odious man! She did not waste time indulging her feelings of outrage. She knew she must make arrangements for the book to be brought to Derek immediately. Tucking the book and the paper carefully in the deep pocket of her gown, she raced from the room to find Mr. Ramsey.

Diana got no farther than the front foyer when she was suddenly grabbed roughly from behind and pushed forward, her face nearly flattened against the wall. There was no one about—no servants, no security men. Just Diana and her unknown assailant. She felt panic setting in and her blood ran cold as an all-too-familiar voice hissed menacingly in her ear.

"Ah, so there you are, Lady Diana. I am afraid, if you don't take your leave soon, you shall be late for our meeting this morning."

Chapter Twenty-six

Diana shrank deeper into the corner of the coach trying to keep her seat while the vehicle tipped and swayed viciously. They were traveling at a rapid speed, convincing her they must have reached the outskirts of London. She also could no longer hear the bustling sounds of the crowded town streets.

Agitated, she wrinkled her nose at the bothersome scarf blindfolding her. The silken material had fallen down over her nostrils and it itched. She very much wanted to reach up and adjust the cloth, but she did not. Although she was fairly certain she was alone in the coach, Marlow had given strict orders not to touch the blindfold, and she did not dare disobey.

It was distressingly easy for Marlow to remove her, seemingly unnoticed, from the house. After surprising her in the foyer, he had boldly pushed her out the front door, down the steps, and into a waiting coach. She'd landed in a heap on the bottom of the carriage. Taking advantage of her momentary disorientation, Marlow had quickly tied a silk scarf around her eyes before she had so much as caught a glimpse of him. Once her eyes were securely covered, he'd slammed the carriage door shut and the vehicle had jolted forward.

Marlow's continuing precautions to conceal his identity led Diana to two conclusions: he was someone known to her and he did not intend to hurt her immediately since he continued to hide his identity. By the time the carriage stopped, nearly an hour after it had started, she had almost convinced herself Marlow truly meant her no great harm.

Her stomach turned over in nervous anticipation, however, when she heard the driver scramble down from the top of the box. Above all else, she told herself, she had to stay calm. Strong fingers gripped her arms tightly as they pulled her out of the coach. She stumbled, but was caught before she hit the ground.

Once standing, she took a deep breath and squared her shoulders. She was immediately nudged from behind and told to walk. The voice commanding her was not Marlow's, but that of another man, perhaps the driver. For a second, she panicked, thinking Marlow had not accompanied them out of town. "Mr. Marlow?" she asked softly.

"Have no fear, Countess, I have not abandoned you." Cool, strong fingers closed around her wrist. She choked, stifling her screams at the unexpected contact and willed herself to remain composed.

They entered a dwelling and Diana nearly tripped as she was pulled up a long staircase. After being shoved into a room, she winced when someone roughly pulled off her blindfold, tearing out strands of her hair in the process.

She blinked several times in rapid succession, allowing her eyes to become readjusted to the daylight. Then she turned with great curiosity to face Jonathan Marlow.

"Mr. Rotherby," Diana whispered in amazement. "What a surprise."

Rotherby laughed with genuine satisfaction. "Shall I comment on your wrinkled gown or your pale coloring this morning, Lady Diana," he mimicked in a high-pitched voice.

She simply stared at him. She could not believe the fawning dandy who had danced with her at Lady Harrington's ball, gossiping so enthusiastically about clothes and fashions, was the notorious Jonathan Marlow.

And what of Henriette? Was she too involved in this notorious deception? "Henriette?" She whispered softly.

"That stupid cow," Marlow sneered. "She knows nothing of this. Her friendship with Rotherby provided me a legitimate excuse to visit with Giles during their marriage."

Diana shivered at the coldness of Marlow's deep voice. Yet she had to credit him: Marlow had certainly perfected an effective disguise. No one would possibly make the connection. Even Derek had insisted she dance with Rotherby at the ball. But now that Marlow revealed himself to her, did he mean to kill her? Her stomach turned at the thought.

"Why have you brought me here, Mr. Mar—"

"You may address me as Marlow, Countess," he said with a broad grin. " 'Tis, after all, my true name."

"Why have you brought me here?" She repeated. She struggled to keep her voice steady. "Your note

345

instructed me to meet you at the King's Arms Tavern."

Marlow's eyes were feverishly bright as he answered. "I also told you not to tell your husband about meeting me at the ball, Countess, yet I knew even before you left the ball that evening you would tell the earl."

"But I—" she said, trying to deny his accusations.

Marlow waved his hand in annoyance. "Please don't insult my intelligence by lying to me, Lady Diana. Any fool can see how much you love your husband. And Rutledge loves you. Couples such as you rarely keep secrets from one another."

"Why did you abduct me?"

"Your husband has a rather fierce reputation for protecting what is his. I can control him easier if you are in my custody. Besides, if any of that nonsense about your being an Ashton cousin is true, I am also up against Tristan and Morgan Ashton, two men with dangerous reputations. With you under my roof, I better my odds."

"What do you want?" Diana whispered with dread, fearing she knew the answer.

He sneered at her, a most unpleasant smile. "I believe we have already discussed this at great length. I want the property Giles stole from me."

"Ah, yes, the famous black book," she said, feeling its outline in the pocket of her gown. She was certain that, as long as she kept the book away from Marlow, she would remain unharmed. "The earl and I found it fascinating reading. I am sure Lord Atherton and Sir Benning are relieved to have the book out of your hands."

Marlow's eyes brightened noticeably at her mentioning two of the names from the book. "I knew you would find it," he said triumphantly. "Where is it?"

"My husband took the book to the King's Arms Tavern, as you requested," she said, terrified he might decide to search her. If Marlow found the book, he would probably kill her.

"I thought as much." Marlow snorted. "I am sure he also devised a brilliant plan to capture me. But I have rather neatly outwitted him, haven't I, Lady Diana? It is too bad that, after I recover my property, I shall have to get rid of you both. Not a fitting reward for such a clever couple."

Her already queasy stomach plummeted. She felt as if she might throw up. "Why the elaborate abduction with the blindfold if you plan to hurt me?"

Marlow walked over to the window, gazing down at the woodlands surrounding the house. "The blindfold was a necessary precaution. I have learned over the course of the past few weeks you are neither a weak nor easily manipulated woman. On the very slight chance you might manage to escape the confines of this room, I had to make certain you would not be able to find your way back to town. After all, your husband will be exceedingly disappointed if he comes to rescue you and finds you have already departed."

"I have no doubt Derek will indeed find me, Mr. Marlow," she replied with complete faith in her husband's abilities.

"Of course he will find you, Lady Diana," Marlow sneered. "I am counting on it. One of my men, a footman in your household, will provide the essential clue, describing the mysterious coach parked outside your house just before your disappearance. I have left a difficult, but not impossible trail for the earl to follow."

"What are you planning?"

Marlow's look was decidedly sadistic. "After I have

recovered my property and captured Rutledge and whoever else is foolish enough to accompany him, I shall dispose of the lot of you. If there are too many corpses, I shall have to resort to torching the entire house; if not, I shall merely remove the bodies and dump them in the river."

She shivered noticeably at the casual tone he used. He acted as if he were trying to decide between two items for dinner, not plotting the deaths of innocent people.

"What could possibly be so significant about this book that would bring you to murder?" she asked breathlessly.

Marlow's face contorted in an expression of anger. "It has taken me the better part of seven years to collect the information contained in that book. It provides an essential part of my income and I refuse to relinquish it without a fight."

Seeing her puzzled frown, Marlow continued. "Blackmail, Countess," he whispered reverently. "There are numerous members of society, as well as government officials, who prefer that their occasional lapses in morality and honesty remain a secret. They pay me handsomely for my silence."

"Was Giles paying you to keep silent about his two marriages?"

Marlow stiffened. "Giles always maintained his marriage to you was a fake. I didn't know he had actually married you until a year into our association. A slip of the tongue while indulging in too much wine and I knew his sordid secret." Marlow smiled mockingly. "I first met Giles when he was searching among the more notorious inhabitants of London for a man skilled in forgery. As Marlow, I assisted him in the sale of many of your properties, supplying the required signatures. Apparently it became too much of an inconvenience for Giles to travel to Cornwall to see you each time he needed additional funds. As Rotherby, I avoided contact with him in society, but he began requiring Marlow's services so often he eventually discovered my secret identity."

Horrified, yet spellbound, Diana asked, "What happened?"

"Giles and I became partners. By then I knew he was a bigamist, so we each had a secret worth keeping. Giles provided Rotherby with access to even higher levels of society. With his help, I was able to ferret out many fascinating bits of information, greatly increasing the value of my black book. Ultimately, however, Giles became too greedy. He stole my book, my living, so I took his life. A fair exchange, do you not agree?"

Diana began backing away from Marlow, repulsed by the reckless desperation she saw lurking in his eyes. "Derek will not allow your evil schemes to continue," she said softly. "He will stop you, Mr. Marlow."

Marlow's mouth curved up in a chilling grin. "I do imagine he shall try, my lady." With a final parting glance, he left.

Diana alternated between deathly calm and unbridled panic as she waited for Derek to arrive. The room she was locked in was small and spartan, with one unlocked window. After examining the window she understood why. It was a long, steep, four-story drop to the ground beneath. Even for someone without her peculiar fear of heights, it was a substantial drop.

Discouraged, she craned her head out of the open window, trying to get a better look at the house.

Although not an overly large dwelling, there were numerous windows, and she knew Derek would have a difficult task trying to locate the room where she was imprisoned.

Diana decided it would be necessary to mark the window for Derek, but how? She shut the window and immediately picked up the single candle fitted tightly in its brass base, intending to leave it in the window as a signal. Yet she hesitated, wondering how her husband would react. A lone lit candle in the window. It might look suspicious. She thought for a moment and then wedged her linen handkerchief between the upper and lower cases of the double-hung window, hoping Derek would be able to see it and understand its meaning. Her task completed, she resumed her pacing.

The linen handkerchief was immediately noticed by Derek, Morgan, and Tristan as they observed the house, covered by the protection of the thick underbrush several hundred feet away.

"It could be a trap," Derek said pointing toward the top floor window where the cloth was clearly distinguishable through the glass.

"Yes," Morgan said. "Or it might be a sign from Diana." He squinted. "How do you wish to proceed, Derek?"

"I'm going to climb up there," he said. He pulled a length of rope from the saddle of his horse, who was tethered to a nearby tree. He crossed the rope over his chest and adjusted his two pistols. "If Diana is up there, I will bring her down. If I am discovered, order the soldiers to rush the house, Tristan." Derek faced Morgan and Tristan squarely. "I want you both to swear you will see to Diana's safety, should anything happen to me."

The two brothers exchanged looks and then nodded in solemn agreement.

"Good luck," Morgan murmured quietly as Derek waited to make his move.

Tristan and Morgan watched as Derek dashed from the cover of the thicket toward the house. Once there, he pressed himself against the building and waited until he was certain no one had seen him before beginning his climb.

Derek brushed aside the thick ivy vines and searched the aged brick for a hold. He dug away some loose mortar and wedged the toe of his boot into the opening. Grabbing tightly onto the ivy vine, he hoisted himself up. He waited breathlessly to see if the vine would support his weight before continuing. Miraculously it did, and within a relatively short span of time, he had successfully scaled the side of the house. He came to rest on the outer ledge of the top floor, pleased to have his feet on the strong, narrow stone.

Carefully inching over on the ledge, he peered cautiously into the room he believed Diana occupied.

Diana's face appeared suddenly in the window. "Derek!" she said loudly. "Have you completely lost your mind?"

What he nearly did loose was his balance, at his wife's sudden and startling appearance. "For heaven's sake, be quiet," he said, wondering if Diana had just inadvertently alerted the entire household of his presence. "And stand away from the window."

Diana ignored his order and stepped forward, throwing the window wide open. She stuck her arm out, trying to grab hold of him, and she almost knocked him off the ledge. "Give me your arm, Derek, so I may help you inside."

It took tremendous strength of will for Derek not to shout at his wife. He knew she was only trying to help, but if she continued with her unwanted aid, she would probably push him off the ledge. "I do not need your assistance, Diana. Kindly step away from the window so I may enter the room." He spoke in a forceful, commanding tone. This time, Diana obeyed.

With Diana no longer blocking his path, Derek was able to easily climb through the window. In a moment, he was standing safely inside the room, not certain if he wanted to throttle or embrace his wife.

"I was terrified when I saw you standing out there," Diana said, throwing herself into his arms. "What ever made you do such a foolish thing?"

He grunted. He was vastly relieved to find Diana here and apparently unharmed. "I have come to rescue you. I was under the mistaken impression you would be pleased to see me."

"Of course I am happy to see you," Diana said with a frown. "I was not expecting to see you outside my window. That's all." She shuddered. "You frightened me, Derek. I was certain you would fall."

He flashed a smile. "I very well might have fallen if my lovely wife continued helping me." He pulled away from her embrace, his keen eyes scanning the room. He quickly removed the rope slung over his chest and tied one end to the base of the fireplace mantel. He then tugged vigorously on it, testing its strength.

Diana watched in silent fascination. When he had completed his task, she asked, "What is the rope for, Derek?"

"Climbing."

"Oh, I see. All your men are going to climb up

here, so you can make a surprise attack from within the house. A clever plan."

Derek raised an eyebrow. "That is a very interesting approach to the problem," he said casually, checking the rope a final time. "But hardly a practical strategy, Diana. Ten men climbing up the side of the house are sure to be noticed. You and I will climb down. Once you are safely out of the house, I shall confront Marlow."

Diana froze. "Surely, you are joking, Derek." She licked her lips nervously when he did not respond. "You cannot possibly expect me to climb out the window, step onto that very narrow ledge, and then climb down the side of the house. I'll break my neck."

"I will help you," he said, acting as if he had not heard her protests. He held out his hand expectantly. "Come along, Diana."

She folded her arms across her chest. "You are not listening to me, Derek. I just told you I cannot go out on the ledge." She let out her breath in a huff.

"Sweetheart, it is not that difficult. The bricks and mortar are old and I have made numerous toeholds. Plus the rope is here to guide and support you."

"I don't care if there are steps in the bloody bricks. I am not climbing out on the ledge."

He threw up his arms in frustration. "Diana, I am not about to debate the point with you."

"You are right. There is no cause for debate," Diana said. "If this is your brilliant plan to rescue me, you will have to rethink it. I must admit, Derek, I am sorely disappointed."

"Diana," he said.

"I swear to you, I would rather face Marlow alone than climb out the window. You will simply have to come up with an alternative plan."

"There is no time for an alternative plan," he said impatiently. "Morgan and Tristan are waiting below for us. We must leave now."

"I cannot."

Derek shot her a look of pure annoyance and strode purposefully toward her. Without uttering another word, he picked her up and hoisted her over his shoulder. She would have screamed if she hadn't been taken so completely by surprise. When he began to climb out the window, she again found her voice.

"Derek, wait. Please listen to me first. I have discovered some very important information that will help you formulate a new plan. To rescue me. And capture Marlow."

"I already have a plan to rescue you," he said through clenched teeth. "It is a fine plan. A sound plan. And it shall be a successful plan, if you will only cease complaining and allow me to execute it."

She grew more apprehensive at her husband's words. He was not going to easily give up on this idea, she concluded with dismay. She started speaking again, but lost her voice when Derek straddled the ledge.

Diana thought she was going to faint. Good Lord, he actually was going to carry her down the side of the house. She pulled hard on his coat, desperately trying to get him to listen. "Marlow is expecting you, Derek. He planned for you to find me here."

Derek paused a moment, and her voice rose with excitement when she realized she had captured his attention.

"I know who Marlow is too. You won't believe it. He is really Rotherby, that foppish dandy. And I found his stupid book. It was hidden in the hunting picture in the drawing room—you know the one with Giles holding a fox. Marlow and Giles were partners in a horrible blackmail scheme. And—"

Derek slowly lowered his wife to her feet, inside the room. He held up his hand for silence. She was starting to babble, and although he was clearly amazed at the array of impressive secrets she revealed, she was starting to confuse him. "Slow down, Diana. You are going too fast for me to make any sense of this."

Diana took a deep breath, and in the ensuing silence, Derek heard the ominous sound of footsteps approaching. "Someone is coming," he whispered urgently. "Quick, stand over by the mantel in front of the rope."

Diana reacted automatically and followed his orders. She gasped loudly as Derek slipped back outside onto the ledge, but her attention was diverted by the opening of the door.

Jonathan Marlow took only three short steps into the room before Derek burst through the window, shattering the top panes of glass as made his daring entrance.

Even though Diana had just informed him of Marlow's identity, Derek was shocked to see the fawning dandy he knew as Rotherby standing before him. His moment's hesitation afforded Marlow time to reach for a pistol hidden in his coat pocket. When Derek saw the weapon, he instantly lunged for Marlow and they struggled briefly for the pistol.

Marlow would not relinquish his grip, and as they rolled on the ground, Derek could feel Marlow's hand tighten on the trigger. He was able to push the gun away from his chest and toward Marlow, just as the other man released the trigger.

The noise was deafening. The smell of smoke and

blood instantly assaulted Derek's nostrils. He felt Marlow's body slump limply, heavily, on his own and knew the other man was dead.

"Derek," Diana said. "My God, are you injured?"

He looked calmly at Diana's horrified face bending over him. "I am fine, sweetheart." He shoved Marlow's body off his chest. At her shocked gasp, he glanced down at his blood-soaked shirt and jacket. " 'Tis Marlow's blood, Diana. I fear he is dead."

"I am glad."

Derek looked at his wife. Despite her bloodthirsty response he knew she was terrified. He wanted to hold her close and comfort her, but he could not, not while his body was covered in Marlow's blood. Instead, he comforted her with gentle words. "It is all over, Diana. Marlow can never hurt you. And the secrets he carried about Giles are gone too."

Diana smiled faintly. "It is over," she repeated quietly. "It is truly over." She closed her eyes. "Thank you, Derek."

"I love you very much, Diana," he said softly as he rose to his feet.

The door unexpectedly thrust open and Morgan appeared, pistols drawn in each hand. Derek shoved Diana instinctively behind him, but grinned with relief when he saw the duke.

"Are you hurt?" Morgan asked, his eyes resting on Derek's bloodstained chest.

He shook his head. "We are both unharmed. Marlow, or should I say Rotherby, is dead."

"Rotherby?" Tristan asked as he joined his brother in the doorway. He too had his weapons drawn.

"Hard to believe," Derek said dryly, nudging Marlow's inert form with the tip of his boot. "He very cleverly fooled us all."

Diana gingerly removed the black leather book

from the pocket of her gown. "I imagine there are numerous people who will be pleased to learn of his death."

Derek took the book with interest. "You said something before about blackmail, Diana?"

"Yes. Marlow told me the book contains numerous bits of sordid information he and Giles used to extort funds from members of society and the government. I attempted to read the book when I first found it, but could not understand the citations. It must be written in some sort of code."

Derek fanned the pages of the small book with fascination before handing it over to Tristan. "I trust you will keep this safe. We shall no doubt spend many hours trying to decipher this code, Tris. After we have determined exactly what information we have discovered, we will decide what to do with the book."

"Fine." Tristan turned to his brother. "I believe the house is secure, but Morgan and I shall check the rest of the rooms to be certain. We will wait for you outside."

After they left, Derek placed a comforting arm around Diana's shoulders. He could feel her trembling.

"Thank God, you are safe," he said softly. "I nearly went out of my mind when I returned home and discovered Marlow had kidnapped you."

"He was waiting in the front hall." Diana shuddered. "I had just discovered the book hidden in the back of the painting and was rushing to tell Mr. Ramsey." She stopped abruptly and searched through the pocket of her gown. "Wait, there is something else. In all the confusion, I forgot about it." She pulled out a sheet of paper and carefully unfolded it.

357

"What is that?" Derek asked.

"I found it with the book," Diana said. "It is the missing church register page. The only existing proof of my marriage to Giles."

Silently, Derek took the paper his wife held out to him. "We were right. Giles must have stolen this soon after your wedding."

Hand in hand Derek and Diana walked to the fireplace. Only a small flame flickered in the grate, but it was sufficient. Ceremonially, Derek tossed the paper into the fire. It caught immediately, bursting into flames.

"Now that we have discovered the truth about Marlow, I strongly suspect we will find your property deeds among Rotherby's papers." His voice deepened with emotion. "It will bring me great pleasure to turn over the stolen deeds to you, my dear."

"Thank you, Derek." She kissed his cheek softly. "I am finally free," she whispered softly.

"It is a glorious relief for both of us, my love," he whispered. Seeking to lighten the mood, he flashed her a devilish grin. "And the very best part of all, my dear, is I won't have to make you climb out that damn window!"

Epilogue

The musicians were poised, their instruments ready, and Morgan, holding his wife close to his chest, waited until the hushed whispers died down before nodding his head. At his command, the strains of a lovely waltz echoed through the vast ballroom, and the musicians played enthusiastically while the crush of elegantly clad guests joined in the dance.

The Earl of Harrowby was not among those on the dance floor. He was trying to persuade his beautiful wife be his partner, but Diana continually rejected his advances.

"Diana, you are being very foolish about this," Derek said.

She grimaced at him and sank back farther into her chair. "For pity's sake, Derek," she said, "stop badgering me. I have no intention of parading about the dance floor in my condition. Now leave me alone."

"Are you feeling unwell?"

She shook her head. She didn't dare tell him the truth. Despite his outward calmness, she instinctively knew he would overreact. Visions of Derek lifting her up in his arms and carrying her out of the ballroom filled her head. What a spectacle! "I feel fine, Derek. Just a bit conspicuous, that is all."

Derek eyed her rounded belly. "Even being eight and a half months pregnant, you are the most beautiful and desirable woman in attendance tonight, Diana. Come, dance with me."

She could not help the smile that tugged at her lips. "You are fast learning how to flatter me, my lord."

Derek grinned charmingly. "I am getting rather good at it, aren't I?"

"Getting good at what?" Caroline asked, joining them.

"Having his own way," Diana said, glancing with envy at Caroline's slim waist. "I presume you were upstairs in the nursery again. How is young Richard this evening?"

Caroline's face took on a radiant glow of happiness. "My son is absolute perfection. Everyone agrees he is advanced well beyond his three months of age. He and his youngest cousin, Victoria, were screaming down the nursery with hunger cries. Alyssa and I have just come from feeding them. Now that they have both gorged themselves like little piglets, they are sleeping soundly. It is a heartwarming sight."

"Quiet, slumbering infants are indeed a heartwarming sight," Tristan said, walking up to his wife. "I do take exception, however, to my handsome son and dainty niece being referred to as piglets, Caroline."

Caroline laughed. "The truth is not always easy to accept, Tristan. When it comes to his meals, our Richard is a greedy little boy."

Tristan glanced boldly at his wife's breasts. "As long as the lad leaves some for his father, I shall not quibble," he said with a lecherous grin.

"Tris!" Caroline colored noticeably.

"Yes, love?"

"I think you had better lead me out on the dance floor," Caroline said. She squeezed his arm forcefully, then turned to Derek and said, "Why are you not dancing with your lovely wife?"

"I have been trying to persuade her, but she continues to rebuff me," Derek said with mocking regret.

Three pairs of eyes regarded Diana thoughtfully. She glanced ruefully down at her protruding belly. She was starting to feel a little better, yet she hesitated, slightly embarrassed. "What will people say?"

"They will probably remark, with great envy, on the astonishing fertility of the Ashton family," Tristan said kindly. "Three babies in one year. We surely are blessed."

Diana could see he was sincere. "You are right," she said suddenly, dismissing her earlier misgivings.

Derek held out his hand to assist her from her chair. Once they were on the dance floor, Diana began to relax. Being held so lovingly in Derek's arms always had a soothing effect on her.

"Feeling better, sweetheart?"

She looked up at him. "I'm sorry I am being so difficult, Derek."

Derek smiled down at her. "You aren't being difficult, Diana. Just very pregnant. Take heart, Diana. This shall all be over soon."

She merely smiled at her husband, as another

cramp gripped her belly. It would be over sooner than he knew, she thought smugly. Her labor pains had begun an hour ago, but she knew it would be many long hours before the child was actually born. There was no pressing need to inform Derek of that.

The annual winter ball held at Ramsgate Castle, Morgan and Alyssa's home, would provide the perfect distraction until her pains became more severe, Diana decided. She gave her husband another enchanting grin and took a deep breath. It was going to be a lovely evening.

At dawn, Diana delivered a small, but healthy baby girl. She lay back against the pillows and listened with pure joy to the lusty cries of her newborn daughter. She felt relief, exhaustion, and euphoria simultaneously.

Derek cuddled his new daughter lovingly, and Diana knew it had been almost unbearable for him to watch her struggle through the last few hours of intense labor. But now that the baby had been born, his face reflected his immense relief.

"Derek?"

"Yes, love." He sat on the edge of the bed, gingerly holding the infant in his arms.

She looked up at her husband, and her eyes filled with tears. "She is rather tiny, our new little girl."

"She is magnificent," he said in a strong voice. The baby opened her small mouth and yawned delicately. Turning to Diana with a teasing grin he said, "Morgan and I have decided to share the costs of constructing a convent."

"A convent?"

"A convent. For all of our daughters. So we can adequately protect them from the world's irresistible scoundrels."

"You mean men like their fathers," Diana said with a mischievous smile.

Derek laughed. "Tristan was correct, my love," he said, leaning over to kiss her damp brow. "We are truly blessed."

AMY ELIZABETH SAUNDERS

Passionate, Sensual Historical Romance By The Bestselling Author Of *Forever*.

Sweet Summer Storm. Rude, snobbish, and affected, Christianna St. Sebastien is everything Gareth Larkin despises, but she's the most breathtaking creature he's ever beheld. Determined to steal the beautiful aristocrat's heart, Gareth sets out to teach her that the length of a man's title and the size of his fortune are not necessarily his most important assets.

_3650-9 $4.99 US/$5.99 CAN

Wild Summer Rose. Torn from her carefree rustic life to become a proper city lady, Victoria Larkin bristles at the hypocrisy of the arrogant French aristocrat who wants to seduce her. But Phillipe St. Sebastien is determined to have her at any cost—even the loss of his beloved ancestral home. And as the flames of revolution threaten their very lives, Victoria and Phillipe find strength in the healing power of love.

_51902-X $4.99 US/$5.99 CAN

DECEPTION AT MIDNIGHT

COREY McFADDEN

When Edward, Earl of Radford, meets a winsome tomboy in a midnight encounter, his only thought is to see the lovely vagabond to safety. But under Maude Romney's dirt-smudged face is an enchanting sprite who ignites his passion like no other woman ever has. Yet once Edward learns of her impoverished nobility and tainted past, unsettling doubts plague him. Is Maude truly in danger—or has she cleverly used her innocence to force him into marriage?
_3520-0 $4.50 US/$5.50 CAN